NIGHT SHIFT

Shift Work: Book One

Split Shift: Book Two

Shiftless: Book Three

By TA Moore

ROGUE FIREBIRD
PRESS

Published by Rogue Firebird Press

Night Shift Collected Volumes
Shift Work: Book One
Split Shift: Book Two
Shift Less: Book Three

Cover Art by **TA Moore**

http://www.roguefirebird.com/

Print

Printed in the United States of America

First Edition

Oct 2021

Dedication

To the Five, all of us and forever, who always said I should do it. To my mum, who always knew I could do whatever I wanted.

Acknowledgements

To everyone in my Facebook Group, Trouble in a Teacup, and all the subscribers to my newsletter: Thank you for putting up with my weird digressions and nattering about this book for the last month.

Also thank you to Penny Rogers and Brian Holliday for being the editorial taskmasters that didn't let me slip in a rogue 'grey' or randomly change a minor character's name mid-book.

SHIFT WORK

You'd think the werewolves would be the worst thing about the Night Shift; you'd be wrong.

All Officer Kit Marlow wanted was a cup of coffee and some downtime before his next night shift. Instead, he got a naked man in the elevator and an unaccounted-for dead girl in the morgue. He's going to need to deal with both before he can head for his bed.

Or anyone else's. Although not much chance of that.

Reluctantly partnered with the acerbic security consultant Cade Deacon—last seen naked in the elevator—Marlow delves into the dead girl's life. Between them, they uncover a new crime scene with the whiff of old corruption. A corruption that, five years ago, nearly took Marlow's life and ended his career.

Finding out who killed the dead girl on the slab might only be the start of this investigation. Oh, and it's the second night of the full moon. So 80% of the city, including Cade, will turn into werewolves in the middle of the case.

So, there's that.

CHAPTER ONE

"HOLD THE DOOR!" someone yelled.

Marlow knew the voice—from the TV, from podcasts, and from sarcastic diatribes against an allegedly incompetent police force. It was a memorable voice. He considered pretending to be deaf for a second. It was the morning after the moon before and he didn't need this, but his better self won out. Life was hard, and it was stupid to pass up a chance at some good karma. He juggled his coat, keys, and coffee as he tried to free up a hand to do as asked. That didn't work. He stuck his foot out instead and let the elevator doors bounce off his shoe.

The elevator dinged at him in reproach and slid open again. The "this" he didn't need, otherwise known as Cade Deacon, grabbed the edge of the door before it could try to close again. He was naked except for the electronic tags that dangled around his throat. His feet were grass-stained, and leaves still matted in his curly dark blond hair.

"Thanks," Cade said in a rough, warm tone as he squeezed past Marlow. The clammy heat of him, all fresh sweat and old blood, washed over Marlow and coated the inside of his mouth. He imagined that was what Cade would taste like if he licked him—salt, copper, and musk—and then tried to focus on the thought of what Human Resources would say if he did that.

He could see the headlines now: "Night Shift cop licks head of private security firm in inter-company dominance display."

They wouldn't be happy. Neither would he when Cade knocked his teeth down his throat.

Marlow hit the button for his floor and watched as Cade selected the fourth floor. The morgue. He took a drink of his coffee—it was cold and had never tasted that good, but it was still coffee—and pushed his sunglasses more firmly up onto his nose. Three floors down from the ground floor and fifteen minutes paperwork, then his good deed for the day would be done. He could clock out and leave the whole building to Cade Deacon.

Neither of them said anything. Cade stretched, reached back, and scratched his ass.

It was rude to make it a *thing* that time of the month. Marlow chewed the inside of his cheek and managed a whole floor before he snuck a quick look at Cade's backside. He wasn't going to pretend he'd not noticed it before. The fitted suits that the head of Cold Winds Security favored showcased it nicely when Cade came in to consult with the chief or rip the Night Shift—including Marlow a couple of times, although he doubted Cade remembered—a new one for throwing one of his asshole operatives into the Crate. This was the first time Marlow had seen it in the flesh, though.

He'd expected the ripe curve of moon-pale skin and tight muscle, but the scars that licked across it were a surprise. Thin raised welts of white keloid crisscrossed his ass, with the tail ends of scars wrapped over his hips and down his lean thighs. He briefly wondered how that had happened. Or when.

"Either ask or look somewhere else," Cade told him.

Marlow felt the flush crawl red and hot from his collarbones up to his ears. It made them sting. He looked down at his feet—the fabric of his worn Converse had started to come away from the sole and had maybe a week left in them—and cleared his throat.

"None of my business," he said.

"You knew that already."

Fair enough. Marlow shifted his weight from one foot to the other and swore under his breath when the elevator stopped on the second floor. There wasn't even anyone there, just an empty hallway and a briefcase left to hold their spot.

He leaned forward and mashed his thumb against the "door close" button. Someone had told him once that it didn't actually do anything except give you something to do, but he held it down anyhow. *Come on, come on, come on.*

"If nothing else, I have to respect the work ethic of San Diego's tax-funded LEOs," Cade drawled, his voice low and clear. "Not only here first thing in the morning, but dressed and already looking like shit."

Sometimes it was hard to tell the difference between dominance games and flirting. Apparently not with Cade. Marlow could appreciate that.

"I've been on shift for … " Marlow paused to figure it out, his brain at that stage of tired where everything worked, but just 20 percent slower than usual. It was November, so the Night Shift was usually split into two. Except Harrison and Toledo had both called in sick, so he'd caught their consecutive shifts. "Seventeen hours. The only thing I want is to sign my kit back in and go home."

And some good coffee. Or more bad coffee. He wasn't fussy.

"Oh, that makes sense," Cade drawled. "You're one of the fun police, tired out from ruining everyone's good time last night."

Marlow's ribs ached from the impact with a skip in an alley down in the garment district. His knee had that loose, overworked Play-Doh feel that might ease overnight or might seize up and leave him hobbled for a week. When he came in tomorrow night, there'd be a stack of paperwork as thick as a dictionary to log the damage to his patrol car after someone jumped onto the roof and crumpled it.

"That's me," Marlow said. He resisted the urge to roll his eyes and just leaned forward to jab the button again. "The fun police. You know, there are lockers on every street corner you can keep a spare set of clothes in."

"I know."

They finally reached Marlow's floor. He decided to believe hammering the button had worked. The doors slid open, and Marlow had never been so glad to see the institutionally green walls. He didn't exactly bolt out of the elevator, but the doors hadn't opened all the way when he dodged through them. He was almost free and clear when Cade cleared his throat.

"Officer… Marlow, wasn't it?"

So much for not knowing who—what—Marlow was.

The cold paw of his grandma's ghost clouted Marlow about the ear. She'd not spent years chewing manners into Marlow for him to be rude to someone higher ranked than him now. Karma, Marlow reminded himself. He would get credit for this.

He turned around, stiff and reluctant, and his brain promptly fell over and flapped like a gaffed fish. Cade had leaned back against the wall of the elevator, his hands braced on the rail, and his smile showed teeth that were a bit too sharp and crinkled eyes that were bright honey brown. It wasn't as if it was a *surprise* that Cade was hot. Marlow didn't like the idea of a private police force, and he didn't particularly like the acerbic CEO of it either, but he wasn't blind. Cade was handsome in a hard, uncompromising way that had nothing soft or pretty about it, with broad, freckled cheekbones and an angular, clean-cut jaw.

The thing was, it was one-way street hot. Marlow had never gotten the sense that Cade had noticed him, or anyone else, as anything but an obstruction. The man only cared about his work and being an asshole.

Until now, when Marlow's breath caught behind his ribs as Cade pinned him with those wild near-gold eyes.

"Get some rest, Marlow," Cade drawled. For a second, Marlow was cynically surprised that Cade actually remembered who he was, until the next thing Cade said gave him something else to be surprised about. "You look like you should be in my bed already."

Marlow stared at Cade, his jaw slack, as he wondered if he'd misheard. Before he could decide or give in to the urge to let his eyes follow the ridiculously perfect triangle of Cade's body down to check directly, the elevator doors slid shut and cut off Marlow's view.

"What the hell was that?" Marlow said out loud and looked around to see if anyone else had seen what just happened.

The hall was empty.

After a moment, Marlow shook his head and rubbed a hand over his face. He should be used to being out of step with the rest of the city, even the other cops. Real cops. Marlow was tired to the bone from the late shift, and they'd spent the night on all fours howling at the moon.

Fun police. Marlow snorted as he turned on his heel and headed toward the armory.

Werewolves didn't know how the other 20 percent—based on the last census, anyhow—lived.

"Forget the wolves," Bennett said. The other Night Shift officer held court in the middle of the armory. She waved a mug of black coffee, probably laced with whiskey, as she talked. "The fucking rabbits have gone feral. Swear to God, I found a full-grown wolf treed by a bunch of angry bunnies."

"Yeah," one of the rookies snorted, sure he'd caught his superior out in a leg pull. He looked around for support. "Right.

Then the squirrels got together and stole your car before you got back, right?"

No one cracked a smile. After a second, the rookie's face fell. He turned back to Bennett, who glared at him.

"Something funny?"

"Oh, come on," the rookie said. He spread his hands in a plea for *someone* to see sense. "*Bunnies*?"

Bennett just shook her head and walked away, toward Marlow. The rookie looked after her with a crestfallen expression, and then jumped when one of the other men chuckled and slapped his shoulder.

"First blue moon? On the job?" Franklin, Bennett's go-to backup, asked. The rookie had a dull flush on the back of his neck as he ducked his chin in a stiff nod. Franklin pursed his lips and gave a low, breathy whisper as he shook his head. "Oh yeah, you have got a lot to learn. Tell you what, buy Uncle Franklin breakfast, and I'll get you caught up. Before the bunnies or Bennett get to you."

The big man threw a companionable headlock on the rookie and marched him toward the door. Marlow paused to watch them go and then gave Bennett a wry look.

"Ever going to tell the kid that 'bunnies' are what you call the beat officers?"

Bennett cracked a grin and glanced after her team as they filed out. "Someday. Probably. C'mon, the kid's new. He needs to learn that blue moon madness is real, for his own good."

"Except it's not," Marlow pointed out. "It's an old wives' tale."

That made Bennett splutter indignantly. She followed along as Marlow headed over to the desk and swung his kit bag up onto the counter.

"That it's an old wives' tale is an old wives' tale," Bennett said. "What? Do you think all the lunar radiation in the air has no effect or something? There have been studies done, and to the wolves, that stuff is like catnip. They lose control. Tell him, Erin."

Officer O'Malley grabbed the strap of Marlow's bag and pulled it to her side of the bulletproof glass wall.

"Last time we had a double bubble," she said, "we used up three times the average amount of ammo for a month. That's a fact."

Bennett slapped her hand on the counter. “There you go. That’s a *fact*. You can’t argue with facts, Kitty-boy.”

The nickname made Marlow clench his teeth. He hated it; that’s why he went by his surname instead of Kit. Bennett knew he hated it; that’s why she used it. Although they had the same rank, Bennett had three years seniority on him. She liked to make sure everyone remembered it. And she was an asshole. Bennett was the sort of person who tickled a kid until they wet themselves. She never knew when to rein it in.

It just made her worse if she knew she’d caught you on the raw, though. Even if you were friends… ish, or at least had no better offers.

“I’m not arguing,” Marlow said in his mildest voice, “just disagreeing. I just do my job; doesn’t matter what color the moon is.”

He took the clipboard Erin slid through the partition to him and scrawled his initials where they were required. The pen had clogged, and he had to scribble in the corner of the sheet to get it to work. The doodle came out as a wolf with black pricked ears and blind white eyes at the top of a long, wrinkled nose.

Bennett lifted her chin and squared her shoulders. “You saying I don’t?”

“I’m saying I didn’t use any more ammo the last time we had two full moons in the cycle.”

A scowl flicked over Bennett’s face for a moment at the dodge. She visibly shrugged the brief black mood off and leaned back against the counter to finish her coffee.

“Lucky you,” she said. That was all. She still managed to convey the impression that he’d somehow slacked off.

There was a pause while Bennett drank her coffee. Marlow took the opportunity to finish the forms. He kept one eye on Erin as she started to unpack his kit, each weapon logged back in as she went. Anything that didn’t tally between her count and what he’d signed out that afternoon—yesterday afternoon—had to be accounted for in his incident report. Technically. In practice, IA didn’t have enough manpower to investigate every dropped bullet. Unless it was flagged in connection with a different active investigation, a few discrepancies weren’t enough to worry about.

It was still a good idea to keep an eye on the clerk as they worked. Last year, one of Callen's kits had been logged back in under McCall's name. It had been cleared up in two days, but the investigation had rolled on for six months before Callen got assigned to active duty again. He'd missed his chance at a leadership position.

Erin lifted out the tear gas carefully and checked them. The armory was sealed, but if one of the canisters went off, it would take three days of scrubbing the walls down with toothpaste and vinegar before they could reopen it. Even adulterated to decrease the potency, the aconite would send any wolf who got a sniff straight to the ER… whether their nose was human or not at the time.

"I hear Harrison has requested early retirement," Bennett said abruptly.

Marlow was startled enough to botch his signature. He swore under his breath, scribbled it out, and tried again before he looked up at Bennett. "You sure?"

"New wife, new life," Bennett said. "I guess she doesn't want him shot. Me, that's the first thing I'd want to happen to my husband and his police pension. Then I could be a Merry Widow."

Bennett winked at Erin, who laughed and then gave Marlow a quick, awkward look before she went back to work. There were still two blotches of high color on her cheeks as she pulled out the ammo boxes and counted the bullets. She had to pause again as one of the other clerks ducked in from the back to murmur in her ear.

"She isn't the first wife who wanted to change him," Marlow said. "Night Shift has always hung on to him before."

"Well, she might be the first one to pull it off," Bennett said. "My source knows what they're talking about. Paperwork was signed and handed in. If he doesn't back out, you going to go for the job?"

Marlow hesitated as he thought about that. As an abstract, one-day thing, he'd always assumed he would, but the reality was a bit more daunting.

"I guess," he said after a moment. "You?"

He got a scathing look for that. Bennett had been acting sergeant for two years while her sergeant was off on extended medical leave. Only, he'd come back as fit as a fiddle and ready to take back the reins.

To her credit, she'd handed them over, but everyone knew she missed it.

"What do you think?"

Marlow shrugged his acknowledgment of that. "Probably Dawson over on day shift too."

"She's night-blind," Bennett said. "What good would she be?"

"OT got her those glasses," Marlow said. "And she needs the money, with her husband."

Bennett had to give him that, with an annoyed twist of her mouth. "Maybe—"

Before she could finish, O'Malley cleared her throat. When they both turned, she slid a slip of paper through the slot in the partition. The other clerk had written the note in loopy, messy letters that were still legible.

"The captain wants to see you," O'Malley repeated it anyhow. "Down in the morgue."

Her finger unconsciously tapped the paperwork she had almost finished, just over the tally of Marlow's bullets. He'd brought back less than he'd checked out. It happened. A wolf was a wolf until it wasn't. It couldn't be talked down or reasoned with. Sometimes silver was the only way to keep its teeth out of someone's throat.

That didn't mean there wasn't hell to pay when someone died.

If someone died. Marlow could have sworn that every wolf he'd crossed paths with last night might wake up pissed off, but they *would* wake up. Maybe he'd been wrong.

"Damn," Bennett said. She clapped Marlow on the back, hard enough to hurt, in rough sympathy. Or close enough to it. "I guess I don't have to worry about you as competition after all."

She chuckled at her own joke as she headed out to the locker rooms.

"Look, take your gear back, and I'll finish up this," O'Malley offered. "It's everything but the last two boxes, and they aren't touched. I can notarize the forms."

Marlow hesitated for a moment, but there was no reason to say no. Or there was, but those reasons were either paranoid or ungrateful.

"Thanks," he said.

O'Malley wrinkled her nose dismissively as she pulled the sealed envelope out from the rack under the table. She handed it over, and Marlow hooked his finger under the flap to rip it open. It contained his badge, personal weapon loaded with non-silver bullets, and his wallet.

Wolves weren't men during the full moon, but they weren't just beasts either. No one on Night Shift wanted to tangle with a wolf and then find out it used their ID to beat them home. There were tragedies written about that.

Not that Marlow had anyone *at* home to put at risk. The worst he had to fear was wolf scat on his sheets.

"See you tomorrow night," O'Malley chirped cheerfully.

Marlow grimaced as he clipped his gun to his belt and pulled his T-shirt down over it. He supposed he would with the current manpower shortage, no matter how much sleep he ended up getting.

"Maybe I'm going to get a pie for all my hard work?" he said. "And the night off?"

O'Malley wrinkled her nose. "I think Jay would have gotten a pie first," she said. Her eyes went big and dreamy. "She's amazing. It wouldn't be fair to give one to you and *not* her."

It took Marlow a second to realize who she meant. Bennett. He rarely used her first name or even thought about it.

"There's no pie," he said as he stepped back. "There's never pie, O'Malley. Or a night off."

It turned out he was right. There was no pie.

There was a corpse.

CHAPTER TWO

THE DEAD GIRL lay on the slab in the SDPD's chill, sterile morgue. She looked dead—her skin slack and sticky-sallow and the faint whiff of decomposition ripe in the air—but at first glance, there was no obvious cause. The sheet had been folded down to her chest, an inked wolf winked from the curve of her upper breast, and there were no visible injuries.

Cade didn't recognize her, but he'd always had a bad memory for faces. If Captain O'Hara had gone to the bother of an early-morning, post-moon callout, he assumed he had crossed paths with her.

"Tragic," Cade said as he pushed the sleeves of his borrowed sweats up his forearms. "But I don't see what it has to do with me."

Dr. Sun, the chief pathologist, half turned to grab a small plastic bag from a tray. She handed it to Cade—inside it was a single black card etched with three wavy silver lines broken by a stylized tree.

"That's a keycard provided by Cold Winds Security, isn't it?" O'Hara said. He already knew the answer, but the dance was—Cade supposed—traditional. "As part of your company's contract with the board up at the Reserve."

Cade turned the card over to check the back. He didn't know the serial number of every card they issued, but he knew what the grouping structure of the number meant.

"She was a guest," Cade said as he gave the card back to Sun. "Not a resident. Based on the card."

"Whose guest?"

It was Marlow who asked the question. Cade glanced around at the slender Night Shift officer who was slouched back against the wall of the morgue and tried not to look like someone who'd just been shot down in an elevator.

The morning after a full moon always made Cade feel larger than life. His muscles were tight, his nerves too close to the surface of his skin, and any self-control he had was replaced with far too much confidence. And it wasn't as if anyone had ever accused him of lacking that the rest of the month.

It usually faded.

Usually, he didn't run into anyone who his subconscious apparently found more attractive than he ever had. That revelation would have been enough to put him in a bad mood on its own; the fact it wasn't reciprocated meant he took a certain amount of pleasure in his answer.

"Even if I knew that off the top of my head, I couldn't tell you," he said. "Client confidentiality, I'm afraid. Get a warrant if you're that interested."

Marlow stared at him for a second through those pretentious tinted glasses of his and then shrugged the refusal off. Literally. With one hitch of a shoulder, Cade was denied a frustrated rant about the right thing as Marlow just accepted it and moved on. Cade felt more cock-blocked than he had earlier.

"Where was her body picked up?" Marlow asked O'Hara.

O'Hara exchanged a look with Sun. The pathologist picked up a clipboard and ran her finger down the crumpled piece of paper attached.

"According to her intake paperwork," she said, "from the Reserve—"

"No," Cade interrupted firmly. He already knew that the dead girl wasn't a wolf. They didn't get tattoos. Not ones that stuck over the full moon, anyhow. "No null residents or guests stay on the Reserve during the full moon. It's policy. Anyone who doesn't shift into a wolf, even spouses and children, is found other accommodations. Not to mention the question of what the Night Shift was doing at the Reserve in the first place."

O'Hara scowled at him. "The Reserve is a private community that employs its own security," he said gruffly. "It's still in the San Diego city limits and falls under our authority. You function up there because we allow it."

"I function up there because very rich people want it," Cade corrected him. "And they don't want local law enforcement interfering with their pretend wilderness. So, unless the Night Shift had a very good reason to be there—"

O'Hara held up his hand. He only had three fingers, his pinky just a shiny nub of scar tissue. Wolves healed from most things—that was the problem with tattoos—but anything cut off didn't grow back.

"They didn't," he said. "And they weren't. That's the problem. The intake form isn't signed, none of the emergency operators logged a call from the Reserve, and nobody transported her body to the morgue. She was just here this morning with paperwork written on a form six years out of date."

He paused like that was supposed to mean something. It didn't. Not to Cade, at least.

"Fuck off," Marlow said as he pushed himself off the wall. His voice stayed even, almost calm, but there was an edge to it. It was the closest to excited that Cade had seen the laidback Night Shift officer get. He ignored the tickle of interest that caught the back of his throat and focused on what was going on instead of his sex drive. "That isn't going on anymore. Internal Affairs dealt with it, and the officers involved."

Sun shifted her weight. Her rubber-soled shoes squeaked on the floor as she did so. "And my predecessor was fired," she said. "I am not with O'Hara on this. That problem was rooted out."

Cade rolled his eyes. "On *what*?" he said. "What are you talking about?"

All three turned to glare at him. The wolf was close enough to the surface that Cade had to struggle not to bare his teeth at them.

It was Marlow who broke the standoff first. "He wasn't here six years ago," he pointed out. "The Reserve contracted a private security firm *because* of what happened with Piper."

Cade pressed his finger to the inner corner of his eye as his patience ran out. "Which was?" he asked in a harsh voice. "And exactly why am I here, because you could have asked my assistant about the keycard."

Marlow bit out a laugh. "You're here because of what happened," he said. "Captain O'Hara doesn't trust the Night Shift, and if he calls in IA, then everyone will know that."

O'Hara looked unhappy, but he didn't even try to disagree. Not really.

"It's not about trust; it's about confidence," he said. "All I want to know is if there's any reason to think we missed something—someone—back then. Deacon can get that process started quickly and discreetly, before I have to bring anyone else in."

Cade raised his eyebrows. "Why should I?" he asked. "Since I assume you can't get that warrant I asked for without whatever this is becoming public."

"True," O'Hara said. "But then the Reserve is dragged into this, the old dirt and the new. Right now, it looks like someone walked straight through Cold Winds' security measures and murdered someone's guest. How long do you think it will take before your contract evaporates? How many will you find to replace it?"

He waited, a wiry, spare man with thinning hair and calm composure. Like it or not, he was right. The Reserve wanted discretion and silence, not mistakes and publicity.

"I could maybe make some inquiries," Cade allowed. "Any intel I share will be redacted, but I don't owe the SDPD anything—contractually or otherwise. So your sins won't be blacked out."

O'Hara's shoulders relaxed as Cade gave in. He nodded his agreement to the deal and opened his mouth. Marlow interrupted.

"And me?" he said. "Why am I here?"

"He's not a police officer," O'Hara said. "You are—and this is still our investigation. Plus, I know that you burned your bridges with Piper when this happened. So this is your case until I tell you otherwise. Right now, you're not Night Shift. You're our new liaison with the Reserve."

"Go fuck yourself," Marlow said and stalked out of the morgue.

The urge to follow him briefly tugged at Cade. He resisted, although he'd be grateful when his unlikely attraction to Marlow went back in the basement where it belonged.

"That was short-lived," he said. "Nice to have a partner while it lasted."

"He'll do what needs doing," O'Hara said. "You just do the same."

Cade recited the string of numbers in a clipped, evenly paced voice into the cracked mouthpiece of the pay phone handset. The plastic smelled like bad breath and bad decisions.

"Okay," Lem said, the "o" drawn out as he scuffled noisily around his desk for something, probably a pen. "Have we gone DEFCON code now, because I think I missed that meeting."

"Which one *didn't* you miss?" Cade asked, an edge of old—so long-standing it was dusty—frustration in his voice. On the other end of the phone, Lem just snorted out a laugh at the joke. Cade looked up for strength at the high cracked ceiling and let it go. There were reasons he kept Lem around; none of them involved his work ethic about admin. "I need to know who was assigned that card."

"It's a guest card. Hold on, let me check the files," Lem said. His voice blurred as he shifted the phone from one ear to the other. Despite the fact Cade had never seen him use more than two fingers to type, the clatter of hit keys was rapid-fire. "A recent one, this year or late last from the numbers. I'd need to go into the office to pull the request paperwork to find a name."

Cade pressed his thumb against his forehead. He never remembered more than bits and pieces of what happened during the full moon. Most people didn't; the rest were liars. He would bet the wolf never had to deal with this sort of thing, though.

"Why aren't you already in the office?" he asked.

He couldn't see it this time, but he'd watched Lem shrug his way out from under something so many times he didn't *need* to see it. His memory provided the visual of a carelessly hitched shoulder for him.

"I called in to say I was running late," Lem explained. "Elliot said you weren't in yet either, so I figured you'd not know if I had a lie-in. Guess I was wrong."

Cade clenched his jaw for a count of five and then decided that was too much to deal with in a public place. He had a reputation to protect, and the CEO of Cold Winds Security couldn't curse out an employee where just anyone could hear. Any offending cop who'd crossed him, sure—he'd called Marlow, or a Night Shift who looked sort of like him, a eunuch with balls full of Kleenex once—but not his own people. They got the dignity of being dressed down in private.

"I'll deal with that, and you, later," he said coldly. "Get to the office and get me the name. *Do not* get pulled over for speeding on the way. I won't bail you out this time."

"Make up your mind, Cade," Lem said, his voice lazy and good-natured. Sometimes Cade wasn't sure if Lem realized when he'd actually crossed the line and didn't care, or just didn't know there was a line. "Do you want me to care about getting to work on time or not?"

Cade sighed as Lem sniggered at his own joke.

"Remind me again why I haven't fired you?" he asked.

"Because firing your own little brother is Victorian mill-worker shit?" Lem said. "What would you do to top that?"

Cade hung up on him. He pulled his tag out of the reader and tucked it back under his sweatshirt. It felt warm and faintly greasy against his skin from contact with the overused machine.

The squirm of distaste that Cade felt made him snort to himself. He used to wake up after a full moon naked in the woods with no idea where he was and no way to call for help, not that any would have been coming. Now he complained that the tags that meant he could pick up his calls, pay for a taxi, or buy new pants—all with a swipe of the chip—felt a bit sweaty?

It was one thing to improve yourself—and Cade thoroughly appreciated how far he'd come and from what—and another to get soft.

"City wolves couldn't hunt a Twinkie out of its wrapper, never mind a hare on the run," his dad's voice cracked between Cade's ears. "You're better than them."

Long practice let Cade hit the pause button on that memory before it played out any further and spoiled the moment. His childhood was best enjoyed out of context. His dad was better as a ghost.

It was typical of the old bastard that he had—so far—refused to make that wishful thinking a reality.

Cade headed out into the street to see if he could find a cab. Now that he wasn't braced to resist whatever O'Hara wanted, he could feel the question of the dead girl catch his interest. People died during the full moon sometimes—shot by the Night Shift, caught by a wolf who'd wake up in the morning with the taste of meat in his mouth and not know it was Jessica instead of rabbit—but not often, and they didn't leave neat corpses.

A woman in a three-piece suit, heels dangled from one hand and phone pressed to her ear with the other, gave him a quick red-lipped grimace of apology as she dashed past him.

"… didn't get them to the courier," he caught as she paused on the curb to wait for a break in the traffic. "I know! I know! It just got away from me, but the judge won't—"

She bolted across the road, dodged a bike messenger, and headed around the corner onto Oakwood.

It was possible that was what had happened to their dead girl, Cade supposed. If she'd died just before the full moon—of natural causes, even—and then gotten lost in the shuffle of the handover. That happened. Not all wolves were created equal. Some were more sensitive to whatever triggered the change from man to wolf than others. Cade changed early and back late; others didn't change until the moon was high in the sky. Some changed at a different point every month.

Mistakes happened. Forms didn't get signed because paws were bad with pens, appointments were missed, and bodies ended up unclaimed when they weren't where they were meant to be.

Cade made a mental note to check the call logs in the hours leading up to the shift as he raised his hand to grab a yellow cab's attention as it cruised past. The driver ignored him. Cade bit the inside of his lip as old insecurities made a bid to rise from the dead. He didn't look lost or poor, just that he'd been caught out like any other wolf who'd gotten the idea to range too far from home turf. The driver had no idea where Cade had come from or how generously he would have tipped.

The next cab stopped. Cade pulled the door open and scrambled inside. The air freshener, cut into a cartoon pork chop shape, dangled from the mirror and filled the inside of the cab with the smell of old stones and moss. It swung as the driver reached up to adjust the mirror so he could see Cade.

"Where to?"

Cade weighed the list of things he had to do that day. He was tempted to go home, start the day out right with a good soak to get the smell of the morgue off him and his choice of freshly laundered outfits. It was a good hour out of the city—not at the Reserve; even if he could afford it, they didn't want the help in residence—but still rural and relatively private. By the time he got there and back, even if he broke some speed laws, he'd have lost half the day.

So, the office shower and a suit that his assistant had gotten dry-cleaned a week ago it was.

"Prospect Tower," he said. "West side entrance."

The driver whistled. "Nice," he said as he pulled back into the flow of traffic. "My cousin worked on that when it was going up a few years ago. He snuck me in one night. Amazing views. You work there?"

Cade pushed his sleeves up his forearms. "I own it."

He watched the suspicion and envy flicker through the driver's eyes as he checked Cade out a second time in the rearview. It would have been more satisfying if he didn't hate himself for needing that validation.

Lem was in his office when Cade got there. Any points he got for that were lost because he also had his boots up on Cade's desk.

He might not know where the line was, but he wasn't an idiot. He caught Cade's glare and swung his feet back down onto the floor.

"Boss," Lem said as he straightened up in the chair. "Rough morning?"

Cade glanced down at the SDPD-branded sweats he still had on. They were clean enough—the only smell worked into them was bleach and the morning after the moon before stink of him—but still.

"What gave it away?" he asked as he pulled the sweatshirt off and draped it over the back of his chair. "Did you find who that card belonged to?"

"No," Lem said. Before Cade could get beyond a breath sucked through his teeth in irritation, Lem scrambled on. "I mean, I found whose allotment the card was drawn from. Wallace Macroy."

"Halfway there," Cade said. "Time to bring it home. Who did he want a guest card for?"

Lem pulled his face into an exaggerated grimace of anticipation. "You aren't going to like it."

"Well, then," Cade said dryly as he stood on one leg and then the other to strip the loose fleece off. "Keep me waiting. That always puts me in a better mood."

He headed for the smoked glass door that led into the small shower room he'd had the architect add to the floor plans when they were drawn up. When you built your own office, you got to have your own way.

"It's for his office, for when he's away. In case he needs someone to get something from the house or water his plants," Lem said. He held his hands up defensively when Cade turned to look at him. "Hey, I didn't approve it."

"Who did?" The minute the words left his lips, Cade regretted the question. He could guess the answer from Lem's reluctant expression. "Son of a bitch."

"Yeah," Lem said. "Him."

Cade scratched his head—and pulled a twig out of his hair—and tried to think past the sour old grudge. His ex-partner had fucked him over worse than this. A shared office card for a wealthy celebrity-adjacent client? That was just Justin trying to curry favor, not actually undermine the company.

"Fine. Get me Wallace's contact details," he said, and almost instantly changed his mind. "Make it his office manager. They're more likely to know. And see what you can dig up on an Officer Marlow. Night Shift. He pulled a few of our operatives in… last year?"

Lem unfolded himself from the office chair, a lean man made of black leather. "Well, that narrows down the suspect list," he said. "Is he a problem?"

Yes.

"No," Cade said. "But technically, this is his case."

"Huh. So why isn't he doing the leg work?"

Cade pulled the bathroom door shut and thought about Marlow's tight shoulders and the way he'd leaned against the morgue wall like it was all that kept him upright. It made a shiver of breathless electric interest run down his spine and tug at his balls. He had no idea where it came from—his type was arm candy, not roadkill—and he wasn't going to work that out in front of Lem.

"Hopefully because he's getting some sleep," he said. "If he's my backup, I'd rather he be able to keep his eyes open on the case."

CHAPTER THREE

MARLOW MOVED BEFORE his brain caught up with the fact he was awake. He stopped mid-stride in the middle of his house, barefoot on sun-warmed tiles with his gun in his hand and his blood loud in his ears. The dregs of old bad dreams had left a sour taste in his mouth.

Dark streets echoed with the eerie howls of wolves. Some of them were his colleagues. His friends. They'd still rip him apart and not even know they had in the morning. Habit made his hand flex around the emptiness where the gun they'd taken off him should have been.

'I'm not going out there."

He sounded scared. He was. For the first time in his life, he knew he was going to die.

"Die out there or die in here. Your choice."

Gunshots deafened Marlow—

Someone hammered on the door again. Okay. That explained that. Marlow scrubbed his hand over his face and went to tuck his gun into the holster. Cold metal scraped along his hip, and he remembered he slept in boxers. The elastic wasn't up to that.

"Hold on." He padded over to the door, slid the security chain on, and opened it a crack. Cade was propped up against the door frame, his face and one sardonically raised eyebrow visible through the gap.

"What would you do if I just kicked the door in?" he asked.

Marlow held the gun up. "Shoot you and deal with the paperwork later," he said. "What do you want?"

For a second, something dark and hot flickered through Cade's eyes, still bright amber even hours after sunrise. It made the breath catch in Marlow's throat with sudden sticky awareness. Then Cade throttled it back.

"Nothing that I'm going to do in the street," he said. His voice was still rough, low, and scratched around the edges, but it was more clipped now as the wolf faded and the asshole was back in the driving seat. "So let me in, before I tell your captain you're not being helpful."

Marlow closed the door on him. The glimpse of deep black offense he saw on Cade's face for the second before the wood blocked it was *very* satisfying. For a second, Marlow considered leaving it at that, but fulfilling as it was to piss off the biggest pain in the Night Shift's collective ass for years…

The captain had assigned him the case, like it or not. Marlow didn't follow orders blindly, but he needed more reason than pissiness to ignore his boss.

Besides, his door was made of plywood and six layers of paint. If Cade wanted to kick it in, it probably wouldn't take long.

Marlow still let the door stay closed a second longer than necessary before he unhooked the chain and opened it again. On the other side, Cade glared at him, those wolf-gold eyes narrowed.

"What?"

"I don't like having doors slammed on me."

Marlow wiped sleep out of the inner corner of his eye. "Yet I bet it happens a lot." He stepped back and gestured for Cade to come in. "And yeah, it was childish. I'm not used to being woken up during the day."

For a second, Cade just looked more pissed off. Then he visibly moved past that as he stepped over the threshold and looked around. His eyebrows twitched up as he took in the open-plan space with the huge, poorly installed French doors that let in the sun most of the day.

"This is… open," he said.

"It was cheap."

"I'm sure."

Marlow didn't bother to bristle at the faintly disdainful note in Cade's voice. His house wasn't to a wolf's taste; that was why it was cheap. Too much light, too much space, no basement. It had actually been an artist's studio when Marlow moved in, bought just for the view of Sunset Cliffs.

"It suits me," he said. "But I'll admit, nobody ever wants to crash here. What do you want?"

Cade turned to look at him and paused. His eyes tracked down Marlow's body, from his head to his cartoon mouse boxers. His attention lingered on the scars that stippled over Marlow's shoulder and spread over his ribs. Just two shots, but they'd made a mess. And Marlow didn't have a wolf's advantages.

After a moment, Cade looked back up. Marlow waited.

"I found whose house the entry card belonged to," Cade said. It wasn't what Marlow had expected, and he was off-balance for a second. Then he caught up, and he felt a pinch of guilt that he'd let the dead girl slip to the back of his mind. "Whoever it is shouldn't have been there, but his business manager is willing to talk to you if you get there in the next hour."

Marlow checked the time and swallowed a groan. He'd had three hours and twenty minutes sleep, and now the adrenaline from his abrupt wake-up call had faded, he could feel it. It would have to do; he'd functioned on less.

He scrubbed his free hand over his face and up into his hair, tangles caught around his fingers.

"Give me five minutes to get dressed," Marlow said as he turned to head into the bedroom. "Then we'll go."

"One question," Cade said before Marlow could close the door behind him. The clipped edge to his voice was close enough to a command that habit made Marlow turn on his heel. "You got the full show this morning, so how come I just get boxers?"

Marlow looked down at himself, past the scars to the wrinkled boxers he'd dragged on before he collapsed face-first into his pillows earlier. Six years ago, and Cade would have gotten his show—no boxers *or* scars. He shrugged and gestured with the gun still loosely gripped in one hand. "Same reason I sleep with this under my pillow, I guess," he said. "If you want to put some coffee on, feel free."

No coffee.

It turned out that Cade wasn't domesticated. Marlow couldn't pretend he was surprised, but when the secretary who'd shown them in invited them to sit down, he decided to stand. Right now, he could have dozed off in one of the station's uncomfortable plastic chairs, never mind in what looked like an oversized, overstuffed cushion on legs.

Cade stayed on his feet too and paced restlessly around the room.

Marlow leaned on the filing cabinets—although the sleek black glass towers had little in common with the dented, sharp-edged steel ones at the station—and looked over the posters on the wall. The office was cutting-edge modernity, monochrome in black and gray, with the only splash of color, the bright red chair. Through the gray tint of Marlow's glasses, everything looked as if it was faintly grubby. In contrast, the posters were explosions of color and block lettering: musicals, rom-coms, and a few kids' movies, based on the "Sheepret Agent" poster.

It wasn't what you expected when you came to talk to a man about a dead girl.

His pocket buzzed. Marlow pushed himself off the cabinets and pulled his phone out of his pocket, a notification from Dr. Sun on the screen.

"The autopsy is finished," he said.

Cade sat on the edge of Macroy's desk, trousers pulled taut over his thighs as he crossed his legs at the ankles. Marlow glanced down at Cade's feet. Boots this time, but same difference. In his opinion, it wasn't fair that Cade in clothes was just as distracting as Cade without.

"And?" Cade asked.

"It was… umm…" Marlow glanced back at the screen and squinted at the aggressively abbreviated message. "Exsanguination."

"Not natural causes," Cade said. He sounded pleased with himself. "Shame I told Macroy it was, but it was the information I had at the time."

That explained why someone from the Reserve had agreed to talk to the police without a whole legal team present to do the speaking for them. It raised the question of why Cade had stuck his neck out to make it happen.

Marlow pulled the pictures up. He had a good phone. The colors were bright and the resolution sharp. It was unforgiving. He'd seen worse.

"They cut off her hands," he said. The sound of someone's voice snapping orders as they approached down the hall filtered through the door. Marlow swiped the photos off the screen and tucked the phone back into his pocket. "Then left her to bleed out."

Cade slid off the desk and pushed the sleeves of his jersey up his forearm. "When?" he asked.

"Sometime between midnight and three."

The door opened, and a short, round woman in a sleek red dress that matched the chair walked in. She immediately begged for one more minute with her finger as she turned to the secretary who'd shown them in.

"Tell Ms. Griffin that we'll pass along her husband's 'advice,'" she said, her fingers hooked in air quotes around the last word. "But the final decision is the director's. Then trash his email and see if there's any starlet from that mystery-girl show that just wrapped available."

The secretary nodded, tapped assiduously on his phone, and closed the door behind him as he left.

"Ms. Farnham," Cade said. "I appreciate you taking the time to speak to Officer Marlow about this. The quicker it's resolved, the better for us all. Once Cold Winds can confirm that Mr. Macroy did due diligence in safeguarding his card, we'll reassure the board at the Reserve that they don't have to take action."

She gave Cade a once-over, head to toe, and then did the same to Marlow as she gripped his hand to shake. He'd been eyed up before, but never quite so dispassionately. It felt more like being measured for a suit than anything else.

"Of course," she said. "Mr. Macroy is in Canada right now, overseeing a production. But he's instructed me to do whatever I can to help, although I'm not sure how. As I told your colleague earlier, that card is for the use of Mr. Macroy's personal assistant… whoever that is. Mr. Macroy is a creative genius, and like many such men, he isn't always easy to work with. His assistants rarely stay after the first bottle thrown at their heads."

"You can't get the work ethic these days," Marlow said mildly.

Farnham raised a perfectly sculpted eyebrow at him, then gave in with a dry smile and let herself be amused. "I don't blame them," she clarified. "But some only last a week. One didn't even make it a full day. It was a trial to have to reapply for a new card, and one year Mr. Macroy burned through his entire allotment of visitor passes."

"Who had it last?" Marlow asked.

"Me," Farnham said. "Or at least I touched it last when I put it back into the file. Mr. Macroy doesn't necessarily want everyone he works with to have access to his house. When he doesn't need them to check on his appliances, make sure his TV was unplugged, or feed his fish, it stays in his safe. His latest assistant left two months ago, so the only one who had access to it was me. I go in once a month and make sure the place is locked up for the full moon."

"You don't stay up there yourself?" Cade asked. "A perk of the job?"

Farnham folded her lips in a tight smile. "Not much of a perk," she said. "I'm null. Like Officer Marlow here."

That made Marlow blink in surprise. His scars itched under his black T-shirt, and he scratched his shoulder without thinking about it.

"How did you—?"

"You look tired." She tapped a finger against her cheekbone to call attention to the puffy skin under her eyes. "Even the most expensive eye cream doesn't make a dent, does it?"

"*You* work Night Shift?" Cade asked. He didn't bother to try and hide the doubt in his voice.

Farnham traded an amused look with Marlow and didn't answer that question. She waved her hand toward the bookshelf, where an inset safe had been left open and empty.

"I checked it this morning after we spoke. The card was gone."

"Anything else?" Marlow asked. He walked over to look at the safe for any sign that the door had been forced or tampered with. Nothing he could see, but the carpet lined interior of the metal box stank of musky, pine-themed perfume. When there was a pause before Farnham answered, he turned to look at her. "I don't care what else Mr. Macroy kept in here, ma'am. I just want to know if the card was all whoever opened it wanted."

Farnham pursed her lips for a moment and then shook her head. "There was some money and… personal items in there," she said. "As far as I could tell, they were untouched. I just moved them for security. The keycard was all they took."

Marlow took his phone back out of his pocket. He pulled one of Sun's pictures onto the screen and enlarged it until it just showed the dead girl's face. Farnham was obviously prickly about her boss's reputation. The minute she heard the messy details, fellow null or not, she'd clam up.

"Do you recognize her at all?" he asked. "Maybe an old employee or…?"

Farnham blanched and pushed herself up from the desk. She reached for the phone, but aborted the gesture as Marlow apologetically moved it out of reach.

"Oh," she said. Her voice dropped in a regretful sigh, filtered through her fingers as she raised one hand to her mouth. "Oh, no. Not her."

"You know her?" Cade said.

Farnham kept her eyes on the screen as she nodded. "For years," she said. "Since she was a little girl. You don't?'

She finally looked up from the photo to give them both an incredulous glance. When they didn't react with any sort of recognition, she gave a thin slice of a smile.

"Ah, no kids, then? Or sisters?"

Cade's face closed down like a slammed door. He wasn't a particularly open and approachable man anyhow—except when naked in an elevator—but the sudden freeze was so brutal it was unmissable. It made Farnham flush and look flustered, not sure where she'd misstepped.

"Only child," Marlow said. He shrugged crookedly in an invitation for sympathy. "And working Night Shift makes it hard to find a date."

For a beat, Farnham couldn't decide what to react to, but Marlow's was easier. She nodded as if what he'd said made sense to her.

"Of course," she said. "Her name's Haley Jenkins. She was the star of one of Wallace's first big shows."

Farnham pointed to one of the posters on the wall. A girl with white flames for hair stood on rocky letters that spelled out *Haley's Comet* against a backdrop that looked like a ruined New York skyline.

"I haven't seen her in years," Farnham said. The shock had faded from her face, and her voice was steady again, though there was a deep scratch of sadness in it. "After the show ended, she had some problems, and she blamed us, the company, for them. She cut ties. We've not had any dealings with her since. I have no idea how she got the keycard or why she'd want it."

"Do you have her contact details?" Marlow asked.

Farnham closed her eyes and swallowed, a wet, slow click in her throat. "I think they're probably out of date." All of a sudden, she sounded as tired as Marlow felt. "But Parker will have them at the desk on your way out."

Marlow nodded. "Thank you for your help," he said. "SDPD appreciates it."

She nodded.

"I'll get an operative to check the house and reset the security system," Cade said as he led the way to the door. "I'm sorry for your loss."

The cell phone number that Parker had given them was dead. The other number connected to an answering machine for an Adelaide Jenkins, who had the warm, happy voice of someone that should bake pies and knit baby blankets.

Marlow left a message for them to contact the station. Night Shift didn't have to do death notifications often—usually only on the scene if they needed people to understand why they had to leave the dead—and Marlow didn't want to start on Adelaide and her warm Montana voice.

He went over to take his coffee from Cade.

"I don't know how you drink that stuff," Cade remarked as he popped the lid on his cup and breathed in the salt and beef steam. "It'll stunt your growth."

"It'll keep me awake," Marlow said, although interest in the case had counteracted some of his weariness. "So how did Haley go from child actress to dead girl?"

Cade left the beverage cart behind and headed down the road to where he'd parked his car.

"Haley Jenkins starred as Haley Comet, a teenage null girl given superhuman powers by… Haley's Comet." Cade paused to roll his eyes as he read the synopsis from his phone. "It was popular and ran for four seasons but was reputedly canceled over a contract dispute with Haley. That was six years ago. Since then, it's been bad boys, booze, and a bed in rehab."

"When?"

"On the bad boys or the rehab?"

"Either. Both."

"Bad boys are ongoing, based on TMZ's coverage," Cade said. "The last rehab was six months ago. Maybe she graduated to something stronger than Grey Goose?"

Marlow slid his fingers up under his glasses to rub his eye. "I don't usually do motive." His gran had loved the old classic cop shows. There had always been one on when he got home from school, and he'd wanted to be one of the detectives. But he wasn't. "You know what they say."

"Night Shift don't have the *nose* for detection," Cade repeated the old jab, with sarcastic emphasis on the right part. "But you're what I've got to bounce ideas off, so give it a sniff."

"In my experience, drug dealers don't usually kill their clients. They don't need to. The product eventually will, and the dealer will get paid for it. And why make it… weird?"

"Good question.'

As praise went, it was brisk and disinterested. Marlow still had to bite the inside of his cheek to squelch the flush of pleasure it gave him. He wasn't a rookie who thought *he'd* be the one to break the silver ceiling anymore. The Night Shift was what he did, and he was good at it.

"Have you ever been to the Reserve?" Cade asked as he thumbed the fob he pulled out of his pocket. The lights on the Tesla flashed twice. It was a state-of-the-art car, synced to Cade's tags so he didn't have to worry about losing the keys during a shift. The problem, as Marlow assumed Cade had learned earlier, was that you could still lose the car.

"Couple of times. I went out with a cook who worked up there. He lived in, so he sneaked me in. The food was good; the boyfriend didn't last." Marlow paused to wash the sudden dry, ashy grit out of his throat with a gulp of sour coffee as he caught up with what had just come out of his mouth. There was no good reason that Cade needed to know Marlow dated men. None that Marlow wanted to admit to himself on this amount of sleep. He cleared his throat, which still felt dry, and took pity on the irritated look Cade had sent his way. "Don't worry, it was before Cold Winds took the contract. Bear Arms Protection was a lot more relaxed about protocol."

Cade didn't look any happier.

"Then you can tell me what you think of my updates," he said. "Farnham just confirmed that Macroy's house was broken into, possibly during whatever attack left Haley dead. That means that you—"

"—don't need a warrant," Marlow finished for him as he ducked down into the car. "I was going to bring that up."

Cade drained his Bovril and tossed the empty cup into a nearby trash can.

"Of course you were," he said, without any attempt to disguise the condescension in his voice. "Now you don't have to."

CHAPTER FOUR

HE KNEW HOW to be nice to people! Despite evidence to the contrary.

Cade flexed his hands around the steering wheel and took a quick sidelong look at the cause of his irritation. Marlow was kicked back in the passenger seat, arms crossed and his chin tucked down toward his chest. He'd been asleep since before they hit the outskirts of the city.

At least he didn't snore. That was good to know.

Yes, Cade thought irritably to himself as he focused on the road, *because this is both a good idea* and *going well.*

There were dozens of people who had no idea that Cade had a reputation for being difficult or that he could be a jerk. His accountant sent him a gift basket once a year. The cleaners who kept his house in order thought him reasonable and an excellent tipper. He didn't need to make sure they knew their place for the sake of his business or his ego.

So he *could* be nice. Except every time he tried with Marlow, the words that in his head seemed witty—even charming—were hijacked by asshole. All he'd wanted to do was impress Marlow with the idea of a visit to the Reserve. Instead, he'd implied the man was stupid and a liar to boot.

Not that Marlow seemed to care, which might actually be more annoying.

The problem with an inconvenient attraction crawling out of the subconscious—aside from the fact there was no putting it back—was that it was a mess. It hadn't been trimmed and tidied, compartmentalized so it fit neatly into his life.

It was just a slop of chemicals spilled all over his brain. He felt like a teenage boy with a crush, who ached at the thought of a mobile mouth and the constellation of scars down a lean torso.

Cade clenched his jaw and swore under his breath as his body reacted eagerly to that image. It was ridiculous. No one got hard over the thought of a man in cartoon mouse boxers.

Next to him, Marlow cracked one eye open. "What's wrong?"

"I thought you were asleep."

Marlow straightened up out of his slouch. "My eyes were closed," he said. "Close enough. Something happen?"

Before Cade had to lie, the red strobe of road work lights flashed ahead, dim in the daylight. He just gestured to them as he tapped the brakes to roll the car to a halt at the boundary.

A dead thing lay in the road. A moose from the ragged mass of it, although the head and most everything under the rib cage had been hollowed out. What the wolves hadn't got last night, the scavengers would today. There was still enough left to wreck a car if you hit it at speed.

"At least I don't have to deal with wildlife," Marlow said. "Well, rats. But they hold their own."

One side of the road was still open. Cade swung wide around the strung-up tape and drove past. He put his foot down as they cleared it.

"It's about ten more minutes away," he said, "if you want to have another catnap."

Marlow gave him an unamused look. "Very funny," he said, dry and just off clipped. "I'm fine, thanks."

Cade gave up with a silent *fuck*. He didn't even know how he'd got that one wrong.

"Who are you here to see?" the younger guard at the Reserve checkpoint asked as he leaned down to look in the car window. His dull brown eyes squinted to see against the sun coming through the passenger side. If Cade had wanted he could have grabbed the wolf's collar and yanked him into the car, shanked him with the ceramic knife he kept in the door, and grabbed the tablet used to interface with the security system. "Invitation only for visitors."

The guard wasn't one of Cade's personal picks. Of course, more weren't than were these days. The company had reached the point he couldn't have direct oversight over personnel. Maybe he needed to carve time out of his day, though.

Marlow leaned over, one hand braced on Cade's thigh, and showed his badge.

"Night Shift," he said. "We need access."

The guard gawped for a moment and then nodded as he swiped his finger over the tablet.

"Of course," he said. "I'll, um, escort you myself. Where do you need to—"

The other guard—Smith—was one of Cade's hand picks. In fact, Cade had personally recruited him from a corporate security firm that ran a refinery up in Alaska. He wasn't on gate duty usually, but Cade liked everyone to take one shift a year in every post, just so they knew the ropes.

Smith tapped his tablet to lock his co-worker out of the system and stepped in.

"Ask for a warrant, Nader," Smith said.

Nader gave him a dubious look. "He's Night Shift," he said, with a jerk of his thumb toward Marlow. "You don't get in their way."

"It's midday, man," Smith said. He bent down to peer into the car. His eyes flicked to the hand on Cade's leg and then back to Marlow's face. "You even on duty?"

"Special assignment," Marlow said.

"That come with a warrant?"

Marlow grinned, a quick, easy flash of charm that lit up his whole face. "No, it doesn't."

He pushed himself off Cade's leg. The warmth of his hand remained, soaked through cotton and down into muscle. Cade definitely hated that.

"So he doesn't get in, not until we see the warrant," Smith said, in the patient voice of someone with a particularly slow-to-learn kid. He pointed at Cade. "Or the boss, who we let in, tells us that the cop is with him. Idiot."

Nader flushed miserably. He was handsome and clean-cut, the sort of looks that had been scuffed off most of Cade's recruits after stints in the army or the police. Another problem of his ex-partner's left behind for Cade to deal with, maybe? He'd thought they needed more "approachable" faces.

"He's with me. By the way, there's a moose carcass on the road," Cade said as he shifted the car out of park. "Five miles back. It should have been cleared already."

It was part of the contract with the Reserve. The state road crews were responsible for repairs, but the Cold Winds' crews ensured the roads were passable. Half of the Reserve's clients were rich enough they only had to work three days out of the year. The other half were so rich they couldn't even take the usual three days a month off.

Leftovers spilled on the road weren't what they wanted to see.

Nader frowned and glanced down at his tablet. He jabbed and swiped with a gloved finger as he checked.

"Nothing on the task sheet," he said. "You sure?"

"I drove past it," Cade said after a dangerous beat. "Pretty sure."

Smith grabbed Nader by the collar and dragged him back out of the way. "We'll get on that, sir," he said. "Sorry for the oversight."

Cade rolled up the window as he headed up the road. Next to him, Marlow laughed.

"Paramount close protection professionals, you get what you pay for," he repeated the blurb from the Cold Winds website. "Truth in advertising, I guess."

He'd looked them up.

Cade wondered if it was because Cold Winds had intersected with one of the Night Shift's operations—which had happened a couple of times—or if he'd considered their recruitment package. They hired a lot of ex-cops and a few moonlighters, although Cade would admit that was mostly to annoy the chief of police.

And maybe he'd looked at Cade's bio page when he was there?

"If you're looking for a new challenge," Cade said, "I can move you to the top of the list."

It was only half a joke. Null operatives were in high demand. While they only made up around 20 percent of the population, there were a lot of very good reasons why there were sign-up bonuses on a null contract—and not just because it was always handy to have someone around who could touch silver or nightshade. But nobody had much success tempting Night Shift officers into the private sector. It took a lot of work to make Night Shift, and anyone willing to put that effort in had a vocation, not a job.

"I would," Marlow said. "But I just can't give up that public servant money. Besides, it's creepy up here."

Cade took his eyes off the road for a second, looked at Marlow, and then turned his attention back to the—carefully cultivated to look untouched—woods around them. It was as close to idyllic as expensive architects and landscapers could make it. Mansions were dug down under hills or disguised with elegant copses of native trees. Wildlife experts maintained genetically diverse herds of moose, bison, and boar for the wolves to hunt, and the only fences were the acres of property they'd bought as a barrier between them and the rest of society.

The Reserve's residents paid exorbitant amounts to have the best of both worlds, with modern comforts like running water and territory their wolves could run and hunt in unfettered.

No fences. No rules. No Night Shift.

As long as they stayed within their property lines, anyhow.

"This is creepy?" Cade asked.

Marlow shrugged. "I've never liked the countryside," he said. "I'm a city boy. Not enough alleys out here, and it gets too dark at night."

"You just need to get used to it," Cade said. "On a clear night, when the moon and stars are out, you could count the freckles on someone's ass if you wanted to."

Cade heard himself a second too late to edit the shit that came out of his mouth. He closed his eyes for a beat but resisted the urge to just keep them closed and drive into a tree. Since when did he flirt—badly or otherwise? He dated (some) and hooked up (more), but when you had money, you didn't need pick up lines. You just picked up the tab.

Of course, he didn't go to dinner with any of his hookups or setups already aware of the faint spray of pale freckles that blotched their lean shoulders. If he did, maybe he would say something just as humiliating.

The road petered out under the car's tires. Cade turned left onto a gravel path and glanced briefly over at Marlow, who was focused on the precarious route ahead, either because he was so disinterested in Cade that he hadn't even noticed the flirting, or just disinterested enough to ignore it politely. Embarrassment clutched at Cade's stomach like a missed meal, and he could taste the bitterness of it.

"Do you—"

"Macroy's place is the next turn," Cade interrupted Marlow curtly, just in case Marlow was going to say something *nice* and *diplomatic* about how he was flattered, but… There was always a "but," and what came after it was never the truth. Cade managed to be a little amused at the discovery he didn't want, not just yet anyhow, to be disillusioned about Marlow. "So, we should be clear on the ground rules. We're here to confirm that, however she got Macroy's keycard, Haley wasn't on the Reserve when she died. Anything else?"

"It's meat of the poisoned deer," Marlow said in mild-mannered agreement. He braced his arm against the car door and gasped as Cade took a sharp turn onto a concealed road. It took him a second to get the air back into his lungs again to finish the thought. "Shit. Yeah, unless it's related to this case, none of Macroy's personal habits are my business. Unless it's kids, in which case your lawyers can fight it out in court."

Cade's smile felt thin and tight against his teeth as he pulled up outside Macroy's property. He killed the engine, and the silence that fell felt almost oppressive. "Oh, it wouldn't get to court. Don't touch anything inside. If you break it, you buy it. And you can't afford to buy it."

"I don't know about you," Marlow said out of the corner of his mouth as he leaned in toward Cade. "I wouldn't take any of this stuff for free."

It was the first joke he'd made around Cade. Unfortunately, Cade couldn't appreciate it. The house was trashed. Empty containers of takeout food were stacked on the tables, rank and stinking of old pork and MSG, the furniture was stained, and the lamps and mirrors were smashed in shards and fragments on the floor. He could smell sweat, the stink of it so strong that it cut through his humanity and hooked whatever bit of wolf hung in through the change.

Fear. Want.

"Son of a bitch," Cade spat as he walked through the mess.

He kicked a pile of wet, soiled towels out of his way and headed down the hall into the huge old-fashioned farmhouse kitchen. The smell of burnt food and scorched metal caught in the back of his throat. He covered his mouth and nose with his sleeve and jogged over to the stove to turn the gas off. The flickering blue-red flames guttered out, and Cade reached for the pot without a thought.

Heat stung his fingers even before he touched the handle. The base of the pot was so hot it glowed a dull cherry red, and the inside of it was cracked and caked with charred black lumps of whatever had been in it.

"Looks like Haley made herself at home." Cade pulled a dirty dishcloth out of the sink and grabbed the pot. It was hot enough to make him wince even through the layers of cloth. "And was a fucking raccoon."

He dropped the pot into the sink, on top of the plates already there, and flicked the water on. A cloud of steam spat out of the pot, and he jumped back, a "Shit" hissed between clenched teeth. Something in the sink cracked with a brittle snap. "

Marlow snorted as he joined Cade in the kitchen.

"I'd assume that there's some sort of vetting process residents have to go through before they throw a party?" Marlow said, his head tilted to one side.

"That's right," Cade said. "It's not prison. They can have people over, but they need to let us know ahead of time. The guards wouldn't have let a bunch of D-list celebs down from LA in just because they said they'd been invited. Even Nader's not that stupid."

"Even if Haley could have done it through Macroy's mail, it probably would have hit social media by now," Marlow said. "It's the Reserve. D-listers would want pictures to prove they were here. So, this built up over a few days."

Cade kicked a cabinet door shut. It bounced back open again. His temper wanted to say it looked like she'd been here for a year, but practically…

"We do sweeps of empty houses," he said. "Once a week, to make sure nothing has been disturbed or needs attention. She could have, maybe, dodged it the first time. Not the second. I'd guess four to five days would be the maximum she was here for, from the debris."

"And she didn't particularly care what Macroy would do to her when he got back," Marlow said.

He tapped his foot on the bin to open it and peered into it, then without a word, headed back out and down to the main room. Cade turned the water off in the sink and went after him.

"What is it?" Cade asked.

Marlow knelt on the floor and leaned down to look under the couch. He stuck his hand in and pulled out a heavy glass tumbler with a residue of sticky cherry-red cordial in the bottom. He sniffed it.

"Cranberry juice," he said. "She might have left the house a mess, but it's a sober mess."

Cade frowned but nodded his agreement anyhow. The relapsed junkie would have made a nice, tidy story, but there were no empty bottles of booze, no drug paraphernalia, and while the place was a mess, it wasn't *trashed* like a tweaker's place.

"So, what the hell was she doing here?"

"Getting her own back?" Marlow said. He moved a cushion and pulled out a dog-eared copy of *Necromancer*. "If Farnham was right, maybe she still blames Macroy for the loss of her career."

Cade thought about the bright-eyed, air-brushed girl on the poster in Macroy's office and grimaced. "Or for something else."

"Maybe."

Marlow opened the book and pulled out a scrap of paper whoever had read it used as a bookmark. He replaced it with a bit of tassel pulled off a cushion—as if Haley would ever worry about a lost place in a book again—and set it down on the floor.

"If your people didn't know she was here," Marlow pointed out, "they wouldn't know she needed to leave. It's possible she was still here when the moon was up."

Cade couldn't argue with that. "Yeah," he said. "But no one here could be held responsible. They didn't know she was here, and there's no sign of forced entry. If she went out that night, she went out on her own."

Suicide by moonlight. It was rare—there were easier ways to go, ones that left a corpse that wouldn't make your granny cry—but it happened.

Marlow scratched his lower lip and looked grim. It sharpened the soft, easy-going lines of his face, pulled the angle of his jaw and cheekbones into high definition. Cade was slightly surprised to realize Marlow was actually handsome. He hid it well, most of the time.

"Unless someone did know," he said.

"Who?" Cade asked.

He didn't expect Marlow to answer; that was why he had Lem digging up dirt on the SDPD Night Shift going back a decade. For a second, as Marlow opened his mouth to say something, Cade thought he might be wrong.

Something shattered in the back of the house. It shouldn't have. The glass windows were reinforced and tempered, able to survive an impact with a pissed-off wolf that had just seen its reflection.

Cade kept his gun in a shoulder holster tucked against his ribs under his jacket. It turned out that Marlow favored a clip-holster in the small of his back. He might have had a second's edge on his draw.

It didn't *matter*. This wasn't the old days. A fast draw wasn't going to give Marlow the edge in a duel.

Cade knew he was still going to put extra hours in at the gun range this month.

He caught Marlow's attention and raised his hand to sign directions that sent Marlow around the outside while Cade went through the house. Technically he didn't have any standing to give orders, but in his experience, the key to leadership was to not give anyone the chance to argue.

Gun held low by his thigh, Cade stuck close to the wall as he headed toward the back of the house. Out of the corner of his eye he saw Marlow glare at him, grimace, and then back up toward the front door to do as he was told.

Cade's feet slid over the tiled floor as he paused at the doorway, shoulder against the frame. The familiar pulse of adrenaline hummed in his ears, a vibration that settled in the bones of his jaw as he checked the hall.

Empty.

He loped down the tall white-walled space, wary of the doors. The kitchen was clear, window steamed up and sink still full of dishes. He paused at the long, curved staircase down into the Macroy's main living area—his memory of the blueprints filled in what was down there, the living room and bedrooms, office, and theatre—but the steps were covered with torn, crumpled papers that looked undisturbed.

Garage, then. Back of the house.

Habit raised his hand to his ear before he remembered that this wasn't one of his operations. Marlow was on his own.

So was Cade, but he was used to that.

He shouldered the door to the garage open and went in, gun raised, just as the intruder—tall and skinny in gray sweats with a hoodie pulled tight around their face—climbed onto the top of a Lexus and climbed out a narrow broken window.

Shit.

CHAPTER FIVE

THE MAN IN gray landed awkwardly on the grass, arms extended to break his fall, and scrambled back to his feet. A bright smear of red ran down the arm of his hoodie.

"Hands up!" Marlow barked as he stopped, feet planted and arms braced as he lifted his gun. "Don't move."

The suspect started to raise his arms slowly, but Marlow could already tell he wasn't going to comply from the way his eyes darted around. That was a man who still thought he had options.

Cade broke the last shards of glass out of the window with the butt of his gun. He swung one leg out and then angled his broad shoulders through the gap. Marlow glanced at him quickly.

It was the closest to an opportunity that the suspect would get. He bolted like a sprinter off the blocks and dashed toward the trees. Marlow sighted down his gun to the nice broad space between the man's shoulders as they jerked up and down with each step. It was an easy target. He wasn't the best shot in the Night Shift—that was Bennett—but he'd not miss that.

His ribs twinged with the memory of shock and pressure. It hadn't hurt. Not at first. He'd just felt winded.

Except this wasn't anything to do with that. Everyone involved was either dead or still in prison, not out for a run in the afternoon sun.

Marlow swore and thumbed the safety back on. He tucked the gun into its holster, snug and heavy against the small of his back, before he gave chase.

Glass crunched in the grass as Marlow cut through it. The long muscles in his thighs flexed as he powered up the slope after the suspect. His knee decided this was the opportune moment to remember it wasn't 100 percent as he navigated the uneven footing. It felt like shards of glass frayed the tendon each time he changed direction.

It was fine.

Or it was functional, at least. Close enough.

The suspect scrambled over a fallen tree, strips of bark stripped off under his sneakers, and landed badly on the other side. His leg folded under him, and he bounced down the steep hill in a tangle of arms and legs.

Marlow vaulted the log, one hand braced on the wet, scabby wood, and followed in a—slightly—more controlled descent. At the bottom of the slope, the suspect dragged himself to his feet and broke into a stubborn hobble toward the empty streambed that cut along the bottom of the valley.

A shabby red 4x4 was just visible through the trees on the other side, caked with dirt and bits of tree from the drive up. The suspect had come prepared.

Marlow skidded down the last few feet of the slope. He heard gravel kick down behind him and took a quick glance back to check that he wasn't being flanked. Instead, it was Cade, stains on his gray trousers, only a few yards behind Marlow with his gun still drawn.

The back of Marlow's neck crawled with suspicion, an itch that ran all the way down to the small of his back, but he ignored it. Everyone at the station knew that Cade was a pain in the ass, but Marlow didn't think he was corrupt. In his experience, corruption made people a lot more concerned with what people thought of them.

He dragged his attention back to his own feet as he reached the bottom of the hill. There was blood on the stones where the suspect had landed and a gray cord where the drawstring had snapped off his hoodie. Marlow hopped over them and broke into a dead run across the last stretch. He hurdled the dry gully and wove through the trees as he tried to cut the suspect off before he reached his car.

Branches whipped at his face, and Marlow swore under his breath as he tried to dodge under them. The side of his neck stung where one of the thinner branches had caught him. This was why he hated the countryside. He could chase a perp down an alley in the city, and all he had to worry about was broken glass on the ground and rats.

Ahead of him, the suspect misjudged his speed and smacked into the side of his car. He bounced off and scrabbled at his pockets with frantic fingers.

Shit.

Marlow might not be entirely sure whether Cade meant to flirt with him or not—or what the hell he'd do if Cade was—but he knew he didn't want to look like an incompetent ass in front of him. Flirt *or* asshole, that would be humiliating.

He put on a final burst of speed and tackled the suspect. His shoulder slammed into the man's side, and they both went down. The suspect kicked out violently with both feet, the heels of sneakers jabbed into Marlow's chest and shoulder, and popped a switchblade out of his pocket.

"Get away from me," he spat as he swung the blade at Marlow. The tip of it sliced in front of Marlow's face, close enough it blurred as it nicked the tip of his nose. "Son of a bitch."

Marlow jerked back and rolled easily to his feet. He stepped backward, his body between the suspect and the car, and waited.

The suspect slashed the knife at him, wild, wide swings of his arm, to try and bully Marlow backward. It didn't work. Marlow just swayed back onto his heels and waited for panic to set in.

"I've got a knife!" The blade trembled in a too-tight clutch as the suspect jabbed it at Marlow's torso. "Just get out of my way, and no one gets hurt."

He thrust again, and Marlow grabbed his arm. He dug his fingers into the suspect's wrist until he ground tendons against bone, then twisted. The knife dropped to the dirt track with a thud as it slipped out of suddenly boneless fingers.

"Be happy you don't know how to use it," Marlow said as he used the suspect's arm like a lever to force him down onto his knees, "or I'd have had to shoot you."

Cade, slowed to a lope now the chase was over, joined them. He held up one hand, a set of keys dangled from his finger for the suspect to see.

"You weren't going to get far without these anyhow," he said.

Not any sort of professional, then. They'd have left the keys in the car. Who was going to steal it way out here? A raccoon?

The suspect lunged forward in an attempt to wrench free that ended in a howl of pain as his arm bent entirely the wrong way. He subsided with a groan, and his head hung forward between his shoulders as he shuddered.

Marlow reached down and pulled the snug, now grubby, gray hood back off the man's head. It folded up around his neck, revealing sandy-ginger hair and a mole off-center on the back of his neck.

"I know him," Cade said. He frowned and tilted his head to the side. "Where do I know him from?"

Good question. Marlow slammed the man against the door of his 4x4 as he dragged a spare zip tie out of his pocket. He looped it around the man's bony wrists—a moderately expensive watch cool under his fingers as they brushed the links—and pulled it to secure them. Once he was happy the tie was secure, he yanked the suspect off the car, turned him around, and slammed him back into it.

Recognition caught him flat-footed. The man looked a lot different from the last time Marlow had seen him, with bruises on his bony well-bred face and leaves tangled in previously gelled-flat hair, but there was no question it was him. It had only been a couple of hours ago that they met, after all, so his face was fresh in Marlow's memory.

"Parker," Marlow said, his voice inflected with surprise as he stared at Ms. Farnham's secretary. "What the hell are you doing here?"

In the gray box of the interrogation room, Parker, hunched over meekly in his gray sweats, faded into the background. He twisted his hands together, which made the cuffs that shackled him to the table rattle, and fidgeted in the chair.

Marlow couldn't blame him for the last part. The metal seats were uncomfortable, like that had been the plan when they were made.

"Are the cuffs necessary?" Elliot Grayson asked as he clicked his pen. "My client is cooperating, he's not a violent felon, and he's hardly a threat to anyone here—"

His client was an interesting way to phrase it. Grayson had been hired by Farnham, sent over when Parker had used his one call to contact the office. It probably wasn't in his best interests, but he'd accepted the representation.

"He might not be a felon, but he did pull a knife on me," Marlow pointed out. "So violent is back on the table."

Grayson raised his eyebrows and looked Marlow over. "You seem fine," he said, "so he's obviously not taken to assault and battery like a duck to water."

"All he needs is practice," O'Hara said as he sat down. "Let's not give him the opportunity. So, Mr. Parker is ready to speak to us now?"

"This was all a misunderstanding," Grayson said in a smooth, pleasant voice. He was better at his job than most of the overworked, under-motivated court-appointed attorneys that ended up in here. It sounded like he actually believed his client. "A well-intentioned good deed that somehow, without Mr. Parker's involvement, went terribly wrong."

O'Hara sat back. "Go on, then," he said. "For the record. What happened?"

Parker glanced at Grayson, got the nod to go on, and took a deep breath as he straightened up out of his slouch.

"We were friends," he said. His voice was a bit too loud against the raw concrete walls, and he stopped for a second to recalibrate before he tried again. "Haley and me, we were friends. Had been since *Haley's Comet* was on air."

"A coincidence that you ended up working for her producer, then," O'Hara noted.

Parker shook his head. "She was the main character, not the only actor," he said. "I played Patton Black on the show. My first job and my last. I'd rather be like Mr. Macroy, make the shows, not just star in them. But that's how I met Haley. We weren't besties or anything, but we stayed in touch after the show ended. A couple of weeks ago, she got in touch with me and asked for help."

"With some handiwork?" Marlow asked.

Parker looked at him blankly for a second. "No?" he said eventually, after another glance at Grayson for reassurance. "Um. No. She needed somewhere to dry out, and she couldn't go back into rehab. She'd landed her first gig in ages, and part of the contract was that she stayed sober. They'd have bounced her if they found she'd toasted someone with champagne, never mind gone on a bender."

Contempt cut through his voice for a second, a sour flick on the end of his sentence. The table jolted slightly as Grayson nudged him with a knee. Parker stopped and looked down at his hands.

"I just wanted to help," he said. "And I didn't see the harm. Mr. Macroy lets people use the house sometimes when he's not there. To learn lines or clear their head."

Marlow carefully didn't look behind him at the long glass mirror. He couldn't imagine that Cade was best pleased with that bit of information.

"So why break in?"

Parker tried to do something with his hands and was pulled up short. He laid them both flat on the table and stared at them.

"I didn't know what was going on," he said. "All I knew was Haley had gotten into trouble again and… and if she'd left anything that implicated me, I could lose my job. I figured you were Night Shift, so there was no way you'd be up there until after the moon waned. The plan was to get in, clean up, and get out."

It wasn't a bad plan. There was a chance that O'Hara would have sent up a detective on days, but at this time of the month, it wasn't likely. Most of the force was too busy dealing with the aftermath of the previous night—towing cars, settling disputes with neighbors, processing anyone hauled in and Crated—before the next full moon clocked them off. If Marlow hadn't been willing to cut his downtime short, Parker could have been in and out without anyone the wiser.

"What we call that," Marlow said, "is getting rid of the evidence."

Parker shook his head. "No. I mean, yeah. I wanted to cover my tracks, but only for letting her stay there." He poked his finger against the table to underline his point. "I didn't know… I didn't know, okay? I thought she'd gone on a bender and crashed her car—again—or something like that. Not that she was, you know… dead."

Grayson put his hand on Parker's arm to quiet him.

"Misjudgment," he said. "Maybe even misappropriation of his employer's property, but not anything as extreme as murder."

"And yet Haley was murdered," O'Hara pointed out. "And your client has just admitted he was the only one who knew where she was."

"Except," Grayson said, "she died last night, according to what you shared with Ms. Farnham. My client is a wolf. As you can imagine, he was otherwise occupied. He'd booked a day package at a hunting lodge up in LA. He was killing boar, and his tags will confirm his location."

Hard to argue with that.

O'Hara didn't cede to Grayson immediately, but they all knew he'd have to. At least for now, on the murder charge. After a brief back-and-forth, Parker was charged with assault on an officer, since Macroy's office had refused to press charges for the breaking and entering.

It wasn't nothing, but…

"Farnham really went to bat for that boy," Marlow remarked as they stood in the corridor and watched Parker limp away. "I wonder why."

"Doesn't matter," O'Hara said. "He couldn't have killed her, so he's a dead end. Move on."

"To what?" Cade asked. He crossed his arms and raised his eyebrows. "Whatever happened to Haley didn't happen at the Reserve. Some overworked Night Shift porter put 'Reserve' down on the paperwork because they found the card on her. No mystery. No conspiracy. No problem."

"She's still dead," Marlow said.

Cade looked *almost* sorry for a second. Then he shrugged, a dismissive twitch of his shoulders.

"That would be your problem," he said, "not mine. Captain O'Hara, I've been more than cooperative—"

"I'd like one more look around," Marlow said before the captain could cave again. "Tomorrow. I've got… a feeling we could have missed something. We were interrupted."

There was a pause. Marlow felt a twinge of guilt at the back of his skull as he wondered if Cade's maybe-flirtation was why it wasn't an immediate no.

"Noon," Cade said at last. He leveled a finger at Marlow. "It's your last freebie. You want past my men again, get richer. I'd suggest a new job."

"I could marry well," Marlow said. "Either way works."

Cade gave him a hot look out of bottle-amber eyes. It made Marlow's mouth go dry, even though it took him a second to catch up with what he might have suggested. Once he caught on, it seemed rude to blurt "Not you!" so Marlow held his tongue.

Sometimes you had to settle for the win and stop chasing the loss.

"I didn't take you for a gold digger. Good to know." Cade brushed at the stain on his sleeve and then checked the time. "I better go. If I see you later, it won't be personal."

He turned without any of the expected niceties and stalked away. Marlow had to admit, as he watched him go, that he gave good stalk. It was loose, with long legs and the cocky swing of his hips. The walk of someone who knew people liked to see him leave for two good reasons.

His personality, and his ass.

O'Hara cleared his throat. "Flirt on your own time," he told Marlow, voice dry and starchily amused. "And go get some sleep. You're on active tonight."

That smacked the distraction right out of Marlow. He spread his hands in protest.

"I was active last night, all night," he said. "And I've been out today. Regs say I should be on call."

O'Hara shrugged. "Franklin had a death in the family, out in Victorville," he said. "And Sergeant Harrison is on indefinite medical leave. His knee isn't coming back this time. We're short-handed, and you're here."

That explanation made more sense of Harrison's retirement than Bennett's version.

"You'll be more short-handed when I get eaten because I made a mistake."

"No," O'Hara said. "Franklin should be back tomorrow. Try not to die before midnight."

Marlow snorted and tried to shove the question of Haley Jenkins and how she died to the back of his mind as he headed down to the locker rooms. She could wait. The moon wouldn't.

The child screamed, a piercing pre-verbal shriek at the discomfort of it all, as the wolf ran with it in her mouth. She barreled through the fences that divided the neat postage-stamp suburban plots. Dirty white hooked claws dug furrows in the manicured green lawns. The bloody curtains from the nursery flapped behind her like a cape, illuminated as a series of security lights flicked on as she passed.

It made it easy to follow her.

"Dispatch?" Marlow clipped into his radio as he vaulted a broken swing set. A bit of plastic twisted under his foot as he landed. He staggered, caught himself, and kept going. "We've got a familial custody dispute on Albina Blvd. In active pursuit. Will need a medic here ASAP."

The radio crackled a promise that the ambulance was on route.

A door opened, and one of the neighbors stepped outside. The distinctive ratchet of a shotgun being loaded was audible even over the baby's hysterics.

"Get back inside," Marlow yelled. He broke stride to grab his badge so he could flash it at the man. "The situation is under control. Go. Inside."

Inside the house, a man tried to convince his husband to listen. The neighbor compromised by staying put. He cradled his shotgun in his arms as he craned his neck after the wolf.

Idiot.

Marlow left him to it. The break in momentum had cost him a few yards as the wolf lengthened her stride and widened the lead. In her jaws, the baby flopped, silent now.

Shit.

"She's headed for Wagner," he said into the radio. "Package is nonresponsive. Need an intercept and seed the road."

It was Bennett who answered, her voice ragged from adrenaline and barked orders.

"On our way," she said. "Fuck."

Marlow scrambled over a downed fence panel and ran straight into a backhand that sent him flying into the garden he'd just left. He landed hard on his back and stared up at the fat, smug ass end of the full moon for a shocked moment as his lungs spasmed around the expelled breath.

He managed to force a raw, scratchy mouthful of air down into tight lungs. It was harder to bully himself to his feet, but he managed it.

The wolf snarled at him as she slunk through the broken fence, slats of wood splintered under her paws. Her ears were plastered flat to her skull, and she snarled, black lips peeled back from bloody, messy teeth. She'd been on all fours as she ran, but now she pushed herself up onto her back legs. Heavy shoulders bunched as she shook her long, wirily muscled arms—thickly sleeved in gingery hair—and curled her muddy fingers into claws.

Blood filled Marlow's mouth, flat and weirdly soup-like in texture. He spat onto the ground and shifted his weight onto the balls of his feet. She'd put the baby down. That changed the rules of engagement. Without the kid to protect, his priority was to get her to leave. Marlow could still kill her if he *had* to, but he'd rather avoid it.

That way, tomorrow, the kid would still have a mom and not a gravestone.

"Annette," he said. The words were ragged as he breathed heavily. That was what her parents had said her name was, between hysterics. "This won't end well. Just go. It's a big city. Lots of places to be. Deer in the park."

Frothy drool dripped from the wolf's mouth as she tossed her head back and howled. The sound echoed in her barrel chest and thinned as it filtered down her long, broad snout. That wasn't a good sign for a peaceful conclusion.

Marlow darted forward, spun on the ball of his foot, and kicked the wolf in the throat. She choked on her howl; the sound trapped in her mangled larynx. Her eyes bulged as she choked, but the wolf's throat twisted and clicked as her body worked to mend the damage. She lunged forward and rammed one of those thick-muscled shoulders into his stomach.

He'd expected a slash, not a tackle. The air whooped out of him for a second time as he backpedaled blind through the garden. Lights flashed out on Wagner, the bright swing of high-powered torches, as backup arrived.

It didn't take long to gut someone, though. He could be dead by then.

The wolf lifted him off the ground, ready to smash him back down again. Marlow grabbed one tufted ear and twisted viciously. The shock of pain made the wolf's grip on him loosen, and he got his feet up. He braced them against her stomach and shoved hard, his knee a sharp "fuck sake" jolt of pain as it absorbed the pressure to free himself.

Marlow hit the ground, got a mouthful of muddy dirt, and rolled back to his feet as he fumbled one-handed at his belt. Claws smacked into the ground where he'd been, dug in, and ripped up a chunk of sod. The wolf shrieked in frustration and threw the clod of ground at him. It hit his shoulder and sprayed sandy dirt and worms down his front, under his shirt, and into his boots.

The wolf's claws were silhouetted against the moon as she cocked her arm back for the last blow. Marlow sprayed her in the face with aerosolized aconite. Where it touched, she broke out in wet red blisters and welts as the wolf tried to peel back from the human within. White scales crusted over her eyes, blind as the moon.

She yelped and pawed at her face, and the inflamed skin split under her claws. Her ears flapped as she shook her head and staggered away in a rough circle.

Marlow unholstered his gun and clicked off the safety. He gripped it in both hands, held it low against his thigh as he waited. The silver bullets would take out a joint if he went for a nonfatal shot, but that wouldn't necessarily put her down.

He didn't need to decide. The wolf pawed roughly at her face one last time before she broke, dropped back onto all fours, and ran blind—or good as—toward the road.

"Charlie-thirty," he said into the radio, the call sign for Bennett's team, as he picked his way through the destruction. "This is Charlie-forty. Let her go or pen her. Package dropped off."

Static and silence dragged out too long for his comfort. Then Bennett came over the air with a curt, "Copy."

Marlow clambered over the broken slats of the fence. It was the only damn house in the row that didn't have a security light. The garden was blurred shades of gray and black. He grabbed his torch and flicked it on to illuminate a single long bar of the garden.

The curtain was easy to find, caught up in the branches of a dry little pear tree, and ripped to shreds once the wolf realized that was what had slowed her down. Marlow panned the light down to a muddy rag next to a flowerbed. Except, once the light hit it, the dull stains turned red.

"Not tonight," Marlow said. He hurried over and dropped onto his knees to shove the thick green stems of the lily of the valley aside. "I did not come out here on four hours sleep for a dead child. Come on."

He found the baby rolled under a rose bush. It was bloody and covered in mud and manure, but when he pulled it out, the rough handling startled another wail from a screwed-up red face. Alive.

"Okay," Marlow said as he got back up. He gave the little ginger head an awkward pat. "You're going to be okay. Those are the rules, right? Bennett! Over here. I've got it."

Bennett boosted herself over the last panel of intact fence in the suburb, lean and dangerous in the Night Shift's full uniform. Even the helmet which Marlow had left in the car.

"I see that," she said as she dropped down on the other side. "She okay?"

Marlow shrugged. "Alive."

"Good enough. Give me a hold."

He handed the baby over and left Bennett to cuddle it while he went to let the medics in. Cameras flashed in his face as the gate opened, a glare of bright light that illuminated Bennett with the infant held against her bulletproof vest.

Very heroic. The picture of a Night Shift sergeant.

She caught his eye for a second and shrugged unrepentantly as she headed for the medics. "She's alive," Bennett answered to the shouted questions from the press. "And tomorrow, she'll be back in his mother's arms. Round here, we call that a win."

Whatever. Marlow brushed dirt off his cuffs. Let her have it. She was right about the win.

An hour later, once the circus had gone, Bennett handed him an energy drink.

"All's fair in love and PR," she said as she lit a cigarette. It was as close to an apology as she'd get. Gray smoke wreathed her face as she exhaled it down her nose. "Good hands, though."

Marlow leaned against the side of the armored van, black metal cold against his shoulders, and took a drink as he listened to the pitch of howls that rose from the city streets. The next call would come in soon; they just didn't know where yet.

"Plenty of night left to impress," he said dryly. She laughed and flicked ash into the gutter.

The rookie who hovered awkwardly on the outskirts of their conversation drained his can and crushed it down into a disk. "I don't get it. We aren't charging the mom with a Depraved Heart felony? It's, like, textbook."

Bennett plucked the cigarette from her lips and let smoke eddy from her mouth. “Only if it’s a shit textbook,” she said. “Jesus, do you even know how to read?”

“Depraved Heart is when a wolf tries to use the limited amnesty of the full moon to get away with murder or insurance fraud,” Marlow said. “That’s not what happened here.”

“Failure to thrive,” Bennett said. “Sometimes, if the kid’s not healthy, the hormones that stop the wolf mom from eating the little piglets don’t kick in. So all the wolf knows is that they want the kid, and when you’re an appetite with teeth… It’s why you should never date a wolf.”

“Date a wolf *and* work Night Shift,” Marlow finished for her. He frowned at her, but she shrugged it off.

“Is that a rule?” the rookie asked.

“No,” Marlow said quickly. He thought about Cade’s sharp smile and low, rough-voiced proposition—if that was what it had been—and felt that dry catch of flustered interest in his throat… mixed with the blood and the dirt. Maybe it wouldn’t hurt to hear a reminder of precisely what that unofficial rule was about. “Just good advice. Hookups, whatever, that’s your business. A wolf, though, when the moon’s up, they can’t tell the difference between love and dinner. Someone usually gets dead.”

Bennett dropped the butt to the ground and shredded it over the pavement with her boot.

“It won’t be me,” she said. “And don’t be fooled by Marlow’s whole mild-mannered thing. It won’t be him either. So, guess who that leaves?”

CHAPTER SIX

ON THE NIGHTS he made it out to his ranch, Cade woke up sprawled out in cornfields with dew-damp skin. In the city, he woke up in the gutter with the taste of rat in his mouth. It wasn't an improvement.

Cade cleared his throat, spat, and pushed himself up onto the curb. His ribs ached, the faint twinge of an old bruise, and he lifted his arm to peer down at his side. New scars scraped from his armpit down to his hip, already faded to white against tanned skin as if they'd been there years.

He'd gotten in a fight.

He poked at the scars with his fingers and hoped they were bite marks. His crush on Marlow was embarrassing enough when he was the only one who knew about it. If it turned out he'd hunted Marlow down in his wolf skin, like the hapless lead in some Shakespearean play, he'd never live it down.

Right *now*, of course, that actually felt like a great idea. Cade could feel the sunny, soft-edged fantasy of it swell his chest and poison his mind with dopamine. It would absolutely end with him rescuing Marlow from another wolf and then *not quite* dying in Marlow's arms—he didn't want to be a Shakespearean hero that much—as the sun came up.

Even for the post-change hangover, that was glowingly optimistic.

The keloid lumps under Cade's skin mapped out the pattern of a bite mark. So not from Marlow. Although a brief fantasy about what it would be like if Marlow did fight him, someday, left the back of his neck hot and sticky. He squashed it before his cock, stuck to his naked thigh with sweat and sandy mud, could embarrass him.

So he'd got into a scuffle with another wolf last night. Close enough to dawn that he'd not had time to heal all the way. It happened. As far as Cade had pieced together over the years, the wolf version of him was the same asshole he was the rest of the month. Just happier about it. And hairier.

Cade reached up and hooked his fingers into the chain around his neck. The tags rattled as he pulled them up and checked the cold metal and glass were intact. They always were these days, but he still liked to check.

He let them drop back to his chest and rose easily to his feet. Except for the ache in his ribs, his body felt loose and light, freshly reknit back together. Energy fizzed through his muscles, and he felt like he could run back through the streets to the Cold Winds building.

Marlow probably felt, and looked, like shit.

Yeah, he didn't buy that. Marlow had the sort of bony elegance that just sharpened under pressure, his dark hair tangled and his mouth set in that grim-edged line it fell into when he didn't remember to soften it. Cade considered the image for a second and then tucked it away for later, when he could decide which of them was going to be shoved into a wall and kissed breathless.

He was easy that way. At least, in his daydreams.

Cade brushed grit off his ass and sniffed the air to orient himself. His nose wasn't that much sharper than usual—people disputed whether it was a faded remnant of the wolf's senses or a side effect of being essentially brand new—but he could pick out salt in the air and motor oil. Combined with the office blocks around him, interspersed with shuttered restaurants, he probably wasn't that far away from the Cold Winds building.

Or he'd made it to LA overnight. But the skyline didn't mesh with that theory.

He headed for the end of the street that was nearest to him. Halfway there, he saw a woman's white, bloodstained leg sticking out from under an overturned, dented skip. He hesitated, a stone wedged in his throat as he tried to swallow, as the idea he'd killed someone welled up in him.

Stupid.

He'd killed before. Consciously, in full possession of his senses and morality. A tour in the army and two seasons up north in Alaska as private security at the rigs and refineries, before he'd decided the private sector would be even better if he didn't have a boss instead of a commanding officer to tell him what to do.

It was different somehow. There was a slow dread to the idea he'd done something without any say or recourse.

Before Cade could steel himself to find out, the toes twitched, and the woman farted. The sound echoed under the skip, and after a second, a slightly amazed voice wondered out loud, "The fuck did I eat last night?"

Cade laughed and broke into a lope.

Kinnock Ave. It sounded familiar. He probably could walk. Instead, he hailed one of the vulture cabs, the back seats practically covered in plastic, that trolled the city for business at dawn.

"You're putting a lot of the businesses resources into this… favor for the SDPD," Lem remarked. "What will you do if the board expects a justification?"

Cade sat down on the couch and swung his feet up onto the coffee table.

"Tell them I had you Google something," he said. "I'm sure they'll see the expense is worth the good relationship I've formed with the local LEOs."

"Slightly more complicated than googling," Lem said, one finger raised to make his point. "Fair enough, though."

"Marlow?"

Lem pulled his phone out of his pocket and flicked his thumb over the screen. The smart screen on the wall flickered to life and the SDPD website loaded up.

"Really?" Cade asked. "A background on one local cop is involved enough that you need visual aids?"

"I don't need them," Lem said. He grinned toothily. "It's just cool."

He tapped the screen again, and the front page of the website was replaced with a picture of Marlow. It had the awkward stiffness of a pose held too long, a tightness around Marlow's mouth that said the smile had started to hurt. Cade leaned forward with interest before he could stop himself. In the photo, Marlow looked mostly the same and much younger. It was something about the mouth. Like the laid-back expression had been completely natural back then.

"Officer Kit Marlow," Lem said. He crossed the room and stopped in front of the screen, a slice of Marlow's face projected on the side of his face and his teal shirt. "Apparently his full name."

That explained the glare over the catnap comment.

"He was born—"

"I'm not writing a biography," Cade said. "Fast forward to anything interesting."

Lem shrugged. "You'll wait a while. Kit Marlow isn't an interesting man. He's good at his job. Top five in his class at the academy, good patrol officer, qualified for Night Shift on his second try, and—"

Cade braced his elbows on his knees.

"Six years ago," he said. "What happened then? Not just with Marlow, something with the Night Shift."

Lem raised an eyebrow. "You could let me finish."

He flicked a screenshot of the *LA Times* website onto the screen. The headline was about cuts the Mayor had made to public spending, but Lem stepped back and pointed to a story about halfway down.

Decorated Night Shift sergeant injured on duty?

"Marlow," Lem said. "He was in a coma for a week. Then the shit hit the fan… only quietly. Public story was that he was shot by a null burglar, who he interrupted in the act. And he might not look like much, but he's a tough bastard. Shot three times in the back, lost a shit ton of blood, needed a bullet pulled out of his *lung*. And he'd managed to blow his knee out too during whatever happened, and that needed to be pieced back together like a jigsaw puzzle. Pretty much nobody expected him to pull through… including Ned Piper."

Cade scowled. The imagery was… uncomfortable. Wolves died or got better from most things. Nobody lingered, except the very young. The idea of Marlow laid out in a hospital bed, white as the sheets and hooked up to all sorts of machines, made the back of his throat itch.

Most people had null relatives, even if only as part of their extended family. The Deacons never had. Not that his dad or grandparents had been willing to claim anyhow. Or who'd been willing to claim *them.*

"I take it Piper was the one who shot him?"

Lem nodded and pulled up a picture. Ned Piper looked like he'd been born in uniform and probably shot a rogue wolf on his way out. Tall and handsome, with dark brown hair and just enough stubble on his square jaw to make him approachable.

"Sergeant Edward Piper, widely assumed to be the next Night Shift lieutenant," Lem said. "Until Marlow pointed the finger at him for the shooting."

"Lover's quarrel?"

Lem shrugged. "No idea. There's no motive on record. Piper made a deal the minute the handcuffs went on. He pled guilty and got a reduced sentence at a dedicated null prison in New Mexico. Hot as hell, but he only has to worry about being shanked, not eaten."

Lem paused and waited, nearly vibrating with smugness.

"But?" Cade asked as he stood up.

"But… suspended. Bounced back to patrol. Bounced to *traffic*." Lem flicked face after face up onto the screen. A woman with a cropped gray pixie cut, her scarred mouth set and eyes focused past the camera. Another woman, much younger, with short red hair and a nervous smile. An ugly-handsome man, one hair shade off ginger. A tough-looking woman with shoulder-length dark hair and a cocky grin. "Early retirement. Disciplinary. Disciplinary. Suspended without pay."

Cade stood up.

"All Night Shift?"

Lem finally cracked a grin as the smug escaped him as he nodded. "They weren't all TAC like Marlow and Piper—there was a clerk and one of the trainee pathologists—but all Night Shift."

"What happened?"

Lem blanked the screen. "Officially, nothing. When I dug into the files, all I found were minor infractions, but instead of wrists being slapped, they got broken. It was a purge. I just don't know why, other than it was something to do with Piper. He signed a deal for a stint in non-carnivore prison, and next thing you know, the department pruned dead wood."

That was… interesting.

"How would that be connected to a dead body with no provenance in the San Diego morgue?" Cade asked.

"The pathologist?" Lem said. He frowned and scratched between his eyebrows with his thumbnail. "I can dig some more."

Cade nodded. "Let's make that discussion of misappropriation of resources worth my while. And send me those files."

"Already sent," Lem said. He tucked his phone into his pocket and raised his eyebrows at Cade. "I thought we'd resolved the issue with how our keycard was involved. Nothing to do with Cold Winds. It was the client's security problem. Not ours."

That was true.

"I don't like leaving things half done. We might be able to pin this on the client, but we both know that this exposed flaws in the security protocols. If there's more, I want to find them now. Next time O'Hara needs my help, he gets to ask nicely."

That was the truth too. It was even most of it. And it bothered him that Haley might have died when she expected him to keep her safe… even if she'd no idea who he was.

"Yeah, well," Lem said as he tucked his hands into his back pockets. "Don't point out too many problems. Our contract with the Reserve comes up for renewal next year. We don't want to have to drop our price."

Cade mock-clutched his chest. "Don't even joke," he said. It came out lightly, but the starved penny-pincher in the back of his brain had already started to figure the run-on impact of a significant discount to the Reserve. Or worse, if they threw the contract onto the open market for bids.

The Reserve was dull most of the time. With the security system designed and in place, most of what passed for excitement up there—a stalker who'd gotten directions from the internet, a particularly pushy reporter, lost hikers—was handled on the spot by his men.

Before Haley's death, the last time he'd had to intervene directly at the Reserve had been two years ago, during a messy divorce when the ex-spouse had shot her wife and then set the house on fire. It had been serious enough he'd had to show his face, but in reality, his particular skills hadn't been needed. He'd never been the man in the company to go to for soft skills.

It was still the best-paid contract they had, high profit for relatively low outlay now that the security system was installed and active, and Cade liked profit. It kept him in the style he'd worked very hard to become accustomed to.

"If anyone asks, call it an abundance of caution," he told Lem. "I doubt I'll find any other glaring security breaches. I'd just rather know… and get them fixed before anyone else works out what they are."

Lem nodded. "Makes sense," he said. "I'll do some more digging into this after I talk to our team in Germany. I need to make sure they resolved the tensions with the local gendarmes."

"That's French."

The correction didn't bother Lem. He shrugged it off with his usual grin. "They all speak, like, five languages. They'll know what I mean. Do you need me for anything else?"

Cade dismissed that idea with a shake of his head as he headed back to his desk. He pulled the sleek black leather desk chair out, sat down, and glanced at his computer to check his schedule.

"Not today," he said. "Thanks for this, Lem."

"It's my job," Lem said. "But you're right, I'm doing it really well, aren't I?"

He grinned into the exasperated look that Cade sent his way and let himself out. As the office door swung shut behind Lem, Cade's computer pinged with an email from him. All his research on Marlow.

Cade opened the file and sat back to read through it. He trusted Lem more than most, but his brother was not a man for subtleties.

A scab stitched Marlow's lower lip together, and the dark smudge of a bruise decorated his cheekbone. It made him look younger. Dangerous.

"What happened?" Cade asked as he got out of the car. Marlow had made his own way there. The patrol car parked on the cultivated greenery cut through Cade's fuzzy infatuation with a flicker of irritation as he tallied the paranoid complaints he'd get.

For a second, Marlow looked surprised, as if he'd forgotten about the marks. He reached up and brushed his fingers along his lower lip until he hit the tender spot. Cade's body tightened with awareness, and he wondered what it would be like to kiss Marlow's bruised mouth. The taste, the texture, the way Marlow would pull back or lean in…

"Got punched in the face," Marlow said.

"You paint a picture with your words."

The sarcastic edge to Cade's voice made him swear silently. Despite the pep talk he'd given himself on the way over, he had not brought his best self to play. He tried to cough up an apology, but the flash of a sudden, unexpected grin from Marlow interrupted his attempt.

It was a nice enough smile—wider and more mobile than Cade had expected from Marlow's lean, sharp-boned face. Nothing about it, though, justified the rush of gooey, soppy warmth that rose from Cade's stomach and filled his chest. It just felt good that he had been the one to coax something more than half a crooked smile out of the self-contained TAC officer.

Idiot, he jabbed at himself with wry disdain. It was true, but it was hard to care much when he could just… enjoy it.

"Yeah, well," Marlow said as he pushed the sleeves of his fitted tee up over his forearms. "The full story would just sound like I was boasting."

"Nothing wrong with that," Cade said as he turned away—he didn't plan on pushing his luck with this whole "not being a jerk" thing—and headed over to the front door. "How else will the rest of us know anything worth a boast or two even happened?"

The building was locked up again after their earlier visit. Cade used his company skeleton key to open the front door.

It still reeked inside—more than he'd remembered—the rancid smell of decomposing sugary sauce thick enough to taste.

"Good question," Marlow said. "Maybe I need to work on it."

Cade found the control panel on the wall and flicked it open. That was as far as he got. It looked like Macroy's uninvited guest had lost her temper with the system and smashed it with—Cade measured one of the divots with his fingertip and guessed—a high heel.

"What are you looking for anyhow?" he said as he turned back around.

Marlow shrugged, an off-kilter hitch of his shoulder that made Cade remember the scars on the other.

"I don't know," he said. "Something?"

"That narrows it down." He didn't get the grin this time, but the amused quirk of Marlow's mouth at his jibe topped up the warm flush that filled his stomach. This time Cade iced himself down mentally with the unromantic reminder that if they ever actually fucked, he'd lose interest quickly enough. They were here for a reason. He should focus on that. "There's no reason to believe Haley died here. No blood. No weapons…"

He stopped the list with one item to go and turned on the ball of his foot as he scanned the room. It had been a while since he'd been here, not since Macroy moved in, but Cade had a good memory for places. He could walk past an ex in the street and not even register he might know them, but he could pull up the layout of the club they'd gone to on their first date.

Very useful at work, less so in his private life.

"Last time I was in here, Macroy had two samurai swords on that wall. A souvenir from one of his films," Cade said as he pointed at the bare concrete. "They're gone."

"Redecorating?"

"Not the sort of man who did things like that himself," Cade said. "And the pegs are there."

He left the living room and headed back to the disaster of a kitchen. The water had spilled out of the sink and onto the floor, greasy and cold on the tiles. Dirty plates and glasses were piled haphazardly on the counter. Plastic forks floated in the sink, between the lumps of burned whatever-it-was that had soaked out of the pan.

No metal forks.

No knives. Not even a butter knife.

The drawers were slick metal, flat and smudged with greasy fingers and smears of sauce. Nothing as pedestrian as handles for Macroy. Cade gave one a push until it clicked and slowly slid open. Empty. So was the next one.

"It's more nothing than something," Cade said as he closed the last drawer. "But it does suggest that Parker didn't tell us everything."

Marlow stared at him for a second, his face unreadable behind those glasses, and then clenched his jaw.

"Fuck," he spat out. "How did I miss that?"

CHAPTER SEVEN

CHAPTER SEVEN

THE BACK OF Marlow's neck was so hot that it felt sunburnt. He should have realized why the idea he'd missed something had gnawed at him. This hadn't needed a nose for detective work; it was what he did. At least it was when he wasn't distracted trying to convince himself Cade had flirted with him.

"Parker broke in to try and get rid of evidence he'd had Haley stay here," Marlow said as he walked around the corner and toward the window. "Right?"

Cade nodded as he followed Marlow's lead. "That's right," he said. "Not exactly a good plan, but evidence suggests he's not a man that makes good decisions."

The flick of contempt in Cade's voice was familiar. It had been directed at Marlow on more than one occasion when Cold Winds operatives had ended up on TAC's radar. Like strong emotions, some skillsets also carried over the change. Not whole, but enough to cause problems for the Night Shift.

It was a lot more palatable aimed at someone else.

"So then, one question." Marlow stopped and rocked his weight back and forth, from his heels onto the balls of his feet. Bits of glass in the carefully unkempt grass crunched and gritted underfoot. "Shouldn't the glass be on the inside?"

Cade stared at him for a beat and then turned to look at the small boarded-over square of a window high on the wall. It was his turn to mutter "Fuck" under his breath. Marlow braced himself for the back-and-forth of counter theories, determined to prove his point.

"Haley Jenkins wasn't here as a guest," Cade said in a low, harsh voice that scraped in his throat like ice on a lake. "She wasn't detoxing. She was a prisoner."

It took Marlow a second to pull the points in his favor that he'd already queued up on the tip of his tongue. He put the defensive arguments back in their mental boxes—he might need them later—and nodded.

"Maybe. We can't prove it… yet," Marlow said. "But yeah, it fits. I mean, you designed the security for this place, right? How hard would it be to turn it from someplace designed to keep people *out* into somewhere to keep people in?"

The muscles in Cade's jaw tensed, knotted under his skin. Then he nodded grimly. "Not hard," he said. "Easier than you'd think. It's the trade-off that people make, part of their freedom in return for peace of mind. It's not something most of them like to think about, though. It looks like Parker had access to Macroy's in-house system—which he probably had through work. He could have locked the house down. The logs showed he turned off the smoke alarms and the motion sensors—which didn't raise any flags because it's not unusual. Someone gets a pet chicken or has a kid, and they don't want to deal with us rolling up in full TAC gear every time one of them gets in through the window."

Marlow crouched down and pulled a shard of glass out of the ground. He turned it in his hand to see the light pick out the streaks of blood on it.

"So, Haley picks the first night she knows that he won't be able to be here." He fished an evidence bag out of his pocket and put the glass in it before he sealed the top again. The bag went into his jacket, zipped into one of the extra pockets. "And she escapes."

It would have been too easy if the story ended there. They both knew it hadn't.

"The only problem is that you're right," Cade said. "Parker wasn't here. Some of those hunt lodges in LA are Cold Winds clients too, and they have good security. They don't want just any Tom, Dick, or Fido hopping a wall and getting a free pork roast. Once he was in, he was in for the night. So how did Haley go from getting away to being dead?"

Marlow pushed himself back to his feet. "I know you don't want to hear it, but how many of the Reserve residents would she have had to dodge?"

"Too many," Cade acknowledged. He turned to scan the trees that pushed close to the sparsely eked out plots of the Reserve. "But you know a wolf didn't kill her, Marlow. A wolf wouldn't take the hands and leave the meat."

He said it matter-of-factly. Marlow wondered if the wolves ever realized how disorienting it was to be reminded that someone you might enjoy kissing, might enjoy ripping your stomach out too. Once a month, at least.

That said, Cade was right. Wolf kills weren't pretty, and they didn't leave much behind.

"It was a null that killed her," Marlow agreed. He half-turned to judge the path back through the woods toward the guard's station. There were null operatives on call, according to the outline Cade had filed with the chief of police, in case they ever needed to intervene, but no one was physically on site. Haley might not have known that. "She might have gone that way, back toward the road. It would be her best chance."

Not much of a chance. Marlow was well-trained, in good condition, and used to being out in the moonlight. Armed and kitted out, he might get back to the city alive. He'd not put a lot of money on it, though.

Haley had been an actress, she'd already been blooded, and she probably stank of fear. Easier prey than deer. She probably wouldn't have even made it to the guard's stop.

Cade put a hand on his shoulder, fingers slid under the collar of Marlow's T-shirt, and pulled him around to face the trees again.

"That's what you'd do," he said. "A scared addict with one chance to get around, they run the direction they're pointed."

Unfortunately, that still left a lot of ground to cover.

"Cold Winds has the resources, and we're already on the ground," Cade said into his mobile as he stalked through the undergrowth. Other Cold Winds operatives were strung out in a chain between the trees, armed with directional radio mics and infrared thermal detection wands. "We're glad to get the search started. Obviously, we'd expect our assistance to be reflected in any statements—"

He paused to listen, nodded, and ended the call.

"Captain O'Hara sends his regards. He said you're still on roster for tonight. If you need overtime that much, the job offer is still open. Private sector pays better, and there's… other benefits to working closer with me."

Marlow yawned, a jaw-crack of a gape, as if he'd needed to be reminded he was tired.

"You know, I am never sure if you're flirting with me or just being an ass.".

Cade turned slowly to give him a disbelieving look over his shoulder.

Because he'd heard that.

Shit. That had been meant to be a *thought*, not something Marlow said out loud.

Marlow closed his eyes for a second and tried to think of a way out of that statement. There wasn't one. He would just have to deal with it. "I mean—"

Someone screamed. It was the shocked, genderless yawp of pain, not surprise or horror. For just a *second*, Marlow was grateful for the interruption as Cade turned sharply away from him. Then his brain clicked back on.

That wasn't good.

Nader lay on the mulch and shed needles in a puddle of his own puke and blood. He was gray under the Cali surfer tan he sported, and his cheeks and chin were slick with tears and snot. Two other operatives had to hold him down to stop him writhing before he made his situation worse.

His right leg was mangled, crushed in the half-moon clamp that had snapped down on it. The razor-sharp teeth had sheared through his black combat trousers and torn through flesh and muscle. The spring-loaded force behind the trap had broken his leg viciously halfway up his shin. A tourniquet twisted around his thigh had stemmed the worst of the bleeding, but blood welled sluggishly out of the wound. There was already enough of it on the ground to be a worry.

"Bear trap," Cade identified it as he crouched down, balanced on the balls of his feet. He put his hand gingerly on the cold arch of the trap. "I haven't seen one of these since I left Alaska."

Marlow swallowed the sickly taste in his mouth and dragged his gaze away from the white stick of bone that jutted out of Nader's leg like a splinter. The old scar tissue between his ribs ached in sympathy.

"Are traps legal in Alaska?" he asked.

Cade laughed harshly. "No," he said. "But no one cares about that. Someone get me a crowbar."

It took three men to hold Nader down as Cade forced the jaws of the trap open. Fresh blood spilled onto the ground as the teeth pulled out of Nader's leg and smeared as he was dragged backward.

"The Reserve's concierge doctor will be here soon." One of the operatives delivered the news as he rejoined them. "There is an air ambulance on the way, too, to take him back to San Diego."

Cade let the trap snap shut once Nader was clear. He straightened up and wiped his forehead on his sleeve—the crowbar, scraped and bloody, dangled from his other hand.

"Great," he said. "Then we can work out how the hell someone just waltzed through our security to drop this off here."

Marlow stepped over the wet smear of Nader's blood as he examined the trap. It was attached to a chain that snaked away from it under a loose covering of mulch and leaves. Marlow brushed the debris off the chain with the side of his foot as he followed it between the trees to a huge, black rock half-buried in the side of a hill. The chain was attached to a heavy metal pin freshly drilled into the stone.

He picked the chain up and rubbed grime off it with his thumb. The metal was smooth and thick, well-forged and crafted. Strong enough to hold a pissed-off wolf if you got one leashed. Very similar chains hung in the Night Shift armory, but the few links he looked over didn't have a maker's mark on them.

"No one dropped it off," he said. "Someone spent a lot of time setting this up."

Cade looked around and snarked, "Well, if they put some effort in, that makes me feel better." He left the others to tend to Nader, though, and stalked over to look for himself. A scowl grooved itself into his face as he took in the worked stone, concrete, and quality of the trap.

"Does this have anything to do with Ned Piper and his mess?" he asked.

The question hit Marlow like a punch. He'd been less shaken the night before when the wolf had coldcocked him.

"I don't—" Marlow stopped mid-stammer and shook his head. O'Hara had already dragged him over the coals for his slip up in the morgue. "That's old business, and it's nothing to do with me."

He started to walk away. Cade stepped in front of him to block him, one hand casually on Marlow's shoulder, and he stopped, irritation rough against the back of his throat.

"What?"

"O'Hara thought Piper was involved. Why?"

Marlow chewed on the inside of his cheek as he tried to work out how much he could say. He already knew that what he *should* say was nothing. A slightly masochistic attraction to a handsome jerk wasn't a good reason to spill this particular secret.

Unfortunately, Cade had a point. The security of the Reserve *literally* was his business.

"Piper was a dirty cop, but he did it for money, not thrills. Besides, he's in an out-of-state prison. I never thought it was him, but—"

That was the cutoff for what he *could* say. Marlow stopped, and Cade finished the sentence for him.

"But he wasn't the only one back then who needed a bath?"

Marlow hesitated, but if Cade had put the pieces together, what point was there in lying? It was up to O'Hara to do damage control. He raked his fingers through his hair, sweaty damp at the roots from the hike.

"The morgue drop during the changeover was right out of Piper's playbook," he said quietly, one eye on the crowd around Nader. "Screwed-up paperwork, confusing provenance, all of it. This, though? Not his style. He didn't have any morals, but he was a professional, and he didn't like… messy. Traps? Kidnap? That's too much chaos for Piper. Anything else you want to know, ask O'Hara."

He stepped to the side to head back over to Nader, and Cade's voice pulled him up.

"How dirty were you?" he asked. "For reference."

Marlow stopped. He was surprised at the sour pinch of anger behind his breastbone at the doubt. The bile of it stung the back of his throat. He'd thought that years of that question had worn his reaction to it down until it was see-through and brittle.

He'd been wrong.

"Like I said, ask O'Hara."

He stalked away and nearly tripped as his heel sunk into a loose patch of dirt. The bloody mud sucked at Marlow's boot as he pulled it out with a muttered curse. So much for a dignified exit. He scraped his boot on the grass to get most of the mire off and then… stopped.

Something bright blue, iridescent as a peacock feather, glittered at him from the thick black mud. He knew what it was right away, but he still knelt down and brushed the dirt out of the way.

Her last manicure must have been just before rehab. It was half grown out, stubs of blue on the end of her nails. Dirt was worked into the pores and lines of her hands and scabbed in a crust over the raw knobs of bone at her wrists.

It wasn't like there could have been any other end to the story. Haley's body was at the morgue; Marlow knew a happy ending was ruled out. It still felt… unfair. She'd gotten away from Parker, avoided the wolves, and made it further than expected through the woods… only to die like an animal in a trap.

"Poor kid," he said as he sat back on his heels. "Not a good way to die."

Cade put a hand on his shoulder. "None of them are," he said.

The hands got their own body bag.

Marlow wasn't sure if it showed respect or just made them more pathetic. Sun unzipped the plastic shroud and peeled it back.

"I'll need to do a proper examination," Sun said as she peered at them over her plastic glasses. When Marlow nodded that he understood, she picked up the left hand in gloved fingers. "But a cursory examination would support your theory. These wounds are consistent with being caught in a trap of the sort that you brought in."

Cade stepped forward to peer at the hand as Sun turned it toward them so they could see the damage dirt had disguised before.

"Did someone sever them postmortem?" he asked.

"I don't believe so," Sun said. She pushed her glasses up her nose with her knuckle. "I had a look at the trap in evidence, and it's a heavy-duty piece of equipment. Compressed, double-spring loaded, twice the size of a normal foothold trap, and the jaws aren't offset with inward-facing teeth."

She crooked her free hand and snapped her fingers together as if that would help them follow.

"It was built for big game," Marlow said. He knew he had missed something obvious, but some stubborn part of his brain was determined that was for the best. "Bears or—"

"Wolves," Cade interrupted. "Right, Doctor?"

Sun set the hand back down and grimaced with the same unhappiness that Marlow had felt.

"Those traps are banned," she said. "Here. In Europe. It's illegal to make or use any sort of snare or trap designed for people, even if they're wolves at the time."

Cade's smile was tolerant. "Of course," he said. "But if you were going to design one—"

"I wouldn't," Sun said sharply. Then she deflated slightly as she looked down at the sad gray hands of the dead child star. "But yes. It's… possible… that the trap started as a normal bear trap but was altered to make it more effective if used during the full moon."

"Against wolves," Cade repeated.

"It wasn't silver," Sun hedged.

"It didn't need to be," Marlow said. "Sever a wolf's paw, and it won't grow back, doesn't matter what you used to make the cut."

This time Sun had to nod. She touched her finger to the heart of Haley's palm. "From the angle of the wound and the scrapes on the heels of her hand, I think she fell, put her hands out to catch herself, and triggered the trap. It wouldn't have taken long after that, without medical treatment, for her to bleed out."

Cade muttered, "Fuck," loud in the sterile tile-and-metal lab, and stalked out of the room without bothering to excuse himself. The doors slammed shut behind him. Marlow turned back to Sun.

"Anything else?" he asked.

She pursed her lips and shook her head. "Maybe once I get the tox screen on her blood back," she said. "For now… there's some bruising to her knuckles that looks a few days old. It's premortem."

"Can you get the tox screen rushed?"

Sun shook her head. "I doubt it," she said. "There are other cases with more urgency in the queue. Sorry."

He waved that off. It wasn't Sun's fault. "Would you give me a call when they come back?" he asked. "Just for my peace of mind."

"You want to be a detective now?" Sun teased him and then relented at his look. "Okay, okay. I'll let you know as soon as I've told O'Hara. Now go on. I have work to do."

She flapped her hands at him. Marlow took the not-even-a-hint and left.

"Continue the sweep." Cade paced back and forth across the width of the hall. The thud of his booted heels as they hit the floor echoed off the walls. "I know we found the girl's hands, Lem, but I want to know if there are any other traps. And I want them removed. Today. Before one of our clients wakes up in the morning with a missing foot."

He hung up and looked like he was going to throw the phone at the wall for a moment. Instead, he grimaced and shoved it into his back pocket.

"Do you think the police department would be interested in a lightly-used ex-Marine who just got sued into bankruptcy?" he asked, in a voice that was too harsh for the joke. "Or would crime be a better bet?"

Cade took a step back and slouched against the wall, his head tilted back and lower lip folded between his teeth as he exhaled raggedly. The last time Marlow had seen him in that pose he'd been naked.

"You want to go get a drink?" Marlow asked.

Cade lifted his head and gave Marlow a suspicious look out of wolf-amber eyes in a human face. It hitched Marlow's heart with a jolt of adrenaline that was half fight and half fuck. He already regretted the question.

"So you went and decided on your own whether I was a flirt or an asshole?" Cade said as he pushed himself off the wall and stalked forward. "Or did it not matter if I'm picking up the check?"

Marlow snorted.

"Don't know where the fuck you think serves whiskey before noon," he said as he turned away. The rest of the sentence he tossed over his shoulder as he walked down the hall. "But trust me, the most expensive bottle behind the bar costs about twenty bucks. If you want me to be impressed at you paying the tab, we'll need to run one for a year first."

He was pretty pleased with that. Then Cade caught up with him. His hand skimmed down Marlow's spine and settled in the small of his back, high enough to be appropriate and low enough it wouldn't take much to change that. The breath caught hot and scratchy in Marlow's throat.

"See how the first date goes first," Cade said in his ear. "Think of it like a job interview."

[illegible]

CHAPTER EIGHT

"JOB INTERVIEW," CADE muttered to himself as he leaned against the bar and waited for the barman to make his way down. He rubbed his eye with his knuckle until he saw blurs of color behind the lid. "Fucking hell."

He *could* have just kept his mouth shut. That had been an option. No, he had to open it and try to be clever. It hadn't worked.

To be honest, Marlow's main flaw, as far as Cade could see anyhow, was that he was still willing to share a table with Cade after that. Low self-esteem was all Cade could put that down to at this point.

And possibly the fact Cade was rich and handsome. That had never hurt.

The barman finally finished dishing out foil-wrapped burritos and bottles of cheap beer to the bone-weary ER doctors. He wiped his hands on the old rag of cloth behind the bar and turned toward Cade.

"What can I get you?" he asked.

"What's the most expensive bottle you have?"

Cade scanned the shelves behind the heavy-shouldered gray-bearded man. He hoped for a good Japanese whiskey, but a cursory glance convinced him he was out of luck there.

The barman looked at him for a second, then bent down to reach under the bar. He came up with a dusty bottle decorated with a bright red ribbon.

"Grey Goose," he said, one beefy hand still wrapped around the neck. "For you, fifty bucks."

"And if it wasn't me?"

When the barman smiled, a gold tooth glittered in the side of his mouth. Null then. Cade supposed that made sense for a bar called the Moon After.

"Twenty-five bucks."

Cade pulled his wallet out of his jeans and counted out the fifty in crisp notes, plus another ten for two of the foil-wrapped burritos.

While the barman rang up the sale, he turned around to watch Marlow with the rest of his team around the pool table.

"Take a shot," the tall, solidly built woman with two stubby, incongruous ponytails coaxed as she rolled the white ball over the faded baize. It bounced off the cushion, and Marlow grabbed it before it could roll back. "Best out of three."

"Another time," Marlow said. He lifted his hand off the ball. "I've got other things to do."

As he walked away, a big blond man—heavy shouldered and thick through the chest—leaned on his cue.

"What?" he jeered after Marlow. "You'd rather hang out with some wolf than us? Chasing tail now, Kitty-boy?"

Anger flashed through Cade at the slur. It tightened in the back of his throat, the old, hot knot of being judged not good enough. He took a step forward.

"Don't," the bartender warned gruffly. "I don't allow trouble in here."

Cade turned to glare at him. "Or what? I could buy this place with my pocket change."

"Do it," the bartender said, unflappable as he set the Grey Goose, two shot glasses, and sweaty foil-wrapped rolls down on the table. "I've been thinking about retiring. Be nice to have a nest egg. Marlow can take care of himself."

That was self-evident. Cade's temper had flared because of his own tender pride, not because he thought Marlow needed him. He supposed that wasn't an explanation that reflected well on him, though.

"I don't like assholes," he said.

"Who does?" Marlow asked as he slid up next to Cade at the bar. He picked up the bottle to look at the label and raised his eyebrows. "Ah, breaking the bank with the mid-priced stuff?"

"I knew it'd impress you," Cade said. He took the bottle back and gestured toward the pool table with his chin. "He going to give you trouble if he sees you drinking with a wolf?"

Marlow shrugged. "Franklin? No. He knows better," he said. "Come on, let's grab a table, and we can talk. Thanks, Jim."

The bartender acknowledged that with a grunt; then, he winked at Cade.

"Hey, if that offer still stands tomorrow, have your people call my people." He chuckled to himself as he headed down the bar to the next customer.

Cade narrowed his eyes and wondered how funny the guy would think he was if Cade did. His people were shit hot.

Not shit hot enough to get him out of it if someone at the Reserve lost a leg, admittedly. If they couldn't intimidate whatever "people" a dive bar owner had, though, Cade wasn't paying their retainer again.

He could decide on that later. For now, he grabbed the glasses and the food and followed Marlow over to a booth at the back, next to the jukebox. The table was scarred and stained, but the leather cushions on the benches were polished and clean.

"Franklin spends a lot of time on those Alpha Wolf dating forums," Marlow said as he sat down. "You know, the ones that say you're either the wolf or the sheep in a relationship? Only he thinks it works in the workplace too."

"Does it work anywhere?" Cade asked.

Marlow shrugged as he twisted the top off the bottle. "He was married, but she divorced him. So, breaking even, I guess?"

He poured them both a shot of clear liquor and grabbed one of the burritos to unroll it. The released smell made Cade's stomach grumble in sudden hunger, and he grabbed his own.

Eggs and peppers spiced with hot onion and carrot. Cade'd been hungry too many times as a kid to let food go to waste, even if breakfast burritos weren't exactly date food.

"Piper was a good guy," Marlow said as he took a bite of the burrito. He chewed and swallowed before he went on. "Nothing was ever too much trouble, you know? He'd help you move, pick you up if you were too pissed to drive, or hide the occasional body."

Cade raised his eyebrows. He'd been confident he could find the information eventually—if Lem couldn't find it online, then there was always someone whose tongue could be loosened with cash or the application of pressure—but he'd not expected it to come from Marlow. So he took a bite of his breakfast and chewed while he decided on an answer.

"He was a fixer."

Marlow took his glasses off and tucked them into his pocket. "Sort of. I guess."

"You've got gray eyes," Cade said, as if it was an accusation.

It got him a look of worn exasperation from Marlow. "I know. People point it out a lot."

They would. Cade had never seen anyone with smoke-pale eyes before. One of his dad's exes had green eyes. Lem had gotten a dilute version of them from her, green splinters in hazel. Gray was even rarer than that.

"This?" Marlow said as he waved his finger back and forth between them. "This is why I wear the glasses."

"I can see that," Cade said as he leaned back and tried to look uninterested. "Better to look like a hipster than have everyone stare at you."

"Yeah," Marlow said. "They were Piper's idea."

Marlow looked oddly lost without the glasses. And young. A lot like the photo of him that Lem had pulled from the police files.

In the back of Cade's brain, that pinched *something* he knew he should pay attention to, but it was pushed to the side by the thought that Sergeant Piper might have been more than Cade's boss. How could anyone ever compete with the lover who'd shot you in the back and left you to die? It might not be love anymore, but the emotional real estate that took up had more acreage than the Reserve.

Also, Cade reminded himself in a tart, irritated mental voice, the secret of a homicidal lover's tiff wasn't going to help work out what was going on at the Reserve, was it?

Even with his hormones in a riot, money took precedence.

"Well, if he wasn't a fixer, what was it?" he asked.

Marlow had lost his appetite. He pushed his breakfast to the side and leaned forward, crossed arms braced on the table.

"He did favors," he said. "Sometimes people knew there were strings attached. Sometimes you didn't realize till later on."

From "people" to "you." What had Piper done for Marlow? Cade wondered. He could push on that later, though. For now, let Marlow keep talking.

"Favors like dumping a body into the system at the changeover?"

Marlow nodded. He picked up the glass and tossed back a shot. He screwed his face up at the bite of it before he swallowed.

It was cute. Cade ignored the sappy part of his brain that wanted to moon over that.

"Never more than one or two a quarter," Marlow said. "Spread out over a couple of precincts where he had… friends who owed him other favors. One corpse, a set of badly filled in paperwork, and people just shuffled them off to the side, assuming that someone would eventually deal with them. When no one did, they just got filed away as full moon deaths. It happens. People get killed. They die during the shift if they have a heart problem or they're old. That was the rule, though. Nothing that would raise eyebrows, nothing that would attract too much interest."

Cade picked up the vodka. The glass was greasy under his fingers.

"You mean, like a dead girl with missing hands?" he asked.

A smile twitched the corners of Marlow's mouth. "Yeah. Piper wouldn't have touched that." He set the glass back down and pushed it over the table. "You want to ask me again?"

They both knew what he meant. Cade thought about it for a second and then downed the vodka. It was lukewarm and thick, with a sweet diesel aftertaste. Five bucks for the bottle would have been an overcharge. Pride made him choke it down without a grimace, while Marlow watched with dry amusement. They both knew it tasted awful, but Cade wasn't going to admit that.

He licked his lips once it was done and studied Marlow's face for a moment.

"So, what did you decide? Asshole or flirt?"

Surprise washed visibly over Marlow's face, and then he laughed as he reached for the bottle.

"Honestly, I still don't know," he said. "A few more of these, and I won't care, though."

Cade caught the bottle too, his hand over Marlow's. His fingers slotted into the spaces between Marlow's knuckles, warm and unexpectedly intimate. Or maybe Cade's brain was finally heading for the gutter, as he wondered how else their bodies would fit together.

"I was flirting," Cade said. It was blunt, but he was done with the messy tangle of respect, lust, and interest that stuck to his brain like taffy. Since he couldn't fit it back into his subconscious, it was time to shove it into a box he was more familiar with.

Future ex-one-night stand sounded about right. He'd white-knuckled through the rubbing alcohol he'd just gulped, so the breathless, dramatic disappointment in Cade's chest at that idea didn't stand a chance.

Two days ago, the only time he'd spoken to Marlow had been to rake the hard-to-read cop over the coals for… show, mostly. Two days from now, once the overdose of serotonin from having all this dragged up unexpectedly wore off, he'd wonder why he stopped.

Marlow licked his lips and looked at their hands.

"You sure about that?" he asked, eyebrows raised.

It was a joke. Cade knew it was a joke. It still caught him on the raw. He drew back. His fingers trailed over Marlow's as he pulled away and shrugged.

"I am," he said. "Although I couldn't tell you why. Maybe I had a stroke last time I shifted."

He could hear himself, and he sounded like an idiot. Like someone who hung out with Marlow's Night Shift friend, Franklin, on forums that convinced them pissing on a tree at the end of the night was the key to a second date. It was a knee-jerk reaction—better to reject someone before they could reject you—and by the time he remembered he was over thirty these days, it was too late to take it back. He poured himself another shot of vodka instead.

"What's your excuse for the day before that, then?" Marlow asked.

Yeah. Cade hadn't thought of one for that.

His shoulders hit the door with a thud as Marlow shoved him back into it. It held for a second until the latch gave, and they stumbled into the bathroom. *Okay*, Cade thought as he hitched in a ragged breath and Marlow chewed hot, sharp kisses over his neck. Now he knew who got shoved up against the wall for any future fantasies.

Except there wouldn't be any, Cade reminded himself. He twisted a hand in Marlow's hair and pulled his head back to claim a vodka-spiced kiss from soft, eager lips. *No more stupid crush after today. Just a normal, casual relationship between two people who didn't like each other that much.*

Marlow kicked the door shut and reached out blindly to lock it. He didn't fumble, and Cade had the thin, bitter thought that this wasn't the first time Marlow had dragged someone into the restroom. It cut through the haze of lust and infatuation like a squeeze of lemon through grease.

Then Marlow impatiently pulled Cade's shirt out of his trousers and ran his hands up under it. He spread warm, callused fingers over Cade's stomach and made a low, rough sound of pleasure in the back of his throat, and clarity gave up the ghost. Heat spread through Cade, prickly and tender under his skin, and he gave in to it.

This wasn't the fantasy. That was a midnight fuck in the soft grass meadow behind his house, under the velvet dark of a moonless sky. No deadlines. Just Marlow sprawled under him and hours to enjoy it. It was a far cry from a cop-bar bathroom that stank of cheap booze and cheaper soap, with the dull background mutter of bickering cops as a soundtrack.

It didn't matter. That was the difference between an adult and a teenager. Daydreams passed the time, but they didn't beat reality. He had Marlow pressed against him, all that dry wit smothered under Cade's mouth, and he wasn't going to pass on that because they'd not get grass stains on their asses.

What he hoped were the last sticky dregs of his stupid crush marshaled themselves to whisper hopefully, *not today.* Cade distracted himself from that particular notion with interrupted messy kisses as he dragged Marlow's TAC regulation T-shirt up over his head. He tossed it into the sink—better than the floor, he supposed—and hooked his fingers into the waistband of Marlow's jeans to drag him in close again.

"*You* sure about this?" he checked, his voice rusty in his throat. "I'm not exactly popular with your colleagues out there."

Cade clenched his jaw a minute too late to shut himself up. His balls ached resentfully at the thought Marlow might realize this was a bad time, a bad place, or just a fucking bad idea. Even worse, he felt the clutch of sentiment in his chest at the possibility that Marlow would pick him over them. Or, even better, defend him.

Since when, he thought viciously at himself, *had he needed anyone to defend him? From anything?* He didn't. He never had. Sure, it would be nice sometimes. That didn't mean he needed it.

Marlow cupped Cade's jaw in his hand and grazed a callused thumb across his lower lip. The slow caress made Cade swallow thickly as he tried not to visibly squirm. "I don't usually ask them to join in," he said. "But if you want me to put it to a vote…?"

"I always knew you had a smart mouth," Cade grumbled. "Just because you didn't run it, didn't mean I couldn't tell."

"Sure," Marlow drawled. "You spent, what, all of ten minutes thinking about me once a year. You know me inside and out."

That was true, but it didn't feel true. Not right then, with Marlow's hand on his face and the taste of the null still in Cade's mouth. Or maybe it wasn't. Cade had—apparently—paid more attention to Marlow than he'd been ready to admit.

"You'd be surprised what I thought about you," Cade said. He turned his head and pressed a kiss against Marlow's wrist. The steady pulse fluttered against his lips as Marlow hissed softly at the contact. "What about you? What did you think about me?"

Another stupid question.

Cade grimaced at himself. He didn't need to know what Marlow looked like when he lied. Or, worse, *didn't* lie.

"Or maybe—" Cade lowered his head to bruise kisses over Marlow's naked shoulder. His mouth grazed the edge of a scar, rough and raised under his lips, and it occurred to him that any mark he left on Marlow would linger past tonight. It could be there for days. Or longer. The thought made his balls clench, heavy and hot, and his voice catch roughly in his throat. "—we just shouldn't talk anymore."

CHAPTER NINE

MARLOW SNORTED AT the flicker of self-awareness from the acerbic Cade.

"Thought or think?" he asked.

"It was a dumb question. Forget I opened—"

"Spectacular ass," Marlow said.

Cade lifted his head to give Marlow a suspicious look out of wolf-amber eyes. Something went tight and wet in Marlow's stomach at being the focus of that attention. People always made a fuss that his were grey, but they never struck him as anything special. It was just the absence of color. For him, it was Cade's, whiskey shot through with bronze, that made his breath catch in his throat.

"I have one?" Cade asked. "Or I am one?"

"Yes."

Cade narrowed those bright eyes for a moment, and then he laughed. It was a low, rich, *warm* sound that rubbed against Marlow's skin. He kissed Marlow's throat, a slow, wet caress of tongue and lips, and admitted, "Fair enough."

Marlow grabbed a handful of thick blond hair—it was probably going to be expensively trimmed as soon as the moon waned, so Marlow was going to enjoy the good grip while he could—and pulled Cade's head up. He grinned at the flash of annoyance that pressed Cade's full mouth together, a harsh comment almost visibly pinned back between his teeth.

"I didn't say I didn't like it," Marlow pointed out.

Cade raised his eyebrows. "That I am one?" he repeated dryly. "Or that I have one?"

"Yes," Marlow said again. He sounded raw. Honest.

He'd never been smooth. Never needed to be when he had a badge and a uniform with TAC stretched over his shoulders. This time, though, he'd apparently got it right. Hunger flashed over Cade's face—a glimpse of the wolf through human skin—and he pushed Marlow up against the far wall. The tiles were cold against his back, hard against bony shoulder blades, and Marlow tightened his fingers around the fistful of Cade's hair out of instinct.

Control. That was how he'd been trained. Always stay in control of a situation, don't let anyone else direct the outcome, always be the one in charge—or you'll end up dead. Hard habits to break—whether on the job or not.

Marlow held on for a moment—Cade's head tilted back against the restraint and the muscles in his neck corded with the strain—and then let go. Cade flashed a quick grin—wolfish even when his teeth weren't sharpened—and then it was gone as he claimed Marlow's mouth.

After that, neither of them did much talking.

It was the sort of kiss that didn't leave room for air, never mind words. All teeth and tongue and chewed-open lips. The sort of kiss that left exactly what you'd been up to written all over tender mouths and stubble-scraped cheeks. Marlow twisted one hand in the collar of Cade's expensive shirt and grabbed a handful of his ass with the other.

For the record, it felt as good as it had looked in the elevator. The memory of the crisscrossed scars made Marlow's fingers twitch as if he could feel them through the fabric, but he brushed that away. Scars like that you didn't ask about unless you had good reason. They weren't like Marlow's—uncomplicated as a spray of bullet holes got—and whoever wore them was the one who chose when to bring them up. It wasn't easy to scar a wolf, and it was never an accident.

Definitely not something to bring up during a restroom hookup.

Marlow got a firmer grip on the taut curve of Cade's backside instead and pulled him closer. His cock throbbed in dull counterpart to the eager ache in his balls as Cade scruffed the back of Marlow's neck with one hand and explored the long, tight muscles of his back with the other. The hard jut of his cock nudged insistently against Marlow's hip as they pressed together.

The kiss had slowed to something less desperate, more deliberate. Marlow leaned into it for a moment as he chased Cade's breath over his tongue to taste it. Then he pulled away and looked down as he tugged at the buttons on Cade's trousers.

"Fuck," Cade groaned, his voice caught low and raspy in his throat.

He dragged his shirt up over his head and off in an impatient, awkward tangle of arms and fabric. Marlow glanced up, and the broad spread of tanned chest nearly made him forget what he was doing. It wasn't fair. After you'd seen someone naked once, by rights, it should lose some impact.

Apparently not.

Marlow got his mind back to the task in hand and finished undoing Cade's trousers. He bit his lip, his mouth dry with expectation, as he started to push them down. His fingers slid over taut, silky-smooth skin and solid muscle that twitched under his fingers as they got closer to—

Someone hammered on the door until it rattled in the frame.

Marlow jumped so hard he cracked his head on the tiles and reached out to slam his hand against the door. Just in case the latch didn't hold. His heart battered against his ribs, the sour hit of adrenaline a buzz in his veins.

"What?" he snapped.

"Something you might wanna see on the TV," Bennett said, her voice conversational for someone on the other side of a locked door. There was a pause, and then she added with a dry edge to her voice, "Both of you."

She gave the door one last thump. Marlow felt the vibration in the bones of his hand.

"And it's meant to piss in," she said. "Some of us don't go in the woods."

The sound of her boot heels against tiles tracked her departure as she stomped off. Marlow, still awkwardly twisted as he held the door shut, looked up the few inches at Cade.

"Rain check?" he asked.

Cade closed his eyes and swallowed hard; frustration pulled tight along his jaw. After a moment, he opened his eyes and pulled up a thin smile from somewhere.

"The mood's kind of gone," he agreed dryly. He dropped a quick kiss on Marlow's mouth that turned into a bite. It was hard enough to sting. When Cade drew away, Marlow tasted blood on his tongue.

It made him shiver.

They scrambled back into their clothes, bumping elbows and hips as they shifted around the limited space. Marlow tucked his T-shirt in and adjusted himself roughly through his trousers. He resigned himself to the ache between his legs. No one had ever died of blue balls. Not directly.

He raked his hair back from his face and unlocked the door.

"Do you want to go first?"

"What, and you follow five minutes later?" Cade asked as he tucked his shirt—wrinkled from its stint on the floor—into his trousers. "I could go out the back and come back in the bar, pretend I just got back?"

A smart response stung the tip of Marlow's tongue. He caught it between his teeth as he glanced at Cade and changed his mind.

Sometimes, not often, Marlow got the idea that it was actually possible to get under Cade's skin. Enough to hurt. He was probably wrong, but he didn't want to risk that.

Don't ask him why.

"I'm not ashamed," he said. "But whoever goes first is going to have to pretend whatever Franklin says is funny."

Cade didn't look convinced, but he did look… relieved? Whatever it was settled the arrogance back over his shoulders like a coat. He dropped a quick tease of a kiss on Marlow's mouth as he stepped past him and out the door.

"I bet I'm funnier," he said and headed back into the bar.

The repeated dull trill of Cade's phone punctuated the NBC 7 news item as it played out on the bar's wall-mounted flatscreen. After the eighth notification, he muted it and stuffed it in his back pocket. Marlow glanced over at him briefly and then back at the screen.

"…teen star Haley Jenkins, best known for her work on cult classic *Haley's Comet*, was reportedly staying at the exclusive gated housing complex the Reserve, on the outskirts of San Diego," the smooth-faced blond news anchor said, as footage of a younger Haley in a black bodysuit bounced athletically around the screen as she fired white bolts of energy at wolf-headed aliens. "Her death during the full moon raises the question, what responsibilities does the Reserve and their private security—"

"Turn it off," Cade said, his voice tight and controlled.

Bennett gave him a flat look as she took a long swig from her bottle of beer. “What if we don’t?” She wiped her mouth. “This isn’t the Reserve. You don’t call the shots around here.”

She always had to be an asshole. Marlow briefly weighed the cost of interfering. He liked Cade—at least, since yesterday—but enough to get on Bennett’s bad side?

What the hell. It wasn’t that much different than being on her good side.

“Since when do you care about the news if you’re not on it?” he asked. There was maybe even a bit of edge under his mild delivery. He’d swallowed last night’s stunt, but it didn’t mean he’d liked it. “Turn it off.”

Franklin snorted and took a shot at the pool table. Balls rattled off each other with brittle cracks that reminded Marlow of the noise the trap had made as it snapped shut earlier. It made the back of his neck itch with sweat. The last thing Marlow would claim to be was squeamish. Not now, not after nearly a decade on Night Shift. It could have been him, though; it was just luck that it wasn’t.

And Marlow’s injuries wouldn’t be wiped away when the moon rose.

Franklin left the balls to ricochet off the green baize cushions as he straightened up. “What if she doesn’t?” he asked. “What are you going to do about it, Kit-kat.”

Bennett grabbed the black ball before it rolled into the pocket, her knuckles white as she clenched them around it, and then fired it back over the table toward Franklin.

“Do I look like I need your help?” she asked. “If I want to start something, I can do it myself.”

They glared at each other for a moment. The report on the screen droned on as they went back over Haley’s bio, including a never-aired detective show pilot and a brief relationship with a Hollywood d-lister.

Cade broke the tension with a dry snort. “Wait, I just remembered,” he said as he pulled his wallet out of his pocket. “I can afford to drink somewhere else.”

He pulled a handful of notes out and slapped them down on the bar. “Drinks are on me,” he said, voice pitched to carry. “To thank you guys for your service.”

Someone whooped. Hands went up as people yelled out orders. Cade pocketed his wallet again and stalked out of the bar. The door slammed behind him.

Franklin laughed, a blurt of awkward, resentful humor, and jerked his thumb toward the door. "Some guys can't take a joke," he said.

Marlow lifted the cue ball off the table and bounced it on his palm. "Yeah, me," he said. "Don't call me Kit-kat, Franklin."

Heavy-lidded blue eyes narrowed over broad, scarred cheekbones, and Franklin leaned forward. He braced his knuckles on the table, shoulders hunched under his shirt, and showed his teeth in a thin, mean smile.

"Or?"

"I'll punch you, and we'll both end up with a disciplinary," Marlow said.

Franklin glared at him for a second and then suddenly laughed. He pushed himself upright and shook his head.

"What the fuck am I supposed to do with that?" he asked of the room at large. "I'm trying to escalate things here, and he's just not working with me. C'mon, man. Call me Frankenstein because I'm tall or something?"

"Frankenstein was the scientist," Marlow told him.

"Fuck off."

"He's right," Bennett said.

"Then why's the movie called *Bride of Frankenstein*?" Franklin asked.

Marlow left them to bicker over that and headed for the door after Cade. It didn't take him long to catch up. Cade stood next to his car on the phone, jaw clenched as he listened to whoever was on the other end. He glanced briefly at Marlow as he walked over, and a muscle in his jaw twitched.

"…is not the level of—" Marlow picked out the tinny voice over the sound of scant mid-moon traffic. He turned away and tried not to listen. After a second, Cade hung up and stuck the phone into his back pocket.

"So much for keeping this quiet in return for my cooperation," Cade said as he pulled the fob out of his pocket and unlocked the car with a flash of the headlights. "I don't expect much from the

SDPD, but I thought they could make it two days before they threw my company under the bus."

It might not have been O'Hara," Marlow said. Even to himself, he sounded detached, his voice aggressively placid in response to Cade's annoyance. That always pissed Bennett off, and from the repeated jump of the muscle in his cheek, Cade had that in common with her. It didn't matter. Marlow couldn't help it. High-pressure situations made him calm. "Leaks happen."

"Do they?" Cade asked, something pointed in his voice. "Is that why Piper tried to kill you?"

He looked like he regretted it the minute he said it, but he had the good grace not to apologize. Some things you didn't get to take back. Not right away. It had to sit on your conscience for a while.

"I would have gone with, 'You should know, after the number of holes Piper put in you,'" Marlow said, still detached and pleasant, despite the bite of sour water in the back of his throat. It shouldn't bother him this much—people had said worse, and some of them had been people he'd known a long time—but it stung from Cade. "But for the record? No, it wasn't. I didn't know enough to leak anything."

Marlow didn't wait for a follow-up question that he had no intention of answering. He turned and walked away, along the well-worn trail from the bar back to the precinct. Most people had the good sense to be going the other way when they took it.

"Hey," Cade called after him. "You never asked me."

Despite himself, Marlow slowed down as curiosity tugged at him. Asked about *what*? What had brought Cade from Alaska to California? The scars? Why he was such a dick?

Marlow didn't stop, but he did turn around and walk backward a few steps.

"Ask you what?"

Cade looked awkward as he scratched behind his ear. "What I thought of your ass."

That stopped Marlow in his tracks as he laughed. He crossed his arms.

"That sounded smoother before you had to say it, right?"

"Maybe," Cade admitted with a wry smile. "Just… I don't like to be angry alone."

It wasn't an apology. Marlow didn't know if he needed one—or would have accepted it if it was. The truth was that his life would be a lot less complicated without kissing Cade Deacon in restrooms.

Somehow, the fact he knew that had no impact on how much he wanted to kiss Cade again.

"That's your therapist's problem, not mine," Marlow said. "I'll find out how news of Haley's death got out. If O'Hara lied, I won't be happy either."

Cade shrugged to that, as if it hadn't just made him storm out. "So, are you going to ask what I think?" When Marlow stared blankly at him in confusion, Cade's mouth tilted in self-mockery. "About your ass?"

Marlow raised his eyebrows briefly and then shook his head as he turned around.

"It's my job to work out twice a day," he tossed back over his shoulder. "I know I have a great ass. Maybe I'll see you tonight—unless you behave yourself."

Cade snorted. "I'll bear that in mind," he said.

CHAPTER TEN

THERE WERE A dozen angry messages and missed calls on Cade's phone from clients and stockholders in Cold Winds. The sad truth about owning your own company—that no one had told young Cade, who hated to be told what to do—was that once it was big enough to be worthwhile, you were back to answering *to* people. Mental health days were for people who didn't have ranch land to pay off.

Back in his office, Cade stood in front of the long window, sun warm as it seeped through the glass, and watched the gulls hang lazily in the afternoon sky over the marina. In the background, one of the Reserve's board rattled angrily about oversight and communication on speakerphone.

"…and what do you have to say for yourself?"

It wouldn't be anything good if he spoke his mind.

Cade finished the Bovril in the cup he'd nursed through two calls so far. It had gotten cold, the meaty taste gone malty on his tongue. He wiped his thumb over his lower lip and turned back to the computer to hit the unmute button.

"That under the circumstances, and in respect for the dead girl, I won't expect the Reserve to pay the full penalty for Macroy's breach of contract."

Acton—transport millionaire, Treasurer of the Board, and generally irritating man—choked on the other end of the call. "What? Macroy *assured* me that Cold Winds had given him express permission to have a keycard for his office, rather than a named guest."

Cade grimaced to loosen his lips from the irritated snarl that pulled at them. Every time he thought he was done fixing Justin's messes, he found some more his ex-partner had squirreled away.

"He was. We did," Cade said, no sign of his annoyance in his smooth, calm voice. "The contractual expectation remained to keep those cards in his, or his proxies', physical possession. He didn't, and as a result, it appears that his employee used his access to commit unlawful acts on the premises. Which, as you know, would allow us to apply the penalty clause… if it didn't seem in poor taste. I wouldn't want Cold Winds to look like it was profiting from this young woman's death. Not once everything comes to light."

Silence. Cade tilted his head. No background noise. It was his turn to be muted while Acton swore at him, he assumed. He took the second to flip through the mail on his desk—one for Justin. On a better day, he'd give it to his secretary to forward it. Today he tossed it into the bin. It had been months. There was no reason for Justin's stuff to still be sent to him.

"We appreciate your restraint," Acton said, his voice ripe with sarcasm. "But nulls who are where they don't belong get eaten. It's unfortunate, but it happens."

"A wolf didn't kill her," Cade said. "Not directly, at least."

This time the silence was just frustration, broken with a heavy sigh. "And you're managing the situation?"

"I'm giving it my all," Cade said. "I have an in with one of the detectives on the case, and he's keeping me on top… of things."

At least, Cade smirked to himself despite the annoyance of the last few hours, that was one way to describe it. He absently reached up to finger the bruises on his neck, still raised and hot under his fingers. They would be gone by tomorrow, but for now, the tender spots conjured the memory of Marlow's mouth on him, and his hands… elsewhere.

"We'll see how this plays out," Acton agreed finally. "We'll speak about it again once the case is closed, and I've spoken to Macroy to see how he wants to go forward."

"Let me know."

Cade hung up. Sometimes he wondered if this job was worth it. It probably wasn't, but the benefits were. He liked money. He liked security. That was why he was good at this job. He knew what the very rich people who hired them wanted: to feel that they'd be safe even if they didn't pay for it. They wouldn't be, of course, but the illusion was important.

He glanced at the clock to check the time. Habit. It was hours until he was likely to change, late enough to break open the whiskey and early enough to enjoy the buzz before it was burned off. His next appointment wouldn't care.

In fact, he'd expect his own tumbler.

Cade set a neat whiskey out on the coffee table and poured one for himself. Two sips in, and his secretary tapped on the door and showed in Benjamin Cooper, the ex-chief operating officer of Bear Arms Security. He'd lost his job recently—after the higher-ups had recruited Justin into the role.

He didn't need a job. Unlike Cold Winds, which was strictly civilian, Bear Arms Protection was a subdivision of the Institute, a private military company that had branches in every global hot spot and war zone in the world. There were plenty of positions to transfer Cooper into.

Of course, that didn't mean Cooper's position wouldn't be strengthened if the Institute thought he might entertain other offers. And job security or not, he probably enjoyed the idea he could make some people sweat.

"Deacon," Cooper said. "I see the shit's hit the fan at the Reserve?"

One of those people being Cade, since he had stolen the lucrative contract for the Reserve security from under Cooper.

Cade pulled a cold smile from somewhere to acknowledge the jab and waved his hand at the whiskey.

"Help yourself," he said.

Cooper snorted and took the seat. He was a big man, solid through the chest and gut despite being closer to fifty than not. His hair had faded from fiery red to a dull gilt shot through with blond streaks, and he had a few wrinkles around his eyes. He looked more comfortable in jeans and a sweater than the suit he'd worn the last time they'd spoken.

"So, you really want me on board?" Cooper asked as he picked up the whiskey and tossed half of it back. "Or you just poking the bear? No pun intended."

Cade sipped his whiskey. It wasn't good whiskey, but it was the best bad whiskey you could get. It reminded him of home. They weren't good memories, but they were a pointed reminder of why he liked who he was now more.

Most of the time.

"I need your help."

Cooper snorted, drained his whiskey, and set the glass back down neatly on the coaster.

"I expected at least some subtlety," he said. "But I appreciate you saving my time. I'll show myself out."

He stood and headed for the door. Cade took another drink of whiskey and licked the tang off his lips.

"It's about Piper," he said.

Probably. Maybe? It didn't matter. Even if Cade wasn't being entirely honest, the name still stopped Cooper in his tracks. He stood there for a moment, in front of the door, one hand stretched out to grab the handle.

"Now there's a blast from the past," Cooper said. He turned around and studied Cade for a second. "He out?"

"No, but he's come up in regards to the Reserve."

Cooper twisted his mouth into a sour smile. "Sounds about right." He scratched his jaw as he thought about it, then finally grunted and sat back down. He nudged the tumbler toward Cade. "I'm not a cheap date. I need more than one whiskey to loosen me up."

Probably not more than two, though. Cade refilled both glasses. The liquor might not be top shelf, but it packed a punch.

"You've seen the news," he said. "The body found at the Reserve?"

Cooper's eyebrows twitched. "I did," he said. "Couldn't miss it."

"It doesn't look like Piper was directly involved," Cade said, "but the body dump came out of his playbook, or that's what I heard from the local cops."

Cooper raised eyebrows that had only faded lightly down from the brick red he'd started with. "Sounds like you've had the whole story, so what do you need me for?"

"The version that tells the whole truth," Cade said. "Instead of the one worried about its reputation."

Part of him balked at the suggestion Marlow had lied to him, but that was sentiment taken too far. The truth was Marlow's loyalties were with the SDPD, along with his next paycheck. It would take more than one heady, sweaty encounter to change that.

Not that Cade wanted that to change, he reminded himself.

"Nobody wanted the lawsuits that would have fallen out of Piper's pockets if he was prosecuted for everything he did," Cooper said. "Short and sweet version is that Piper made things go away, and no one wanted them to come back. Not the LEOs, sure, but the rest of us were glad when Piper went away quietly too."

"Not sure that Officer Marlow would agree," Cade said.

Cooper looked blank for a moment, then lifted his chin as recognition dawned. "The kid who got shot? Yeah, well, not like Piper did that without cause. Just because Marlow didn't have blood on his hands didn't mean they were clean."

That shouldn't have bothered Cade. He kept to the straight and narrow these days—most of the time, officially—for the sake of the company's reputation. That hadn't always been an option. He'd done things he wouldn't want people to know about. He'd done things he wasn't proud of.

None of that mattered. He still felt the sharp sting of disillusionment at the thought Marlow wasn't the good cop he seemed, even though it shouldn't have been a surprise. Marlow had told him himself; Piper hadn't shot him to keep him from blowing the whistle.

"That's the SDPD's problem. Or was," Cade said. "What I want to know is what Piper did for the Reserve."

Cooper sipped his whiskey and frowned. "Favors," he said. "Ones we paid for under the table. But nothing… unseemly. You've probably got a few moonlighting cops on your payroll?"

He raised his eyebrows as he waited for an answer. Cade acknowledged the point with a nod. That was enough to satisfy Cooper.

"We didn't bother with null staff during the full moon," he said. "Cost-benefit analysis said it wasn't worth it; what the fuck was going to go wrong? Of course, sometimes things did anyhow, and Piper dealt with it. It was his job, *anyhow*. Even though the Reserve pays for private security, they still fall under the local's jurisdiction. So, if Piper detoured a few patrols to keep an eye on the Reserve, well, what's the harm? Our 'donations' went directly to support the local police, after all. It just turned out that we should have kept a bit of a better eye on him."

"The bodies he made disappear."

Cooper nodded. He tapped his thumbnail against the rim of his glass for a second. "That's where it started," he said. "He also did favors for some of the residents."

"Like?"

"Guess."

"Murder?"

Cooper didn't bother to mug shock at the suggestion. "No. Thankfully, we didn't have to cover that up." He didn't bother to pretend they *wouldn't* have covered it up either. "A null spouse that was being difficult about a divorce got a scare on the road when her car broke down and got pulled out by Night Shift just in time. A few creditors that didn't plan to pursue a payment plan through the courts were invited up, then hunted by Night Shift through the woods. Most of them learned their lesson after they lost a finger. Or two."

"To traps?"

"I heard about your man," Cooper said. "Is he okay?"

"He's at the hospital. His foot's still attached," Cade said. "Tonight should set him right."

Cooper rubbed his leg absently at the thought. "I can't imagine being lamed like that. As far as I know, it was a step too far for Piper too. I don't know if that was morals or just because everything else he did, he could, mostly, pass off as just Night Shift business as usual. Once it came out what Piper'd been up to, some of it, we fired everyone on our side who we thought might have been involved. And then the Reserve fired us. That's the whole story. So unless you have better whiskey or a real job offer…?"

There was something Cade had missed. He could feel the itch of it in the back of his head.

"If it was real, would you entertain it?" he asked.

Cooper pursed his lips for a moment, then shrugged it off. "Old dogs don't learn new tricks," he said. "It doesn't pay. Anything else?"

The pieces clicked into place. Some of them, at least.

"Any of those creditors after Macroy?" Cade asked.

Cooper chuckled. "Sure," he said. "But he never dealt with them, or Piper. It was that woman he worked with, the one that runs his office. Fucked if I can remember her name…"

"That's okay," Cade said. "I think I can guess."

That obviously intrigued Cooper, but he didn't ask before he left. Cade finished his whiskey and turned the glass in his hand absently as he sat there. Then he picked up the phone to call Marlow.

The trill of the ring tone dragged out before it finally cut off without the courtesy of a voicemail message.

Cade snorted. It saved him from a recording of him being an asshole, he supposed. He hit redial and put the phone on speaker as he sat down at his desk. While he waited, Cade pulled up the Tracers' database and logged in. Most of the time he delegated this stuff to Lem, but he was more than capable of doing it himself.

He'd just finished typing when the phone rang.

"What?" Marlow mumbled at him through a yawn.

"I thought you'd want to know," Cade said as he scanned the screen. "Olivia Farnham knew all about Piper and his… extra-curricular activities. She did the dirty work—or commissioned it—while Macroy kept his hands clean."

Silence. Cade was just about to ask if Marlow had fallen asleep again when the man groaned.

"Fuck," he muttered. "And Farnham's a null."

So she'd have been up and around on the night in question.

"Pick me up at the office," Cade said. "You know where it is."

Marlow's bed creaked as he, Cade assumed, rolled over. Cade wondered if he had boxer shorts on again or was naked this time. Either worked for him.

"You're not a cop," Marlow said. "And you said that we weren't working together anymore."

A thin smile tugged at the corner of Cade's mouth as he reached the end of the report and found the bit of information he'd been after. Or at least, the shape of it.

"I changed my mind," he said. "And I know something you don't."

"What?"

The only answer that deserved was a snort. Cade downloaded the report and closed the database down as he got up from behind the desk.

"Don't take too long getting here," he advised, "or you'll have to wait until tomorrow."

CHAPTER ELEVEN

IT WAS A DIFFERENT assistant that met them at the elevator this time. The young woman looked flustered and uncomfortable as she clutched her phone in both hands.

"I'm sorry," she blurted before either of them could say anything. "But Ms. Farnham isn't available right now."

"Why not?" Marlow asked.

The assistant pretended that she had to clear her throat. "She's in a meeting," she said. "Outside. Not in the office. It's important."

Apparently, they hadn't had time to find someone who was a good liar.

He flashed his badge at her. "Night Shift, TAC team," he said. "We've permission from Mr. Macroy to search the offices."

Or Cade had. He'd drawled a promise to waive some penalty clause, and Macroy had nearly fallen over himself to agree. Marlow had a feeling that the phone call had cost Cade more than just international calling fees.

The assistant looked cross-eyed at his badge and then over her shoulder. The corridor behind her was empty. No one else at the company wanted to get involved.

"I think I should check," she said. Her chin went up, stubborn now she'd decided on the right course of action. "Just in case there's been a miscommunication."

"If there has, file a complaint," Marlow told her. "Where's Parker's office?"

Her mouth opened and stayed like that for a second. She raised her hand jerkily and pointed half-heartedly over her shoulder.

"Thirty-two B," she said. "The comet."

Cade made a rude noise under his breath and stepped around her to head down the hall. Marlow took a moment to say "Thanks" and followed him. He bit the side of his tongue to hold back a reminder that he was the cop, not Cade. That could wait until he found out what Cade knew.

The assistant—after a dithered second—tagged along at their heels.

Each door they passed had stylistic graffiti etched in bright colors. A caricature of a young man on a skateboard, a cartoon dog, one that was just teeth picked out in distressing shades of yellow and gray.

Parker's had a comet in blue and red.

"I guess he peaked early," Cade said. "And didn't want anyone to forget it."

The assistant fretted behind them. "I think I should call someone," she said. "This is Parker's private space. You need a warrant to—"

"It's Macroy's private space," Marlow corrected her. He tested the door. It was locked. "He just lets you use it. Do you have a key?"

He turned toward the assistant expectantly. She started to answer and then changed her mind, lips folded over to pinch her mouth shut.

"If you don't give him the key," Cade said, his voice almost as easy and warm as it had been that morning in the elevator. "Officer Marlow will kick the door in."

The assistant gave Marlow a shocked look. "You can't do that," she said. "It's not the full moon!"

Marlow shrugged. "Yet I still have feet," he said.

Being put on the spot made the assistant squirm. She wrung her hands around her phone, white-knuckled and sweaty, until she finally decided. "I'm going to call someone," she said. "You can ask them."

She walked away to make the call, her back turned to them. Marlow glanced at Cade, shrugged, and stepped back. He braced himself and donkey-kicked the door. His heel hit the wood right next to the handle, and the flimsy lock snapped in half. The door burst open and cracked into the wall behind it.

The assistant yelped and dropped her phone at the bang. She spun around and gasped, "Shit," one hand raised to cover her mouth.

Cade caught the door against the flat of his hand as it bounced back. "I didn't actually mean for you to do it," he murmured in an aside to Marlow. "It was just meant to be a threat."

"What's the point of being TAC if you don't get to kick in doors?" Marlow asked. He pointed his chin toward the shocked assistant. "There's no point trying to put pressure on her. She's always got her back to the wall. I'll pay to fix the door if it comes to that."

He stepped around Cade and into the office. It was small and cluttered, files piled on the desk and folders stuffed with forms stacked haphazardly on the shelves. There was a window with a straggly spider plant on it, crisped from the sun.

No smoking gun.

Marlow hadn't expected one, but it would have been nice. He walked over to the desk and started to look through the files. There was a frame by the monitor, LOVE spelled out in carved calligraphic white letters across the bottom of it. It was a picture of Haley, alive and smiling flirtily over a cocktail at someone. *Not* the person who'd taken the picture, though. They'd been far enough away that the zoomed-in photo blurred at the edges when you looked at it closely.

"They were friends," Farnham said from the doorway. The assistant hovered at her shoulder, nervous and fidgety. It hadn't taken her long to find her boss after all. "That's why he broke the rules so he could help her. People have pictures of their friends."

"You made it back quickly," Cade said. He didn't bother to hide the edge in his voice. "Meeting go well?"

Farnham gave him a dirty look, dismissed the nervous assistant with a curt "You can go," and then stepped into the room.

"Officer Marlow," she said. "Shouldn't you have spoken to Parker's lawyer before you—"

"No," Marlow said. He went through the desk drawers quickly—stationery, lip balm, assorted dried-out sharpies—until he reached one that was locked. "I don't think so."

He pulled a butterfly knife out of his pocket and flicked it open with a snap of his wrist. The drawer held for a second as he jimmied the lock with the blade, then broke with a dull crack. It took some muscle to pull it open. Inside was full of crumpled-up newspaper cuttings, a discarded dress with blood dried crusty and brown on the sequins. And photos. Lots of photos.

"This is what you found?" Marlow said as he lifted out another long-range photo of Haley. The equipment was better this time, and Haley wasn't smiling. She was hunched over in a gray sweatsuit behind the gates of what Marlow was pretty sure was the rehab facility. Another of her with a hot dog. With a man, his face angrily scrawled out with a pen until the paper had torn. At the bottom of the drawer, Marlow unearthed a black journal, its pages full of cramped, tiny script that started every entry neatly and then got messier and larger. Every page had HALEY written on it at least once, in letters three times as large as the rest. "These photos. This diary. Is that when you realized what he'd done?"

Farnham stared at him for a second. Her face was set like flint, hard but brittle. "I don't know what you mean."

"No," Cade said. "She knew before that. That's why you paid for him to be committed, right? And for Haley's rehab—so he'd not feel he had to rescue her."

Color stained Farnham's cheeks, two bright, angry blobs of it like someone had pinched her.

"That's private information," she said, her voice strangled in her throat. "And I want you out of here. This is a private company, and we have—"

"Permission," Cade said. "From Mr. Macroy."

He turned the monitor around. His fingers tapped over the keyboard as he pulled the main screen up and searched for something. It didn't take long. Parker didn't seem to have tried that hard to hide it.

"Look at that," Cade said as the still filthy interior of Macroy's house appeared on the screen. "He tapped the security feed. Took photos of her there too."

Farnham swallowed hard. "I had no idea," she said. "I helped Parker when he had some… problems… because he was one of my kids. The same reason I helped Haley. Back then, I was a casting director. I put those kids in front of the camera. I felt responsible for what happened to them."

Her hands pleated at her cuffs as she talked, neat, nervous motions that concertinaed the good silk into tiny folds. When she saw Marlow's eyes on her, she stopped.

"I didn't get why you went to bat for him so hard," Marlow said. "No matter if you got him a job as a teenager or not, he'd put your job on the line. Your reputation with your boss."

"I told you," Farnham said. "I felt responsible because—"

"Because he was your son," Cade said. The statement made Farnham's face go slack and expressionless. "You had him when you were fifteen, and you left him behind with your sister when you were eighteen to come to LA. Eventually, he came to find you, and you weren't going to give him up again. That's why you got him that job on *Haley's Comet*. This job too. Covered for him, over and over."

Farnham closed her eyes and… *relaxed*. The high-strung tension that had kept her shoulders squared and her back straight seeped away, and she sagged into a more comfortable version of herself.

"Only about this," she said. "Only ever about this. She ruined Parker, and she never even had to try."

"This is what you found," Marlow repeated. He tapped his finger on the desk. "That night."

She nodded, a minimal dip of her chin. A tear ran down her face, and she wiped it away from her nose with one hand.

"He'd been better. Stopped… all that," she said. "Or so I thought. Then I found out about this. I knew. I knew he wasn't *well* again."

"He killed a girl," Cade said.

"Or you did," Marlow said. "Is that why you went out there? To make the problem go away?"

Farnham opened her eyes. She looked genuinely shocked, but then she'd looked the same way when they'd told her Haley was dead in the first place.

"Of course not," she said. "I'm not a murderer. How dare you!"

"But you were out there," Marlow said.

When she didn't answer immediately, Marlow leaned on the table. Nulls might not make good detectives, but they were good hunters. "There are fifteen speed traps between here and the Reserve. Security cameras at every other shop and fancy house. And I'm pretty sure at least a few of Mr. Deacon's very wealthy clients have some very expensive game cameras set up in those woods for selfies. It won't take me long to find the proof you were there."

Farnham rubbed her forehead. "I didn't go out there to hurt anyone," she said. "I didn't find all of… that …until afterward. When I made Parker show me. That night, I just saw the feed on his computer when I came in to leave him a note. The mess. The girl."

"Haley."

Farnham shook her head and looked around for a chair to sit down in. She smoothed her hand over her thighs to press the wrinkles out of her skirt. "I didn't recognize her," she said. "I truly didn't. I hadn't seen her since the first time she went into rehab, and she was seventeen and strung out. Blamed me for it. Blamed Parker. He loved her. He really did."

"That's called stalking," Cade said, "when they don't love you back."

"And she was already gone when I got there," Farnham said, as if she'd not even heard him. "She'd run off into the woods… like she thought she was still on the show and could fight off wolves barehanded. I was going to take her home. That's why I drove out. To get whoever it was out of Wallace's house and pay them off. Get rid of them. If she'd just stayed put, she would have been fine."

Maybe.

Maybe not. Marlow glanced at the furious mess Haley had made of her prison, the defiance of it. He didn't think she'd have taken Farnham's money, and Farnham had proven she would do a lot for her son.

"You followed her into the woods," he said.

Farnham looked at him for a second. "Of course," she said. "She was going to get herself killed. I wanted to get her to come back with me, and I could have locked us both in the house until morning. Explained that Parker didn't mean any harm. I yelled after her, but she wouldn't stop. I don't… I don't know why not. She must have known it was me."

She sounded genuinely baffled. As if she couldn't imagine why Haley wouldn't have trusted her.

"Then she fell," Cade said.

Farnham nodded. "The trap killed her," she said. "Not Parker."

"Except it didn't," Marlow said. The back of his throat tasted like old trauma—the sickly-sweet taste of gas cut through with salt—as Farnham avoided his gaze. "She bled out. It would have been quick, but not immediate. She'd have been screaming for a minute or two."

Nobody said anything for a second. It was quiet enough that the wet click of Farnham's throat as she swallowed sounded loud.

"She didn't scream. Not much," she said, her voice pinched thin as it squeezed through her throat. "We both knew that would bring the wolves. How was I supposed to help her? To get her back to the house? I barely made it myself. Maybe if I'd known who she was, I'd have tried, but I never got that close."

"And when you got back to the house, you called for help?" Cade said. "To an old friend who'd make the problem go away. Or you *thought* would make it go away, like they had before."

Farnham wiped her face with both hands and then smoothed her skirt down again. A small, damp smile curled her mouth for a second, and she leaned forward slightly. "Now *that* I don't think you can prove."

"Not yet."

Marlow made a disgusted sound and shoved the creep drawer shut with his knee. He didn't get angry often. Not that deep, hot anger that felt like it might catch you alight. This had brought him close. Haley had been defiant and brave, and determined. She'd wanted her life, and she'd not deserved what happened to her. Wouldn't have even if she'd been some random girl like Farnham had thought, who could have gone into a pauper's grave with no one all that interested in who she was.

"Olivia Farnham, you're under arrest," he said. It wasn't often he got to do this part of his job, but he remembered the highlights. He gestured for her to stand up and turn around so he could read her rights while he cuffed her. "Do you understand these rights as I've read them to you?"

She shifted her wrists against the constraint of the plastic ties. "I do."

Marlow pushed her back down into the chair. She sat obediently, slightly slumped as if all the steel had left her backbone and it couldn't quite hold up anymore.

"Where's Parker?" he asked.

She took a resigned breath. "At home," she said. "His home."

"No," Cade said. "Not his. Not yours. It's been checked. Where is he, Olivia? Come on, you know there's only one way it ends if he runs."

She licked her lips and looked up at Cade, her expression suddenly hard as she lifted her chin. “I know how this ends if you catch him, where he’ll end up,” she said. “He’s not a bad boy. He’s not well, that’s all. And he didn’t kill anyone. All he wanted to do was help her. That shouldn’t ruin his life, even if he went about it the wrong way.”

Marlow shook his head in disgust. Love was one thing; blind was another. He grabbed the screwed-up dress from the table, blood and old curds of vomit crusted on the sequins, and threw it at Farnham. She turned her face away in disgust as it hit her in the chest and dropped into her lap.

“He stalked her,” Marlow said. “He kidnapped her—”

“She went willingly!” Farnham yelled at him. The roughness of her voice seemed to surprise her. She stopped, licked her lips, and tried again. “He didn’t kidnap her. She got in the car of her own free will.”

“He didn’t let her leave,” Marlow told her. “Did he tell her that when she went with him? When she got in the car, did she know she’d be his prisoner?”

Farnham grimaced and hitched her hips so the dress slid off her lap. She didn’t answer him, but her eyes flicked past him to the window.

It was another two hours before the earliest shift. All good nulls were on their way home to lock the doors behind them, but… not in a panic. Not yet. Marlow turned. Habit made the window catch his attention, but it wasn’t the only thing on the wall. There was a clock—red with silver hands and a tick he’d not noticed until now—and the minute hand had probably ticked off five minutes since they’d come in.

Marlow swore flatly and pulled his gun. The bullets were just lead and copper at this time of the day, but everyone flinched anyhow. Farnham made a small, shocked sound in her throat. He ignored her as he met Cade’s wary amber eyes.

“He’s downstairs,” he said. “In the garage.”

They took the stairs. Marlow’s heels clipped off the raw concrete as he went down two steps at a time. People thought the elevator was quicker, but that was because it was easier. If someone was in shape to run flights of stairs without a break—and motivated enough to move fast—the elevator would usually ding in late.

Marlow's ribs ached as each step pulled the old scar tissue that tangled through them, and his knee didn't hurt yet, but it was hot and the joint too elastic for comfort. He wasn't sure he was in shape anymore, but he clenched his teeth and pushed through the pain. It would pass, and he was still half a flight ahead of Cade.

Pride was better than Tiger Balm.

"Are you sure?" Cade asked him. "We're going to look assholes if there's nothing but a couple of Lexuses down here."

Marlow stuck his arm out to push himself off the far wall as he hit the first-floor landing. "There hasn't been time to come up with a better plan than the one she had," he said. His voice was slightly ragged as his lungs objected to multitasking. "Farnham said it herself. She was going to pay the girl off and get rid of her. Money in the car. Keys, for Parker, in her office. Probably tickets for a Greyhound down to Mexico too."

The door into the garage was solid, black, and locked with a fire bar. Marlow hit it with both hands and slammed it open. He slowed to a jog as he breathed in the damp, stale air of the garage.

"He could have gone already," Cade said.

They fell easily into step. The habits had been trained into them in different places but meshed well enough now. Cade took the left, the gun he'd produced from under his jacket held low and ready in both hands.

Farnham drove a black Prius, according to the assistant who'd been shocked into being helpful. She usually parked by the back wall because she was always the first to arrive and last to leave.

Marlow didn't hear anything, but Cade cocked his head suddenly and circled to the right. The full moon was only hours away; Cade's hearing wasn't wolf sharp yet but probably better than Marlow's.

They split up to cut between the rows of parked cars and down another level. Halfway down the ramp, Marlow caught the bounced echo of anxious voices as two men argued. He gave Cade a quick nod of acknowledgment and followed the sound.

"Just move the truck," Parker begged. "I'll pay you, okay? Here, look, a hundred bucks. Just move?"

Marlow gestured for Cade to go along the wall while he approached from the side. A catering truck was parked in front of a row of cars, the driver's side open and a shifty-looking teen behind the wheel.

"I'm not allowed to drive the truck," the teen said, even as he held his hand out for the hundred and started the engine. Parker swore under his breath and shoved another handful of notes at him.

"Don't move the truck," Marlow yelled. His voice bounced back from the bare walls. "SDPD. Take the keys out of the ignition and get out of the truck."

The kid blanched and bolted. He stuffed the money into his jeans as he dodged between the cars. Cade grabbed him by the collar on the way past and shoved him up against the wall.

"Stay," he rasped.

The kid held up both hands and did as he was told.

"You know the drill," Marlow said as he stepped out from between a Land Rover and a Porsche. "Hands up."

Parker licked his lips. "I won't go to jail," he said. "I know what it's like for wolves. We go mad."

"You locked up a girl," Marlow said. "I don't think you're that well now."

Sweat glistened visibly on Parker's face. "I helped her," he said. His voice cracked with his need to make Marlow understand. "That was the truth. She just… she didn't realize she needed my help. Not yet. She would have."

"No," Marlow told him. "She wouldn't. Hands up."

Parker stared at him. "I'm not a wolf yet," he said. "I'm still human. You can't just kill me."

He turned around and scrambled up into the driver's seat of the catering truck. He slammed the door and revved the engine, which coughed and screeched as Parker ground the gears. Whatever was in the back of the truck rattled and crashed as it jolted into motion and screeched away between the rows of cars.

"Shit," Marlow muttered.

He turned on his heel and broke into a jog as he cut through the closely parked vehicles. It didn't matter how fast Parker gunned the engine, he still had to circle back around to go up the ramp.

Marlow skidded to a stop in front of the ramp and turned to face the truck as Parker drove toward him. He planted his feet on the oil-stained ground and lifted his gun. On the other side of the grubby windshield, Parker looked sick to his stomach. That didn't stop him from hitting the gas.

As the truck barreled toward him, Marlow narrowed his eyes and held his aim on Parker's forehead until *almost* the last second. Then he lowered the gun and took out the two front tires instead. The truck veered wildly as the rubber burst, sparks thrown up off the battered rims, and crashed into the cars on one side and then, as Parker wildly overcorrected the wheel, the other.

Marlow flung himself out of the way, up onto the hood of a Lexus, as the truck lurched past him and crashed into the wall of the ramp. He slid back down onto the ground as Cade loped over to the truck and yanked the door open. Parker was slouched over the steering wheel as blood dripped from his nose.

"You could have killed him," Cade pointed out as he dragged Parker out of the truck. "No matter what he thought."

Marlow tucked his gun back into the holster.

"He kept her a prisoner," he said as he walked over. "Only fair he gets to experience it himself."

The kid in the white coat ventured cautiously out from behind a dark red SUV. He stared at them with a slack mouth and wide eyes.

"Shit," he said, as he took in the wrecked truck. "My boss is going to kill me."

EPILOGUE

"JUST DON'T DROP me off at the beach," Cade said as he got into Marlow's car. It was a nice car, a '69 Impala with black paintwork and original leather seats. Maybe too nice for a cop on an officer's salary, but Cade didn't plan to ask. "I'd rather not wake up with a belly full of sea lion again."

Marlow snorted as he started the engine. "Mission Trails do?"

"I suppose," Cade said. "Hopefully, I won't run into my ex-partner."

Marlow glanced at him for a moment as he pulled away from the curb. He didn't ask.

"Business partner," Cade clarified anyhow. Just in case. He tilted his head back and studied the roof of the car. He still wasn't over that crush, then? "What about you? Surely, after all this, you get tonight off?"

"I would have if I'd shot him," Marlow said. He flicked the indicator and took a left, past a black van and an Apple store. "I'm on call. Which means I can catch up on my sleep but not my drinking."

"Good. You look like you need to be in your bed more than you do the bottle."

Marlow glanced over at him. He had his glasses on again, but it didn't matter. Now that Cade knew the precise silvery-gray of his eyes, he could pick it out through the tint.

"My bed?" he said. "Not yours?"

Reluctance clogged the back of Cade's throat, but he pushed through it.

"Well, there's no reason for us to see each other after this, is there? And that's probably best. My clients aren't exactly your biggest fans."

Marlow hung one hand over the steering wheel, wrist braced on the leather curve and fingers loose as he stopped on red. The streets were empty, but technically you could still get a parking ticket from the cameras. He shrugged one lean shoulder.

"Yeah, same could be said for my superiors," he said. "I guess the spirit of cooperation died with that shitty email you sent O'Hara."

Cade snorted. It was for the best. He didn't need any of this. Maybe the crush would starve to death once the only Marlow fantasies it had were Cade taking him to task over throwing one of Cold Winds' men into the Crate.

The thought made his mouth dry and his balls tighten for some reason. He'd dressed a lot of people down over the years, and it wasn't his kink. Not usually. But the thought of turning the rough edge of his tongue on Marlow in public, while the TAC officer listened with that placid, unreadable expression of his…

Ah, there it was—the thought of what he'd do to Cade *after* that, when they were in private.

"I mean," Marlow said, "there's the sex."

There were a lot of legends about nulls. None of them were that they were telepathic. Cade still felt heat wash up to his ears as he tried to shove his brief fantasy to the back of his head.

"What?"

Marlow kept his eyes on the road as the lights changed, and he threw the Impala into drive. His profile was all sharp lines and smooth skin, the corner of his mouth tucked up with wry humor

"Someone doesn't have to actually die before we can fool around," he said as they pulled up onto the interstate. "Or that's what I've heard."

If someone had asked, Cade wasn't sure he could have described the feeling in his gut. It was a tangle of overinvested excitement and the sudden nervous pressure to not fuck this up and be an asshole. But there was a grab bag of other stuff too.

He reached out and curled his hand around the back of Marlow's neck, and his thumb grazed along the tight line of tendon.

"Is this just because you want a shot at my spectacular ass?" he asked.

Marlow glanced at him quickly—a flicker of gray visible as he looked over the top of his glasses—and then laughed.

"Maybe," he said. "Besides, we still don't know who has stepped in for Piper to clear up—"

Behind Marlow, through the driver's side window, Cade saw the truck barrel through the red light and roar across the junction toward them. It was low-slung and black, with armor-plated sides and glare-bright lights.

Instinct made him tighten his grip on the back of Marlow's neck and drag him forward. He twisted his body over him, arms folded over both their heads. All he had to do was survive the night, and he'd be good as new. Marlow wouldn't be so lucky.

The truck smashed into the side of the Impala. If it had been a newer car, it would have been t-boned. The old muscle car's framework groaned but held, even as metal tore with a raw, almost organic sound.

A window shattered—Cade felt splinters hit the back of his hands—and the car lurched sideways as whoever was driving gunned the engine.

"What the fuck?" Marlow spat, voice muffled.

Cade looked up and squinted at the dust-grimed windscreen. On the other side of the glass, a man in SDPD TAC gear stared back as he threw the truck into reverse. The Impala rocked as the truck pulled free. It backed up a few feet and then roared forward again.

The Impala's tires scraped sideways over the road as the truck rammed it until they hit the barrier. Cade felt the car shift under them, and then the world spun around them as they tipped over the edge.

He braced one hand against the roof as they dropped. A jolt of pain pierced down into his armpit as his wrist snapped. Cade snarled, furious for a second, and then the Impala hit the road, and his head hit the window.

The world went gray around him. Cade did his best to fight the wash of grogginess, although he couldn't quite remember why it was important he stay awake, but it dragged him under.

The car finally scraped to a stop on the street beneath and slowly spun on its scored roof like a shocked beetle. Overhead the moon rose, fat and inexorable, into the dull purple sky.

SPLIT SHIFT

The hard thing about Night Shift is when you realize werewolves are bad news, but people can be worse.

After Night Shift officer Kit Marlow solved the murder of child star Haley Jenkins, he figured he was due a little down time. Maybe even a dinner date with Cade Deacon, the sarcastic security consultant, very good kisser, and werewolf who'd helped with the investigation.

That was before someone in a Night Shift uniform drove them both off the road. With the full moon up the only dinner date Cade is interested in...has Marlow served up on a plate. And not in a sexy way.

It's the second time that corrupt Night Shift officers have tried to kill Marlow. If he has his way, it will be the last. Problem is he only has twenty-eight days before the next full moon. If he hasn't identified who wants him dead by then, he'll have to take to werewolf filled streets with a team at his back he can't trust.

First things first, though. Get through the next twelve hours alive and uneaten, and hope that if a second date is still on the cards it's less eventful.

CHAPTER ONE

THE CAR HAD been built for open roads and speed—long, cool, and black. It had been left cracked open at the side of the road, stranded on its back while hot fluid dripped out slowly and ran over the scarred concrete. A scraped-thin reflection of the fat white moon wavered greasily in the shallow puddle.

Marlow opened his eyes and squinted at the abstract collision of color and light that filled his field of vision. Nausea hit him in the throat, and he squeezed his eyes closed. That didn't help. It only made him aware of the fact his heartbeat hurt in his sinuses and it felt like someone had shot him in the shoulder again.

He tried a second time. The nausea curdled unpleasantly in his chest, but after a couple of hard blinks Marlow realized what was wrong with the world.

It was upside down through a broken windshield.

Or rather, he was upside down. Lines of light from the streetlamps smeared over the road at angles he didn't usually see.

Marlow exhaled hard and watched a fine splatter of blood droplets spray over what was left of his windshield. That wasn't good. Marlow registered that and filed it away for later. There wasn't much he could do about it right now. Not until he got out of the car and worked out what had happened.

His thoughts were scattered. The last thing he remembered was… the rough scrape of Cade's hand on the back of his neck, the heat and heaviness of him as he dragged Marlow away from the wheel.

"Shit," Cade hissed against his ear. Then Cade's arms tightened around him until it hurt. Sharp knuckles dug into his shoulders, and the awkward angle made it hard to breathe.

Then something smacked into them hard enough that, for a second, Marlow felt weightless. Until he wasn't.

Marlow reached up and fumbled with the seat belt. It was jammed—the nylon tangled and the metal buckle battered and twisted under Marlow's fingers. Panic washed over him, a salt-sharp realization this was bad, and he wrenched violently at the buckle for a second. It gave slightly—although that might have been his imagination—and locked again.

The panic crested and faded. He could still feel the effects. His breath was hot and ragged in his throat, and his heartbeat—still echoing painfully behind his eyes—was too fast. It was just, the more adrenaline his body pumped out, the quieter his mind was.

Post-Traumatic Stress Disorder. Everyone Marlow knew had it. When you spent your nights fighting seven-foot-tall werewolves with impulse-control problems, things gave. It would probably be easier for the department therapists to treat if it wasn't useful sometimes.

Cade groaned next to him. Sort of. It started as that, anyhow, before it thickened on its way out through his teeth.

Marlow glanced over at his passenger. Blood plastered Cade's hair to his skull, dark against the shaggy blond curls, and stained his shirt in thick, wet patches. His arms hung limply over his head, one sleeve of his shirt torn off completely, along with a good chunk of skin.

What was left of his arm suddenly prickled with goosebumps, stark against tanned skin, and the fine scruff of pale hair visibly darkened.

Marlow swallowed a mouthful of blood and spit and went back to the problem of how to unbuckle himself. If he couldn't do that, it wouldn't matter how long they'd been here. Eventually, it would be too long.

He kept a pocket knife in the compartment on the driver's side door, but being upside down had added more variables to that. Marlow twisted around the best he could—pain radiated out from his ribs as they grated against each other—and scanned the roof of the car.

Nothing.

Shit.

He swallowed the slow roil of nausea and reached down to fumble over the roof of the car in search of something he could use. All he came up with was a pen, which wasn't much use.

It could have been thrown out of the car. Marlow checked the window next to him. It was shattered, chunks of diamond-sized pieces scattered over the road outside. In the middle of it, the bright red handle of the knife stood out in the moonlight.

Which reminded Marlow…

Next to him, Cade sucked in a quick, eager snort of breath that didn't sound quite… right.

Not quite human.

"How long?" Cade asked.

"Welcome back," Marlow said, his voice strained as he stretched his arm out of the car. His fingers nudged against the pocketknife, but he couldn't quite get hold of it. He braced his foot against the console and pushed himself out as far as he could, the seat belt a vice across his shoulder and ribs as he strained to reach it. Close. Closer. Marlow finally managed to grab it and pull it back into the car. His hand felt numb from the pressure of the seat belt, but he managed to get his thumbnail into the notch on the blade to pull it open. "You okay?"

Cade laughed, a rough, not exactly amused sound. "I will be," he said. "How long do we have?"

The dashboard had cracked on impact, the instrument panel buckled in and broken. Marlow pointed at it with his chin as he worked on the seat belt. The handle of the knife was cracked too, the sharp edges rough against his fingers as he sawed. "Clock isn't working," he said. "How long do you think?"

"Not long," Cade said. He coughed and cleared his throat. Or tried to. It sounded like something was stuck in there or had been damaged in the crash. "If I can get far enough from—"

"From the can of fresh meat bleeding out next to you?" Marlow snorted as he sawed against the edge of the strap. "You can't move that fast."

"You think you can?" Cade asked. "How's your knee doing after being T-boned?"

Good question. Marlow couldn't answer it yet. He could feel the steering wheel where it dug into his thigh, uncomfortable but not painful, but had no idea how functional anything was. He guessed he'd find out.

The strap split under the edge of the knife and snapped. Marlow grunted as the lap belt took his weight. He dangled for a breath, and then it went slack as the fabric scraped through it. He pulled his leg out from under the wheel and dropped awkwardly onto the roof of the car.

The knee was… not great. Marlow clenched his jaw as he squirmed around in the space until he was flat on his stomach. Glass dug into his elbows and knees as he squeezed through the window, arms stretched out in front of him to narrow his shoulders. The road was wet as he pulled himself out.

"Marlow. Kit," Cade said. His voice was thin, like it had been dragged through his teeth on a wire. "I really liked you."

"You don't know me," Marlow said. He rolled over and scrambled onto his knees. His back was sweaty despite the evening chill, his T-shirt stuck to him. "That probably helps."

It was the wolf's smile that flashed over Cade's face, wild and careless. Then Cade's face was gone. Marlow sucked in a sharp breath.

Ten years on the Night Shift, his whole life as a null, and Marlow had never seen a wolf shift before. Why should he? It wasn't a crime to be a wolf, so until they did something that meant Night Shift got called in, they weren't Marlow's business.

He didn't think he'd missed anything.

Bone shattered and reformed, then broke again as anchored muscle thickened from cords into heavy ropes. Skin split and peeled as coarse, tawny fur burst through in matted, slimed tufts. Humanity peeled back like a shed hoodie as the wolf's broad muzzle and heavy skull pushed through. Torn clothes were dragged off impatiently by clawed hands as the previously tailored fit suddenly pinched and rubbed.

Marlow exhaled. That was how quickly the man was unmade and the werewolf stitched over what was left. It felt like it should have taken longer.

The huge sandy wolf was crushed into the low-slung black wreck, half-strangled by the seat belt that dug into the flesh of its broad, thin-furred chest. He snarled, exposed teeth white and jagged, and the car jolted violently from side to side as Cade thrashed against his constraints. The seat belt went first, snapped in half, and then Cade shouldered the door out. It burst off its hinges and flew across the road to smash against the metal shutters drawn down over the storefront opposite.

Cade shrugged the car off like it was a too-small jacket. He shook himself and shed splinters of glass from his thick coat. He threw his head back, ruff thick and knotted around his neck and shoulders, and howled at the moon.

A few other wolves answered from around the city, drawn up and stretched out between the high-rise buildings and down from the buttes. Not many yet. There would be more as the moon rose higher, until up to 80 percent of the city were ready to throw their heads back.

Marlow scrambled to his feet. He took a step backward. Then another. His heel hit a puddle. The splash was faint, barely there, but it was enough.

One of Cade's pointed ears twitched toward the sound, and his broad muzzle followed. They stared at each other for a second.

"I liked you."

The words repeated in Marlow's head. If he thought about it, he could still pull the taste of Cade's mouth up from his short-term memory. Under normal circumstances, it would be a nice way to pass the time. Not so much when those same kisses were buried somewhere in a wolf's hungry brain.

Cade cocked his head to one side and then lunged forward. He leaped easily up onto the undercarriage of the car, balanced on the frame, and snarled at Marlow. His eyes hadn't changed much, still amber and wolfish.

Marlow pulled his gun in one smooth movement and took aim. The silver ammo was still locked up back in the station, but the hollow points loaded in the magazine would blow a hole the size of his fist in whatever they hit. Werewolves included. The problem was that would only slow Cade down.

And not enough.

"Sorry," Marlow said.

The first shot punched through the side of the car and took out the radiator. It exploded with a crack of stressed metal and a spray of overheated steam and rusty water that forced its way up through the undercarriage to blast Cade's feet and legs. The pain of scalded flesh made Cade snarl and lash out at the car. He ripped the suspension out, muscles corded over his shoulders, and swung it like a hammer. The car rang with a flat, off-tune note as Cade battered it.

Marlow winced. The Impala might have survived the accident—eventually. He had a good mechanic—but not Cade's temper tantrum.

Or this.

He dropped his aim a few inches and skipped a bullet off the road. It sparked as it chipped a divot out of the concrete. And that was it. Marlow clenched his jaw against the jitters that his body decided he needed and tried again. Two bullets into the road and another into the ticking engine. This time the spark caught and the fumes from spilled gas went up with a flash. It was a fast burn, thin and smokey, but the glossy ribbon of oil caught like a wick and flickered back to the breached tank.

The explosion knocked Marlow on his ass. His chest ached, and his lungs cramped as he tried to suck in a breath of hot, unsatisfying air. On top of the car, Cade burned. Tawny fur singed black against red skin as he threw his head back and screamed.

"Sorry," Marlow rasped out, his voice raw and hoarse.

He grabbed the gun he'd dropped on the way down and picked himself up. Cade tore one of the tires from its moorings and threw it into the street with a roar. Strings of rubber stuck to the road like taffy as it bounced.

Marlow ran.

That was step one of his plan. He hoped that step two would come to him soon. He cut diagonally across the road and took a right into a narrow, high-walled alley that smelled of cigarette smoke, fried cauliflower, and greasy water. A rat, well-fed and healthy despite the missing half of its tail, watched him with glossy ink-drop eyes from the top of a dumpster.

It held its ground until Marlow was close enough to kick it; then it flicked that truncated tail and scuttled up the wall to the fire escape. It swung briefly from the steps, like a rodent gymnast, and then shinnied up the railing toward the second floor.

Marlow broke stride for a second as he tilted his head to track the rat's progress. Half a plan flashed through his mind—climb onto the dumpster, grab the bottom rung of the fire escape, head up—and was rejected. It might have worked… if the wolf wasn't Cade.

A chance hunt might be abandoned if the trail went cold or it got too hard. There was other meat to be had in the city. But

Cade's wolf had imprinted on Marlow when the moon pulled it out; the memory of an interrupted kiss and the delicate tension between flirtation and complication refined down to simple, hungry want.

It was hardly the sort of doomed, bloody romance that Shakespeare had written Romeo and Juliet about. Cade wouldn't follow the ache in his chest across a whole city to find Marlow and eat his heart. But he didn't need to. Marlow had been right there, ripe with sweat and fresh blood, to whet Cade's appetite.

And then Marlow had set him on fire.

That was the sort of thing that kept a werewolf on your heels all night long.

Marlow pushed himself back into a run. It was hard. The brief pause had filled his legs with lead, heavy and sore as he dodged around the dumpster and loped past sealed delivery doors and padlocked garages. A sprawl of graffiti over the brick wall back of a building, paint sprayed thickly over small square windows, caught his attention. A cartoonish Ganesh hung placidly in the middle of a swirl of symbols and images. In the daytime, he'd be vivid bubblegum pink and cyan, but the moon dimmed him to grays and flesh tones. He was supposed to be lucky, protection against the wolves.

Either way Marlow recognized it. He'd been here before. Last time there'd been more blood and a half-dead boar someone had let loose in city limits holed up in someone's garage.

He'd known roughly where he was—the impact couldn't have thrown the car that far—but this was a solid landmark. The mental map of the city in his head reoriented around it, and he might even have a plan.

Not a great one, but a plan.

There was a homeless shelter at St Anne's over on Irving. If he could get there in time, they'd let him in. Father Bellamy was told a couple of times a year to keep his doors locked once the moon was up, leave the Night Shift to deal with any problems, and he'd never listened yet.

It was a ten-minute run. Five, if he cut through the skate park.

Marlow risked a glance over his shoulder. A greasy pillar of smoke from the burning car eddied up into the air, but he couldn't hear Cade's enraged howls anymore.

He didn't have ten minutes.

The end of the alley was a few yards ahead of him when something dropped out of the sky and landed in front of him with a wet splat. He stepped on it, and it gave under his boot with a crackle of thin bones. Blood and guts squeezed out of it, and instinct made Marlow stagger as he tried to shift his weight off the thing.

It was a rat. Most of a rat, anyhow. The head had been torn off, and it still only had half a tail. Marlow hopped away from the little corpse and looked up toward the rooftops. A shadow hunched up there, half lost in the darkness, and then it was gone.

"Shit," Marlow said softly.

If Cade had caught up with him already, he probably didn't have five minutes. He didn't have any other ideas though, so he bolted for the end of the alley. His focus narrowed to the ground immediately in front of him and the route he'd laid out in his head. Two yellow stripes flashed by under his feet, and he stretched his legs to take the curb in his stride.

A narrow path jinked down between two black cast iron fences—overgrown grass on one side and a cracked patch of concrete on the other, bleached patterns on the ground to show where the playset had been dragged in out of harm's way. A gate swung off warped hinges, something to repair in the light of day, and blocked the way.

Marlow vaulted it. It cost him when he landed, a jolt of pain in his knee that spiked up to his groin and nearly buckled his leg. He forced the next step and the next. By the third, his body accepted the pain wasn't going to make a difference and rerouted it to a less insistent ache.

A naked man, a joint between his lips, watched placidly from the roof of his garage as Marlow raced past.

Six minutes now. The gate had cost him.

He crossed another road and into the car lot outside the skate park. A ragged pennant for the Conquistadors from Serra High School flapped from a pole near the football field, a long shadow that snapped and stretched over the pocked, uneven ground.

Maybe he'd make it after—

Something slammed into him from the side, and Marlow lost his train of thought as he went flying. He hit the chain-link and went through it, the nails-on-chalkboard scrape of broken metal on metal loud in the relative silence. Skin scraped off against the metal hooks as he rolled on the other side. The air left his body on a croak, and his lungs cramped shut behind his ribs. He wheezed as he tried to suck in air and get to his feet at the same time.

"Cade," he tried, the words hoarse and trapped in his throat. It never worked; he always tried. "Don't—"

It wasn't Cade.

The wolf opposite him was wiry, muscle and skin shrink-wrapped over bone, with thick black fur and a missing ear. He grinned, lips skinned back from broken teeth, and waited.

He wanted Marlow to run.

"Fuck you," Marlow told it.

He drew his gun for the second time and blew out the wolf's kneecaps. Flesh and bits of bone sprayed out behind him, and his legs crumpled under him. The earless wolf went down with a frustrated snarl and clawed at the ground as he dragged himself forward. Black claws raked deep ruts in the road.

It wouldn't have bought Marlow enough time with Cade, but he had less distance to cover now.

Marlow turned and ran. This time it took a few more steps to convince his body to quit it with the news he was doing himself harm. Half his attention was behind him, and the rest was on the thin black bars of the cross he could see silhouetted against the moon.

Nearly there.

Sweat itched at the back of his neck and under his arms. He vaulted a fence and cut through a garden, over empty flower beds. On the second floor of the house, a curtain twitched behind the heavy bars as someone looked out. Marlow saw a thin slice of a face, and then the curtains jerked closed again.

Marlow didn't blame them. He was the one stupid enough to be out after the moon rose, and he wasn't even getting paid for it.

The sound of voices raised in soaring chant drifted from behind the heavy shutters on the church. It nearly drowned out the hot snort of a predator's breath as it bore down on him.

Marlow tightened his grip on the gun. It was empty, but he curled his finger around the trigger anyhow. The Night Shift went down swinging.

He reached the edge of the church's lot and spun around, empty gun half-raised out of habit. The earless wolf crouched, muscles like steel cables in its legs, and sprang.

Marlow braced himself. That would do about as much good as the empty gun. The wolf hit him, and then both flew backward until they crashed into the fire hydrant. It snapped off, and water sprayed up. Marlow got his arm up, braced against the wolf's throat, as teeth snapped together an inch from his nose. Slobber dripped, warm and sour with the stink of meat, on his face as the wolf bore down on him.

Then it was gone. Marlow blinked at the sky and then looked over. Cade, fur still singed and crisped, and the black wolf tore chunks out of each other as they fought in the road.

Marlow let his head drop back against the pavement and then levered himself up onto his elbow. This wasn't even close to the worst night he'd ever had. He didn't get to give up tonight.

He clenched his teeth and limped up the steps to the doors. The song inside crested and then broke off abruptly as Marlow hammered his fist against the wood.

"Night Shift," he rasped through the crack. "I'm on foot and fucked."

There was a pause. It dragged on long enough that Marlow wondered if Father Bellamy had finally listened to one of the lectures. Then he heard the bolts on the far side slide back.

He risked a glance back.

Cade punched a clawed hand into the black wolf's stomach and ripped up toward the barrel chest. Bright chunks of intestine bulged through the tear, vivid pink as the Ganesh graffiti, and the wolf finally backed off with an attempt at a defiant snarl. The black werewolf retreated slowly, head down and mouth open as it panted, but once it was gone, Cade looked around at Marlow.

"Thanks," Marlow said. He'd be the only one who remembered the sentiment, but he still felt better to have it said.

The sound of his voice made Cade cock his head curiously. For a moment, Marlow entertained the ridiculous idea that somehow Cade recognized him for a single breath. Then Cade snarled and threw himself at the steps, just as the parishioners pulled the door open for Marlow.

He was dragged inside by impatient hands, and the door slammed shut behind him. Cade hit the century-old wood with his full weight, but it held.

"Thank God," Father Bellamy, a tall, gray-haired man with a round, soft-cheeked face, said as he crossed himself piously. "I wasn't sure we'd get to you in time."

"Neither was I," Marlow said. He sagged down onto a pew and leaned forward, elbows braced on his knees and fingers buried in his hair. The adrenaline had started to fade, the aftertaste of it acidic in the back of his throat, and all the aches and pains he'd collected made themselves felt. His mind wasn't still anymore either, as the full significance of the last few hours finally sank in. He rubbed his thumb over his forehead and wondered aloud, "What the fuck happened?"

CHAPTER TWO

CHUNKS OF HALF-DIGESTED meat and hair splattered the ground between Cade's bare, filthy feet. He spat the sour taste out of his mouth and then replaced it as he retched again. There wasn't much left to expel from his guts, just watery bile and the sharp dregs of yesterday's whiskey.

He braced his forearm against the grimy wall and rested his sweaty forehead on it. It hurt to swallow, his stomach ached, and for some reason, he stank of meat grease and burnt hair. Cade let out a ragged, shaky breath and swallowed hard to dislodge the lump of gristle and regret stuck in his throat.

"You okay there?" someone asked him. They put a hand on his shoulder and rubbed an awkward circle, as if he was a baby that needed to be burped. "Do you need me to call someone?"

"I don't need anything," Cade lied between clenched teeth. "I'm fine."

"You don't look it."

Cade looked up from under the thick straggle of his hair, grimy from the muddy puddle he'd been using as a pillow when he woke up. He curled his lip back from his teeth. It wasn't a smile.

"Did I ask you?" he rasped, voice cold and very precise. "And if I did, was that when I told you that you could fucking touch me?"

The man looked embarrassed and a bit offended as he pulled his hand away. "I've never seen a wolf be sick before," he said. "Not after they shifted, anyhow. That's all."

"Now you have. Change your life?"

The man glared at him as he stepped back. "I hope you choke on it," he said over his shoulder as he stalked away.

"You too," Cade muttered as he pulled himself together and stood up straight. "Fuck."

It happened.

Nobody liked to talk about it—it wasn't exactly nice dinner party conversation to have with your null neighbors—but that didn't mean they didn't know. Sometimes, during the full moon, you ate someone you knew. A neighbor. A spouse. That one asshole from the HOA that wouldn't shut up about your lawn. Not often. Most nulls either stayed locked up this time of the month or were Night Shift and could take care of themselves….

That was the wrong train of thought.

Cade's stomach wrung itself out like a filthy flannel and found a last handful of puke to add to the puddle on the ground.

It happened, but you weren't meant to know. The wolf took the details of the night's menu with it, and unless someone found an earring jammed in their back tooth, they never knew. Suspect, sometimes. A guilty itch that gnawed at them when the cops arrived to inform the neighbor's widow. A shared, queasy "maybe" when the papers reported on a body found in the same area you'd woken up in. Not for sure, though.

Legally, though, the cause of death in those cases was "the moon." It made it easier to face the widow when you dropped off a casserole, to get on with your life.

It turned out it wasn't so easy when you'd killed the man you loved.

Cade snorted, and a sour mix of stomach acid and puke stung the back of his nose. No. He couldn't shed his guilt by pretending this was some tragic moon-crossed romance like Bonnie and Clyde. It had been a crush and the taste of Marlow's breath on Cade's tongue and maybe a date one day. He'd liked Marlow.

Then Cade had torn him apart and gulped down the soft bits.

Fuck.

Tears stung Cade's eyes. He scrubbed them away impatiently on the back of his hand. Crying never helped anyone.

"Grief is just self-pity in a fancy coat," the memory of his dad's voice clipped out harshly in Cade's mind. "Anyone really gives a shit; they get mad."

Cade twisted his mouth into a joyless smile at how easily that came back to him. He'd tried to unlearn his dad's lessons for years, but scratch the surface and there they were. This time, though, his father had a point.

It might have been Cade who killed Marlow, his teeth that sank into the flesh he'd kissed earlier that day. That just made him the weapon. Whoever had forced them off the road and left the moon to do his dirty work for him, they were the murderer.

And once Cade didn't have a bit of Marlow's liver caught between his teeth, that might actually feel true.

His stomach cramped again, but he'd milked the last bit of bile out of it already. Nothing came up. Cade spat again—the back of his tongue tasted foul—and wiped his mouth as he stepped away from the puddle of puke. He headed back into the street and stalked toward the nearest liquor store.

First of all, he needed cheap sweats and a bottle of whiskey. Those were easy. Then he'd work on answers… and payback.

When he found out who was responsible for what happened to Marlow—for what they'd made Cade do for them—he'd show them why he always did his own dirty work. It was illegal to use the moon as a deadly weapon, but only if Night Shift found out what you'd done.

Lem was good company for a black mood. He didn't ask a lot of questions, and he liked to talk about himself.

"…Beth is awesome. Don't get me wrong." Lem sprawled along the gray leather couch that took up one wall of the office, his boots propped up on the arm. His self-centered ramble was a comfortingly familiar background drone. "But what if I miss cock, you know?"

Cade pulled a gray Henley on over his head and tucked it into the waistband of his jeans. His cheap sweats had been tossed in the trash to be burned. Usually, he'd just have them laundered and thrown into one of the clothes banks around the city—for the indigent or people who couldn't afford to replace outfits they lost the night before—but the cheap fleece was stained with blood and sweat.

In the eyes of the law, Cade hadn't done anything wrong. It still felt like evidence. He wanted it gone.

"You broke up a year ago," he pointed out to Lem. "If you want cock, take your feet off the leather and go get it."

Lem snorted and moved his feet but nothing else. "I mean if we got back together, obviously," he said. "Keep up, old man."

Cade paused in the middle of pushing his sleeves up his forearms and gave Lem a steady look.

"What?" Lem asked, one eyebrow quirked. "You are older than me."

Vanity prickled under Cade's skin. He was older than Lem, but only by five years—enough that he'd always felt responsible for his kid brother, even as Lem coasted through life unflappable and unfazed, but not enough to pass comment on. And older didn't mean old.

Besides, Cade didn't plan to look his age for a very long time. He paid a very expensive dermatologist a lot of money to take care of his skin and make sure of that.

Unlike Lem, who got tired of burning the candle at both ends and just tossed the whole thing in the fire.

"I was thinking of bidding on a contract back home. For the refinery security," Cade said idly as he tucked his hands into the pockets of his jeans. "It would make sense to send you since you know the area."

Lem finally straightened up from his sprawl. He draped his arms over the back of the couch and made a placatory gesture with both hands. "Okay. Okay. I just thought I'd float it, a brotherly in-joke, see how it went down."

"Like the Titanic," Cade told him. "I don't need a nickname."

Guilt scratched at Cade. He'd killed someone that he… cared about—that struck the right balance—and yet here he was, distracted by a jab about his age from his idiot brother. Even if only briefly. He combed his fingers through his hair and grimaced at the knots he found.

Lem looked down at his nails and picked at the quick of one with his thumb. A frown pinched his eyebrows together, as if the rough tag of skin took all his focus.

"You okay?" he asked off-handedly.

The "no" stuck in Cade's throat like a stone. It nearly choked him, but he was more surprised that he wanted to say it than that he couldn't. He had never been the sort of man who talked about his emotions. It wasn't how he'd been raised, and it wasn't what people looked for in his line of work

No one wanted a thug who needed to "talk it out." Or a CEO, for that matter. They wanted someone who'd suck it up and get on with the job. Cade had always been good at that.

"It's nothing," he said. "Morning after the moon before."

Lem didn't look convinced, but then he was an idiot, not stupid. He didn't argue. They had, after all, been raised in the same house and by the same bastard.

"Yeah. I get that," Lem stretched his legs out in front of him and crossed them at the ankles. "So, you think Beth is serious about that guy she's with or—"

"I think you should stop dating co-workers," Cade said. He held his hand up to interrupt whatever Lem had been about to say and changed the subject. "And remember I had you dredge up info on what happened with the Night Shift under Piper?"

Lem cocked his head to the side. He looked interested. "Sure," he said.

"I want more."

"Like?"

Cade took a seat. The whiskey he'd bought in the store sat between the two tumblers from last night. It wasn't open. Cade remedied that and splashed a measure on top of the dregs he'd left.

"So that nothing needs drowned, huh?" Lem said.

Their dad had plenty of vices, but he'd not been a drinker. His women had, though. Not an easy man to live with, Benny Deacon. It had never helped, but there was a first time for everything.

"It's worth a try." Cade took a swig of the whiskey. It wasn't cheap, not for a wake, and the burn that spread down his throat and into his chest was mellow. The taste of oak and tannin lingered on his tongue as he leaned back into the chair. He turned the glass in his hand and watched the sun shine through the amber liquid. His phone buzzed politely on the desk. They both ignored it. "I want everything on Piper. Stripmine his life. Who's his lawyer, who visits him, who sends him money? If there's anyone he cares about—a mother, an ex, a child—I want you to turn their financials upside down to find any money that they can't account for."

Lem wrinkled his nose dubiously, "I'm good," he said. "But—"

"Requisition whatever resources you need to get the job done." Cade drained the whiskey and didn't bother to refill the glass. Lem was right; the drink could wait. It hadn't worked anyhow. Cade could still taste the bloody grit of guilt in the back of his throat. "By the time you're finished, I want to know Piper better than his mother does. He might be in prison, but someone in San Diego is still doing his dirty work. This is how we find out who."

"Okay." Lem pushed himself up off the couch in one easy, angular movement. He hooked his thumbs into his jeans pockets and pulled a thoughtful face. "Shouldn't take too long. Piper burned bridges when he went down. He can't have that many friends left."

Cade drummed his fingers absently on his thigh. "Don't depend on it," he said. "Piper made a lot of money doing odd jobs for bad men. The courts clawed some back, but he was a smart man. He'll have enough cached away to buy himself friends."

"Not good ones," Lem said.

"For this sort of work?" Cade said dryly. "The last thing you want is good."

Lem snorted acknowledgment of that. Before he could ask anything else, someone rapped on Cade's closed door and waited.

"What?" Cade asked.

The door opened, and his assistant leaned in around the jamb. Her gaze flicked from Cade to Lem and then back again. "Sorry to interrupt," she said. "Captain O'Hara from the SDPD is on the line. Are you here?"

"No."

She looked slightly surprised at the answer. Cade didn't often dodge the opportunity to remind the cops that he was an asshole with a smart mouth or the satisfaction of reminding them they couldn't touch him until he went a lot further out of bounds than he did.

Not today. Cade doubted there would be anything satisfying about his next conversation with O'Hara, and it wasn't one he wanted to have over the phone.

Lem cleared his throat. "Do you want me to go down and bail any of our guys they scooped up out of the Crate?" he offered.

A miracle, Cade thought dryly. Lem wasn't lazy, but he didn't look for work either. And, come to think of it, he was actually pretty lazy too. Lem was lucky he was blood, and more importantly, good at his job when he wasn't slacking.

"No," he said again. Lem opened his mouth to argue, but Cade cut him off roughly. The last thing he needed today was for Lem to find out what had happened from angry cops that didn't have the whole story. "I already told you what to do, Lem. I'll deal with O'Hara in my own time."

Lem stood his ground for a minute—while Cade's assistant discreetly made herself scarce—until Cade scowled at him and growled, "Do you need something else?"

"Do you?"

"Get out," Cade told him.

"Now you just sound like our dad," Lem cracked. He held up his hands in surrender when Cade started to get up. "I'm going. I'm going. Take a cab to the station if you're going to try and drown anything else while I'm not here."

Lem left, the door closed behind him, and Cade was alone with his thoughts. He slouched down in the chair until his knees nudged against the coffee table. Usually the shift left him energized, but not this time. His mind was full of things that might or might not have happened.

Cade rubbed his eyes. It wasn't the first time he'd killed someone. That was part of the job, although it had been a while. He didn't know if this bothered him more because he'd liked Marlow or because he didn't remember it, as if it were something the wolf had stolen from him.

Or maybe, he thought bleakly, it's because you ate him.

He opened his eyes and looked at the whiskey. The sun caught in the curves of the bottle and winked at him. The idea of another glass—just the one—sounded better by the second, and this time it might work.

Or maybe the glass after that one.

Cade grimaced and got up before he gave in to temptation. He didn't want to let O'Hara pick at this particular scab, but it wouldn't go any better if he was drunk. He stashed the whiskey in his desk drawer and grabbed his keys.

Might as well get it over with.

The vending machine had a list of drinks available. Cade would lay money that they all tasted like his cup of Bovril, thin and vaguely greasy. He tossed it in the trash and patted his pockets down for the mints he'd grabbed earlier.

He thumbed the last square capsule out of the wrapper and popped it into his mouth. By this point, he barely tasted the mint as he crunched the sweet, just registered the wintergreen sting of it in his sinuses.

"Deacon," O'Hara said as he opened the door and held it. He gestured with his free hand for Cade to go with him. "We can talk outside. I need a smoke break, anyhow."

It wasn't, Cade supposed as he rubbed the crumbs of mint against the roof of his mouth, the sort of conversation you wanted to have overheard. O'Hara probably didn't want his men to listen to how one of them had been torn apart, and Cade didn't want to give whatever fuck had used him as a weapon the satisfaction.

The two of them headed down the hall to the elevators—O'Hara broke the stilted silence with a few awkward questions that Cade answered brusquely—and took it up to the ground floor. It was quiet. Most people still had today off to recuperate. A food truck pulled up to the curb passed out fried rice and broth so salty that Cade could feel his nose dry out from feet away.

One person was ahead of them in the queue, a slender man in jeans and a T-shirt. His dark hair curled around the collar, and Cade squashed the sentimental ache in his chest under a mental boot. He wasn't going to spend the rest of his life, not even the rest of the month, flinching every time he saw a man in black with untidy hair.

O'Hara stepped in front of him.

"You didn't order me coffee, did you?" O'Hara asked in a disgruntled voice as he picked up a cup and sniffed suspiciously at the lid.

"No. That's mine," Marlow said as he turned around. He plucked the cup out of O'Hara's hand and replaced it with a different one. Then he turned to Cade and held out a cup toward him. There were bruises on the backs of his hands and scabs on his knuckles. He wasn't wearing his glasses, and his eyes looked very pale squinted against the morning light. "Chicken broth?"

He was alive.

The relief of it felt like a roller coaster as it squeezed the air out of Cade to make room for a breathless delight. He took a step forward, ready to forget about everyone else there and drag Marlow into a probably inappropriate hug. Then a second realization grabbed him by the scruff and pulled him up short.

Marlow was alive, and the little bastard had let Cade think he'd killed him.

It hurt.

Cade hadn't expected that. Anger, sure, or frustration at the incompetence of it all. Instead, his chest ached uncomfortably with old adolescent vulnerability.

He hated it. The guilt had been better.

Luckily, it didn't last. Or it wouldn't. One thing Cade had learned over the years was act like you didn't care enough and eventually it would be true. Indifference could be a shield. Or a weapon.

He took the cup out of Marlow's hand.

"Dinner and conversation," he drawled. "You'd think this was a date."

The chill in his voice seemed to register as Marlow gave him a curious look. Maybe he'd have asked, but O'Hara was already at his shoulder.

"Marlow told me what happened last night," O'Hara said. He waved them toward an empty stretch of railing opposite the stairs that led down to the street. Cade let himself be herded in that direction. "But he didn't see the accident itself."

Cade leaned back against the railing, one arm braced on the metal rod. He sipped the broth—thick enough with salt it had the tang of blood—and studied O'Hara.

"That's because it wasn't an accident," he said.

"I told him that much," Marlow said dryly.

Cade ignored him. He sipped his broth and watched the people milling around them over O'Hara's shoulder. The Night Shift hadn't been the only cops that Piper had in his pocket, and they weren't the only people in San Diego he could ask a favor of. Even from prison.

"One of your men tried to kill us," he told O'Hara.

"You sure about that?"

Cade raised his eyebrows. "Maybe not," he said. "It was someone in SDPD gear, behind the wheel of a Bearcat. I guess it could have been anybody. Maybe you should ask your friends at the TV station to put the word out and find them?"

A muscle ticked in O'Hara's cheek, and his mouth tightened in annoyance. Cade had been wrong. This was satisfying, after all.

"The SDPD was not responsible for that leak," O'Hara said.

"Please," Cade said with a sneer. "You don't even know which of your officers are corrupt. Yet Cold Winds takes the flak for

Haley's death while you and the Night Shift stay above reproach? That leak worked out well for you, didn't it?"

O'Hara stared at him for a moment and then tossed what was left of his broth into the shrubbery. He'd caught on. This wasn't a friendly conversation anymore. A lizard appeared from the roots to lick at the greasy sheen on the leaves.

"I'll give your attitude a pass, after what happened,"

"It's the same attitude I always have," Cade said.

"I've noticed," O'Hara said bluntly. "Mr. Deacon, if the SDPD are involved—"

"If?"

"—they'll be dealt with. The same way Piper was."

"What? Too late?"

Marlow snorted at that jab. He shrugged when O'Hara turned to scowl at him. For a moment, it was hard to remember why Cade was angry with him. Then Cade thought of the greasy knots of half-digested meat as they slipped out of his throat, and it all came back to him.

"But let us handle the investigation," O'Hara said flatly. "The SDPD appreciate your help on Haley's case, but that's where it ends. Stay out of the case, keep a low profile, and as soon as we can, the SDPD will make sure that the press have the full truth about Haley's death. More than that, we'll make sure Cold Winds comes out of this looking good."

"And what if I don't do that?"

"Then you're an idiot," O'Hara said. "We know what we're doing, and just because Cold Winds calls itself a private police force, and acts as one in some locations, doesn't give you jurisdiction to operate in San Diego. I am trying to give you every opportunity to make all our lives easier. Don't stand in my way."

A variety of sarcastic remarks occurred to Cade. He discarded them all. It might be fun to tweak O'Hara's, and by extension, the SDPD's noses, but that didn't mean it was smart. He gave in instead, with a shrug and a thin smile.

"Fair point," Cade said. "I don't get paid to fix the SDPD's fuck-ups, after all. Clean your own house, Captain, and keep it away from mine."

He drained his cup and tossed it into the nearest bin as he stalked away.

Marlow didn't chase after him, which meant there were at least six withering put-downs that Cade wouldn't get to use. That was definitely what he ground his teeth on as he headed down to the street to find a cab.

CHAPTER THREE

MARLOW LANDED HARD. It knocked the air out of him and made his ribs—bruised but not broken—cramp painfully. He ignored it as he rolled to the left, and Bennett's knee bounced off the padded mat instead of his gut.

It would have popped Marlow's kneecap off like the cap off a beer bottle. Bennett just grunted and managed to lurch back to her feet. She hobbled backward, favoring her jarred leg, and brought her fists up to guard her face. Hanks of dark hair had been pulled loose from her tight braid, and her lip was split and puffy. She dabbed it with her tongue.

"Slippery little bastard," she said without any malice in her voice. "Living up to your name, Kitty-boy."

Marlow was too winded to jibe back at her. His ribs ached dully with each breath he forced in, and she'd wrenched his arm when she threw him. He just grinned at her and edged around the outside of the ring, weight balanced on the balls of his feet. Bennett moved counterclockwise ahead of him, her full weight back on her right leg.

Neither of them wanted to commit to an offensive. Marlow knew that Bennett would break first. She didn't have the patience to wait him out, not in front of half the Night Shift. They both knew that. So Marlow made his move first.

He took two long steps forward and threw a jab at Bennett's face. She caught it on her forearms, already mottled with bruises, and Marlow feinted a low kick at her leg. If it connected, he could take her already tender knee out from under her. Bennett jerked her knee up to block with her shin, and Marlow shifted his weight fluidly to his forward leg.

Hung over the ropes on the far side of the ring, arms dangled over the top one, Franklin saw it coming and yelped, "Watch out."

It was too late. Marlow's low sweep kick skimmed under Bennett's raised foot and caught her behind the knee with just enough pressure to make it fold. She started to go down, and

Marlow grabbed her by the shirt, spandex thin and sweaty between his fingers, and helped her on her way.

Bennett hit the mat harder than he had, and Marlow followed her down. He got one knee planted on her chest, his full weight on it, and punched the heel of his hand down toward her nose. It didn't connect—Marlow pulled the strike with plenty of time. But it would have smashed her nose if he'd connected—and he would have.

"And out!" the ref called it as he slapped his hand against the mat. "He takes the match. That's one each. We've got a draw."

Franklin groaned and threw himself backward, held up by the bowed rope he had a grip on. "Fuck sake!" he said. "You had him, Bennett!"

Bennett gave Marlow a wry look from her prone position. She hadn't. Not that time. They both knew that. Even if she had, there wasn't a lot of status to be earned beating up the guy just back from medical leave. A draw wasn't worth getting bent out of shape about.

"Nice throw," she said. "You'll have to show me sometime."

"And lose the advantage?"

Marlow pushed himself off her and hopped to his feet. He stuck his hand out to help her up. She grabbed it and, for a second, the muscles in her arms tightened as if she was going to try and throw him. In the end, she just let him yank her up, taking the weight she was wary of putting on her jarred knee.

Franklin ducked under the ropes and jogged over with a bottle of water. His eyebrow was split and one finger splinted after his sparring match with the rookie earlier. The kid wasn't half bad.

He handed the bottle to Bennett. She took a swig and fended Franklin's offered shoulder off as she cocked an eyebrow at Marlow. "What do you say? Best two out of three?"

Marlow shrugged and stepped back, ready to agree. Before he could, O'Hara stepped in through the door of the gym and looked around.

"Captain," Bennett said. She loped over to the corner of the ring and leaned out. Unless someone was close enough to see the tension in her jaw, they'd not know she was in pain. "Down here to show us lot that you've still got it?"

O'Hara gave her a dry look. "Trust me, Bennett," he said, "I don't, and I don't miss it. The day I was promoted high enough I'd never have to run again? Best day of my life."

She leaned folded arms on top of the padded post and grinned at him. "I don't know if I'll appreciate being off the streets as much," she said. "I'll let you know one day."

O'Hara just shook his head and then looked past her. "Franklin. Marlow." He jerked his thumb over his shoulder for them to follow him. "With me. Now."

He turned on his heel and left. Marlow stared after him for a moment and then traded a baffled glance with Franklin.

"Who have you pissed off lately?" Marlow asked Franklin as he headed over to jump down from the ring.

He went between the ropes and hopped down from there. Franklin vaulted over the top of them and landed easily on the other side. He reached up on the way past to trade a fist bump with Bennett.

"Not Richie Rich and his pals up in the Reserve," Franklin said as he dropped his arm back to his side. He strode toward the door as he tossed back over his shoulder, "So I'm one up on you."

He wasn't wrong. Marlow looked up at Bennett. She had her split lip folded between her teeth as she worried at the raw skin.

"They're not going to promote anyone before Harrison announces his retirement," Marlow said.

Bennett pulled her attention away from the door and looked down at him. "Really?" she drawled in a voice ripe with sarcasm. "Wow, that's a relief. I really thought they were going to make you and Franklin co-lieutenants because of your great working dynamic."

"Try and be nice, see what it gets you," Marlow said to the passing rookie, who looked like he'd rather not get dragged into this. "Go and ice your knee, Bennett."

Bennett tossed the half-drunk bottle of water down to him. "Go soak your head," she advised as she pushed herself off the post. "And watch your back. You're the one that someone tried to kill recently, remember?"

She limped away back to the corner she'd left her gear in. Marlow wiped the top of the bottle on his T-shirt before he took a swig. The label said the water was lemon-flavored, but after knocking around the gym all day, it just tasted flat and tepid.

"I'm not likely to forget," he said quietly.

Around him, a dozen other Night Shift officers sparred, worked out, or hung out by the juice bar. The long, low-ceilinged room was full of the sounds of knuckles on flesh and the rattle of weights. Some of them were friends, more or less, some of them he had never much liked, but he knew them all one way or another.

Any of them could have been the mystery driver who left him to die.

O'Hara tossed two folders onto the desk.

In a rare moment of agreement, Marlow and Franklin both eyed the apparently innocuous paperwork with suspicion. It wasn't like Night Shift only worked three days a month. The rest of the time, they were deployed along with the rest of TAC to deal with hostage situations or warrants.

That meant they worked as a team. They didn't get cases handed to them individually. Even Day Shift TAC didn't get their own cases. Any deviation from standard operating procedure was not a good thing.

"Pick one," O'Hara said as he pulled his chair back from the desk and sat down. It creaked as he leaned back in it. When neither of them jumped to do what they'd been told, he sighed and reached over the desk to push the folders toward them. "One each. Or I just hand them to you."

Marlow glanced sidelong at Franklin, who squinted dubiously back at him.

After a moment, Marlow shrugged and reached for the nearest file. Franklin grabbed it before he could touch it. Of course. Marlow resisted the urge to roll his eyes and took the other folder instead.

"Days requested Night Shift's help on both of those," O'Hara said. "I'm tapping you two to provide it."

"Why?" Franklin asked.

"Because medical hasn't cleared Marlow for operational readiness yet, so he's on restricted duties," O'Hara said. "And you called Homicide a bunch of 'over-hyped morgue techs' yesterday, and now I have to deal with their hurt feelings."

Franklin snorted. "They call us worse."

"Not to your face," O'Hara pointed out. "And you don't get an appeal here. Just do it. Now."

The edge to his voice cut off any hope of negotiation. Franklin stuck the file under his arm and groused his way out of the office. He slammed the door behind him. Marlow let him go and then turned back to O'Hara. He tapped the file on the edge of the table.

"Any updates on *my* case?" he asked.

O'Hara sighed and rubbed his thumb over his temple. "You know better than to ask that," he said. "All I'm going to say is that we're still investigating."

"If I could just—"

"Internal Affairs took over the case," O'Hara reminded him. "And you're the victim in this one, not a cop. They'll let you know when there's something to know, but you can't be involved in the investigation. You have a case. Focus on that."

Marlow just looked down at his folder and stood there for a second. How the hell, he wanted to ask, did they expect him to just do his job like nothing had changed? Except, he supposed, nothing had. He'd known that the purge might not have cleared out *all* of Piper's crew; he'd just… gotten used to it.

"Anything else?" O'Hara asked.

Have you heard from Cade? The question itched on the tip of Marlow's tongue, but he didn't know if he wanted to know for professional or personal reasons. It was stupid. Every null knew better than to put any faith in what was said during the honeymoon period when the wolf was still hot in the blood. Yet here Marlow was, hurt that a known asshole had ghosted him once the prospect of a dinner date was on the table.

"No," Marlow said after a pause. "Nothing."

He turned to go. The sound of O'Hara clearing his throat stopped him in the doorway.

"Internal Affairs *will* find out what happened," he said. "Do like Deacon; stay out of it and let them do their job."

Marlow glanced at O'Hara's dim reflection in the glass of the door. It hadn't occurred to him that O'Hara might believe that had worked. Since no one had asked him, though, he guessed it wasn't his business.

"Sir," he said and left.

You could always tell when it was a null household that made a call. The coffee was good. Strong, in this case, since Victor Clemons had no creamer in the house, but good.

Marlow took a polite sip from the mug and leaned forward to set it down on the kitchen table.

"Unfortunately—"

"I have a restraining order," Victor blurted out before Marlow could finish. "He's not allowed to come anywhere near me."

"He didn't."

Victor shoved himself to his feet. The legs of his chair scraped over the tiled floor as he pushed it out of the way. He stalked across the room and grabbed a folder from the top of the microwave. His hands were shaking as he pulled out grainy printouts of security stills and dealt them out in front of Marlow like cards.

"Tell me he wasn't here now?" Victor demanded. He slapped one picture down in front of Marlow and jabbed his finger against it hard enough to tear the paper. "That's him. That's Barney. Every. Fucking. Night this month."

Marlow gently slid the photos out from under Victor's hand and paged through them. He'd seen the grooves in the stucco on the side of the house when he arrived. Now he saw how they had gotten there. A lanky graphite-gray wolf tore at the wall, pissed on a tree, and threw itself against the heavy metal shutter over the door.

"That's a wolf, Mr. Clemons," Marlow said gently. "You can't put a restraining order on a wolf. I don't see Mr. Lyons in any of these pictures. Unless you saw him in the vicinity of the house last night—"

Victor kicked his chair in frustration and knocked it over.

"It doesn't matter where he is!" He slammed both hands down on the table and glared at Marlow. "As soon as the moon is up, the wolf comes here. To *my* house. To find *me.* Every month. Every night. I can't live like this."

Then he shouldn't have dated a wolf. Marlow flicked through the images to check the time stamp and date. Dumped in a pile, the wolf's attentions looked overwhelming, but it worked out to something like fifteen minutes a night over the three nights.

"When did you break up?" Marlow asked.

"Not soon enough?" Victor said tartly, in a brittle voice. He raked his fingers through his dark chin-length hair and took Marlow's mug as if he'd finished it. The coffee went down the sink, and Victor flicked the tap on to rinse it. "Two months. Three months?"

"How long were you together?"

Victor half turned to frown at him. "What has that got to do with anything?"

Marlow sat back and hooked his arm over the chair. He watched Victor as the man turned to the sink and rinsed the cups with impatient, jerky movements.

"It influences our profile of the wolf's behavior," he said. "What we can predict."

Victor's shoulders stayed tense for a second and then relaxed reluctantly. He flicked the tap off and dried his hands on his trousers.

"We dated for three months," he said. "Three and a half. I cheated on him with my boss at work. He acted like a jilted housewife instead of little more than a hook-up and threw a tantrum *at* my job. Got us both fired and then came back here to trash my stuff. He left, I got a restraining order, and I thought it was over—until he came back at the end of the month and pissed on my car. So, is that enough information, or do you want to know how our sex life was?"

He asked the last question in an intense, chirpy tone, then grimaced and looked away. The muscles in his jaw were tight, visible under his tanned skin and faint stubble.

"No. That should be enough," Marlow said. He stood up and tucked his notebook into his belt. It was a grudge, and maybe some leftover lust, not love. That was more volatile but also more likely to pass. "I'll speak to your ex—"

Victor made a disgruntled sound in the back of his throat and shook his head. "Of course you will," he said. "And *this* time, that will make all the difference. I don't want you to talk to him; I want you to stop him. Make sure he doesn't come here again."

"That's what the restraining order is for. If he breaches it—"

"He breaches it every month!"

"Unless he deliberately leads the wolf here, he isn't responsible for what it does," Marlow said. "I'll talk to him, but if it happens again, you might want to consider leaving town over the full moon. It could break the compulsion."

Victor sneered. He was a good-looking man, pretty rather than handsome, but not with that expression on his face.

"Why should I have to do that?" he asked. "Why should I have to be the one to leave? He's the one tormenting me."

Victor had a point. The problem was, wolves didn't listen to reason or restraining orders, and they couldn't make Barney Lyons do anything he didn't want to do until he did something wrong.

"Just a suggestion," Marlow said. "Hopefully, it won't be necessary."

The cleaver slashed and embedded itself in the bloody chopping board. A freshly severed fish head wobbled in place and stared at Marlow with blind black eyes. Barney scooped it up and tossed it in the pot with the rest.

"I'm well rid of Victor." Barney wiped his hand on his apron and then grabbed the fish to butcher it. The knife sliced along its underbelly from tail to gills, and he scooped out the innards with hooked fingers. "Did he tell you what he did to me?"

"He did."

Barney snorted and swung the cleaver again, this time to sever the fish's tail. The flicker of light on the razor edge made the back of Marlow's neck itch. It was a reasonable conversation so far, but his instincts twinged each time Barney's arm tensed.

"Bet he didn't," Barney grunted. "Not all of it, anyhow. As far as I'm concerned, I'm lucky that I only wasted a few months."

"Three, wasn't it?"

"I suppose." Barney scraped the cleaver over the board and flicked the tail into the trash by his foot. "Better than three years."

Marlow leaned against the counter, just out of arm's reach. The din of the kitchen eddied around him: the splash of running water, hiss of gas, and sizzle of fat on a skillet. Waiters delivered orders through the pass-through in rapid-fire shorthand that the chef then chopped up into brusque, barked orders.

"The wolf doesn't seem to agree," Marlow pointed out. "Mr. Clemons thinks you're doing it deliberately."

Barney smacked the cleaver down on the cutting board and turned to face Marlow. He wiped his hands on his apron, pink blood and scales smeared over the gray-white fabric.

"You know why he thinks that? Because everything is about Victor in his world," he said, an acidic bite of sour humor to his voice. "That house? That's my house. My garden. My neighborhood. I lived there first; he was my roommate. That's why the wolf goes back there. It's nothing to do with him."

He pointed a finger at Marlow's face to underline his point and then went back to work. Two quick strokes of the cleaver filleted the fish into neat steaks, and he started on the next.

"It might be an idea to go away next full moon," Marlow suggested. "Out of town. Break the habit."

Barney snorted. "Why should I do anything?" he asked. "It's his problem. Get him to go away somewhere."

The sullen resistance in his voice was familiar. Marlow bit his tongue. It was the easiest, proven way to avoid problems with a passive compulsion—one that neither side was encouraging—but if neither party would budge, he couldn't make them. There was a legal difference between being okay with the idea your ex might get eaten and taking steps to make it happen.

"Just a suggestion," Marlow said. He stepped to the side to let one of the porters reach through and grab the pot of fish heads. "However, if you do consciously use the wolf to break the restraining order, then that is a serious offense."

"Yeah?" Barney slapped the fillets down on a metal tray and grabbed a bottle to drizzle lemon-tinted oil over them. "Prove it."

He used the tray to jostle Marlow out of the way as he headed for the ovens. Marlow let him pass and dropped his hand to his belt, fingers looped through the clip of zip-cuffs attached to the leather.

If he wanted to be difficult, that was close enough to a confession, and he could pull Barney in over it. The charge wouldn't stick, not when Barney could claim he had just talked big, but it might scare the man enough he'd actually take Marlow's advice.

Probably not, though. Not with a couple of weeks between the lesson and the full moon. The *blue* full moon.

Marlow made a mental note to tag the neighborhood as a place of interest next month. *He* didn't believe in moon madness, but he wasn't the problem. People that wanted to do something stupid would jump at the first excuse they got to justify doing it. If Barney broke the restraining order, they could grab him before the wolf turned a crime into a tragedy.

He flicked a stray scale off his sleeve and headed out of the kitchen. One of the porters caught him at the door and pressed a package of what smelled like fresh fish cakes into his hands.

"For your service," the woman said.

Marlow juggled the waxed paper parcel—they were *hot* fresh fish cakes--and tried to give them back, along with an awkwardly grateful refusal, but the woman put her hands behind her back.

"Night Shift saved my neighbor's life," she said. "What's a fish cake to that?"

She turned on her heel and went back to work. Marlow looked around to see if anyone else looked like they'd take the food off his hands. He got an apologetic shrug from the dishwasher, elbow-deep in the sink, but that was it.

Department policy was to accept unsolicited gifts under twenty bucks—it was a cultural thing in a lot of places, and refusal could offend—and then fill in the requisite forms in triplicate back in the office.

Well, at least he wouldn't have to stop for lunch.

Marlow offered a clumsy "Thank you" to the kitchen and ducked out. He held the parcel in one hand as he cut through the tables in the restaurant. The bells over the door rattled as he let himself out into the muggy, salt-sharp air on the street.

He unwrapped the fish cakes and took a bite out of one as he walked back to where he'd parked the car. Halfway there, mouth full of cheese, potato, and fish, someone strode out of a building and directly into his path.

Marlow tried to dodge back out of the way and stepped on the man's foot instead. He overcorrected and stumbled.

"Christ," the man growled as he grabbed Marlow's arm. "Watch where you're going—"

Cade broke off mid-sentence and narrowed his eyes as he stared at Marlow. His eyes were still wolf-bright, the color of clear amber, even nearly a week after the wolf was out.

"What do you want?" he asked, his voice abruptly cold instead of rough.

Marlow abruptly, unexpectedly, wanted to say the right thing. It wouldn't even be that hard. People knew he was laconic, and Cade wouldn't expect poetry. It just had to make the corner of Cade's mouth twitch with reluctant appreciation and remind him that, despite what he liked to believe, Marlow wasn't an idiot.

Unfortunately, his mouth was full of fish cake and grease. He had a feeling that the "right thing to say" didn't include flaked haddock.

Marlow chewed twice and then swallowed hard to force the food down his throat.

"Lunch?" he said.

Cade chuckled humorlessly. "Of course, what else?" he asked, the mockery dry on the edge of his words.

The tone put Marlow's back up. Cade was the one with the problem; why should Marlow do the legwork to find out what was wrong? So he just shrugged his agreement with Cade and took another bite of his fish cake.

Cade stared at him for a moment and then snorted softly as he shook his head.

"Well," he drawled, then tightened his grip on Marlow's arm, "while you're here, you might as well make yourself useful. I need some information. About Piper."

The smart answer was "no." It might sting to have been ghosted, but that didn't mean it had been a bad decision. Never mind that Captain O'Hara had just told Marlow not to interfere in the case.

Instead, Marlow caved to the temptation of a little more time with Cade. It was stupid—Cade was an abrasive jerk at his best—but he felt like home. Somewhere—someone—that made your shoulders relax from being up around your ears.

"I'm on duty," he said as he wrapped the rest of his free lunch up. "But I can give you a few minutes."

"Lucky me," Cade said, sarcasm thick as butter on the words, as he gestured toward his office door.

CHAPTER [illegible]

[illegible]

CHAPTER FOUR

"O'HARA REALLY THOUGHT I was going to do as I was told?" Cade asked. He nudged the chair out of the way with his knee and leaned one hand on the table as he pulled his emails up on the screen. Too many from various clients. "I didn't take the man for an idiot."

"Liar."

He was. That didn't mean he wanted someone to call him on it. Except Marlow's off-hand delivery slid under Cade's guard and caught his sense of humor. He felt his mouth try to slide into a smile and bit the inside of his cheek to stop it.

"Most people wouldn't call me that to my face," he said.

"I've only got fifteen minutes," Marlow said. "I don't have time to do it behind your back."

Cade couldn't help the laugh that escaped him. The black sludge of his temper loosened its grip on him, whether he liked it or not. That was the problem. It wasn't that he *wanted* Marlow, or that he'd played out the vodka-sharp kiss and what might have happened next a couple of times since the full moon. Over the years, Cade had fucked a few people he'd not piss on if they were on fire. Some of them, that was why he'd fucked them.

The thing was, he *liked* Marlow. The Night Shift officer was easy to be around. He was laid-back enough that Cade had to shift down a gear to spend time with him without feeling like he'd lost some sort of advantage. Even the occasional jabs of wit at Cade's expense were unexpectedly tolerable, as much as Cade hated being the butt of the joke.

It made it hard to stay angry with him.

That was okay. Cade was willing to chew over the sour memory of puke and bile to keep the grudge fresh.

"What about you?" he asked. "Have you toed the line?"

"Unlike you, O'Hara *is* my boss," Marlow said. The corner of his mouth tilted up slightly, a flicker of sly humor, and he added, "Of course, Haley's death is my case. So I've put feelers out to see if anyone else has turned up traps or logged any suspicious injuries or deaths after the full moon."

"And?" Cade asked, his voice clipped and deliberately abrupt.

Marlow pulled an annoyed face. "It's hard to pin down," he said. "A wolf wakes up one morning missing half a foot, it could have been caused in an accident, a fight with another wolf, or—"

"Or a trap," Cade finished.

"Exactly," Marlow said. "One thing is that there has been an uptick in moon-hangover deaths in the last few months. Three train-related deaths, one suicide, two deaths by misadventure when they took a wrong turn in the desert. More than usual this time of year, but not enough to raise any red flags. I've put a request in for their files. If there's something there, maybe I can pinpoint it. What about you? Anything?"

Cade flicked the images from Lem's report up onto the screen on the wall. Photos slid over each other and slotted into a rough grid-like pattern of faces pulled from a variety of sources—selfies, work IDs, mugshots. Three women and four men, all of whom had maintained some sort of steady contact with Piper since he'd been in prison.

"Do you know any of these people?" he asked. "Did you ever see any of them around, back in the day?"

Marlow got up and walked over to stand in front of the screen. He absently pulled his glasses off, the smoked lenses and wire frames dangled by one leg from his fingers as he studied the faces.

"Well?"

"It was ten years ago," Marlow said. He didn't bother to look around at Cade. "And we didn't exactly move in the same circles. He didn't become a crooked cop to hang out with guys working with a rookie's salary."

Cade came around the front of the desk and leaned back against it. He crossed his arms and made a soft sound of disgust in the back of his throat.

"He sounds like a great boss," he said, without any attempt to dilute the sarcasm.

Marlow glanced around at him. A wry smile tugged at the side of his mouth as he raised his eyebrows. "If I asked, would you know the janitor's name?"

"We don't have a janitor; we have a cleaning service," Cade said. He nodded to the screen to redirect the conversation before Marlow could ask what anyone else was called. "Think back. Anything?"

Marlow scrutinized the faces again for a moment. Finally, he shrugged and pointed to two of them, one in the right corner and one just slotted in left of center. One man. One woman.

"These two look familiar."

The man in the middle was wiry and miserable-looking, with one dull brown eye and three raw-looking scars livid on the right side of his face. He was a wolf, so he'd got them young… same as Cade, and without the chance to hide them. At the top, the woman was bright-eyed and glossy, her face blurred with carefully applied makeup until she looked airbrushed. She had a hard line about her mouth.

"Lance Rilkes and Maria Cafolla," Cade identified them confidently. The background checks had been thorough; he probably knew them as well as any of their relatives did. "Both nulls. Lance gets a call from Piper once a month, and the next day he gets a grand deposited in his account. Do you have any idea why?"

"No, but I know who he is," Marlow said. He paused for a moment and then hedged that statement with a shrug. "Maybe. Piper used to tell this story about when he was a kid. Him and a bunch of his friends used to hang out at each other's houses during the full moon. One night, one of them shifted unexpectedly—an early bloomer. It happens sometimes; puberty isn't great at schedules."

The back of Cade's throat felt raw and itchy, like he'd eaten peppers. He'd been twelve the first time. Early, by most people's standards, but not his dad's. The Deacons all shifted early—he'd sworn that up and down and called Cade a bastard when he was eleven and still hadn't changed. He'd thought that self-preservation could force the turn, and he'd dragged Cade out into the snow naked and left him up a tree. Change or freeze. He'd not cared which.

It hadn't worked, neither one. The wolf came out when the moon wanted, and his step-mother always cached a key to the front door and one of his coats in a hollow tree stump the day before.

"How many died?" he asked.

"Nobody," Marlow said. He didn't look around to catch Cade's skeptical look, but he shrugged like he'd seen it anyhow. "According to Piper, they all grabbed the kid as it started and tried to drag him outside. They might have managed it, but one of the kids panicked and got all cut up. Piper saved him, led the wolf outside, and they ran straight into the Night Shift."

The idea of someone touching you mid-shift made Cade's stomach turn uneasily. He probably wouldn't remember it, but the thought made the back of his neck itch as if he still had hackles. Cade scrubbed his hand roughly over the bare skin to try and redirect the discomfort.

"Well, that's an inspirational tale," he said.

"He told it better," Marlow said.

Cade curled his lip and mouthed, "he told it better," sarcastically to himself. The man had tried to kill Marlow, for fuck's sake; why defend his reputation?

And, Cade reminded himself with resigned amusement as he pushed himself up off the desk, hadn't he decided not to care what Marlow did anymore? It had been a lot easier to amputate his feelings for people when he'd been young and desperate.

The memory of Lem's *"old man"* smirked in his head. Young*er*, Cade corrected himself. It placated his offended vanity—for now. He stopped beside Marlow, crossed his arms over his chest, and frowned at the screen. Lance stared, half-blind and disinterested anyhow, past them.

"Fascinating glimpse into a corrupt public official's past," he said. "What does it have to do with Lance, perennially under-employed kitchen porter?"

"The scars." Marlow traced the photographed scores out on his own cheek, from his eyebrow and down over his cheekbone to his jaw. "The friend that got cut up lost an eye, and Piper said he'd been left with stripes to remember his stupidity. It was his 'shape up or ship out' speech. He always said either do what needs to be done or stay out of it from the beginning. No second thoughts…"

He trailed off as he thought about that.

"For reference?" Cade said. "That's a bit of a red flag."

"I suppose, in retrospect," Marlow admitted. "At the time, it just seemed like good advice. Hesitation can get you killed."

"So could Piper."

It was meant to be cruel. Marlow just laughed at the jab, a soft huff of humor, and pointed at the woman's face.

"I know her face," he said. "But I can't place *how* I know her face."

"Maria Cafolla. She's a Spanish teacher who also volunteers with convicts to teach them life skills. Piper ever show any problems with basic literacy, numeracy, or cooking a microwave dinner?" That got him a smirk from Marlow, but he otherwise ignored it. That was fair enough, Cade supposed. It had been petty. As low as he claimed his opinion of the SDPD was when they inconvenienced him, he doubted they'd promote someone to Night Shift that couldn't do the basics of the job one way or another. "Her and Piper are penpals. He writes to her monthly, and she visits him once a year. Conjugal visits, apparently."

Marlow went "huh" as he absorbed that and stared at Maria's picture a moment longer, his eyes squinted as if that would help him place her. Apparently it didn't work because he finally turned away from the screen.

"Sorry," he said. "I could ask Bennett? Her and Piper had a thing for a while."

Cade raised his eyebrow. That hadn't turned up in the background. Jay Bennett dated women—mostly redheads, but she wasn't prescriptive—and there'd been no suggestion she'd broken that streak for her boss. Marlow caught his surprise and misinterpreted the reason for it.

"If there's anyone in Night Shift I can trust, it's Bennett," he said. "She's the one that turned Piper in to IA after he shot me. Even if she had a change of heart, she knows Piper doesn't give second chances."

Marlow trusted her. Cade knew it wasn't fair to let that put his back up; it didn't take anything away from him. It felt like it did, though. It was meant to be the two of them against the corruption in the Night Shift, after all. What other reason did Cade have to talk to Marlow?

Cade winced to himself at that. What was this? He was calling himself on his own shit now? Okay, so when he'd run into Marlow, he'd just grabbed at the first excuse to keep him around that he could think of. It didn't mean anything—nothing he was going to deal with right now, anyhow.

Still, Cade wasn't sure if it was common sense or that prickle of jealousy behind what he said next.

"What if she didn't ask him?" he said. "You said it yourself; Piper flew under the radar. He didn't leave bear traps in the woods or dump corpses with no hands in front of the cops. Maybe whoever did this just took up where he left off, whether Piper left it or not."

Marlow opened his mouth to argue, but only got as far as "She…" before he had to give up. He grimaced sourly and rubbed his hand over his face.

"Do you know what sucks?" he asked.

Cade did. It was being left to think you'd killed someone you cared about. He didn't say that, though.

"What?"

"You're still pissed at me," Marlow said.

That… That was not what Cade expected. He'd workshopped a dozen versions of this conversation. Most of them ended badly. In a few, Marlow had apologized profusely and physically, and none of them had been that straightforward.

"I'm… not," Cade lied. Poorly.

Marlow didn't even bother to call him on it. He just raised a dark eyebrow pointedly and then shrugged.

"It's up to you," he said. "But if you want to talk about it, I'm—"

His radio crackled. "Dispatch to Charlie-forty. Charlie-forty, respond."

Marlow swore under his breath in exasperation, pulled an apologetic face at Cade, and reached up to his shoulder to thumb the button.

"Charlie-forty," he said, chin tucked down toward his chest. "What is it?"

"We have an FTA for a court-ordered custody mediation," Dispatch said. "Can you do a 10-91?"

Marlow screwed his eyes shut and rubbed his thumb over his temple. "Seriously?"

"Records show it was your case originally. Is that a 10-4?"

"Yeah," Marlow sighed as he opened his eyes. "10-4, Dispatch. Send me the coordinates and details of the pickup. I'll send my ETA once I'm on the road."

He flicked the radio off and shifted his attention back to Cade. "I—"

"Duty calls," Cade said.

Marlow's crooked smile was rueful, but he didn't argue. "Keep me updated if these"—he gestured to the photos on the screen—"yield anything useful."

"I'll think about it," Cade said as he uncrossed his arms. "Good luck finding your parolee."

He waited.

Marlow turned to go, and Cade's stomach sank with disappointment. That wasn't what he'd been waiting for.

"You forgot your fish," he said abruptly. The words hadn't sounded great in his head—they'd just been the first thing that occurred to him—but they sounded worse out loud. Marlow hesitated mid-step, just for a second, and Cade decided, "fuck it." Anything that stopped him from running his mouth was a good idea.

He reached out, grabbed Marlow's arm—the tinted glasses he still hadn't put back on slipped out of his fingers—and pulled him around into a kiss. It was a dry, awkward buss, mouths smashed uncomfortably together and heads at clumsy angles.

Then Cade ran his hand up Marlow's arm and curled his fingers around the nape of his neck. Marlow shivered at the contact and stretched up into the kiss. His mouth was sweet, warm, and slightly fishy. Cade grinned against Marlow's mouth at the brief distraction. It was the weird details that made reality better than imagination.

Well—he remembered exactly how far things had gone in his last sticky late-night fantasy—sometimes.

Marlow grabbed a handful of Cade's shirt and pushed him back against the desk. The hard ridge of it dug into the backs of his thighs. Heat knotted through Cade's stomach as he thought of what his daydreams could make of this.

He shifted his weight and pulled Marlow closer, his lean hips slotted between Cade's spread thighs. The dull weight of arousal tugged at Cade's cock as he worked his fingers up to tangle in Marlow's hair.

Then Marlow pulled back from the kiss. He was still close enough that Cade felt the tickle of his breath as he exhaled raggedly. It might have been regretful too, but that stank of Cade's dead crush, so he squashed it.

"Duty," Marlow said, the corner of his mouth tucked up in a rueful smile, "and all."

Cade twisted his fingers tighter around dark curls and pulled Marlow's head back. For the first time, he noticed the faded bruises stippled along Marlow's throat, the long line of it taut and vulnerable. He'd known nulls didn't heal with the moon. Obviously. It just hadn't occurred to him to look for the marks he'd chewed into Marlow's skin.

It was even hotter than he'd thought it would be.

And Marlow might need to leave, but he still hadn't pulled away.

Cade ducked his head and pressed a wet, messy kiss against Marlow's throat. He felt the quick flutter of a pulse against his mouth, and he had to resist the urge to bite down. The moon had waned; he couldn't even blame the wolf for the urge to send Marlow out of his office looking well-fucked.

"Far be from me to keep you from doing the job my taxes pay you for," Cade said. He untangled his fingers and leaned back on the desk, muscles bunched in his shoulders and pulled tight across his chest. The bulge of his cock was on full display under the thin fabric of his trousers. He wasn't sure if it was an offer or a tease, but Cade knew he looked good. He smirked smugly at Marlow. "You know the way out, Officer."

Marlow bit his lip and made a soft sound in the back of his throat as he took in the view. He still took a step backward and tugged the neck of his T-shirt straight. It didn't cover the bruises, now damp and slick from Cade's mouth.

"Next time," Marlow said, then rubbed the back of his neck self-consciously. He gave Cade a questioning look. "I mean, if this means you're not pissed at me anymore."

That reminder worked on Cade like a cold shower: not that well, but it reminded him it was a bad idea. He pushed himself up straight and raised his eyebrows at Marlow in his best amused dismissal.

"What makes you think I'm pissed?" he asked.

Marlow grinned, a flash of quick, unexpected humor, and glanced down at Cade's fly. "Well, you haven't lost interest," he said in a mild voice. "But you haven't gotten in touch either. So…"

"Maybe I wanted you to do the running," Cade said, "or I lost your number?"

Marlow nodded and tilted the corner of his mouth up in a rueful expression that didn't quite qualify as a smile. "So, still pissed."

There wasn't much to say to that. Cade shrugged and glanced down at his desk, tapping his finger on a catering receipt as if it suddenly interested him.

"Fair enough. Call me if you find anything."

Cade looked up in surprise and scowled at Marlow. He wasn't sure how he wanted this to go, but he'd not expected Marlow to give up.

"You're not going to ask why?" he asked.

Marlow glanced back over his shoulder. "Are you going to tell me?"

Probably not. Not until Marlow begged—which *did* have its appeal—and jumped through a series of hoops to prove he'd do it. Then Cade would just bring it up occasionally, whenever Marlow thought he was finally over it.

It sounded exhausting. He could spend that time with his tongue down Marlow's throat. Or elsewhere.

"I'm not mad," he said. Marlow looked skeptical. "We're good. This is good. Next time."

Marlow tapped his fingers on the jamb of the door for a moment and then nodded. "Sure. Sounds good."

He left.

Cade rolled his head from one side to the other to crack his neck. He'd never taken the high road before, but it had been easier than he thought. Maybe the next thing he'd do was give up his grudge against Justin—who had apparently thrown one last blowout party in LA on the company dime before he'd been congratulated on his new job out the door. Cade pulled a sour face at that as he balled the invoice—already paid—and tossed it in the trash. Or not. He wasn't that generous.

He got up off the desk and walked over to grab Marlow's abandoned fish cakes from the table. They had tasted good second hand, after all. Cade finished them off and folded the wrappers up neatly before he deposited them in the bin. He buzzed his assistant to bring his car around. It was time to find out if Lance was so grateful to Piper that he'd turn down a job offer rather than spill his secrets.

"I'll have it brought around now," his assistant assured him. "It'll meet you downstairs."

Cade pulled his jacket on. The other good thing about forgiving Marlow, of course, was that now he had the upper hand. Now, instead of him being the idiot with a crush trying to get the Night Shift hero's attention, Marlow would need to prove that Cade hadn't made a mistake when he handed over a second chance.

Yeah.

Cade definitely thought he'd done the right thing when he let Marlow off the hook.

CHAPTER FIVE

THE BABY SUCKED on her own fist contentedly and stared up at Marlow with vague blue eyes. It didn't seem that her late-night adventure last full moon had done any lasting damage. Marlow really didn't want to break that streak by dropping the kid.

He shifted the baby's squashy weight into the crook of his arm and cleared his throat. None of the people mid-fight in the torn-up yard paid any attention to him.

"I don't need to go!" Annette yelled. She folded down onto the ground, long legs in yoga pants bent into sharp angles, and pressed her hands flat against her ears. "I wouldn't do that. I wouldn't hurt my baby."

The last time Marlow had seen her, she'd nearly kicked his ass, seven feet of misfired hormones and claws. She was younger than he'd vaguely expected, fresh-faced and freckled, with long red hair and bitten fingernails painted bright yellow.

Her mother grabbed Annette's wrists and tried to pull her hands down. When that didn't work, she used her grip to give Annette a frustrated shake.

"It's court-ordered," she yelled into Annette's tearstained face. "If you don't go, they can take Billie away from you. Is that what you want?"

Off to the side, Annette's father shooed the family's pet rooster back indoors. The rust-colored bird churred indignantly and tried to scoot back out round the man's legs. Marlow kept a wary eye on it out of the corner of his eye. Even with their wings and spurs docked, the spur breeds were aggressive. He didn't support breed bans, but he didn't want a beak in his eye either.

"It would be a temporary hold," Marlow downplayed the threat diplomatically. "And that's what we're trying to avoid."

The father finally closed the door in the rooster's face. His hands were scratched from manhandling the alarmed bird, and drops of blood seeped from the torn skin. He blotted it against his muddy jeans as he jogged back over.

"Mary, calm down," he said as he patted his wife's shoulders ineffectually. "It'll be fine. She's fine. This is just a formality."

She turned on him. "They don't send Night Shift for a formality! You know that. Your father was Night Shift, back in New York. Did they send him out to serve summonses often? Of fucking course not."

"California does it differently," Marlow said. "During the full moon, I'm Night Shift, the rest of the month, I'm just another cop. Annette failed to show up today, and I'm here to make sure she does. That's all."

For now.

Marlow could soft-soap this as much as he wanted, but if Annette didn't engage in the process, it would escalate.

"You can't blame me for what happens during the full moon," Annette wailed as she curled in on herself, face buried in her crooked knees. "It's not my fault."

"It's not what you did; it's what you'll do," Marlow said. "Next full moon. The state needs to know what measures you'll take to safeguard Billie."

The baby picked that moment to hiccup its way into a grouchy, croaky wail. Red flushed up to its scalp, bright under the fuzz of hair, as it squirmed against his grip. It was stronger than he had expected.

Annette jerked her head up and stared at him with swollen, teary eyes. She swiped at her cheeks with both hands and scrambled to her feet.

"Why does he have my baby?" she asked.

"It doesn't matter," Mary said impatiently. She grabbed Annette's shoulders and tried to pull her around. "You have to—"

Annette hit her. The crack of her palm against her mother's face was sharp and nearly knocked the older woman down. It was hard to tell who was more surprised. Annette snatched her hand back and clutched it against her chest as if it had gotten into trouble on its own. Mary didn't move for a moment, her face turned away as she absorbed it.

"Mary!" the husband gasped. He grabbed her elbow and put his arm around her shoulders. "Are you okay?"

"I'm sorry," Annette babbled. She reached out with shaky hands. "I didn't mean—"

Mary shoved her husband roughly away from her and slapped Annette across the face. She used the back of her hand and put her shoulder into it. It staggered Annette. She stumbled back a step, nearly into the freshly replanted flower bed, and raised a hand to touch her bruised cheek with trembling fingers.

Shit.

Marlow took a quick look around. The baby's carrier was set under the table, in the thin crescent of shade. He bent down and tucked Billie into it, getting a spit-wet fist in the eye as Billie wriggled while he strapped her in.

"You nearly killed us too, you selfish little brat," Mary yelled, her voice cracked and flash-paper furious. "We've lived in fear since you first shifted, and you won't even do this for us? For Billie?"

Marlow straightened up just as Mary cocked her hand back for another slap, while Annette cringed. The dad hovered on the sidelines, frozen in place by the outburst of violence. Marlow put himself between them, one hand on Annette's shoulder and the other raised in warning for Mary to stop.

"That's enough—"

She hit him. The heel of her hand cracked against his jaw hard enough to make his teeth click together. From the taste of salt on his tongue, he'd caught the edge of his cheek or tongue as well. That would sting later; right now, all he could feel was the heat that scalded the side of his face.

Mary blanched as she realized what she'd done. Her mouth opened slightly and stayed that way as she took a step backward. The movement finally jarred her husband from his paralysis, and he stepped in to wrap an arm around her shoulder. His fingers dug into her upper arm as he pulled her back.

"It was an accident," he said. "That's all."

"I'm sorry," Mary said. She wasn't looking at Marlow; her pleading expression was directed over his shoulder. "I just… I just…"

Damp fingers touched Marlow's wrist. "I'll go," Annette said, her voice small and tight in her throat. "Okay? That's what everyone wants. I'll go."

Annette ducked out from under Marlow's arm and headed back to the house. She didn't look at her parents on the way past. Mary tried to reach her, hand outstretched pleadingly, but the dad pulled her back.

"Not yet," he said into her hair. He patted at her shoulders in nervous comfort, although it might have been for himself instead of her. "Let everything settle, love."

Under the table, Billie didn't seem to have noticed the atmosphere. She'd somehow managed to shed both her socks and waved her chubby-toed feet triumphantly in the air.

"The mediator won't want to see Billie this time," Marlow said. It sounded officious, but he couldn't think of how to soften it. "Next time, they might want to see all of you."

Annette's father gestured uncomfortably at Marlow's face. "And…"

It had been Marlow's tongue that had taken the worst of the hit. He absently grated the edge of it against his molars to check the sting.

"An accident," he said. "No harm, no foul."

He went after Annette. She was waiting for him next to the patrol car, her hands in her pockets and her head tipped forward so her hair hid her face.

"You could press charges," Marlow said in a neutral tone.

Annette rubbed her cheek. "I hit her first. She didn't mean it. She's just… it scared her."

They didn't speak as they got into the car; then Marlow tried again before the silence settled.

"Some null parents, if they aren't Night Shift, they take it hard," he offered. His experience had been from the other side, the child left behind while the moon stole his family one by one. Maybe that had been better. It hadn't felt like it at the time. "They spend every full moon focused on keeping their family safe from the wolves, and then suddenly their kid is out there with them. It's scary."

Annette swallowed and stared down at her hands. She picked at the dirt under her nails. "They think I'm scary," she said. "Now. They were okay, but not now."

Marlow pulled away from the curb. "No one can blame you for what the wolf did," he reminded her.

She crossed her arms and slouched down in the seat. "I could," she said. Fear softened her voice for a second, made it tremble, and then denial snapped back in. "*If* it was true. If I did hurt Billie… if the wolf did it? I'd blame myself. But I didn't. It was a mistake. Night Shift made a mistake. Because I couldn't live with hurting her."

Half the petals on the Bloomin' Onion had already been plucked. Bennett broke another one off with greasy fingers and dipped it in the ranch dressing.

"Well, that's sad," she said as she crunched into the fried batter. "Because she's just going to have to, isn't she?"

Marlow slouched in his chair, one arm hooked over the back, and wrapped his fingers loosely around the neck of his beer. He should have known better than to bring this up with Bennett, but he'd not been able to shake Annette's misery over the last couple of days.

"It's just something that happened," he said, "not something she did."

"You would believe that, Kit-cat."

Marlow shook his head and looked away from Bennett to the pool table. His gaze landed briefly on the sign for the restrooms, and he felt heat flush his temples. He pretended he'd not noticed and watched Franklin harass the rookie for beer money.

When he didn't take the bait, Bennett made a disgusted noise.

"Whatever. She doesn't come to terms with what 'happened,' then we'll be out there at the end of the month, and maybe this time I won't be there to save the baby."

"You didn't save her this time," he pointed out.

"I would have. Probably quicker once my maternal instincts kicked in."

Marlow laughed. Bennett kicked him under the table. In the shin, not the knee, so she hadn't taken it to heart.

"I've got maternal instincts," she said. "My pet rat ate my favorite bra, and I didn't yeet it out the window."

"Mother of the year," Marlow drawled. He took a drink of beer and wiped his mouth on the back of his hand. "You ever wonder how Piper got started?"

Bennett paused mid-chew and reached for a napkin as she finished off the onion bloom. She wiped her hands on the paper fastidiously.

"Not because he wasn't sympathetic to doe-eyed mommies who nearly ate their kid alive," she said. "If that's what you're getting at."

"I wasn't." Or maybe he was. Marlow didn't know anymore. It was just too strange to be here eating bar food and drinking beer with someone who maybe tried to kill him. "Just—"

He shrugged. Bennett studied him a moment longer and then grabbed a limp, tepid fry from the dregs left in the basket. She swabbed it through a puddle of ketchup.

"I heard about the case with that actress," she said. "It sounded like something out of his playbook, but no one's bandied his name about since then. I thought it was just some rich bitch who thought her son should *never* be blamed for anything, full moon or not."

There was nearly as much contempt in her voice for Farnham as there had been for Annette. No one got much slack in Bennett's world.

"Sort of," Marlow said. He took another drink of beer and tried to work out how much he could share without just… trusting her again. "She was one of Piper's clients. Or was the go-between for him and a client, anyhow."

"Fuck," Bennett said. "So when the shit hit the fan, she just figured if it had worked once…"

"I guess. Just made me think."

"You're Night Shift," Bennett said. "They don't pay you to think, they pay you to hit stuff… and in your case chauffeur them places when they bat their baby browns. Didn't think that was your type."

Franklin dragged a chair over and straddled it, arms folded over the low carved back of it.

"What are we talking about?" he asked as he grabbed the beer he'd left behind. "Marlow befouling the restroom of our sacred brotherhood with paid help?"

Bennett grabbed the neck of the beer and yanked it out of Franklin's grip. "I look like your brother?"

He rolled his eyes. "Turn of phrase."

"And we're talking about Marlow getting all soft-hearted over that wolf-bitch that tried to kill her kid," Bennett said. She drained his beer while Franklin mugged indignantly at her. "Like he won't have to put a bullet in her next full moon if she doesn't learn."

Franklin shrugged. "Whatever," he said and jerked his thumb over his shoulder. "Unless we're roasting Marlow for his bad taste in boys, we got a rookie to initiate."

They looked over. Half of Bennett's team were clustered around the kid. They'd kept his glass full and his blood high all night. Dawson had him in a headlock, and he laughed along with the others even as his face went red.

"That we do." Bennett handed the empty bottle back to Franklin and slid out along the bench. "I need to piss first; then we can go."

"Fuck sake, there are ladies present," Franklin mock-protested as he waved a hand at Marlow. "Mind your language!"

Bennett gave him a friendly punch on the shoulder and sauntered away from the table. The expression on Franklin's face as he watched her was soft, his mouth creased with something rueful. Marlow looked away. There were some sore spots you just didn't poke at, because people would never forget it.

"So am I a 'lady' now because I like guys?"

In the time it took Franklin to look around, he'd rearranged his face into cockiness.

"No," he said. "I'm not a *dick*. It's because you're all soft and sentimental inside and get all, you know, up in your feelings about some girl that's sad she nearly ate her kid."

That was good. Marlow had been worried that Franklin had upgraded his jerkiness to the point it couldn't be ignored as banter.

"That's a surprise," he drawled. "You and Bennett agreeing that she doesn't deserve sympathy."

His phone buzzed in his hip pocket. Marlow reached down to grab it while Franklin snorted at him.

"I think she doesn't *need* sympathy," Franklin said. "Nothing happened to her. She doesn't even remember it, so it might as well never have happened. That's one thing that Piper got right. The wolves have it made. It doesn't matter what they do or why they do it. Nothing sticks. She could have eaten that kid, and as long as no asshole told her, would she even know?"

It was Cade's number.

"I think she'd notice the kid was missing," Marlow pointed out as he got up. He fished his wallet from his pocket and pulled out about thirty bucks. He dropped the bills on the table in front of

Franklin. "That should cover my share of the pot. It looks like I'll have to duck out."

Hopefully. Cade *could* have called to tell him that all their leads had fallen flat. That wouldn't take the rest of the night to deal with, but it wasn't like Marlow had really wanted to be here in the first place. Bennett had dragged him along, so he'd take the opportunity to get out of it painlessly while he still could.

Franklin picked the notes up and folded them over and over again into a thick wad. "What? The wolf whistles and you go running?" He laughed at his own joke as he tucked the money into the inside pocket of his jacket, then sobered. "Don't go soft on the wolves just because you're fucking one, Marlow. You start thinking about who they are in daylight, you're going to flinch. Then you're going to be dead."

"I don't flinch," Marlow said. He plucked his coat from the back of the chair and slung it over his arm. "And I didn't know you cared."

Franklin shrugged and glanced around at the bar. "I don't trust the rookie to watch my back," he said. "Not yet."

The call rang out. Marlow swiped to call back and lifted the phone to his ear as he stepped away from the table.

"You probably could if you weren't an asshole."

Franklin's snort of laughter followed Marlow as he headed out of the bar and onto the street. He dodged through a group of Day Shift cops who'd retreated outside to smoke, their liquor decanted into plastic glasses. A few of them tried to stop him for… something… but he pointed at the phone to put them off.

Just before the call disconnected again, Cade answered.

"I can't remember the last time someone let me go to voicemail," he said down the line. "Next time, pick up."

Marlow laughed. "Sure," he said. "That sounds like something I'll do. Why did you call, Cade?"

There was a dry pause on the other end of the line. Marlow could *feel* it as Cade decided whether or not it was worth it to follow through on his attitude. He must have decided not.

"I tracked down Lance. It turns out he's not an easy man to find," he said. The cold edge was gone from his voice and what was left was practical. Businesslike. "My plan will work better if I have someone tied to Piper with me when I talk to Lance."

He didn't actually ask. It was easy to assume that he had, but he never did. If Cade couldn't order you to do something, he expected you to volunteer off your own bat. Marlow stopped next to a half-empty newspaper rack and looked through the greasy glass at the headlines. The tally of full moon damage had been pushed off the front page days ago; now it was sports, scandals, and politics.

"What if you had to ask nicely?"

"I won't."

Cade didn't bother to try and sound ashamed. It was probably strange that Marlow found that blunt embrace of his flaws attractive. The abstract guilt of knowing he'd done something, even if he wasn't sure exactly what, didn't help.

"When and where?" he asked.

He heard a car door open and slam shut. Tinny music and loud voices filtered into the background of the call.

"Now," Cade said. "I'll text you the address."

The insurance company had cut Marlow a check for the full amount when they wrote the Impala off. He wasn't ready to let go yet, so the money sat in his bank account while the charred carcass of the Impala sat in his mechanic's lot. Until it was either fixed or he got around to checking the gear-head message boards for a project car, Marlow was behind the wheel of a primer-red and matte-black junker.

His mechanic wasn't going to forgive him for a while.

Still, the junker fit in around Cortez Hill. The only cars around here were wrecks and the drug dealers' shiny Ford Flex minivans. Marlow parked two blocks away from the address that Cade had given him and walked. The last of the heat had seeped away, and it was cold enough he could feel it settle into his knee.

The address was for a shop called Silver Bullet Solutions. Home security. None of the security companies could—legally—sell the actual metal, but all of them liked to imply they would. Instead, they sold heavy-duty shutters and motion-sensor alarms, hollow-point bullets packed with delphinium extract. It was the same family as wolfsbane, but less potent.

Marlow tried the door. It was locked.

In the glass, he saw the reflection of the dusty sedan as the door swung open. He turned around and went over to look inside. The inside was nicer than the dinged-up off-white exterior, with leather seats and top-of-the-line electronics.

"My gran always told me not to get in cars with strange men," he noted as he climbed in and slammed the door.

"You just did," Cade pointed out.

"She told me not to join Night Shift too," Marlow said. He took the drink that Cade offered, the sides of the cup warm against his cold fingers. "I don't listen."

He took a sip. The bitter tang of burnt beans and sugar surprised him. He was used to cups of Bovril from TAC colleagues when he pulled a day shift.

"Thanks," he said. "Where's Lance?"

Cade pointed over the road at the squat white stucco building on the corner of the street. The sign over the door read SKINNED in hot pink letters that flickered unsteadily, and a naked wolf, all pink and red lines, did a stuttered dance in the window.

"That's—"

"Yes," Cade agreed as he pulled a dubious expression. "Not the classiest establishment, but it's the cheapest place in town for slap and tickle that's heavy on the slap."

"And Lance frequents…"

Cade shook his head. "Apparently, he's a performer," he said. "Some people like scars."

"And your plan?" Marlow asked. It was maybe a good thing he'd changed out of his gear before he left work. His second-best Converse—less worn-in but sole still fully attached—didn't exactly make him look like a high roller, but they'd fit in better than a stab vest. "Ask for a private dance and doorstep him when he's off-balance?"

Cade snorted and drained his cup. "I don't pay for it," he said, that edge of brittle dignity sharp in his voice. "And if I did, they better keep their balance. No. We just have an opportunity for him to help out his old friend and, ah, frequent benefactor."

"Oh?" Marlow asked.

CHAPTER SIX

LANCE'S SCARS LOOKED softer in real life than they did in photos. Less livid. The edges blended into his tan, except where a curl of scar roughed the skin. He'd pulled a T-shirt on after his performance, and glitter smudged over the black cotton.

"Barman said you wanted to talk to me," he said as he sat down. He lifted the glass of clear liquid, cherries floating in it, that he'd brought with him."And I guessed you wanted to buy a round too."

Cade glanced at the bar and saw one of the staff on their way over, two glasses of whiskey and a bowl of salsa and chips on the tray they carried. He shrugged as he turned back to Lance.

"I'll call it a business expense."

Lance laughed and took a drink. "Yeah, me too."

"They charge that much for the water here?" Cade asked.

He'd never stripped, but his stepmother had after Dad threw her and Lem out. The first rule was to get in good with the bouncers; the second was the customers got pissed and she got hydrated. It was a lot easier to take advantage of a drunk when you were sober.

"I finished my shift," Lance said. He necked whatever he had in his glass and plucked one of the tumblers from the server's tray. The woman gave him a disapproving look but didn't say anything as she unloaded the salsa and the last glass. Lance waited until she was gone before he took another drink. "What do you want? Private shows are no-touching and—"

"We wanted to talk, not watch," Marlow said. He took a chip from the bowl. Cade took it off him before he could eat it and gave Marlow an exasperated look. SKINNED was not the sort of strip club where the food was part of the draw, and he doubted good hygiene was either. Cade tossed the chip back in the bowl, and Marlow gave him the finger. He ignored that. "About Ned Piper."

What expression there was on Lance's face shut down. He took a long drink of the whiskey and then set the glass down with a click, his fingers loose around the rim.

"What about him?"

Cade smiled, the professionally empty one he deployed at board meetings, and laced his fingers together.

"Certain individuals within the SDPD and outside it have encouraged me to take a look at Piper's conviction," he said. "They question how fair and measured his sentence was, considering all the good work he did and how many other people were involved."

Lance pulled a sardonic face; the scars twisted at the expression in odd ways.

"Yeah, he was a saint. Does Piper know about this?"

"How else would we find you?" Marlow asked. "You're not exactly on his list of known associates."

"I'm not an associate."

"Employee?" Cade suggested. "Contractor?"

Lance absently turned the glass in small, tight circles on the table, a wet trail dark against the scarred laminate. After a second, he picked it up and smacked it back down again with a click.

"I'm the fuckin' help," he said. "I just do what I'm told, and I guess, finally, he's got something to tell me. So what is it? What's he want me to say?"

Marlow's knee tapped against Cade's under the table. That didn't sound like someone who'd been doing Piper's dirty work. Willing to do it, maybe, but it wasn't the dynamic that they had tailored their play for.

It wasn't exactly a problem. Cade could think on his feet, and Marlow's usual laid-back demeanor was useful for hiding whether he was flustered or not. But it would have been nice, just this once, if Cade got to look like he knew what he was doing.

Although, wasn't Marlow meant to be the one doing the running now? That had been why Cade had forgiven him, hadn't it?

The question hung around in Cade's head as if it expected him to realize how profound it was. He dismissed it impatiently—he liked to be respected, he'd take envy as the next best thing, and that wasn't new or exclusive to Marlow—and focused on the current problem.

"He told us you could get us what we needed," Cade said as he worked on the mental edit of their approach.

"What?"

"Evidence," Marlow said. "His safety net. All the people he could bring down if things don't go his way."

Lance rubbed his scarred socket with the knuckle of his thumb. "Hasn't he wrung that well of favors dry already?"

"This is what happens to a spent favor," Cade said. "It becomes leverage. It becomes a trading card."

Lance's eye flickered from Cade to Marlow, and he bit his lower lip as he shook his head.

"Yeah, fuck off," he said. "I'm not biting."

Cade let himself look annoyed. "I didn't come here to waste my time," he said. "If you want proof of my bona fides, I can get it—"

"I'm sure you can," Lance said. He braced his hands on the table to push himself up. "Until Piper tells me otherwise, go fuck yourself."

Marlow reached over the table and grabbed Lance's wrist. "Sit down," he said. "Or I'll call Vice and have this place raided."

"Go ahead," Lance sneered. "It isn't illegal to dance."

Marlow smiled faintly. "But the place *will* be shut down for a week—or more—if I tell them I'm sure there's something to find. And I came up under Piper, so if I'm sure I can find something? I know how to be sure I find it."

Doubt flickered over Lance's face. He sat down hard, as if his knees had given way under him, and Marlow let go of his wrist. Lance sat back and rubbed his wrist as if Marlow had gripped him hard enough to hurt.

"Piper didn't send you," he said. "He made sure I don't know shit about that stuff anyhow."

"So what's the money for, then?" Marlow asked. Cade gave him an irritated look. He'd been ready to edit the plan; Marlow had just ripped it up entirely. Marlow hitched a shoulder in response and pointed out, "He knows we're not working for Piper. Might as well cut to the chase."

"Run errands," Lance said. "Spy on his ex-wife, deliver messages. That sort of thing. Give the big hero something to feel good about while he's locked up."

The mix of gratitude and resentment that twisted through Lance's words was acidic. It might be useful too.

"What?" Cade asked. "Don't tell me he still expects you to grovel just because he saved your life once?"

Lance stared at him for a second and then twisted his mouth into a bleak grimace of a smile. The music dropped in volume as the redhead grabbed the last notes from a customer's hand and hopped off the stage. The music cut out, and a bored voice introduced the next dancer. She took the stage to a remix of what sounded like choral music and Madonna, all wild curls and aggressive hip action.

"That's his version, yeah," Lance said. "Maybe I don't remember it the same way. In my version, I might just get what I'm due."

"What is your version?" Marlow asked.

Lance looked up, honest surprise on his face for a moment. "You know what, no one ever asked that before. Not back then. Not since."

"And?" Cade asked.

It took a moment, but finally, Lance shrugged. His voice softened, the rough edges burred off the words as he remembered. He sounded younger.

"I've heard the story he tells, and it's pretty much true. Close enough that no one ever questioned it. Except he's the one who froze, who freaked out. I was the one who dragged the wolf out the front door and managed to get back inside to pass out in the hallway. By the time I woke up in the hospital, though, Piper had told his version of the story to everyone. He got to be the hero, and I got this."

Lance dragged his thumb along his jaw, just under the uneven, roughly raised scar.

The part of Cade that wasn't entirely sure how Marlow had felt about Piper—once upon a time before the murder attempt—reveled in the revised story. So, Piper wasn't a good cop who'd made some bad choices; he'd always been an asshole.

"You didn't tell anyone?"

"Couple of people. No one believed me. I was just some music nerd, and Piper already looked the part."

"The other kids—" Marlow started to ask.

"Didn't see anything or didn't want to get involved. The only one who could have corroborated was Raymond—the wolf—and he obviously didn't remember anything after it started." Lance looked bitter for a second and then shrugged. "It didn't matter anyhow. Not like being called a hero in the paper would make my eye grow back. Piper could have it."

"And he paid for the privilege?"

"Not till it went down with him shooting that rookie." Lance picked a chip from the bowl and broke it between his fingers. "I guess prison worked, made him think about everything he'd done wrong. The people he'd done wrong. First time I'd heard from him in years. So, you want something on Piper? You're talking to the wrong guy. All I know about him is how much he'll pay to feel like the big man."

He was wrong. Or maybe just lying.

Piper had run his racket out of the heart of the SDPD's Night Shift for years without a single complaint or flag on his file. That wasn't the sort of man to be suddenly overcome with regret. Never mind that there were plenty of people who should have been ahead of Lance on the amends list. Marlow for a start.

No. The reason that money dropped into Lance's account every month wasn't altruistic; it was self-serving. Lance was someone that no one had any reason to tie to Piper's racket and who was bitter enough to accept the idea that his payday was "reparations" without any questions.

Errands. Messages. The ex.

Cade got his phone out of his pocket and pulled up a picture of Maria. He turned it around to show Lance.

"Do you know her?"

Lance glanced at the photo and then back at Cade, his face set in a studiously blank expression.

"Even if I did, why the hell should I do anything for you?" he asked.

"Why do anything for Piper?" Cade asked.

For a second, Lance looked like he didn't know the answer to that question. He started to answer, changed his mind, and took a drink instead.

"He pays me," he said. "Why else?"

Cade raised his eyebrows. "Is that all?" He leaned back in the chair and reached into his jacket for his wallet. "I can pay you. How much will it take? Ten grand? Twenty?"

Behind Lance, the dancer on stage drained the bottle of champagne and wrapped up the act to whoops and applause. The

DJ lowered the music to a distracting background drone and announced it would be ten minutes till the next act.

Lance licked his lips and stared at the wallet as if Cade had that much in actual twenties stuffed into the leather folds.

"I don't know. I mean, Piper's basically got me on retainer. It's, like, steady employment… I mean, if he finds out—"

"I won't tell him," Cade said. He pulled a business card out and pushed it over the table. "Give me a price."

Marlow provided the pen, rolling a black ballpoint over the table. It bumped to a stop against Lance's fingers. It took a moment, but he picked it up and clicked it twice in nervous succession.

"I get the money?" he checked. "Whether what I know is helpful or not?"

"As long as you answer our questions the best you can," Cade said. He tucked his wallet back into his pocket and smiled wryly. "As long as I think your quote is reasonable, of course. I want to know what Piper is up to, but there's a limit to what any information is worth."

The tip of the pen hovered over the paper as Lance tried to work out how far to push it. He started to write, the scrawled loop of a dollar sign carved into the shiny card, and then paused as he looked up at Cade.

"He'll never know, right?" he said. "I know he's in jail, but he still—"

Lance stopped mid-word as he looked at something over Cade's shoulder. His face went slack and then flushed, a quick tide of color that didn't touch his scars.

"Did you see—?" He stopped mid-question and gave Marlow a quick, hard stare. "I know you. You're Night Shift. I know you. You work for Piper!"

For a bright, suspicious moment, Cade considered the accusation. It would explain… absolutely nothing. In fact, it would raise more questions. The only thing that theory had to recommend it was the punch of adrenaline that paranoia released into the bloodstream.

"Trust me," Marlow said. "He'd not have me, even if I'd have him."

He sounded the way he always did when he talked about Piper—the familiar protective guard of his dry humor laced through with something astringent. Regret? Anger? Unresolved sexual tension? Cade wasn't sure he could tell, with his own emotions in the way of practicalities.

Lance crumpled the card in his hand and threw it at Marlow.

"Fuck you," he blurted as he bolted to his feet. The backs of his legs hit the chair and knocked it over backward. Lance clutched the pen in his hand, his knuckles white through the taut skin, as he glanced over Cade's head again. His eye flickered as he tracked something. "I never told you *shit*. You tell him that. I didn't tell you anything."

Cade started to turn around to see if he could pick out what was so interesting. Before he could, Lance snatched up his glass and tossed the dregs of it into Cade's face. Cheap liquor stung his eyes, and Cade recoiled with a spluttered "Fuck" as he tried to wipe it away on his sleeve.

Through the blur of tears and booze, Cade saw Lance back away from the table.

"Nothing!" the scarred man repeated, his voice cracked with tension. "You tell him that!"

He turned on his heel and bolted toward the back of the club through the maze of scantly occupied tables.

"You get him," Marlow said as he stood up. He stretched up onto his toes as he scanned the dimly lit club and the clots of customers clustered around the bar. "I'll see if I can find who spooked him."

The hem of his T-shirt rode up. The narrow slice of pale skin, drawn taut over lean muscle, made Cade's mouth go dry. He grimaced at himself—there was a time and place, and this was neither—as he gave his eyes one last scrub.

"The way Lance reacted, the connection he made," he pointed out. "Whoever he saw—"

"Is Night Shift," Marlow finished for him. "We already knew that, though. It's fine."

"Is it?" Cade asked.

It was one thing to believe that someone you worked with—that you might be close with—was corrupt. It was another to come face-to-face with the evidence. Cade had been there, back in

Alaska on the private-security circuit. He'd not even bothered to learn half of their names, and it had still been unsteadying.

Marlow hitched the corner of his mouth up in a wry shrug. "Close enough."

He headed toward the bar. People got out of his way. Even when he wasn't dressed for the Night Shift, Marlow moved like someone who knew their own body. Cade filed that away for later and went after Lance.

The floor was sticky underfoot as Cade wove through the tightly placed tables. A waitress in high-waisted short-shorts and a furry bikini top dodged back to get out of his way, one arm crooked protectively around the champagne some mug had paid for. Her eyes widened as she checked him out, and she tossed a worried glance over to the barman.

Angry men in expensive clothes didn't bode well in a place like SKINNED. Or anywhere, for that matter.

Cade ignored her. He didn't plan to hang around long enough for them to have to deal with him.

The DJ kicked the volume of the music up. The first beatboxed kick drum notes of "Mrs. Officer" pumped out of the speakers, undercut by a static buzz from one, while the stripper crawled onto the stage. Cued by the song, other dancers got up from the tables with whoever had bought their time to writhe to the music. Dark hair flicked against Cade's face as one of the dancers tossed the long rope of a ponytail over their shoulder. He batted it out of the way and pushed past her.

"Fuck off," she hissed at him through glossy red lips. "I'm working."

He ignored her and craned his neck to catch a glimpse of Lance. From the back, without the scars to set him apart from the crowd. Cade cursed under his breath as he tried to remember what color Lance's hair was.

It hadn't seemed like something he'd need to know.

The hard crack of the flat of someone's hand against his ass made Cade jump a moment before he felt the sting of the slap through his trousers. He turned sharply, grabbed the man's wrist before he could retrieve it, and squeezed.

"Don't touch me," Cade warned him flatly.

The baby-faced man—razor burn on his throat and body paint on his shoulder—had the good sense to look uneasy. It passed, drowned in the fumes of whatever he'd drunk that night.

"Free world," he said.

Cade brought the man's arm down against the edge of the table. The sharp line of it caught him just under the joint of his thumb. Something cracked—loud enough to hear over the music—and the whiskey-flush blanched from the man's face. His mouth opened, but whatever strangled shriek came out was drowned under the police-siren vocals of the song.

Asshole.

The man doubled over, clutching his wrist, and Cade left him to it. He loped over to the heavy double doors that led backstage and stiff-armed them open. The kid on the other side yelped and swung his mop up.

"Where's Lance?" Cade asked. He let his old accent out from under a decade's worth of elocution lessons. It sounded more hick than ever to his ears, especially with the punch of anxiety he put behind it. "He's in trouble. There's someone looking for him."

Sometimes the most believable lie was just the truth… as if you weren't part of it. It kept things simple, and it always fit the situation.

The kid gawped at him for a moment and then turned to point down the hall.

"He went that way," he said. Cade shoved past him and loped along the grubby carpet. Behind him, the kid raised his voice and called after him, "He went outside. I heard the fire door slam."

Cade broke into a proper run. He rounded the corner and scanned the hall. The fire door was halfway down, two heavy metal doors painted a dull red. He slowed to a stop in front of them and gave them a shove. The safety bar depressed under his hands, and the doors started to open—until they hit something on the other side.

"Fuck," Cade muttered under his breath.

He took two steps back and rammed the door with his shoulder. The doors scraped open a couple of inches, and the sound of Lance's voice, pitched thin and nervous, filtered in from outside.

"I didn't speak to them. I swear. All these years, I've kept my mouth shut. Okay? Why would I talk now?"

"I'd think of a reason," a rough, unfamiliar voice said, "before I give you one. Get in the car."

Whoever this new player was, they weren't Piper's man, then. Cade threw himself against the door again. He could see the grubby yellow paint of the dumpster that Lance had pushed in front of the door. Luckily it wasn't full, and it scraped reluctantly over the ground as he put his weight to it. It almost drowned out the sound of the scuffle in the alleyway.

"Get away from me!" Lance yelled, his voice muffled. "Who do you work for? Piper will kill you for this!"

The other man laughed. "Piper couldn't kill a cat in a sack," he sneered. "Open the fucking trunk."

Cade squeezed through the crack in the fire doors and boosted himself up over the edge of the dumpster. Cheap black plastic bags puffed and split under his weight, the reek of burned oil and cheap liquor sour in the air.

The alley was dimly lit by a yellow light over the club's back door that flickered and buzzed. Lance was on the ground, blood matted in his hair, as a man in a black hoodie dragged him toward a car that was parked, open trunk first, in the mouth of the alley.

"Let him go," Cade said.

The man in the hoodie let go of Lance's arms and swung around. He pulled a gun from the small of his back and aimed in one smooth motion. So did Cade as he dropped into a crouch on the trash. A bullet tore past his head as he went down, close enough he could feel the burn of it kiss his temple, and a bottle cracked under his knee. The dumpster rang like a cracked bell as bullets punched into it, and the metal dinged in shiny puckers.

Cade counted three shots. Most people, unless they were in a frenzy, paused at three. The first spike of adrenaline had worn off, maybe they had second thoughts, or their hands hurt. It didn't last long, but if you needed a window, it was a way to pick your moment.

He pushed himself up and fired twice. Once at the space where he'd last seen the hoodie-wearing thug, and then he corrected and shot the man in the torso. The man staggered back into the wall as he absorbed the impact, one hand up to clutch his chest.

After a moment, the man's knees gave way under him, and he slid down the wall, his legs folded at awkward angles. He wheezed for air, his face gray, as he dropped the gun by his feet.

On the ground, Lance rolled over and tried to prop himself up on his elbow. He touched his head with one hand and flinched away from the sting of raw flesh.

"Lance," Cade said. "Come here."

He braced his hand on the edge of the dumpster and boosted himself up and over. The smell of the dumpster came with him. Something slimy and halfway to rancid had soaked through the knee of his trousers and plastered it to his leg. Cade had woken up after the full moon and smelled worse.

Sweat itched on the back of his neck as he kept the gun pointed at the man in the hoodie. Cade's shot had hit the man in the center of his body mass. If it had penetrated, the man would be well on his way to being dead. At this distance, even with a Kevlar vest, he'd have broken ribs at least. He could still get back up once the numb shock of a hammer blow to the sternum wore off.

Cade held his free hand out and crooked his fingers. "We can't help you if you don't come here."

Lance lifted his head enough to stare at Cade, his eye narrow and grim with suspicion. He spat a thick wad of phlegm on the ground, the strings of spit dangling from his lips, and scrambled gracelessly to his feet. For a second, it looked like Lance was going to make the smart choice as he half-turned toward Cade; then he bolted for the mouth of the alleyway.

It was a clumsy run. Lance bounced off the brick wall twice as he staggered woozily, but he managed to squeeze past the bumper of the car there to kidnap him. Cade glanced quickly at the man in a hoodie—still down, still gray about the mouth, all that was really visible under his pulled-down hood—and took the risk. He went after Lance and was almost close enough to grab his shoulder when the idling engine revved.

There had to have been someone to pop the trunk, Cade realized with a flash of frustrated self-recrimination. He'd spent too much time behind a desk. That wasn't a mistake he'd have made when he was in the field more often.

The car screeched forward, veered at the last minute, and clipped the back of Lance's leg with the corner of a bumper. He was thrown into the air and came down on the windshield. It shattered on impact, cracks spiderwebbed across the glass, and Lance rolled off to the side. He bounced when he hit the ground, and this time he wasn't going to push himself back up anytime soon.

Cade leaned down and tucked his fingers under Lance's jaw to check his pulse. It was thready—and something in his jaw felt gritty and loose under Cade's fingers—but it was there.

The car turned sharply onto the street outside, reversed backward, and the back door swung open. Cade cursed under his breath, grabbed Lance by the collar, and hauled him unceremoniously over toward the wall. A woman, hat pulled down over her ears and leather jacket zipped up to her chin, climbed out with a gun.

Bullets stitched at Cade's heels as he ducked behind a couple of old, charred oil drums. It wasn't much shelter. It would have to do. Cade propped Lance up against the wall and crouched there for a second.

"For fuck's sake," the woman yelled. "Get him."

Through a crack between the drums, Cade saw the man in the hoodie grab his gun and drag himself up the wall. The woman stayed by the car, ready to jump back in for a quick getaway.

Cade weighed his options. He could get out of this. Not unscathed, but alive. Lance wouldn't, though. And apparently, he was more valuable than any of them had expected.

The sound of the door as it hit the dumpster interrupted his grim calculations.

"Put your hands up," Marlow's voice snapped.

Cade rolled his eyes at Marlow playing by the rules as the man in the hoodie swung around, one hand still clutched to his chest as he raised the gun in the other. Before he could fire, Cade kicked the oil drum out of the way and shot the man in the leg.

No Kevlar there. A plug of flesh blew out the back of the man's thigh, and he gave a high-pitched wail. He staggered backward and fired wildly in Marlow's direction. For a second, Cade's heart seized in his chest. It wouldn't be as bad as when he thought he'd *eaten* Marlow, but he didn't want him killed.

The woman at the car screamed, shrill and a bit hysterical, and strafed bullets along the alley.

“Get in the car!” she yelled. “Get in the fucking car.”

Hoodie lurched down the alley in a hobbled lope and was shoved unceremoniously into the back of the car. The woman scrambled in after him and slammed the door. Smoke belched out from around the tires as the driver hit the gas and reversed back into the wall with a crunch.

Marlow stepped out into the middle of the alley and shot at the car. Bullets punched shiny-edged holes along the back panel and through the doors. Both side windows smashed and sprayed glass into the interior.

A yelp of pain escaped through the broken window—it sounded like the woman—and then the car fishtailed over the road and was gone.

CHAPTER SEVEN

THE PARAMEDIC STEPPED in front of Marlow. He held up both hands, still encased in bloody latex gloves, to stop him in his tracks.

"He's not in any condition to answer questions right now," he said.

"One minute," Marlow said. "The people who did this to him got away."

"That's your job," the paramedic said. He jerked his thumb over his shoulder at the ambulance. "Mine is getting him to the hospital before he codes. If you want to talk to him once he's stabilized, we're going to Kaiser. You can ask his doctors when he'll be fit to be questioned."

Marlow bit the inside of his cheek in frustration. He debated whether to claim it was Night Shift business, but that didn't have the same weight during the crescent moon. Besides, that was the sort of overstepping that might get back to O'Hara.

He shrugged his acceptance and stepped back. The paramedic looked relieved as he stripped his gloves off and balled the bloody latex up between his fingers.

"And get your friend to clean that cut on his cheek," he said as he handed Marlow an alcohol wipe in its wrapper. The paramedic turned and loped back to the ambulance as he tossed over his shoulder, "Wolf or not, it can still get infected. Two weeks is a long time to live with a seeping face."

Marlow snorted at the idea he could make Cade do anything and tucked his hands into his pockets. He waited until the doors to the ambulance slammed and it drove away, its red and blue lights splashed over the ousted customers of the strip club as they milled sheepishly around outside. Their IDs and excuses were being collected by the patrol cars who'd responded when Marlow called the incident in to Dispatch.

Only one of the two was needed, but people always wanted to justify themselves to the badge.

Marlow certainly had. The veteran beat cop who'd taken his statement had absorbed the awkward lie of an interrupted date and heroics with the impassive face of someone who'd heard it all before.

Night Shift's mistakes were not Officer Dioli's business. Marlow envied him that. It seemed like his whole career had been about mistakes they'd made.

He headed back toward the club. Cade stood in front of the window and idly rubbed his freshly uncuffed wrists as Dioli ran down the "don't leave town" and "we may need to speak with you again" spiel.

"Of course, I'm always happy to help the SDPD," Cade said smoothly, his voice like honey. "If you guys can't protect your citizens, then I can step in whenever you need me."

Dioli made the face. The "oh, one of these assholes" face. Marlow couldn't blame him. He'd taken his turn behind the same look when he'd dealt with Cade in the past. He wasn't entirely sure he didn't have it on right now.

"Ignore him," he told Dioli. "He's a dick."

Dioli looked nonplussed for a moment and then let a quick, controlled grin slide over his face. He scribbled something in his book and then flipped the cover over.

"Noted," he said. "He can pick up his gun at the station once the lab is done with it. We'll let him know."

"That's okay," Cade said. "I have others."

Dioli looked at him for a second and then turned to Marlow. "I see what you mean."

"Right?"

"I've got your statement too, Officer Marlow," Dioli said. "If we need anything else, I guess I know where to find you."

He turned and headed back to the patrol car. His partner looked relieved as he disengaged himself from one of the flirtier dancers.

"I'm a dick?" Cade asked.

Marlow tilted his head and raised his eyebrows. "You're saying you're not?"

"Maybe," Cade admitted as he pushed himself off the wall. "But that's between us. It's not Officer Dioli's business."

"I just assumed you had better things to do than get arrested for pissing off a cop," Marlow said. "Like all of this."

Cade snorted, and the patina of humor faded from his face. "Did you see who spooked Lance in the bar?"

Marlow grimaced and shook his head. "No," he said. "Whoever they were, they didn't hang around. You? Did you see who was in the car?"

"Not well enough to identify them," Cade said. "But that doesn't matter. They told us what we needed to know."

Marlow raised his eyebrows at that. When he'd gotten there, it hadn't looked as if much talking had gone on.

"What?" he asked.

"That they aren't working with Piper," Cade said. He pulled his keys out of his pocket and headed for his car. "The people in the car wanted the same thing from Lance as we did—whatever secrets Piper kept. They just weren't going to negotiate on price. Your ex-boss just went from a potential threat to an asset. We need to speak to him."

"Run."

The old command echoed in Marlow's ears as he stood on the sidewalk and watched Cade cross the road. His throat was dry, sticky when he swallowed, and his chest ached as if he'd just finished a race. That night had been the last time he'd spoken to Piper. It had been the last time he'd *seen* him. Since Piper had cut a deal with the DA, Marlow hadn't needed to face him in court.

It wasn't something that Marlow wanted to change, but he supposed no one had asked what he wanted.

The headlights of Cade's car flashed as he unlocked it, reflected back from the steel and glass in the security store window. He pulled the door open and then turned around to see where Marlow was.

"You in or not?" he asked.

Marlow rubbed his shoulder. It was an old habit. The scar tissue meant he couldn't feel much but dull pressure as he dug his thumb into the flesh. "Not" was probably the smart answer; tap out now and leave the investigation to IA. Instead, he checked for cars and jogged over the road.

"Easier said than done, talking to Piper," he said. "He's refused to talk to anyone from the SDPD or the DA's office since he was sentenced."

Cade smirked and slid into the driver's seat. "Lucky for us, I'm neither. We just have to wake someone up first."

It turned out Maria wasn't asleep. Her hair and makeup were perfect, even dressed in neat pink sweats and fluffy mules. In person, she couldn't hide that under the soft edges, there was something hard.

"How dare you," she said. "I'm a teacher. I have a reputation in this community, and your disgusting implications about my voluntary work are out of line. Get away from my house."

She tried to close the door. Cade blocked it with his foot.

"I'm not a cop," he said. "And Ned Piper isn't much of a charity case, is he?"

Suspicion flickered over her face. "I don't know what you're talking about," she said in a flat, uninflected voice. It was an obvious lie. "Or who. I have a lot of penpals. Now get your foot out of my door before I call the police."

She stamped on Cade's foot. It would have been more effective if she wasn't in her slippers.

"Go on," Cade told her. He tilted his head toward Marlow. "It won't take him long to get here."

Maria glanced at him and then pinched her lips together. There had been something familiar about her when Marlow had seen her photo on Cade's wall, but he'd not been able to put his finger on it. Not until she recognized him and pulled that sour, lemons on her tongue, expression.

The last time he'd seen her, she'd been a brunette with track-marks on her arms and thrift store jeans. Her eyes had been hard then too. She'd been Piper's confidential informant—apparently, he'd pulled her out of an even worse situation—and always had the goods on trafficking schedules and bad blood between gangs that would spill over during the full moon. It had been profitable, since she'd also been paid by Piper's less-than-savory clients to drop off that information about their rivals.

It looked like it still was profitable. As McMansions went, her house was on the low end of the scale, but it was a nice property for a Spanish teacher.

"Maria," Marlow said. "Got the tattoos removed?"

She raised her hand to her face and then pulled it away as she thought better of it.

"That's what the makeup is for," she said. The careful polish on her vowels peeled off, and her old accent turned her voice hard. "You know this was a mistake, Marlow. Even if I knew anything, and for the record, I don't, I'd not squeal. Not on Piper. I still owe him, and so do you."

Marlow snorted. "He tried to kill me, Maria."

Maria mugged surprise. "Did he?" she asked. "And how many times did he save your life? I figure you're still the one in the red, Marlow. And I still know my rights. You probably aren't even supposed to be here. So piss off."

She shoved the door again. Cade grimaced as it crushed his foot and started to snarl something. He held his tongue when Marlow nudged him.

"Do you decide what Piper needs to know now?" he asked. "Because when I knew him, he liked to make his own calls."

Maria looked sour and stepped back to let the door swing open. "Fine," she said. "Let's get this over with."

She waved her arm in an exaggerated invitation for them to step inside. Once they were over the threshold, she glanced out into the street, pulled a face at the houses opposite, and slammed the door behind her.

"This'll give them something to talk about." She pushed between them and walked down the whitewashed hall to the kitchen. "I hope you don't think I'm going to offer refreshments."

Cade snorted as they followed her into the large room. It was all glossy red cabinets and stainless steel appliances. Maria took a bottle out of the fridge and poured herself a glass of wine; red liquid nudged right up to the lip of the glass.

"So?" she asked as she climbed up onto a stool next to the island. "What do you want? So I can tell you that you can't have it."

"We want to talk to Piper," Marlow said. The words felt weird in his mouth. It wasn't something he'd expected to say.

"Well, he doesn't want to talk to you," Maria said. She held up a finger to shush Marlow when he went to speak. "And before you ask, that's straight from Piper's mouth. He said everything he was going to say to the San Diego Police Department when they arrested him."

Cade leaned back against one of the counters and crossed his arms.

"That's fine," he said. "Marlow's the cop, not me. I don't give a fuck what Piper did or why. I care about who's taken over from him."

A sly smirk tucked the corner of Maria's mouth. "Yeah, you don't need to worry about that."

"Because it's you?" Marlow asked.

"I'm not an ambitious woman," Maria told him. She gestured to the books laid out in front of her. "You think if I was a kingpin, I'd be marking Spanish homework for suburban kids who don't know how to conjugate irregular verbs?'

"Do you know Lance Rilkes?" Cade asked.

Suspicion flickered over Maria's face for a second. She covered it with a gulp of wine, then wiped the corner of her mouth with her thumb. Once she'd gotten control of her reaction, she shook her head.

"Doesn't ring a bell."

"Liar," Marlow said off-handedly. She glared at him, and he mirrored the corner-of-the-mouth wipe for her. "Your tells haven't changed."

She made a sour face at him and turned back to Cade.

"So maybe I do," she said with an annoyed shrug. "What's it to you?"

"Nothing," Cade said. "But Piper kept in touch with him, didn't he? So he'll probably want to know that someone from the Night Shift tried to grab him tonight. They wanted to know what he knew about Piper, about the business."

Maria pinched the stem of the wineglass between her fingers and turned it in small, nervous circles on the counter.

"I can't imagine he'd know anything."

"Are you sure about that?" Cade asked. "Enough to make the call on your own?"

She licked her lips and then lifted the glass to drain it in one quick, abrupt toss of her head.

"He'll want proof," she said. "That it was Lance."

"Check the news," Cade said.

Marlow straightened up and took a step forward. He pulled a sheet of someone's homework toward him and picked up a pen. It was green, not red. He supposed that was meant to make corrections friendlier. He flipped the page over and scrawled on the back of it.

"He told me who really did what needed to be done."

At the end of the sentence, he hesitated. It felt like there should be something more to add, something he needed to say to the man who'd tried to kill him. He underlined it instead.

"Tell him that," he said as he slid it back over the table. "Exactly."

Maria glanced at the paper and pulled an unimpressed face. "I'll see what I can do," she said. "But he's a busy man, lots of demands on his time. Anything else?"

No. Marlow supposed there wasn't. Not here, anyhow.

"Coffee?" Marlow asked as Cade pulled up to the curb outside his house. It sounded awkward and out of place, too normal for the adrenaline that still itched under his skin and made his knee bounce.

Not to mention, he remembered, that Cade didn't drink coffee.

The offer hung in the air as Marlow tried to think of a way to rescue it. Cade turned the engine off and unclicked his seat belt.

"Actually, I thought I could get even," he said as he leaned over into Marlow's side of the car. "I've still not seen you naked, and you've seen everything I've got."

Marlow tilted the corner of his mouth in a smirk. He could feel the warmth of Cade's body as it *almost* touched his. "At the time, I was trying not to stare," he pointed out.

Cade plucked Marlow's glasses off. "Tried and failed."

The last few weeks of silence and unspoken grudges should have given Marlow pause, but whatever *that* had been about, this was still easy. He hooked his fingers into the waistband of Cade's trousers and closed the distance between them for a quick kiss.

It was a hard brush of dry lips, and there shouldn't have been anything sexy about it. The promise of what was next prickled in it, though, and made Marlow's breath catch in his throat.

"Never let it be said I needed an unfair advantage," he said as he leaned back. Cade handed him his glasses, and he tucked them into the pocket of his jacket. "Come in, and we can level the playing field. I only wear underwear in bed."

Cade laughed, a careless snort of amusement without any of the usual caution Cade brought to any emotion.

"That's not going to work for me," he said. "In bed is when I want you naked."

They got out of the car and got two steps up the drive before Cade pulled Marlow back in for another kiss. His mouth was hard, rough with impatience, and he ran his hand down Marlow's back to squeeze the curve of his ass.

"At least this time no one is going to overhear us," Cade muttered as they stumbled toward the house. He glanced up briefly at the other houses on the street and amended his statement. "No one I care about, anyhow.

Marlow shrugged and grabbed the hem of his T-shirt to pull it off.

"Me either," he said as he stepped backward.

Cade swore, soft and ragged, under his breath and didn't wait for Marlow to finish stripping. The two of them stumbled backward up the step onto the porch, tangled in the T-shirt and each other. Marlow managed to drag his T-shirt up over his head, the night air cool on his skin, and leaned into the kiss. Cade's hand slid down his back and tucked into the waistband of his jeans; his callused fingers just grazed along the curve of Marlow's ass. The T-shirt draped over Cade's shoulder, still tangled in Marlow's hand, as he cupped the back of Cade's neck to pull him down.

The broken board—the one that Marlow had gotten so used to sidestepping it didn't seem worth the hassle to fix it—gave under his foot. He muttered a curse into Cade's mouth and yanked his sneaker out of the hole. His laces got caught on a nail on the way out, and he had to hop in place for a second to catch his balance.

Not quite the seasoned Night Shift officer aura of cool competence someone might expect.

"You should get that fixed," Cade told him. The curve of his mouth was smug under Marlow's as he edged them both around the gap and pushed Marlow up against the door.

"Good idea," Marlow deadpanned. He tilted his head back against the wood and looked up at Cade. "Amazing, I never thought of that."

"I know a man," Cade offered.

Marlow laughed, hooked his fingers into the collar of Cade's shirt, and pulled him down for a tease of a kiss—a brush of lips and a quick scrape of his teeth over Cade's lower lip. "If you're looking to set a record, I have been dumped after a first date before."

His brain caught up with his mouth a second too late, and Marlow felt his ears sting with sudden, embarrassed uncertainty. That wasn't what this was. Not that either of them had actually discussed what "this" was in any sort of detail, but nobody had mentioned "dates" before now.

"Is that what this is," Cade said. He nudged his thigh between Marlow's and used his hips to pin him in place. This kiss wasn't a tease. It was insistent, possessive, and sharp enough that Marlow tasted the tang of blood on his tongue. His or Cade's, he couldn't tell. When Cade finally lifted his head, his eyes dark and hard to read in the dim light, Marlow was breathless and hard enough to make him squirm. "A date? Most boys want dinner, not a shootout."

Marlow reached back and twisted the knob that dug into his hip. He had locked it when he left this morning, but that was mainly just to discourage opportunistic kids who snuck up the path to rattle the door. The mechanism was old and loose. All you had to do was hold the knob all the way around and give the door a nudge with your knee. Or hip, this time. But it still worked.

The door swung open and they stumbled inside, clumsy as they traded kisses and pulled at each other's clothes on the way through the living room. Marlow toed his Converse off and left one on the mat by the door and the other kicked under the bookcase. His T-shirt was tossed over the TV. Cade's jacket was dropped on the floor, and his shirt ended up over the back of the couch as they fell onto it.

"Not how I expected the night to end," Cade said as he sprawled on top of Marlow. He nudged Marlow's head to the side and kissed his throat. "Not that I'm complaining."

Marlow stretched out under Cade, their legs twisted together, and cupped the other man's head in his hand. The curls were soft and thick under his palm. He tilted his head back against the couch cushion to bare more throat to Cade's mouth.

"How did you want it to end?" he asked.

Cade laughed, his breath cool against damp skin. "Like this," he said. "But sooner. I just didn't expect it."

Marlow's cock throbbed in dull counterpoint to the eager ache in his balls as Cade shifted on top of him. It nudged insistently against Cade's hip as he settled his weight. He slid his hands down Cade's back to explore the long, taut straps of muscle under tanned skin.

"Maybe next time you take me to dinner instead of a gunfight," Marlow suggested, his voice ragged. "It won't take up so much of the evening."

Cade's mouth slowed down against his throat, and after a moment, he lifted his head. The light from the crescent moon that filtered through the window picked out the gold flecks in his amber eyes.

"So," he said in a voice that sounded carefully skeptical. "This really has been your idea of a date?"

Marlow cupped Cade's face in his hand. He ran his thumb along the scabbed-over line that skimmed along Cade's cheekbone and up into his hair.

"Not a typical date," he admitted. "Date-adjacent. If you want it to be."

He waited. Cade turned his head and pressed a kiss to the pulse point in Marlow's wrist. Some atavistic instinct twitched as Marlow had a borderline tactile thought about how easily Cade's wolf would have taken his hand off. He ignored it. Some things you just couldn't dwell on.

"What would move it over into a real date?"

"Ask me to dinner."

The challenge in that sentence hung in the space between their lips. It was Cade's turn to ignore something he didn't want to look at. He rolled them both over so he sprawled out along the couch, one leg dangled off the side to brace against the floor, and Marlow straddled him. Cade's face looked softer from this angle, the hard lines blurred, but his expression was still carefully noncommital.

"Why don't you ask me?" Cade asked, as if the answer didn't matter.

And maybe it didn't. It might *feel* like Marlow had seen a side of Cade that other people didn't, but a couple of kisses and a conspiracy was no way to get to know someone. Even if Cade was the only person in Marlow's life he could trust right now. Maybe especially because of that.

He pushed that itch of thought away and smiled crookedly down at Cade.

"I could, but you're rich, and I can't take overtime until I'm cleared to go back on active duty."

Cade laughed, a startled and inelegant snort of a sound. It caught in his throat, and he choked it down. His hands stilled on Marlow's hips, placed gingerly as if he thought he could snap something.

"Are you… Were you hurt?" he asked. "That night?"

Oh.

There was a reason that nulls with ambition on the force wanted onto the Night Shift. It was common knowledge they didn't have the nose for a hunt a detective needed. Eventually though, Marlow supposed, as all the puzzle pieces clicked together, even the most oblivious had to see what was right under their nose.

"Shit," Marlow said as it finally dawned on him. "That's what I did. Why you didn't want to see me."

Cade scowled, his face all sharp lines and impassive beauty again, as he tilted his head back against the cushions. It let him look down his nose at Marlow with a dismissive sneer. "Don't put words in my mouth. Not many people are smart enough."

"Don't be an asshole."

Cade took a breath, and Marlow was pretty sure he was going to do the opposite of what Marlow had just asked him. So he kissed him to shut him up. There were worse ways to do it, less enjoyable too.

The kiss started out deliberate and then turned into something desperate. Cade's hands tightened on Marlow's hips, hesitation forgotten as he pulled him down. Marlow leaned into it and chased the taste of Cade between his lips and over his tongue. It felt like something he needed, like a man needed a drink of water on a warm day.

Marlow wasn't going to think about why. Or about how long it had been since someone, anyone, had cared if they'd hurt him.

He pulled away finally, his lips tender, and looked down as he tugged at the buttons on Cade's trousers.

"Fuck," Cade groaned, his voice caught, low and husky, in his throat. He got his elbows under him and hitched his hips off the couch to make Marlow's job easier.

Marlow hesitated for a second as the taut play of muscle under tanned skin made him fumble as he forgot how buttons worked. His mouth went dry, and his breath caught in his throat as heat crawled up his neck.

It wasn't fair. When you'd seen someone naked once, by rights, it should lose some impact.

Apparently not.

Marlow got his mind back to the task in front of him and finished undoing Cade's trousers. He dipped his hand inside and curled his fingers around Cade's cock. It was heavy and warm against his palm, the thick weight of it solid under a layer of thin, velvet-soft skin. Blood pulsed quick and eager against his palm. He dragged his thumb over the head, slick and wet with precome, and leaned in to swipe his tongue up Cade's throat at the same time.

He tasted like salt, a film of sweat faintly bitter on his skin, and he groaned out another soft "Fuck" as Marlow tightened his grip on his cock. Fine skin creased under Marlow's calloused fingers as he stroked the hard shaft.

"I should have called you," he said. "Let you know I was okay. I just… I knew wolves didn't remember what happened the day after. I guess I just didn't think what that meant. It always—the Night Shift always talks about it like a 'get out of jail free' card."

Cade tilted his head back, the line of his throat taut and smooth, and stared at the ceiling.

"The last thing I remember was seeing you," he said. "Night Shift or not, I knew you couldn't have gotten away. Not with no gear. No weapons. No backup."

"I did, though."

"How?" Cade asked as he looked at Marlow. The genuine curiosity in his voice cut through the anger like a splash of lemon. "When I woke up, I knew—I *knew*—I had to have killed you."

"I blew the car up and ran like fuck while you were on fire. Sorry."

It took a second, but Cade started to laugh. It left him breathless and whooping as he tangled himself around Marlow, chuckled kisses warm and ticklish against Marlow's throat and jaw.

"You're a dangerous man," he said. "But I guess I knew that."

"I am sorry," Marlow said.

"For setting me on fire or for not realizing I thought I'd eaten you?"

Marlow exhaled against Cade's lips, a tickle of breath against kiss-damp flesh. He dragged his hand along Cade's cock, a slow, lazy stroke, and felt Cade tense under him in response. "Both?"

"I told you before," Cade said. "It's okay."

"Tell me that tomorrow," Marlow said. "When you ask me to dinner."

Cade laughed, low and rough and warm as honey, and Marlow's cock ached under his jeans. He slid his hand down to the base of Cade's cock and cupped his balls, tight and hot in Marlow's palm as he squeezed them. He could *feel* the thrum of the string that sent a bolt of pleasure from them to the back of Cade's skull, the wire-taut tension of it under his fingers.

Sweat slicked their skin, sharp with the salt and the stale adrenaline from the fight earlier. Cade bit kisses along Marlow's neck and shoulder, wet and messy and careless. There was no real sensation in the white welt of scar tissue on Marlow's shoulder, but he could still feel the pressure of Cade's teeth as he bit down and the wet of his tongue.

His own balls were heavy and tight between his legs, a dull pressure that spread out into his gut, and he ground against Cade's thigh. It was almost silent, all soft grunts and gasps and bitten-back whimpers. Cade came first, with a hot-breathed groan against Marlow's ear. He clenched one hand on the edge of the couch, fingers dug into the worn fabric and the tendons in his wrist taut, as he spilled himself, wet and sticky, into Marlow's hand. When he finished, he licked his lips and pushed himself up into a sitting position. Marlow was perched on his lap, his knees braced either side of Cade's hips.

"Your turn," Cade said, his voice rough in his throat from being quiet until now.

Marlow leaned back, one hand braced against Cade's heavy thigh, and lazily wiped the other on his stomach—come smeared across pale skin.

"Go on, then," he said.

Cade raised his eyebrows at the lazy goad but took the bait anyhow. He leaned in and… almost… kissed Marlow. He pulled back before their lips touched and shoved Marlow down onto the couch.

Marlow sprawled out on the cushions, so hard it hurt. A lazy, wicked smile curved Cade's mouth as he looked down at him. After a moment, he leaned over and trailed kisses over Marlow's shoulders and chest.

Then further down.

Wet, openmouthed kisses laid a trail down Marlow's body, between and across the spray of old scars and down to the salty gloss on his abs. Heat puddled after them.

Lower.

Shit.

Marlow bit his lip and tilted his head back, his breath tight as it squeezed through his throat when Cade reached his stomach. Soft lips and a wet tongue teased his belly button as Cade tugged at his trousers.

Expectation hitched in Marlow's chest and in his balls, a tug of pleasure that held him ready for—

His phone rang, a hard rattle against his hip bone as it vibrated. Marlow should have ignored it—he wanted to ignore it—but a decade of ingrained habits made him shove Cade back so he could grab it instead.

"Sorry," he mouthed as he swiped over the screen to accept the call. His thumb, sticky with sweat and come, left a smear on the glass. When he lifted it to his ear, it smelled like sex. He ignored that. "Marlow."

"Is that fucker with you?" Bennett demanded.

The question made Marlow glance at Cade, who'd slouched back against the cushions with an expression of sullen patience on his face. Marlow opened his mouth to say yes, but Bennett talked over him.

"Franklin crashed my car," Bennett ranted, too furious to realize Marlow had misunderstood her at first. "Totaled it, complete write-off. Now the shithead has gone to get drunk and lie low. Like he can avoid me when we're on the same shift."

"You want me to call you an Uber?"

"Yeah," Bennett said. "To your house. He's still got my keys."

Marlow scratched his head, his hair sweaty and matted as he dug his fingers into it. There was a good chance she'd tried to kill him, that she'd worked for Piper all these years.

"Look, if it's a problem, I can go to a hotel," Bennett said. "Whatever. Enjoy your Hungry Man microwave meal."

"Okay."

She snorted down the line at him. He heard a door slam behind her and what sounded like a bar in the background. "Come on. I need a shower and a good night's sleep."

"Text me the address," Marlow sighed as he swung his legs off the couch and stood up. His balls ached in complaint as his jeans pulled tight over them. "I'll come and get you."

Bennett sighed in relief. "See?" she said. "This is why you deserve that promotion—and why you aren't going to get it at the same time."

She hung up.

"Seriously?" Cade asked as he slung one arm along the back of the couch. His jeans were still undone. "You're going to pick her over me?"

Shit.

"I know. I'm sorry," Marlow said as he padded over and bent down to pull his shoe out from under the shelf. "It's just—"

Cade shoved himself up off the couch and tucked himself in. "I'm teasing. I get it. She's your squad. You show up. I'd do the same for my people. Probably."

The Converse sneaker dangled from Marlow's fingers by a grubby lace as he looked at Cade. It felt like something in his chest had just unclenched for the first time in years. Since he woke up in the middle of the night to someone hammering on the door. He hesitated for a second, but one of them had to do it. "Do you want to go out with me?" he asked. "On a date."

Cade zipped up and came over to pull Marlow into a slow, sweet kiss. His thumb stroked up Marlow's neck to the tender spot under his ear. After a moment, he leaned back.

"I'll think about it," he said as he grabbed his shirt and headed out.

Marlow caught his breath and stepped back to pull his shoe on. "Asshole."

CHAPTER EIGHT

IT WAS EMOTIONAL edging.

Cade sprawled in the leather chair behind his desk, legs stretched out in front of him. Most of his attention, 90 percent, was on the contract to provide personal security for a Russian politician's family when they came to California. So far, they had agreed to Cade's moderately inflated quote with no haggling but refused to discuss the reason they thought they needed protection. So either they just wanted bodyguards for the bragging rights, or they owed money to the Russian mob. One or the other. It didn't make much difference, the operatives would be briefed to expect the worst and enjoy the uneventful, but Cade wanted to cover all eventualities in the Client Responsibilities rider.

The rest of Cade's attention was on the fact that he could, at any moment, call Marlow and agree to that date. He would—soon enough—but for now, he enjoyed the pleasant, restless itch of anticipation. The breathless excitement of it felt like one of those kids in Christmas movies, ready to tear into a stack of presents for the one they knew Santa had brought.

So far, he'd kept himself on the hook for a week.

It wasn't better than reality. The reality was Marlow's mouth on his throat and his hand on Cade's cock. It would take a lot to beat that. That didn't mean that Cade couldn't savor the satisfying knowledge that all he had to do to get what he wanted was say "Yes."

Cade had played out a few scenarios in the back of his mind during slow meetings over the last couple of days, but he hadn't quite decided on any of them. Maybe he'd just toss a coin… or decide what felt right in the moment.

Despite his efforts, he was still as infatuated as a teenager who'd had his first kiss.

The door to the office opened, and Lem came in. Halfway in, anyhow. Lem stopped on the threshold, one foot in and one foot out, and eyed Cade suspiciously.

"You look like the cat that saw the sunrise," he said. "What happened?"

Cade pulled his attention back to the here and now. He saved and docked the file to keep it out of a mis-mashed keystroke's way.

"Maybe I'm just in a good mood," he said, "for no particular reason."

"Yeah," Lem said, the word dragged out over his tongue. "That is not how we were raised, and you know it."

True. Cade leaned back in his chair and crossed his arms over his chest. The cuffs on his shirt rode up and flashed the heavy steel band of his watch around his wrist. "Fair enough," he said. "Maybe it's none of your business."

Lem laughed and came the rest of the way into the office.

"Yeah, that sounds more like you," he said as he threw himself down on the couch. There was a chair in front of Cade's desk, but Lem liked to have room to sprawl. He slung his arms over the back of the couch and stretched his legs out in front of him. "It looks like the hospital finally brought Rilkes around this morning. The cops haven't been let in to see him yet, but if I were them, I wouldn't hold my breath that he's going to be useful. Between the trauma and the induced coma, he'll be lucky if he knows his own name."

Maybe.

From the story he'd told in the club, Rilkes had come back from worse.

"Keep an eye on the situation," Cade said. "If he does talk to someone, I want to know about it."

Lem grinned, a wicked slant of his mouth, and put his hand over his heart. "For Cold Winds? I'll go and charm the nurses myself."

"Try to catch a surgeon," Cade suggested. "They make more money, and you have expensive tastes."

"Oh, and Night Shift officers are rolling in money?" Lem asked.

Cade felt himself blush. He scowled at Lem and tried to ignore it. It was one thing to be infatuated, another to act like he was fifteen again. Worse. At fifteen he'd had more sense and too big a chip on his shoulder to admit he wanted anyone to like him.

"Was there anything else?" he asked in a clipped voice.

Lem grinned at him but had the good sense to drop it. He sat up and pulled his phone out of his pocket so he could swipe his thumb over the screen.

"Yeah, I pulled what I could on Rilkes's comings and goings over the last year," he said. "Quick and dirty, but I grabbed his text messages and pulled location data from his cellular plan. Most of it is pretty mundane. He dated a woman for a while, but they broke up amicably enough, and he hasn't left town this year. The Mexican place near him is going to get worried when his orders stop coming in, and he owes bits and pieces of money to a variety of people."

"So that's most of it," Cade said. "What did you leave out?"

Lem looked smug. "Once a week, he texts the same mobile number. It looks like updates on a to-do list." He glanced down at his phone and started to read from the screen as he swiped the screen up. "So he says stuff like, 'Left the package where you asked,' and 'J is dating a redhead from work,' and… drumroll please… 'Went to Rankins. They said they paid your new guy.' Rankins, by the way, is a car shop over in Mesa Verde that is a front for Joe Gazaryan, the Russian mob's point man for drugs run up over the border."

"So not quite as innocent as he claimed."

Lem shrugged. "He was an errand boy," he said. "And a good one. Never asked any questions. Except once."

"Oh?"

"A week ago," Lem said.

He unfolded himself from the couch and walked over to the desk. He handed the phone to Cade so he could read the captured text. Cade scanned it quickly and repeated it aloud.

"Did you send them?" he said.

"And the only time the other mobile messaged back," Lem said. He flicked up to the one-word reply. "They told him 'No.' Not that it did him much good. The sender was in New Mexico."

Piper had a burner phone. That was unsurprising but useful. Cade tossed the phone back to Lem, who nearly fumbled the catch. It didn't wipe the smug look off his face.

"Nice work," he said. "And the surveillance footage?"

Lem looked disappointed at the abrupt shift in topic. He scowled and shoved his hands into the pockets of his jeans.

"Nothing useful," he said. "Plates were treated so they couldn't be picked up, and they ditched the car in a blind spot a few streets over, so that made it harder to track them."

"It was a long shot," Cade admitted. "They're Night Shift. They're not known for making mistakes. Good work."

Lem gave him an amused look at the compliment. "You need to marry that guy," he said firmly, a finger pointed at Cade's nose. "Lock him down. I don't think you've been in this good a mood since…."

He trailed off and blew his cheeks out as he tried to think of an example. Finally, he gave up with a shrug.

"It's not like he's my first boyfriend," Cade said defensively. "I've been happy."

Lem shrugged. "You enjoy stuff," he said. "But happy? I don't know."

"Don't you have any other work to do?" Cade asked.

"Lunch," Lem said. He checked the time on his phone. "For another two minutes. So you're my brother, not my boss. Seriously, call the man. Before *he* gets a better offer."

Cade shook his head and pulled the contract back up. "Go eat a sandwich," he told Lem. "Stay out of my private life. We'll both be happier."

He finalized the wording of the contract and sent it on to the legal department to process and send. There were three other non-urgent but time-sensitive emails in his inbox to answer and an invitation to attend a dinner party at The Reserve from one of the board members. Cade grimaced. That had always been Justin's role to play. It always put Cade's back up, because no matter how nice his suit or how impeccable his manners, he was there as the hired help. It didn't bother Justin. He'd smile as they talked down to him—and take their money as an apology.

Unfortunately, Justin wasn't on deck anymore, and after the bad press around Haley's murder, someone needed to go to keep them onside. Since Lem would probably sleep with a board member's wife, or son, to get out of ever having to do it again, that left Cade.

He supposed he could ask Marlow. It wasn't an unpleasant idea—although Marlow probably wouldn't turn up in full Night Shift gear… despite Cade's brief fantasy of exactly that—and it wasn't a bad one either. People respected the Night Shift.

If he hadn't changed his mind. The snide voice of his inferiority complex wormed through Cade's brain. You would have by now, it pointed out, if you'd asked him out and he left you hanging.

His inferiority complex had a point. And it was a smug bastard.

Cade reached for his phone again. This time he hesitated, fingers just above the case, as he tried to convince himself it would be better to ghost Marlow now than risk being rejected. If Marlow chased him, then he'd get what he wanted without having to admit he wanted it.

Or he'd not get anything.

Cade grimaced to himself at that old craven impulse. He wasn't the school reject anymore. If Marlow turned him down, he'd survive. And he was successful now, so he could find someone new easily enough—someone better.

There was something satisfying in the bitterness of that. It lingered on Cade's tongue like sour candy, even though he couldn't *quite* come up with any idea of who would be better.

He grabbed the phone. It buzzed to life the minute he touched it, and he thought, for a second, that Marlow had caved first. Which would still mean Cade won. The screen claimed it was an Unknown Number. He didn't get cold calls, so that didn't leave a lot of options.

There was only one way to find out.

He answered the call.

"You wanted to talk to me," a man said. "So talk."

Ned Piper had been born and raised in Phelan, California. He'd not kept that accent. In the various bits and pieces of footage that Cade had found—news interviews, a single appeal for witnesses, a feature on his work breaking the local packs, and one ironic PSA where he told kids to stay indoors and trust the Night Shift—Piper had acquired a convincing coastal drawl. Not perfect, but most people would have believed he came from La Jolla or even up past LA.

Five years in New Mexico had worn the edges off that. He sounded like he came from nowhere now. But he still sounded like someone who could talk you into doing anything without asking any questions until it was too late.

"How's Rilkes?"

"Dead," he lied.

"If you want anything from me, I need to trust you."

Cade stood in front of the long glass windows and stared out over the marina and the flat gray strip of ocean.

"You're a convict, a crooked cop, and you called me on a contraband phone to ask about the man you paid to do your dirty work while you were locked up," he said. "I don't think I'm the one whose character is in doubt."

Piper snorted. "You don't get to be where you are without breaking some rules, Mr. Deacon," he said. "How far would I have to dig to find the bodies?"

"See, that's the difference," Cade said. "In my line of work, the bodies go on my CV. Not in shallow graves."

"They weren't that shallow," Piper said. "And don't bother with the bleeding heart routine. I might have made money from it, but no one I… dealt with… was innocent."

"Even Marlow?"

It was a genuine question. Cade guessed he hadn't dismissed those initial doubts about how deep Marlow's involvement in Piper's gang had gone.

"Yeah, well," Piper said. "There's an exception to every rule. I'd not go so far as to call him innocent, but that was the only call I regret. Not just because it put me in here. Maria said he was with you. Is he still a stubborn little bastard?"

There was a flicker of something in Piper's voice. It wasn't quite affection, but it was close enough to put Cade's hackles up. Admiration, maybe, or pride. As if he was still Marlow's commanding officer and could take credit for *anything* Marlow was.

He wasn't wrong, though.

"Yeah," Cade said. "He is."

"So telling you both to stay out of this and let me handle it, that's going to work?"

Cade smiled thinly. He could see the dim reflection of it in the glass, sharp and unhappy. It was over a week until the next full moon. He couldn't blame the wolf for how feral it was.

"He won't," Cade said. "And they tried to use me as a murder weapon on the full moon, so I have my reasons too. Who is it?"

Silence for a second. Cade could hear the low background noise of the prison, the sound of hundreds of people breathing in concrete boxes. It made him feel claustrophobic by proxy.

"How's Rilkes?" Piper repeated the question.

This time Cade answered. "In hospital," he said. "Still critical. They didn't want to kill him, but they weren't too worried if they did."

"Poor bastard was always in the wrong place at the wrong time," Piper said wearily. Then he cleared his throat. "I don't name names. That's what kept me alive. As long as they trust me to keep my mouth shut, it's not worth risking any fail-safes I might have set up in case I met an unfortunate end. Once I start talking to the authorities, killing me is worth the risk."

"You think whoever is out there, taking over what's left of your empire, is going to let you live?" Cade asked. "Whatever deal you had with them before, it's obviously been broken. They found Rilkes. How long before they find Maria? Once they find her, they get everything, and then what good are you?"

Piper laughed. It was a short huff of sound, bitter but genuine. Apparently, he could still see the funny side.

"Sorry to tell you, but there's not much left for them to find," he said. "Back when I was first sent away, sure. I still had fingers in pies and debts to call in. But attrition is a terrible thing. People retired, got caught. Died. Fuck, one woman I could have hung a dozen… bad things… on got religion and joined a nunnery. These days? I could make some mid-level gangsters' lives uncomfortable. Maybe. People still think I have juice, but… five years is a long time in a high-risk profession."

"And the people in Night Shift who were still loyal to you?"

Piper sucked his teeth. "I know my legacy is going to be this," he said. Cade imagined the gesture that took in his cell, the cot, and whatever luxuries his reputation had kept him in. "But even if I wasn't a good cop, I was good at being a cop. My people knew that I'd take care of them—that what I did was to make our job easier. Make people safer—"

"Line your pockets," Cade corrected him. He had no control over what Piper told himself, but he didn't have any reason to go along with the revisionist history lesson.

"Every month, we go out and put our lives on the line," Piper snapped. "You're a wolf, Mr. Deacon. You don't know what it's like to see your family, your friends, the fucking plumber become a killing machine that won't even remember murdering you the next day. New York pays Night Shift a stipend and a bonus if they are hurt on the job. We get basic pay. Night Shift can't even claim overtime during the full moon. So what if I found a way to make enough money that it was worth our while? No one got hurt. No one who mattered."

"Liar," Cade threw Piper's accusation back in his teeth. "And I don't care, so why are you telling me this shit?"

"People were loyal to me because I kept them alive and kept a roof over their head," Piper said. "And I looked the part doing it. Been a while since I did anything other than pass the time between waking up and going to sleep. Hard to inspire much loyalty that way. Not when there's someone else on the scene pulling their asses out of the fire and putting cash in their pockets."

"And who's that?" He didn't get an answer. "Piper, whoever it is put the closest thing you have to a friend in the hospital. You and them? You aren't working together anymore. They've left you behind."

"I left them behind," Piper corrected him. "That mess in The Reserve, with the traps? That wasn't my style. It wasn't *business*; it was personal. That was always their problem. Me, I like to keep things… transactional."

Cade clenched his free fist in frustration and thumped it against the window a couple of times.

"What do you want?"

"My life back."

The glass was cold against Cade's knuckles as he leaned on it. "Try again."

"I'm not here to bargain."

"No, you're there to pay," Cade said. "You did what you did, and you didn't do it well enough to get away with it. Now you expect me to fix that for you? This is the hole you dug for yourself."

"Yeah, well, now I'm in that hole, it's full of shit," Piper said. "I want out. Out of prison, out of the system, and out of *fucking* New Mexico."

"I can't get you that."

"If I were you, I'd try," Piper said. "I talk to you, I end up dead. I don't talk to you, same endgame. So you better have an ace in the hole to change the course of this game."

Cade stepped away from the window before he tried to put his fist through it. The glass wouldn't break, it was bulletproof and reinforced, and he'd just look stupid.

"The funny thing is, Piper, that Marlow is probably the only person in San Diego who still remembers when you were a good cop."

"That's his problem. I tried to kill him; he should know better."

Resentment tasted like iron on Cade's tongue, like the apples his stepmother pierced with nails to let the metal leech out into the flesh. Growing up in Alaska meant being short of some sort of vitamin or mineral during the year—unless it was one that came from game meat and beer.

"Yeah, I'd have learned my lesson," Cade said. "Marlow, he likes to think the best of people."

"Yeah?" Piper said. The background noise got louder as the prisoners shouted abuse at the guards on their rounds. The lazy drawl left Piper's voice, and his words came out clipped and deliberate. "Well, get me what I want or real soon Marlow's going to be disappointed in someone else. One thing my… associate… told me before he left? Third time's the charm on killing a cat. Marlow isn't going to see another full moon out without my help."

He hung up.

Cade gave in to the urge and punched the window. He split the skin over his knuckles and dripped blood on the wooden floor as he called down to the legal department.

"Two?" the guy behind the counter asked, two fingers held up to check the order. When Cade nodded his agreement, the man turned and yelled it back into the kitchen, voice pitched to carry over the din of service. Then he gestured for Cade to move along to the other end of the shop, where he joined the short queue of people ready to pay.

Cade rolled his eyes in annoyance at the wait and checked his phone. His last message to Marlow was still unread, without even a flickering row of dots to show willing. Doubt made the back of

Cade's neck itch as he considered the unpleasant prospect of having to choke down two bowls of shrimp noodles on his own. Just in case anyone thought he'd been stood up.

The woman ahead of him handed her money over and took her tray in exchange. Cade stepped back to give her room to get by, and a lean black-clad arm reached past him to pay. Two crisp twenties and a "Keep the change" from Marlow won a quick nod of thanks from the woman behind the counter before she turned her attention to the next in the queue.

"I had it," he said, his voice stiff in his throat as he lifted his carton from the tray. "You didn't need to pay."

Cade could have bought the restaurant, if he wanted, and made the staff make him mac and cheese. With the cash in his wallet, he could have paid for the next two hours of customers to eat on his tab. Yet he could still feel the dull ache of kicked pride in his chest and a weird sort of panic clutch at his throat.

If Marlow didn't want his money, wasn't seduced by the lifestyle, then what the hell did Cade have to offer him?

Nothing.

That answer came from the scrawny seventeen-year-old he'd been, who'd too much pride and not much else. Cade had come a long way from then, but he'd need to think about it for a while before he could come up with a better one.

"I asked you out," Marlow reminded him. "My shout. I did expect you to pick somewhere fancier. With seats, maybe?"

Cade considered that for a second and decided he could live with it.

"According to Piper, you guys don't get paid that much," he said as he popped the styrofoam lid. Savory fishy steam rose from the sauce-covered shrimp piled on top of the bed of sticky noodles. Cade grabbed a pair of chopsticks from the small table at the door and stripped the paper off with his teeth. "So I thought I'd cut you a break."

Marlow paused mid-reach for his utensils.

"You spoke to him?"

"He called me." Cade glanced at the cluster of people by the counter. They all had their attention, one way or another, on the food. He gestured with the sticky chopsticks for Marlow to follow him outside. There still weren't any seats, but there was a wall to lean on. "Bit of an asshole, isn't he?"

"That's one word for him," Marlow said. He poked absently at the food until the shrimp was half-buried under the noodles. "What does he want?"

Cade raised his eyebrows. "What makes you think he wants anything?"

"If he'd told you anything, you would have led with that. So, what does he want?"

On the street, a cop car drove slowly by. Cade watched it pass and only relaxed when it turned the corner. His spats with the local LEOs were a game. They might not have thought so, but Cade knew just how far to push it. He was a thorn in their side they couldn't afford to touch.

This was different. Whoever had taken over from Piper in the Night Shift wasn't constrained by the SDPD's rule book.

"Let me worry about that," he said.

Marlow gave a humorless bark of laughter. "Easier said than done. Whatever it is, however he wants out of prison, tell him no."

"I've not promised him anything," Cade dodged around the truth. "And you're wrong, he did tell me something."

"What?"

"He wouldn't give me their name, but he said whoever it was planned to kill you."

Both of them made a living out of violence one way or another, so Cade didn't expect Marlow to faint. But he had expected more reaction than the shrimp's brief pause in midair, dangled from cheap chopsticks, before Marlow popped it into his mouth.

"We knew that."

Cade jabbed a chopstick in Marlow's direction. "During the next full moon. In a week. You need to fail your next physical. Give us time to find more leverage on Piper."

"No."

"He thinks he has the upper—" Cade stopped as he realized what Marlow had just said. "What?"

"I'm Night Shift," Marlow said. "I can take care of myself. Besides, I wasn't on duty the first time someone tried to kill me. I'd rather be armed and combat-ready if anyone is going to try something. Not balls-out naked and half-asleep."

It sort of sounded like it made sense. It didn't *feel* that way, though.

"Stay at mine," he said. "Out in the sticks. No one around but wolves."

Marlow ate the last shrimp tangled in thick, ribbony noodles, and neatly boxed up what was left.

"If they try and kill me, we'll know who they are," he said as he walked away to toss his leftovers in the bin. "Then Piper won't have anything to trade, will he?"

"Or you'll be dead," Cade pointed out.

Marlow considered that as he wiped his hands on a napkin on the way back.

"Well, then you can talk to Piper," he said after a moment. "I won't care anymore."

Cade growled under his breath. He could feel the itch along the nape of his neck where it wanted to be hackles. The moon wasn't full enough to turn him inside out and let the wolf out, but he could feel it turn under his skin.

"I'll be careful," Marlow promised. "Besides, if you couldn't kill me, what hope do they have?"

Cade swallowed, the taste of spicy shrimp gone rancid on his tongue as he remembered the greasy puke he'd *thought* was Marlow.

"That's not funny." Cade caught Marlow's waist and pulled him closer. He leaned down until their foreheads touched, his mouth not quite against Marlow's lips. "If you get killed, I'm going to make O'Hara's life a misery. The whole SDPD is going to regret that I ever moved here."

Marlow kissed him. It was rough and desperate, the only break in Marlow's cool composure, and his hand dug into the back of Cade's neck. Cade held his food clumsily to the side, the sauce hot enough to sting his fingers through the styrofoam.

"They already do," Marlow said as he finally stepped back. "And I'm not going anywhere. Next date's on you, remember? I want to see if you can actually ask me out *without* insulting me somehow."

He grinned at Cade's glare and left.

Cade watched him go for a heartbeat; then he tossed the remnants of his meal away. Sauce and shrimp splattered the sides of the bin and soaked down through the trash and discarded objects. He pulled his phone out of his pocket and called back into the office.

"Get Maria Cafolla off the streets," he said as he headed away from the restaurant. "I want her safe, and I want her out of communication. It doesn't matter how."

He hung up before Lem could protest. It was time to turn the heat up on Piper.

CHAPTER NINE

"I WASN'T EXPECTING you tonight," Captain Mila Gil, the Night Shift version of O'Hara, said as she stopped in front of Marlow's desk. She narrowed her eyes, a spray of wrinkles creased into the corners, as she looked down at him. "Have they cleared you for duty?"

A casual tap of the mouse hid the files that Marlow had pulled up. No one had told him he couldn't look into the recent spate of post-shift deaths, and that wouldn't change as long as no one knew what he was doing.

"Yes," he said. "I'm fighting fit."

"Good," Gil said. "Because I don't care if your liver just fell out your ass. It's a blue moon tonight, and if you don't have a death certificate and a note from your mother, I want all hands on deck."

"I'm getting a head start," Marlow said. He pointed to Victor Clemons's file on his desk. "Captain O'Hara asked me to follow up on that complaint. Nothing actionable, but it's worth keeping an eye on over the next few nights. Acrimonious breakup, and the wolf still sees the house as his territory. His ex disagrees. There's been a few incidents."

Gil looked sour. "Breakups like that?" she said. "They're why I work on my marriage. Divorce isn't worth that. Add it to the briefing folder and go get some coffee. I don't want you dying on me halfway through the night."

"Me neither," Marlow said with a wry smile.

She snorted and walked away. Marlow stared after her while his mind tangled itself in erratic, suspicious knots. It could have been a chance choice of words, or it could have been a taunt at someone she thought was still oblivious to the plan to kill them. Who better to run a gang of corrupt Night Shift officers than the person who ran the rest of the Night Shift?

Except, Marlow reminded himself, Gil had transferred from Vegas nine months after Piper's arrest. It didn't mean she was clean, but it meant she wasn't in charge. Whoever that was, they'd known Piper. Until recently, they'd worked for him. Or at least kept in contact.

So, he could eliminate Gil from the list of suspects. That just left the rest of the Night Shift. Not a comforting thought.

Marlow pulled the files back up and flicked through the tabs. They were the deaths he'd talked to Cade about, finally collected in one place after Sargeant Windsor in San Marcos unearthed the last one filed in the system with the wrong case number.

People died during the full moon. Not many, not like in the old days, but always a few. Even with the Night Shift on their A-game, they couldn't stop that.

Mostly nulls. People misjudged their curfew or just wanted the thrill of outrunning a wolf and got caught out on the street. Or they rolled the dice on a wolf picking their home out of all the other houses on the street and didn't put in proper security.

Wolves died too, though: a bad enough accident, a fight with another wolf that did more damage than their bodies could stitch back together, or a trap. Not often, though. Mostly, if wolves died, it was the morning after. They'd shift back and find themselves naked and somewhere they might not recognize. They didn't often leave their territory—although there were always a few cases a year of someone who headed north and got as far as LA, or sometimes even San Francisco—but that still left plenty of opportunities to get lost. They woke up in the wilderness and didn't have the wolf's survival instincts or healing ability to get home.

So, other than the number of them, most of the deaths weren't unusual.

Except for Clara Walker. She'd jumped off the Coronado Bridge, and that was weird. Wolves committed suicide during the new moon, not during the honeymoon period after the shift. The wolf was too close to the surface then, and it wanted to live.

In the photo, Clara was a pretty woman with clear brown eyes and curly black hair. Or she had been. The other photos were more brutal, but the autopsy hadn't shown any sign of foul play.

She'd done it herself. But why?

Marlow read on down through the report. No history of depression, her job had been secure, and while there was a recent breakup, her family said she'd started to date again. Halfway through the transcript of the interview with Clara's sister, the woman said that the breakup hadn't been a surprise.

"…they never talked, he was always at work, but she said he'd at least given her a good idea for her podcast."

Marlow flicked back up and then down to the bottom of the file. There was no other mention of the podcast. He pulled up Google and had just started a search when the door swung open and the rookie stumbled in, laden down with half the squad's packs.

"I got it!" the rookie said gamely as he headed for the locker rooms. He didn't look like he had. "It's okay!"

Marlow closed down the files and pushed himself back from the desk. He intercepted the rookie just as the closed door broke the kid's forward momentum and his carefully balanced burden started to shift. Marlow relieved him of four packs, one after the other, and stacked them on Bennett's desk.

"You don't have to do everyone's scutwork, you know," Marlow said as he pulled a rifle slipcover from under the rookie's arm. "Just your job."

"Speak for yourself, Marlow," Franklin corrected him as he loped into the room, big, blond, and genial in a Raider's hoodie. "Senior officers get to call the training shots."

"I'm senior to you," Marlow pointed out.

"Really?" the rookie asked.

"Six months," Marlow said.

Franklin scowled at him and grabbed his bag off the table. He swung it up onto his back in one easy movement.

"Marlow was Night Shift's backup choice after I got injured in the line of duty before my first shift," he told the rookie. "He took my slot, and I had to wait until I was fit for duty again. Same thing that would have happened to you if you'd broken that arm a month ago. So you should count yourself lucky you're even allowed in here to do scutwork."

The rookie flushed and hitched his shoulder up to hold the kit bags in place as he scratched at the frayed edge of his cast.

"I do," he said. "I know I fucked up. I should have been more careful. It's my fault you're going out there short-handed."

Franklin looked conflicted. Marlow had seen the look before, as Franklin's desire to be a dick butted up against his hatred of the city bureaucracy. The hatred won.

"I'll tell you a little secret about how this town is run," Franklin said as he clapped his hand on the other man's shoulder. "And when I say run, I mean run into the ground. The—"

Marlow had heard this one before. He unearthed his kit—just the Kevlar and weapons, anything silver he had to sign out himself—and headed to get changed. Rude, maybe, but he might get killed tonight. He didn't want Franklin's opinion on where city funds should be spent to be one of the last memories he made.

"Fuck me. I got it in my mouth," Bennett said. She took a swig of water, swilled it around her mouth, and then spat it out. The red-tinted liquid splattered over her boots and dribbled into the cracks in the pavement. "What the hell?"

Marlow holstered his gun and held his hand out for the bottle. She twisted the cap on and tossed it to him. It slapped, cold and heavy, against his palm, and he bent over to pour it over his head. Blood and a few furry chunks hit the pavement.

"Urban farm?" he suggested.

The bottle went to Franklin next. He rinsed off his hands and shook them to shed the water and mess. The flip of his fingers was oddly fastidious for the situation. "Hoarder?"

Bennett crouched down to wipe her boots off with a tissue. "Still think the Blue Moon is an old wives' tale?" she asked.

"Yes," Marlow said.

"After that?" Bennett jerked her thumb back over her shoulder toward the house. The windows and doors were broken to let out the stink of the aconite tear gas they'd used to clear out the feeding frenzy. "You ever seen a clusterfuck like that on a normal night?"

"Two hundred guinea pigs did not just manifest themselves overnight," Marlow pointed out. "They were already there, and it's just chance the wolves found them tonight, rather than last month or two months from now."

"Bullshit," Bennett said. "One wolf maybe, but six of them, just gorging themselves like that? They hadn't even eaten all of them; they were like foxes in a henhouse. And it's a coincidence it happened on the double bubble? I repeat, bullshit."

She had a point. Marlow stuck a finger in his ear and wriggled it. That had been weird. It had been like… gory confetti, and the wolves drunk on the thrill of it. On the other hand, she might plan to kill him tonight, so he wasn't in the mood to admit anything.

"We've had weird calls before," Marlow said. "What about those guys that left out chicken carcasses stuffed with weed butter before they turned? Six stoned wolves with the munchies, and three on the worst trip of their lives. Nothing weird about the 'lunar energy,' just garden-variety stupid."

Bennett pulled a face, but there wasn't time to argue further. Their radios crackled with another call, and she caught it.

"Dispatch, throw us a good one," she said. "We've a blue-moon skeptic on our hands here."

A guinea pig, fat and fuzzy, with two asymmetrical rosettes on its backside, scurried out of the gates and along the pavement between their feet. Franklin grabbed it on instinct and then stood awkwardly, as if he didn't know what to do with it.

"I've got just what you're looking for, then," Dispatch drawled. "Reports of a half-naked woman staked out on her lawn. Neighbors called it in. Apparently they tried to get her to come inside, but she won't give them the keys. Elim and Church Street, white house, red door, lady on the lawn. Can't miss it."

"We're on it," Bennett said. She turned to Marlow. "See? Told you. Blue moon brings out the crazies."

Marlow snorted. "She's a null," he said as he loped back over to the van. "This is garden-variety stupid."

They piled into the back. With the rookie on desk duty at the station, it was Franklin who brought up the rear. He gave them all a quick leer as he slammed the doors shut.

"At least the scenery is gonna be nice for once," he said as he dropped the guinea pig in an empty ammo box.

"Don't be gross," Bennett said as she fastened her seat belt.

She slapped the metal next to her and yelled, "Go, go, go!" to the driver. Marlow was nearly thrown out of his seat as the van took off with a guttural roar of the engine. He hung on to the straps of his harness and managed to get himself wedged back into position and strapped in. Franklin swore at Bennett as he bounced off the sides before he managed to fall into a seat.

Marlow tilted his head back against the cold metal behind him, the thrum of the engine loud as it vibrated through the bone, and tuned out the familiar bickering. He focused on the staccato monotony of calls as they came through the driver's radio.

Fire at a Target over in Mesa Verde.

Two robberies under cover of the moon. Three reports of pack activity. One call up at the Reserve to collect a handful of paparazzi who'd thought it was a good night to try and catch a photo of a naked celebrity mid-shift. That made Marlow think briefly of Cade, somewhere in the city—unless he'd made it out to the ranch he'd offered Marlow as a bolthole.

Marlow checked the gun in his holster, as if it might have fallen out since last time. It was an old habit, but the buzz of low-grade anxiety that made his heel bounce and his skull ache was not new. He remembered it from his first shift after he'd been put back on active duty after the shooting. The brass had been confident they'd cleaned out the department, but the back of Marlow's neck had burned all night long with uneasy suspicion.

It had faded over the years, tamped down as he dealt with the very real, toothy, and easy to identify threats right in front of him. He'd actually thought it had gone away, but now it had been turned back up, he'd realized it had always been there as a low background hum.

Maybe he should have taken up Cade on his offer, pulled a hamstring, and sat this month out in the country. Except if he'd done that, Marlow wasn't sure he'd have been able to come back.

One good thing about it, he supposed as he braced around a corner, at least Cade wouldn't get to say "I told you so" if he was right.

According to the neighbors, the woman on the lawn was Vera Brannick, and she was usually very nice. Not tonight.

"She bit me!" Franklin said as he recoiled. He shook his hand, then examined the bite mark. "Damn it. She broke the skin. I'm gonna need a shot or something. Fuck sake."

Vera screamed and, as Bennett finally managed to get her feet unshackled, kicked.

"Get away! I want this!" she yelled as blood soaked through the pink teddy from the gouges on her stomach. She'd done them herself. "I want to know wild, feral love. I want him to come for me! He can't resist."

Marlow threw a blanket over her like she was an angry canary. She fought them as they tried to get her on her feet, so they just picked her up and hauled her over to the ambulance.

"She's on something," Bennett said. She stopped and pulled a cautious face, then spat a tooth out into her hand. "Shit."

The paramedic plucked it out of the froth of bloody spit with gloved fingers and held it up to check it in the light.

"Came out in one piece," he said. "I can insert it back in if you want?"

Bennett gave an exasperated look. "Oh, I don't know," she said. "I always thought I could rock a gap tooth."

The paramedic looked at her. Behind him, his partner had Vera strapped down to the stretcher and had slid a needle into her arm. Her screams slid away to dozy mumbles.

"Put it back in," Bennett said, the words enunciated. "You idiot."

He absorbed the insult with a shrug and got her to perch on the back of the ambulance and tilt her head back.

"Her neighbor says she was out there nearly an hour," Marlow said. "I can't believe she lasted that long."

Franklin snorted. "You ever see a wild animal eat something rabid? No way. They give that crazy, frothing squirrel a wide berth. I figure it was the same with her. Any wolf that came by could smell the bad idea on her." He held his hand up and flapped it toward the paramedics. "I guess no one cares about my hand, huh? Just let it fall off, yeah?"

The paramedic glanced over his shoulder. "Put antiseptic on it."

Bennett growled something at him around the fingers in her mouth, and he looked back down at her. He'd just wiggled the tooth back in when the radios crackled again.

"Dispatch to Charlie-forty, we have an incident at an address you flagged," Dispatch said. "A Victor Clemons. Do you want to respond?"

Shit. That was all he needed. Marlow cracked his neck to loosen the muscles and glanced over at Bennett.

"Dispatch," he said. "We're taking five to get Bennett patched up—"

“Take it,” Bennett said as she pushed the paramedic’s hand away from her mouth. “I’ll catch a ride with another squad once they’ve splinted this.”

The spot between Marlow’s shoulder blades itched as he tried to work out why Bennett would give him a chance to look good in front of their superiors. She wanted the promotion—either for the usual reasons people wanted to be promoted, or because it would make it easier to run a corrupt protection racket with less oversight—and she’d never played fair before. Maybe this had been planned?

He hesitated. Dispatch crackled an impatient request for an answer.

“Do it,” Bennett said. She wiped blood off her lower lip and gave him an annoyed look. “Since when do I need babysitting. Go. Make sure no one is getting killed.”

That was his job.

“On our way,” he said as he depressed the button on the radio. “Two-man team, Bennett’s trailing.”

Victor Clemons was a prudent man where full moon safety was concerned. Surveillance cameras, heavy-duty shutters, reinforcements to the walls and ceiling. His door was open.

Marlow signaled to Franklin to go around the back while he edged up onto the porch and checked the hall around the corner of the door. Thick gouges were ripped out of the plaster on the wall, dug down into the drywall beneath, and the wooden flooring was splintered and torn up. The flat, metallic scent of blood hung on the air.

“Victor?” Marlow said, voice pitched to carry but not too far. He unclipped the flashlight from his belt and flicked it on to illuminate the dimly lit space. “Are you still in there?”

He edged around the door and down the hall, one hand on the butt of his gun. The stairs were clear. Living room too. The TV was smashed and the couch torn to shreds, but no sign of blood or bodies.

The house felt empty. All Marlow could hear as he made his way steadily down the hall was his own footsteps and the faint controlled sound of his breathing.

He stepped in something that slid under his boot. Marlow hopped back and tilted the light down. A splatter of blood on the floor, bright red as the light hit it, with his boot print in the middle.

The wolf had come through the front door. He had probably hit the living room first, maybe while Victor hid. Then, when Victor thought Barney was occupied, he'd… What? Marlow turned the beam of the torch onto the stairs and tracked the route of escape straight down and out the front door. If he'd been in the kitchen instead, why not go straight out the back door?

Marlow filed that question away to answer later and pulled his gun. He held it low and ready by his side as he edged into the kitchen, weight balanced on the balls of his feet in case he had to move fast.

Most of the blood was in here. It splattered the floor and over the kitchen surfaces, a single long spray of it up the wall. Marlow was careful not to step in it this time as he circled around the island.

Barney lay on the ground in front of the kitchen sink. He was dead. It was the only time a wolf was human under a full moon. He was also naked, which made cause of death easy to pinpoint—a bullet hole in his chest, the skin singed around the edges. Marlow crouched down to check his pulse anyhow, fingers pressed against the slack, still-warm skin.

Nothing.

"Charlie-fifty, you there?" he said into the radio. "We've a dead wolf in here and no sign of a null. Where are you?"

"Door's locked," Franklin said, his voice sullen. "If a wolf can't kick it in, I can't either. Open up."

Marlow stood up and headed over to the back door to let Franklin in. It wasn't locked. The handle turned easily when he grabbed it.

So what the hell had taken him so long to make entry?

The pieces came together just as Franklin rammed his shoulder into the door from the other side. It smashed into Marlow. He'd already started to back up, but it was reinforced metal, and it hit his chest hard enough that he was knocked backward.

He hit the floor and skidded until he smacked into the base of the fridge. He felt the curved metal dent under the impact, and the gun slipped from his hand.

"I'd hoped the wolf would do you in," Franklin said as he walked into the kitchen. He rubbed his shoulder with one hand as he talked, his thumb dug down into the joint. "Give you a bit of dignity; let you go out the way you want to go."

Marlow snorted. Or tried to. His lungs hadn't quite recovered from the door yet. He got his elbow under him and tried to push himself up.

"I don't want to die by wolf," he said.

Franklin kicked his arm out from under him. The ground came up fast, and Marlow saw stars as his head bounced off the floor. His voice stayed conversational as he put his boot on Marlow's wrist and pressed down."Then why are you fucking one? I mean, seriously? You know better. If I didn't kill you tonight, he would have sooner or later. At least you know I'll remember your face."

The pain in his wrist actually helped. It was immediate, occurring, and Marlow had abused his body enough over the years that it knew what to focus on. The ache from being clotheslined by the door faded into the background, and the hot, fresh pain that radiated up his arm cleared the fog from Marlow's head.

"You're Piper's second?" he said. "And I thought it was Bennett. I owe her an apology."

"You owe me an apology," Franklin said. "You thought I was an idiot, right?"

Marlow shook his head. "You don't get to Night Shift by being stupid," he said. "I just thought you were unlikeable."

Anger thinned Franklin's lips over his teeth for a moment, and he put his weight on Marlow's wrist. Then he got himself under control again.

"Always a smartass," he said. "I do what needs to be done, and I *know* what needs to be done. It's a wolf's world, Marlow, and if you want to live in it, you have to live by their rules. It doesn't count if it happens under the full moon."

"You tried to kidnap Lance Rilkes under a new moon," Marlow pointed out. "How does that fit?"

Franklin looked at him for a second and then grinned. It was wide and seemed entirely genuine.

"That's your problem, Kit," he said. "Too smart for your own good. The others buy that shit, but you see right through it. Too clever to be conned, and too moral to corrupt."

"You could try," Marlow said. "Who knows. I went along with Piper for way too long."

Franklin shook his head. "The penny-ante stuff," he said. "Piper always said you'd balk if you got too deep. That's why he was so easy to convince that it was you who'd squealed."

He winked.

Marlow drove the heel of his hand into the side of Franklin's braced knee. It wasn't *exactly* how he'd wrecked his, but the torn-gristle pop of it sounded very similar. Franklin made a wet retch of sound in the back of his throat as his knee bent the wrong way. He lurched backward, and Marlow scrambled to his feet.

He tackled Franklin, shoulder aimed at the vulnerable slice of flesh where the Kevlar vest rode up, and took them both to the ground. Franklin grunted and hammered punches into Marlow's ribs and back as they scuffled in the blood. He managed to flip them over and pinned Marlow down, his forearm jammed into Marlow's throat.

"Fuck it," he said. "Why let you go out clean. I'll tell them you got scared. That your famous nerve finally broke. There was no need to kill that wolf, no lives in danger, but you did it anyhow. Then you attacked me to cover your tracks, and I had to kill you. With my bare hands. Think they'll buy it?"

Red smeared at the edge of Marlow's vision. He peeled his lips back from his teeth in a snarl at Franklin.

"My nerve, maybe," he rasped out. "That you could beat me?"

He sucked air through his teeth to express his doubts about that lie. Franklin snarled and leaned harder on his throat. That brought him in close enough for Marlow to reach up, grab an ear, and dig his thumb into Franklin's eye.

Franklin screamed and recoiled. Blood dripped down his face from his torn eyelid as he scrambled away on his hands and knee. He blotted at his eye with the back of his sleeve as he cursed Marlow.

"You really think you've got nine lives, huh?" he rasped as he grabbed Marlow's gun and scrambled to his feet. "Well, trust me. Three's the charm."

Franklin squinted through the veil of blood as he aimed at Marlow, finger curled around the trigger. He licked his lips.

"Probably for the best," he panted. "If you were corrupt, you'd be competition, and I learned from Piper where that leads."

His finger tightened on the trigger, and then Bennett's voice echoed down the hall.

"Marlow? Franklin?" she said. "What's going on?"

Habit twitched Franklin's head in her direction. The gun wavered for a second, and Marlow lunged for the back door. He scrambled out over the threshold on all fours and then staggered to his feet in the garden. The cool night air stung his raw throat as he sucked in lungfuls of it. He scrambled up the wire fence at the bottom of the garden and dropped down the other side.

A window twitched in the house opposite and quickly closed again as the neighbor took in the scene. They were probably on the phone to 911 now, which would just help Franklin's story.

Marlow grimaced and put that aside to deal with later. He pushed himself into a dead run down the long concrete rat run of the alley. At the end of it, he paused for a second to orient himself.

Behind him, he heard the distinct double-tap report of shots fired.

Bennett?

There was nothing he could do now. Marlow stripped his radio off and tossed it, then folded one arm over his ribs as he jogged away into the darkness. The wolves were waiting out in the city for him, but tonight they weren't who he was worried about.

SHIFTLESS

Night Shift is the city's thin, silver line - and some nights it's thinner than others.

It isn't the fact he almost died last night that's thrown Night Shift officer Kit Marlow. He's used to that. It's the fact that instead of a werewolf trying to rip his throat out, it was his friend and colleague who tried to put him in the ground.

Well, 'friend.'

Now Marlow's been framed for a murder he didn't commit by a man who's committed more than his fair share. Half the cops in San Diego want to see Marlow behind bars for what he's supposedly done, and the other half want him dead before he can tell his side of the story. The problem is that he can't tell them apart.

There's only one person in town that Marlow can trust, even though he knows he shouldn't drag Cade Deacon into his problems. The sharp-tongued CEO of a private security firm might have gotten close to Marlow over the last few weeks, but taking on the SDPD is a lot to ask.

Marlow doesn't have much choice, though. If he can't clear his name before the last full moon of the month sets, he might not see another one. That'd be a shame since Marlow would really like to spend the night with Cade without needing protective gear.

CHAPTER ONE

SPLINTERS OF GLASS washed out of Cade's hair and fell onto the tiled floor between his feet. They glittered in among the suds the water swirled around the drain. Cade curled his toes and felt grit under his feet.

Most of the time, Cade was glad he didn't remember what the wolf did. No one needed to know exactly what it was like to eat a seagull; the taste of the leftovers between his teeth when he'd woken up had been bad enough. And if Cade *had* eaten Marlow last full moon, the last thing he'd have wanted was the gory details.

Cade would put money on *that* being one of the rare times that reality really would have been worse than anything his imagination could come up with. And his imagination had worked overtime on that one.

Sometimes though—Cade flicked the pressure on the shower to high and let needles of hot water batter his head and shoulders—he had to wonder what the hell his furry self had gotten up to.

"…."

The white noise of the shower almost drowned out the sound of someone's voice. Cade just caught the ghost of it from the other room. He slapped the water off and raked his fingers through his hair to squeeze the water out.

"Hold on," he said, voice pitched to carry, as he stepped out of the shower. "I need to get dressed."

"It can wait," Lem said. There was a pause, and then he added, "You won't be happy if it does, though."

Clean clothes were folded neatly on the table next to the sink. It would take Cade a couple of minutes to dry off and get dressed. There wasn't much that couldn't wait that long… But Lem knew that, and he'd still interrupted.

Cade grabbed a towel and slung it around his hips as he padded out into the office. The morning sun bathed the stark gray and black room with stripes of honey gold light. Lem was perched on the arm of the couch, a tablet balanced on his crooked knee.

"What?" Cade asked.

"You know," Lem said. "If you aren't going to take the full moon off, you could get an apartment in the city. Houses, even. Nice ones."

There were. Except the farmhouse was the dream. Everyone had one in their line of work: The girl back home. The boy you messaged every night. Parents you wanted to help in their old age or prove wrong about everything. It didn't matter what it was; you just had to have something to make the shit parts of it all—the bag jobs, the dirty jobs—worth it.

For Cade, it had been a farmhouse in the country with room for family and a BBQ on the back porch that he lit every weekend. Now he had the farmhouse and the BBQ, but he'd never gotten around to lighting it.

No family either. Except for Lem, who considered the suburbs a trip into the wilderness.

"That feels like giving in," Cade said. "Once I get a new COO in, someone to take up a bit of the slack, I'll be able to get out there more."

From the skeptical look on Lem's face he didn't buy that assurance, but he didn't argue the point either. Instead, he tapped the tablet screen, turned it around, and held it out to Cade.

"…of course, it was a Blue Moon," a rigorously handsome man with carefully unobjectionable styling told the camera. Or his phone. One of the two. "Perhaps that had something to do with the unfortunate events that rocked San Diego's Night Shift last night."

Despite the heat that lingered in his lightly scalded skin, still pink from the shower, Cade felt a cold sweat break out on him. He felt his throat tighten as he prepared himself for the blunt announcement of Marlow's death. No one ever bothered to sugarcoat it when someone on the Night Shift died. It wasn't as if anyone would be surprised.

The camera shifted to a grainy, zoomed-in shot of a big blond man perched on the back of an ambulance. He was shirtless, with stark purple and blue bruises blotched over his pale chest and smeared down over his stomach. The paramedics kept trying to slip an oxygen mask over his mouth and nose, but he pushed it away impatiently as he talked to the woman next to him.

After a moment, the camera pulled back to show the Night Shift in formation around the ambulance, as wolves snarled and tested the line around them.

"Officer Cordell Franklin, a veteran Night Shift officer who served in both San Francisco and San Diego, was reportedly *shot* tonight during the performance of his duties," the man said. His voice wobbled with borderline inappropriate excitement. A lot happened during the full moon, but most of it only had limited local interest. People tuned in the morning after to find out what happened to their house/wife/neighbor's extension, but this could get some airtime. "At the moment, we don't know exactly what happened, but we have heard that another Night Shift officer was on the scene and is now being sought by his colleagues. A source has told us that the officer in question is Kit Marlow, who was involved with the corruption scandal that saw Lieutenant Ned Piper stripped of his commission and imprisoned. Perhaps, in light of tonight's events, there was even more to that story. This is Dalton Reeves for—"

The clip ended abruptly. Relief washed over Cade, and he felt his knees weaken with it. He'd worry about what had gone down last night later. Right now, Marlow was alive and the Night Shift was corrupt. Same as yesterday. That was better than what Cade had expected to hear.

A frame-up could be fixed; death couldn't.

"Okay," he said as he handed the tablet back. "When you said it couldn't wait, I thought someone was dead."

Lem shrugged and tapped at the screen. "Well, the word on the neighborhood forums has it that someone is," he said. "The resident's ex-boyfriend, Barney 'Something,' was brought out in a body bag after the Night Officer who got shot. The verdict is that Night Shift killed Barney and that it was about time. He'd apparently come to piss on the property every full moon since he broke up with the guy that lived there."

"It happens," Cade said. "Night Shift won't kill him for pissing, but if he escalated—"

Lem held up a finger to shush him. "One problem with that," he said. "I got the ex's name from his rental contract and ran a quick background check on him. He made reservations at the Hilton

Bayfront for three nights, the full moon getaway deal. Sunset check-in."

So no one had been at the property when Barney got there. That would make it hard to justify the kill. Technically, Night Shift's remit allowed them to deploy deadly force in defense of themselves or another, but self-defense was a hard sell. The Night Shift's lives were in danger from the minute they went out on the streets, so they could kill who they wanted and claim self-defense.

They were the only ones who'd know if it was true or not. The same way they were the only ones who knew if the accusation against Marlow was true or not.

"Is there any news on Marlow?" Cade asked.

Lem shook his head. "The cops are looking for him, but they just say he's a person of interest. No details. So he's in the wind, but why and where we don't know."

The "why" didn't matter. Cade didn't care if Marlow *had* murdered someone. To be honest, it would pull some of the teeth from the background worry that, despite everything Cade had built up to keep him-now and him-then apart, Marlow could do better.

The "where" could be solved, but it would take time—

"You *cannot* go in there!" Cade's assistant objected from outside the office. Her voice was shriller than usual. "Unless you have a warrant or—"

The sentence ended on a startled "eep," and the door swung open to let O'Hara stalk in. A few paces behind him came Bennett, her face set in an unhappy scowl despite her split lip.

"Captain," Cade said, his voice coldly impersonal. "This is unexpected. Did we have an appointment?"

"Shut up," Bennett said.

O'Hara held his hand up to quiet her. She clenched her teeth, the tight muscles visible along her jaw, and held her tongue.

"Have you seen or spoken to Marlow?" Cartwright asked.

Cade raised his eyebrows and glanced at Lem. "What time is it?"

"Six a.m."

"So if I did, I ate him," Cade said. He tasted bile in the back of his throat for a second, and it stung when he swallowed. Apparently, it wasn't funny yet. O'Hara didn't need to know that. "Is that all?"

"No." O'Hara reached into his pocket and pulled out a photo of a dead man to show Cade. His hair was wet and sandy brown, slicked severely back from his lax, sallow face. "Do you know Barney Lyons?"

Cade glanced at the photo briefly and shrugged.

"No."

"Really?" O'Hara said. "Because he worked just down the street, in The Fat Fish. That's not even a block away. You've never been there?"

The memory of the unexpected encounter with Marlow on the street outside was so vivid that Cade could feel the warmth of Marlow's kiss on his lips. He remembered the crumpled sticker on the wrapper he'd tossed in the trash for the cleaners to sort and dispose of.

Anyone who watched TV knew it was surprising the amount of things you can find out from someone's trash. Not many knew how easy it was to actually track your discarded bags from the backyard to the dump if you were motivated enough. If the SDPD were on the ball—even if it was the wrong ball—it wouldn't take them long to find out he'd been there. Once or twice, at least. A blunt denial could be used against him later.

"I'm bad with faces," he said. "I might have seen him around, but we never got beers together. Why?"

"He's dead."

"…obviously," Cade said. "They wouldn't have let him work with food if he looked like that under normal circumstances."

The corners of O'Hara's mouth twitched with repressed annoyance. He tucked the photo into his pocket.

"You have been a royal pain in the SDPD's ass since you arrived in town," he said. "So I get that you have invested a lot in this knee-jerk anti-authoritarian persona that you've cultivated. This isn't the time."

Lem snorted and shrugged when both O'Hara and Bennett glared at him. "Don't flatter yourself," he said. "You aren't the first cops he's thought were stupid. The SDPD isn't even in the top five."

"Maybe that says more about him," Bennett said.

"Well, duh."

Cade ignored both of them as he looked at O'Hara. "What is this about, O'Hara? And can it wait till I have pants on?"

There was a long pause as O'Hara weighed his response. Finally, he nodded briefly to himself and stepped forward into Cade's personal space. So apparently, "no" on the second question.

"Last night, one of my best officers killed a man and tried to kill another Night Shift officer when they tried to stop him," O'Hara said, his voice grim. "And when I start to dig, your name turns up every time one way or another. Lyons worked a few doors down from your offices. Haley was killed on property you provide security for. And, despite the fact you nearly killed him, Officer Marlow keeps turning up in your company. I don't believe in coincidence."

Cade crossed his arms. His elbows nudged against O'Hara's chest as he did so.

"A hundred people work within a few doors of my offices," he said. "Some of them probably died in the last month, but that doesn't mean I had anything to do with it. Same goes for Haley. If I had anything to do with that, I wouldn't have solved the crime for you, would I?"

"You have an answer for everything, don't you?" O'Hara said. "People with something to hide usually do. What about Marlow? You have been very vocal about your contempt for the police. What makes him the exception to the rule? Why do you suddenly enjoy his company?"

Cade leaned in until their noses almost touched. He could smell the sourness of a long night and no time to catch a break on O'Hara's breath.

"I want to fuck him," he said. "That answer your question?"

The blush was unexpected. It crawled up into O'Hara's cheeks, under the scruff of graying gingery stubble, and turned his ears bright red. Despite the barely repressed anger that fairly seeped out of Bennett, she gave a brief snort of amusement at the jibe.

O'Hara ignored her. He stepped back out of Cade's space and cleared his throat.

"I'm afraid not," he said. "Not all of them. We'd like to speak to you down at the station."

"Are you asking or telling?" Cade asked.

O'Hara popped his knuckles absently. "Until you refuse, we're asking," he said.

There was too much wolf under Cade's skin—antsy with the promise of another two night's mayhem—for him to swallow the implied threat easily. The back of his neck itched, and his teeth felt very sharp against his tongue.

O'Hara had been right about one thing. Cade did like his antagonistic relationship with the local LEOs. For one thing, he didn't have much use for cops—in his personal experience they were either useless or in his way—and it also tested well with Cold Winds' target market. Someone who hired private security generally didn't want the police involved in their business.

That didn't mean they wanted a straight-up dark web mercenary either, and there were conduct clauses in the contracts. So far, no one had ever used them against Cold Winds. But they could.

"Well, since you asked so nicely," Cade said. "If you don't mind, I'm going to get dressed and call my lawyer first. You can wait in reception unless you want a show."

He untucked the towel from around his waist and rubbed it over his soaked hair. O'Hara didn't look. Good for him.

"Don't take too long," O'Hara told him. He checked the time on his wristwatch briefly as he turned to leave the room. "Courtesy expires in twenty minutes, Mr. Deacon. After that, well, the station has seen your ass before."

Bennett hung back as he left. "Only guilty men need lawyers," she said, "in my experience."

The door closed behind O'Hara and left the three of them alone.

"Please," Cade said. "Does that ever work? Everyone *needs* a lawyer. The guilty just know it."

Her bruised mouth twitched in a cold smile. "So you admit it?"

"Not without my lawyer present," Cade said. "Now, get out of my office."

Bennett took a step back. "You think you're slick," she said. "But I knew Ned Piper, and he played this city like a drum for years. You aren't on his level. So I don't care *how* you talked Marlow into this shit storm; you're going to pay for it. I'll make sure of that. Lawyer or not."

She turned on her heel and stalked out of the office after O'Hara. Cade waited for the door to swing shut behind her with the solid click of good craftsmanship and reinforced metal under the polished layer of wood.

"Find him," Cade said.

"What?" Lem said.

"Marlow." Cade slung the damp towel around his neck and gave his brother an exasperated look. "By the time I get back from my…. completely optional… chat with the SDPD, I want to know where he is."

Lem made an exasperated gesture as he stood up and nearly knocked his tablet to the floor. He grabbed it awkwardly and rested the edge of it against his hip.

"And how do you think I'm going to do that?" Lem asked, frustration in his voice. "The Night Shift and half the city are looking for him, but I'm just supposed to 'find him'? How do you expect me to do that, Cade?"

"I don't care how you do it. I just want it done," Cade said. "I've spent years telling our clients, the press, and various local government officials that Cold Winds is better funded, better staffed, and just plain better than the SDPD. So don't make a liar out of me. Find Marlow before they do."

Lem grimaced and looked down at his tablet. When he looked up, his face was set in determined, unhappy lines.

"You sure about this?" he asked and held up a hand to intercept whatever Cade was about to say. "And don't just tell me to mind my own business. This is Cold Winds money and man-hours you're sinking into this personal interest of yours. I remember how pissed you were at Justin for doing the same. Maybe you're letting your personal feelings—for a guy you've known a *month*, Cade, or not even a month—get in the way. I want you to be happy, big brother, but this Marlow might turn out to be a bad bet. Maybe he did what they say he did. Maybe we shouldn't get involved."

Cade dropped the towel onto the floor to sop up the moisture from his wet feet.

"Maybe you should do your job," Cade said. "Which, unless I've missed a memo, is cybersecurity, not the personal angel on my shoulder."

"So you admit I'm right?" Lem asked. "This is a bad idea?"

Cade shrugged as he turned and headed back into the small bathroom to get dressed. "It could be," he said over his shoulder.

"But this is my company, and I get to make that call. Not you. And tell Beth to meet me at the police station. I don't want this to take any longer than it has to."

Lem sighed, loud enough to still be heard as Cade closed the door behind him.

"So now I have to do the impossible *and* talk to my ex?" he said. He slapped his hand against the door twice. Their father had done that when he was done with their shit. It had been the double-tap on his ability to control his temper. All these years later—and even knowing it was Lem, who'd never raised his hand to anyone—Cade's shoulders still tightened at the sound. "Maybe I should take Justin up on that job offer, huh? At least I wouldn't have to care if he was fucking himself over."

They both knew Lem wouldn't. They—probably—both knew that Cade didn't want that. Lem was the only family he had, and neither of them had the emotional skills to maintain a relationship if they didn't work together.

None of that helped Cade not be a dick at the moment.

"Go ahead," he said. "You might be looking for a new job anyhow if you don't get off your ass and do what you're told."

There was a pause, and then Lem snorted. "Fine," he said. "But I hope this guy is worth it."

Cade hitched his jeans up over lean, damp hips. "Me too," he said, but he'd waited until he heard Lem leave. The problem was—Cade glanced at his reflection in the mirror and rubbed a hand over his stubbled jaw as he debated a shave—he *knew* Marlow was worth it. He had no doubts.

That scared him.

CHAPTER TWO

"WELCOME TO *BONES* *and Broth.* How can I help you?" the girl behind the counter rhymed off the question by rote. "Today's special is tilapia and pupfish broth, sourced from the Salton Sea. You can add a fat bomb for only another dollar, and that will pick you up until the moon's up."

The "do you serve coffee" was on the tip of Marlow's tongue. He choked it down as he glanced at the board behind her, the day's offerings almost unreadable in hand-written chalk.

"Grande beet kvass," he ordered instead. "And a yogurt."

She rang it up on the till. "That will be $12.40," she said. "Do you have a loyalty card?"

He did not.

He hadn't exactly expected to be asked to pay either.

Usually he did—fairly often, anyhow—but it was easier to just let people buy you a coffee during the full moon. *For your service.* Not that he'd be able to tell one wolf from another in the dark, but people seemed to like the idea that keeping the Night Shift sweet had some impact.

Marlow patted down his pockets as he tried to recover. It took him a second to remember that his wallet—along with his ID and his house keys—was still in a lockbox in the armory. The girl behind the counter started to look annoyed.

"If you need to go and get your—"

"No," Marlow said. He fished the emergency fifty-dollar bill out of his back pocket and handed it over. It had been in there—one pocket or another—for five years. The creases were so set that when the girl unfolded it, the paper was threadbare in places. "Sorry. My ex is a dick."

It wasn't actually a lie—a number of them were—but it wasn't an explanation either. The girl took it as one, though. Most people did. The details got filled in from their own experience, and they were either sympathetic or decided not to get involved as a result.

It was one of the things you learned when you were economical with words. People would read more into what you didn't say. For once, it was useful.

"Ugh," the girl said as she counted out his change. "I've been there."

Marlow tipped reasonably, took the kvass and yogurt, and retreated to the back of the cafe. They had stools instead of seats, rickety on thin metal legs. He perched on one that let him keep his back to the corner and let himself relax—a bit.

The sun was up, and the wolves were back to buying bone broth and flirting in the morning sun. Marlow still had problems to deal with, but he had time for that now. None of them were going to rip his throat out the minute he let his guard down.

Marlow dipped a spoon in the yogurt and stirred to dredge up the peanut butter and jelly sludge at the bottom. His stomach grumbled, loud enough to make him look up awkwardly. No one else in the cafe had noticed.

He'd broken into some wolf's house last night to wait for the dawn. It hadn't been difficult. Null houses had metal shutters, deadbolts, and security cameras with dedicated streams, because if someone broke in, it was probably to eat them in their bed. The wolf had a cylinder lock and a sash window he'd left half-open because most burglars weren't desperate enough to risk working during the full moon.

Marlow had raided the wardrobe in the master bedroom for the jeans and shirt he had on—pale pink with a gray check, the sort of shirt that everyone who knew Marlow knew he wouldn't wear. The rucksack he'd grabbed to stash his Night Shift gear in was currently locked in the trunk of his wrecked Firebird in the mechanic's lot.

He could have picked a worse house, but the cupboard had been bare. All he'd found was gauze bags of bone broth and a stash of saltines.

Marlow spooned the yogurt goop into his mouth. The edges of the plastic spoon were sharp against his lips as he sucked it clean.

He'd never thought what it was like for wolves the morning after. Even those who got Crated for the night weren't his problem once the sun came up. Day Shift dealt with them, and Marlow was usually on his way home. He'd dated a couple of wolves back before he got his shot at the Night Shift—when it was just risky and not borderline idiotic—but never seriously.

Now he wondered what it was like when they woke up on the sidewalk—or the pier or beach—as he ate. Were they stuffed from the wolf's gluttony? Too starved to make it home to eat?

For a second, he remembered the raw look—a thorny tangle of gutted, relieved, and angry—that Cade had given him the morning after the *last* time that Franklin had tried to kill them. Marlow hadn't understood it at the time, but now he did. Or at least he understood it a bit better.

Wolves didn't remember what they'd done under the full moon, but that didn't mean they couldn't work out some details if they tried. If they worked out what—who—they'd eaten, maybe it left them too sick to the stomach to think about food again.

It would explain the saltines.

Marlow felt a pinch of guilt at the reminder of how easily he could have made Cade's bad morning better. He ignored it. It was probably deserved, but Marlow couldn't afford to dwell on it right now.

He finished the last of the yogurt, smears of peanut butter scraped out with the edge of the spoon, and picked up the kvass to wash it down. The drink had warmed up enough that he could taste the earthy ripeness of the beets, almost stronger than the salty bite of fermentation. Marlow grimaced to himself, but he'd not gotten it because he expected to enjoy it. It was to give him an excuse to linger as he nursed it so he could try to come up with some sort of plan for what next.

Franklin.

Marlow rubbed his shoulder absently, bruises tender under his stolen shirt, as he contemplated that discovery. Out of everyone on Night Shift, he would have never suspected Franklin.

Of being corrupt? Sure. That had always been on the table. Franklin had been tight with Piper. He'd kept his job after the SDPD cleaned house, but Marlow had always assumed that was a trade. Information in return for a clean slate. And he hated wolves nearly as much as he wanted to be one.

Marlow wouldn't have been surprised to find out that Franklin had fallen in behind somebody else.

Behind Bennett, that would have made sense.

The idea that Franklin was the mastermind, the brains behind all of this? That was hard to swallow.

Nearly as hard as the mouthful of kvass Marlow absently took. He coughed into his hand to clear the taste out of his throat and glanced toward the counter. The girl was preoccupied with taking photos of a fresh hunk of leg bone, the marrow blistered and dusted with paprika. She didn't have any attention to spare for Marlow.

For now.

Marlow leaned back so his shoulders rested against the wall, his heel hooked over the rung of the stool to steady him, and grimly wondered how long it would be until a notification popped up on her phone about a rogue Night Shift officer. He'd made the news this morning, obviously, but they'd not shown his face.

In cases like this—there weren't many, even Piper hadn't run—Internal Affairs would rather not have the suspect's face on the news. No one wanted a civilian injured trying to take down one of the most highly trained fighters in the country, or the Night Shift mythology dinged by a lucky swing to the back of the head.

They'd prefer him to turn himself in or be brought in quietly, but when that didn't work, they'd release the photo to the press. If that didn't work… well, that depended on how Franklin spun the story.

He probably wouldn't try and pin the corruption on Marlow. That was the sort of thing that IA wanted to talk about at length, and the last thing Franklin wanted was for Marlow to be brought in alive. It'd be a hate crime, the old myth of the murderous null in the night and the poor wolf who'd never known what hit it. That was the sort of crime where IA didn't want the perpetrator to talk too much. It wasn't like O'Hara would give the order to bring Marlow in dead, but he'd not have the political capital to raise a fuss when Marlow's corpse was laid out on the table.

A blond man nudged the door to the cafe open with a tinkle of bells. It *wasn't* Cade—he didn't have the shoulders or the swagger—but Marlow's breath caught in the back of his throat anyhow. Just for a second.

Because he'd expected it to be Cade.

Some part of him anyhow. Marlow pushed his glasses up onto his forehead and rubbed his eyes in tired exasperation. What was that about? Since when did he need anyone? Night Shift worked in teams, but Marlow always went in first or split off. He appreciated backup, but he preferred to work solo.

It was how he worked *best*... Always had been. He didn't sit around and wait for anyone to save him.

A statement, he thought wryly as he tilted his cup to see how much kvass he still had to get through, that would have more bite if he had any other idea of what to do. Last night had been easy. He was Night Shift. All his training revolved around not getting killed in streets full of things that wanted to kill him. Usually they were wolves, but other than the element of surprise, Franklin hadn't brought anything new to the table. Everything from the fight in the kitchen to Marlow bolting the minute Bennett distracted Franklin had been instinct and adrenaline.

Now the sun had come up, and he was tired, sore, and framed for a murder he didn't commit by his corrupt teammate.

Night Shift boot camp had not prepared him for this.

The blond man looked over at him. Then back to the clerk. She looked at him and shook her head as she bagged egg tarts and rolled the paper down. The man took a second look and then shrugged. He paid for his breakfast and left.

Marlow drained the last of his kvass—it was thicker at the bottom, almost rubbery—and unhooked his foot from the stool. Coffee would have helped him come up with a better plan. Any plan.

The door opened, and two uniforms came in, hands on their guns. The clerk chirped her scripted welcome, and they turned toward her automatically. They said something quietly and showed her something on their phone. Probably a picture.

Marlow could just turn himself in, put his faith in the system. Except that left him with the same problem he'd had last night: who could he trust? Franklin didn't work alone, and he absolutely couldn't afford to let Marlow give his side of the story.

Gloved fingers dug into Marlow's cheeks to hold his mouth shut as they cuffed his hands behind his back. Someone slapped his ass, and the hot, bright shame of it choked him. He'd never work out why that bothered him so much. Something ripped, and then they pulled a bag over his head. It was only when he choked on feathers that he realized it had been a pillowcase. Two held him while the two he'd taken down worked him over.

His bruises ached, and gravel scraped his bare feet as they dragged him out. The night air was cold on his skin. He made frantic mental notes of that as if it mattered, as if it might help at some point. It was all he had. His neighbors were mainly wolves. The few nulls spent the full moon at the local church. He knew because they always tried to talk him into joining them. No one was going to see him.

Hands grabbed his arms and legs to bundle him into the trunk of a car. It slammed shut, and he squirmed against his bonds. The cuffs were too tight to pull his hands free, but he managed to use his shoulder to shove the pillowcase up over his head.

It was dark, but after a few bumps, the driver had to stop for something. In the dim red glow cast by the brake lights, Marlow could see the SDPD gear bundled up under him.

There'd been four people there that night by Marlow's count. The only thing Marlow knew for sure was that none of them had been Piper; he'd been at the warehouse when they got there. It could have been some of the cops who got fired when the department cleaned house. Or they could have slipped IA's net and still be on the force.

Two of them could be in the cafe with Marlow right now. Probably not, but Marlow didn't want to bet his life on it. He got up, tossed his empties in the trash, and grabbed one of the nice metal knives from a table—there was a reason not to hole up in a McDonald's for you--as he headed toward the single restroom at the back of the cafe.

The back of Marlow's neck itched, but he resisted the urge to look around. That would just slow him down and draw attention to him. If he'd misjudged his exit, a heavy hand on his shoulder would let him know soon enough.

"Hey," a cop said. Marlow didn't need to look around to know it was one of them. He recognized the way they projected their voice, the assumption of authority. "Sir. You at the back. Stop right there."

Marlow didn't. He stiff-armed the door open, ducked inside, and slammed it shut behind him. The lock was built into the handle. It wouldn't hold long, but it would buy him a few more seconds than a latch. Marlow turned the lock *just* before he felt the impact of someone slamming into the other side of it. It hit his shoulders hard.

"Sir," the cop said. He tried the door again, rattling it in its frame. "Officer Marlow. This isn't the way to do it. Just turn yourself in."

There was a big metal bin against the wall. Marlow dragged it over and wedged it under the handle.

"I didn't do it," Marlow said. He'd cased the cafe before he came in earlier. The bathroom had a small window that opened into the alley. "Tell Bennett the guy was dead when we got there."

He lifted the toilet seat—rookie mistake to stand on that—and climbed up to stand on the bowl. The sour, off-putting smell of a well-used toilet poorly covered up with bleach rose around him as he felt around the window. It was painted shut, layers of heavy white paint crusted over the wood.

"Then how come your bullet ended up in the corpse?" the cop asked.

Marlow paused for a second, the blunt edge of the knife half wedged into the crack of the window. His mind replayed the double-tap concussion he'd heard as he made his getaway. A bitter smile twisted his mouth. Franklin always had improvised well, the bastard.

"Course it was," he muttered and yanked back on the knife.

Paint cracked, and old wood splintered.

"Look, I'm a wolf, but I get it," the cop said. His voice was carefully measured, reasonable and engaging. "I've seen the footage. Being out on the streets on a full moon, every full moon. That has to get to you."

"Does it?"

"It obviously did. Then you met this guy, and you could see how it was going to end, right? He was going to get killed, and you just wanted to save him. You just wanted to stop the wolf."

Behind the measured "talk him down" cadence of the cop's voice, Marlow could hear the soft mutter of another conversation. The clerk's voice, pinched tight and nervous, cracked high and sharp as she said, "I don't know. I guess so. Yes. There is. Yes."

They knew about the window.

Marlow gave the knife one last yank. The window was loose in the frame now, chips of paint scattered over the sill and Marlow's boots. He shoved against the window. The latch creaked as he put his weight against it, but held. Marlow pulled back and slammed the heels of his hands against the frame hard enough to sent a jolt of pain through his wrists.

"Hey!" the cop outside yelled and hit his shoulder against the door. "What are you doing, Marlow? Don't run. You won't get far."

Wood splintered and gave at one side. The gap was wide enough for Marlow to get his fingers into it and wrench it open the rest of the way. Cold air blew into the bathroom as Marlow dropped the glass to the ground outside. He got his elbows on the sill and boosted himself up to climb out.

A broken splinter of wood caught in Marlow's shirt, just under his arm. He felt it dig into his skin as he twisted around so his back was to the alley. The door rattled as someone on the other side threw themselves against it with a thud of muscle against wood.

Once. Twice.

The door popped open and jammed against the bin. Marlow reached up, dug his fingers into the crevices between the bricks, and hauled himself up. He braced his feet against the brick ledge and glanced around.

This part was where he was either lucky or not. The alley ended behind the cafe in a blank concrete wall, dumpsters shoved up against it behind the "wolf proof" cage. Marlow hadn't been able to see what was on the other side. Now he crab-walked along the metal edges of the cage, steadied by his grip on the brick, to the wall.

"Hey!" the cop barked from behind him. "Think about this, Marlow. You can still hand yourself in. You said you didn't kill that man; this is how you can prove it. Tell us who did."

Marlow took a quick glance back. The cop leaned out the broken window, body twisted around and a gun aimed at Marlow. If he'd been one of Franklin's, he'd have probably taken the shot already.

"Yeah," Marlow said. "Good idea. Give me a couple of days, and I'll get back to you on that…"

A shadow of begrudged amusement crossed the cop's face. "Not how this is going to play out," he said.

"Kit Marlow! You're under arrest!" the second cop skidded into the alley, gun out and held low in front of her. "Don't fucking move, or I'll shoot!"

The first cop pulled a frustrated face and jerked his head around. "Cartwright, stand down," he said. "This is under control."

Marlow saw Cartwright start to raise the gun, the tension in her shoulders and the decision in the set of her mouth. He pushed himself off the side of the building and jumped over the wall.

Or Cartwright saw him start to move and took her shot.

It happened so quickly that even Marlow couldn't swear his interpretation was the right one. Either way, his feet hit the metal roof of the lean-to garage on the other side as a bullet bounced off the wall where he'd been a second ago. It was close enough that a chip of brick caught his cheek.

The garage roof creaked as he landed, but it held under his weight. He slid down it on his ass and dropped over the edge into the alley, into a stack of old car parts. It wasn't his most graceful landing ever, half pratfall and half tumble, but he hadn't broken anything.

Marlow kicked a broken headlight out of his way and scrambled to his feet. He brushed himself off as he jogged down the alley, turned left as he reached the street, and slowed his pace to a steady walk. The adrenaline that hit his bloodstream wanted him to run, but that would draw attention. He ignored the twitch of muscles in the backs of his thighs and the over-clocked thump of his heart as he walked calmly along.

He stole a hoodie from the back of an unattended chair outside a cafe and shrugged it on. It smelled of someone else's sweat—fresh and sharply salty—and a faint underlay of smoke that itched in his nose. He stuck his hands in the pockets and found the original owner's lighter, but not his cigarettes.

It took a block before Marlow saw his next opportunity. A man in a hastily donned suit—the tail of his shirt was untucked and there was a price tag still on the sole of the trainers as he tugged them on—ranted into the phone he held against his ear with one shoulder. Annoyance lilted in his voice as he tied the laces.

"…I *did* rent a locker. No. I did," he said. "Will you listen? Just… Well, if you'd let me finish. Yes. That's what I said. I *did* rent one. Yes, like you said, one by the office. When I got there this morning, someone had broken into it and stolen my shoes. Just my shoes. Obviously not my phone. I'm on my phone. Anyhow, I'll be there soon. Okay? Fuck sake."

He hung up with an irritated jab of his thumb and dropped the phone into his pocket. After an irritated sigh, he picked up the cup of hot broth. He held it in both hands, fingers interlaced, and breathed in the steam.

Marlow bent down on his way past—and had to bite the inside of his cheek against the oof of pain as his shoulder twinged—and lifted the phone out of the man's pocket. The screen was still on. Marlow took a second to remember Cade's number and then pulled up the man's texts to send a quick message.

2nd date? Same as the first. Noon.

He paused for a moment, thumb poised above the Send button. It was a lot to ask. Cade had already gone above and beyond what was reasonable in trying to track down who'd taken over from Piper. Now he was supposed to help a fugitive who might, for all he knew, actually be a murderer?

Cade wasn't a cop, and wishful thinking aside, he wasn't Marlow's anything.

But he was the only person Marlow trusted right now. So Marlow hit Send, deleted the message—it could be retrieved if the techs looked for it, but it would slow them down—and gave the phone a quick wipe on his sleeve before he dropped it onto another table.

Whether Cade got back to him or not, at least he had a plan now.

Like the cop had said, the best way to prove Franklin was a liar was to find the real murderer.

CHAPTER THREE

"PART OF ME doesn't blame him," Bennett said. "Every full moon, we go out and put our asses on the line to get clawed up and bitten, beaten and killed, all for a government salary. You know the department doesn't even have to pay us overtime if they call us in to cover a staff shortage? Essential duties."

Cade crossed his arms and rocked onto the back legs of his chair. "Really?" he said. "You should talk to our recruitment agent. Cold Winds has a very generous benefits package for any null employees who pick up the slack during the full moon. Plus, we have a very generous compensation scale for employees injured in the line of duty."

Without looking up from her notes, Beth added in a dry voice, "We also have full dental."

Bennett ran her tongue over her teeth behind her scabbed, still-swollen lip.

"You think I'm going to sell out Night Shift for a nicer smile?" she asked.

"Fair enough," Cade said. He gave Bennett a toothy, empty grin. "I don't suppose you'd get much use out of that."

Beth kicked him under the table. The toe of her expensive shoe—Cade wasn't that interested in women's fashion, but he could recognize money—clipped his ankle. He managed not to grimace at the unexpected pain and held his tongue as Beth underlined something on the page and looked up.

"I think we've gotten off track." She tugged her sleeve back to look at the slim leather-banded watch on her wrist. "And your time with Mr. Deacon is running out, I'm afraid. So, to recap? Your theory is that Officer Marlow, a veteran Night Shift officer with numerous commendations on record, turned to murder because of overtime?"

"I didn't realize we were on the clock," Bennett said.

"Oh, don't you hate it when that happens?" Beth asked. "When people have different expectations of something and don't realize it? It's how so many Tinder dates end. So no one ends up blue-balled, let's clear up the ground rules now. Mr. Deacon's time is valuable, I'm here to safeguard that, and you have exactly ten more minutes before I get snarky and ask if he is free to leave. You'll have to say yes, since you have absolutely no cause to hold him, and then we'll be done here. So, now we're all on the same page. Yes?"

Bennett raised her eyebrows. "You'll *get* snarky?"

"You have no idea," Beth said. She tapped the pen on the table. "So again, your theory is that one of the SDPD's best and brightest went off the deep end because he didn't get overtime. Too bad and so sad, but how does that involve my client? It's nine minutes now, so… be succinct."

Nine minutes. By Cade's count, Bennett wasted a good five seconds of them in a staring match with Beth. Then she gave a thin twitch of a smile and looked down to flick through the file in front of her.

"You see, I don't know," Bennett said. "Maybe he was just sick of being the clean-up crew. Or he saw this Clemons guy being harassed month after month, with nothing we could do to help him, and just… made the wrong call. At the end of the day, though, I don't know why Marlow, who was a good cop, did this. I don't know what pushed him to it or what pressure finally made him snap. He wasn't talking to me. He wasn't talking to any of us, anyone in the department, not really. The only person he talked to was Mr. Deacon, here. We have phone calls, messages, secret meetings—"

Cade shifted his weight and brought the front legs of the chair down with a thud.

"We were going to fuck," he said. "Sometimes I like to talk first."

"I'm sure you talk during, as well," Bennett said. She held up her hand in front of Beth's face to stop whatever comment she'd been about to make. "I know. Seven minutes. Did you have any idea that Marlow planned to do something like this?"

"No," Cade said.

"At any point did he talk to you about Victor Clemons's problem with Barney Lyons? Did he express sympathy for Clemons's situation or seem frustrated at Lyons?"

"No."

"Did he seem upset about anything when you last spoke? Angry? Depressed? Conflicted?"

Cade hesitated for a second before he answered. He glanced at the one-way mirror that took up one wall of the interrogation room and wondered who was on the other side. O'Hara? One of Piper's one-time goons? If Cade put his cards on the table right now, would it make the situation worse or put some reasonable doubt in people's minds?

It was hard to tell, but if he spat out something like that without running it past his legal counsel, Beth would kill him.

He flicked his attention back to Bennett. "He seemed fine," he said.

Bennett licked her split lip and pulled a report out of her file. She glanced briefly—performatively—at it and set it down in the middle of the table.

"And the last time you saw him?" she said as she tapped the paper with a bruised finger. "That would be at the strip club where you were involved in a shootout, and a stripper ended up in hospital?"

Beth cleared her throat and reached out to grab the sheet. She ran her gaze down it quickly.

"Okay," she said as she held up one finger to stall the conversation.

"That wasn't the last time I saw him," Cade said. "The last time I saw him was later that night, when he had his hand around my—"

"Time's up," Beth interrupted him, one hand on his forearm to remind him why she was there. "My client's free to leave? Isn't that where we left it?"

"By my clock," Bennett said. "I've another five minutes."

Beth gave her a thin smile as she stood up. "Your clock is wrong, Officer Bennett," she said as she gathered her stuff up. "We're leaving. Unless you intend to detain my client, in which case I can schedule in an extra few hours to bring the SDPD's roof down around your collective ears."

For a second, it looked like Bennett, the muscles in her jaw clenched so hard her teeth had to ache, would try and call Beth's bluff. Then she grimaced sourly and stood up.

"You're free to go, but don't leave town."

"Didn't plan on it."

Bennett walked them out to the elevators. She pressed the button for them and turned to go. Before she went, she leaned in too close to Cade and dropped her voice to a murmur. A cop stepped out into the hall, forms held clumsily in the fingers that stuck out of his scribbled-on cast, and then backtracked through the door as he saw the confrontation.

"Attack lawyer or not," she said, "I will find out how you're involved in this and how you dragged Marlow into it. You're lying, and I can tell."

"I'd be more impressed with your insight," Cade said, "if you didn't actually believe that Marlow would do this."

"I don't believe it," Bennett said with an angry crack in her voice, "I *know* it. Franklin caught him red-handed, and Marlow tried to kill him. Guilty or not, though, he's not going down for this alone."

The elevator chimed, and the doors slid open.

"Mr. Deacon," Beth said. "We should go before you give them anything for free."

Cade glanced at her and nodded. You didn't pay a lawyer and ignore her advice. He stepped around Bennett and into the lift. Habit made him step back and lean against the wall, his hands braced on the railing.

The glass was cold against his shoulders, and the taste of blood was on the back of his throat.

In front of him, Marlow stood, weight shifted to one side to accommodate the heavy bag slung over his shoulder. The hair on the back of Marlow's neck was prickled with awareness and tight with his determination not to look around at Cade.

Heat unfurled in Cade's stomach with slow, pleased-with-itself inevitability. How had he not noticed this Marlow before? he wondered.

"I have a question for you," he said, ignoring Beth's aggrieved hiss of "Not now" as she jammed her finger against the ground floor button. Bennett set her jaw, tucked her hands in her pockets, and waited. "If Marlow wanted Franklin dead, why didn't he aim for the head?"

Bennett opened her mouth to answer and then closed it again as a frown pinched her eyebrows together. She shook the doubt off with a visible twitch of her shoulders, but the elevator doors shut in her face before she could rebut him.

"If you want someone to defend the man, Cade," Beth said as the lift started up, "hire someone. 'He didn't try to kill that guy because he's a good killer and would have succeeded if he wanted to' isn't actually the staunch support of his innocence that you think it is. Besides, aren't cops taught to aim at center of mass?"

Cade snorted. "Not if they know someone is wearing Kevlar. Then you're just going to—" He stopped mid-sentence as his brain caught up with his mouth.

"What?" Beth said.

"Knock them on their ass in an alley," Cade said. In his head, he replayed the fight that Bennett had talked about, the way the bullets had thrown the mystery attacker on his ass before he'd escaped. Something else picked at his memory too. An insistent nudge from his subconscious that he'd missed something.

The woman in the car? No, that hadn't been Bennett. Marlow trusted her, and Cade resented that enough he'd like her to be thoroughly implicated. She'd not have hidden in the car, though, or missed. Bennett wasn't someone to stay out of a fight.

Ah. There it was. It had been before the alley, when Cade had followed Lance out of the strip club. The guy who'd grabbed Cade's ass had probably taken a broken wrist home that night, just like the cop that had nearly tripped over himself to avoid… not Bennett, but Cade.

"What?" Beth repeated, irritated now. "Why do you look like the wolf that got the snout?"

"Because you forgot your phone," Cade said.

"Doesn't sound like me," Beth said.

"I'll owe you one," Cade said.

Beth hesitated for a second and then sighed as she took her phone out of her pocket. She hiked her skirt up to expose the knife she wore strapped to her thigh. Cade looked away as she tucked the slim square of the phone under the strap. It only seemed polite, even if Beth's leg wasn't going to do anything for him.

"What do you need me to get?" she asked.

"Did you see that cop that decided he didn't actually need to leave the room he was in?"

"Broken wrist?"

"That's the one. Get his name," Cade said. "He's involved in this."

Beth cleared her throat to let him know she was finished. She smoothed her skirt down over her legs with both hands.

"Lem thinks this isn't Cold Winds business," she said. "That it shouldn't be your business either. I'm good at my job, Cade, but not a lot of people who take on City Hall, or the police department, come out of it happy with how things went."

The elevator stopped as it reached the ground floor.

"Are you and Lem back together?" Cade asked.

Beth snorted. "No."

"Then what do you care what he thinks?" Cade asked as the doors swung open. He stepped out as the handful of people waiting to get on shuffled out of his way. "Are you coming?"

Beth shook his head—to the question or the situation, could be either—and stayed put.

"I forgot my phone," she said as she leaned in to press the button to go back down. "Go on ahead. The office will send my bill over."

He left her to it and checked his messages as he headed back to his car. A text from an unknown number made him frown, the back of his neck itchy as it missed his hackles. Piper? He'd not been in touch since he put his deal on the table. Cade had tried to get in touch, but no one answered the contraband phone, and Maria insisted she had no other way to contact him.

He swiped the screen and broke stride briefly as he stared at the cryptic message.

Not Piper.

Probably Marlow, but Cade wasn't sure. One month, however intense, wasn't enough time to build that sort of code on.

That said, if it *was* Marlow, then Cade knew exactly where he meant, and he had half an hour to get there.

The restaurant didn't open for lunch.

Cade sat three buildings down, on a rickety metal chair outside an Italian café, and let his pasta get cold as he waited. He picked at the congealed ragu idly whenever the server came out to glare at him and tried not to check the time.

It had been twelve-thirty the last time he looked, and Cade didn't want to know exactly how long Marlow could keep him on a string—or dwell on the other reasons that Marlow might be delayed. Cade snorted to himself and ate a bit of the duck he unearthed from the sauce. Look at that; he'd rather Marlow had stood him up than gotten himself killed.

Maybe this was true love after all.

He waited for the cynical snort to chase that thought like the bite of lime after a shot of tequila. Nothing. Just the twee, teenage yearn of the idea. Cade felt a sort of unmoored panic for a second. But before he could commit to it, Marlow slid into the seat opposite him.

"Sorry I'm late," Marlow said as he rested his elbows on the table. He looked younger without his glasses, softer. The flick of freckles on his nose was more obvious, and there was nothing to disguise the tiredness that bruised under his pale eyes. "Traffic."

There were a lot of threads tangled up in the relief that relaxed Cade's shoulders. He decided to focus on the one he wanted to deal with.

"I know you didn't shoot Franklin," he said. "Did you kill the wolf?"

Marlow shook his head. "Lyons was dead when I got there." He picked up the cold coffee and took a long, appreciative drink of the tepid brew. Once he was done, he wiped his mouth on the back of his hand and gave Cade a curious look. "How do you know that I didn't shoot—?"

"I suppose the romantic thing would be to say I know you'd never do something like that," Cade said dryly. He paused to let Marlow snort at him and then admitted the truth. "But I happen to know who did shoot him."

"Who?"

"Me."

Marlow stared at him for a second, eyebrows raised. "I appreciate the thought," he said with a flash of dry humor. "Not so sure of the logistics. Those urban legends about wolves shooting themselves with unsecured guns aside, paws aren't designed for triggers."

"Did you see the footage?" Cade asked.

Marlow shook his head as he finished his cold coffee with every sign of enjoyment. He set the cup down and leaned back in his seat as he casually glanced down the street. Without the coffee to keep his hands occupied, he tapped his fingers absently on the table.

"No," he said. "I caught bits and pieces, enough to get the gist of how they've spun the story, but I've not seen any footage. Drone?"

A couple walked out of a side street down the block. The blond woman pushed the baby stroller with one hand while she pulled her partner's hand down so she could look at his phone. They bickered as they walked. From the way they squinted at street signs, it was over whether they were going the right way.

Both Cade and Marlow stopped what they were doing and pointedly didn't watch as the two approached.

They were probably tourists, but they could be cops.

Apparently unaware of the tension, the couple bickered their way past two more streets before they finally agreed to take the next left.

"I *told* you," drifted back, sharp with satisfaction, as they shoved the stroller up the hill.

Marlow exhaled slowly and visibly slouched down in his chair. He pushed his hood back and scrubbed his fingers through the tangled mess of his hair.

"Shit," he said tiredly.

Cade reached into his jacket for his wallet. He counted out money for lunch, with a tip generous enough to make up for his extended stay, and tucked it under the plate of picked-over pasta.

"We should get out of here," he said. "I don't think your colleagues followed me here, but they do suspect we're in contact. All it will take is one sighting by a patrol car to confirm that, and then I'll be in the same position as you."

Marlow's shoulders slumped for a second, the weight of his exhaustion almost visible, and then he lifted his chin. "You're right," he said as he pulled his hood back up and got to his feet. His boots scuffed the pavement as he stepped back. "This is my problem, one I should have handled a long time ago. I shouldn't have—"

He turned to go.

Cade tucked his wallet into his jacket and sat back to see how long it would take Marlow to realize that tactic wasn't going to work here. No one negotiated protection contracts for a living and made a profit if they let the other parties yank on their heartstrings.

He enjoyed the smug feeling of superiority for a heartbeat. Then he remembered this wasn't an oil baron who wanted to make sure his wife didn't get paint thrown on her by protesters. It was Marlow, and he was already halfway across the road.

"Shit."

Cade got up and chased after him. He stopped in the middle of the road, toes on the white-painted lines, to let a repair truck by. The guy in the passenger seat yelled "Stupid fucker!" at him on the way by, the words drawn out thin by the wind.

The minute the truck was past, Cade ran over the rest of the road and found Marlow waiting for him on the curb, hunched into that oversized hoodie with his hands shoved in his pockets.

"What do you—?" Marlow started to ask.

Cade grabbed the front of his hoodie and dragged him into a kiss. Even cold coffee tasted better when it was on Marlow's tongue, the bitterness mellowed out and sweetened with a faded dash of salt and copper. After a moment's surprise, Marlow laughed against Cade's mouth—a low, rough sound—and leaned into the kiss. He hooked his fingers into the waistband of Cade's trousers to pull him closer so they were pressed against each other.

There wasn't time, Cade reminded himself reluctantly. He tilted his head back out of the kiss. Marlow—briefly—chased Cade's mouth but then remembered the situation.

"Idiot," Cade said. It could have been meant for him or Marlow. Both of them, maybe. That worked. "If I didn't want to be involved, I wouldn't be here."

Marlow tilted the corner of his mouth up wryly. "Still," he said. "I should go. Franklin is like herpes in a lot of ways, but he's not communicable by kissing. This isn't your problem."

"*You're* my problem," Cade said.

He heard it. It wasn't that he didn't hear it. The problem was that it was always too late to rethink it by that point.

Marlow tilted his head. "Thanks?" he said.

"I want you," Cade said. His voice was low and thick, the back of his throat scratchy as if he might just be allergic to honesty. "In a lot of ways. I want you in my bed, on your knees, out to dinner with me in a restaurant that has tables and plates. That's personal. And while you getting killed by Franklin would throw a spanner in the works, it's not why I'm here."

Color had crawled up into Marlow's cheeks and turned the bridge of his nose pink as he listened. He flicked his tongue over his lips.

"So why?"

"Because Franklin isn't someone that I can coexist with professionally," Cade said. "And more importantly, I'm pretty sure he feels the same way. So right now, we have the same problem."

Marlow raised his eyebrows. "I thought *I* was your problem," he said.

"Remember when I told you to flunk the physical so they'd not approve you for duty this month?"

"Fair point," Marlow said after a second. He scrubbed his hands through his hair under the loose drape of the hood. "Okay, so what next?"

"We get out of here together," Cade said. "I have a property nearby that's not exactly… on the books. Even if the cops are looking, it should take them a while to find it."

Marlow nodded his agreement as they headed back toward Cade's car. Despite that, Cade kept his hand on Marlow's back, spread over the space between his shoulder blades, as if he thought the other man was still a flight risk.

CHAPTER FOUR

MARLOW SHRUGGED THE stolen hoodie off. It probably smelled more like him than the original owner by now. He still felt better once he'd shed it. He tossed it over the back of a chair and looked around. His gaze took in the heavy, soft leather couches, the smooth plastered walls decorated with black-and-white line art, and colorful 3D sculptures of geometric animal heads mounted on the walls.

"I know you have a low opinion of the SDPD," he said, "but I think we'll be able to find your apartment."

They would. Marlow didn't care. He'd hit empty about two hours ago. Right now, if Bennett turned up with a warrant, he'd take two hots and a cot as a good deal. He wasn't tired, not any more than usual, he was just *done.*

"Give me some credit," Cade said. "This is a Cold Winds safe house for clients or operatives that, for one reason or another, don't want anyone to know they're in town. It's owned through a shell company, and I've never been here before. I don't have an apartment in the city."

There it was, that faintly prickly note in Cade's voice that meant he felt his status had somehow been called into question. Marlow supposed it was weird to find that flash of insecurity endearing, but he did.

"I remember," Marlow said. He gave in to temptation and sat down on one of the overstuffed couches. It wasn't actually as soft as it looked, but close enough. "You own a ranch outside of town. It's probably very expensive, and I am appropriately impressed, don't worry."

Cade gave him a hard look. The raw wound to his ego that drove him to flash cash and shove his way to the front of every line probably wasn't at all amusing from his side.

"Sorry." Marlow straightened up and scrubbed his hands over his face. "In my head, that was not… being a bastard."

Cade studied him for a second. Then he tilted the corner of his mouth up in a wry smile.

"I was actually annoyed you wouldn't remember everything I told you about myself," he said, "for the record."

Marlow folded his arms behind his head. "You've not exactly told me a lot," he pointed out.

"All the more reason to hoard what information I do share," Cade said. "Also, not sure anyone would describe you as an open book, Marlow."

"What do you want to know?" Marlow asked with a shrug. "Why my gran called me Kit? How she ended up raising me? Do the eyes run in the family? Or—"

"How involved were you in Piper's organization?"

That question knocked the wind out of Marlow. He could feel the old ache in his chest, the dull shock of impact the second before the bullet hole in his shoulder had started to hurt. It wasn't something he wanted to talk about, not now.

Too clever to con and too moral to corrupt. Franklin's judgment—*Piper's* really—bounced around the inside of Marlow's head. It should have felt like some sort of dispensation, he supposed, but all he could think about was the uneasy ground in the middle and how long he spent there. Every time he'd looked away or gave Piper the benefit of the doubt. It had to be a hundred easily justified little compromises over the years. More.

"Less than I could have been, more than I should have been," Marlow said after a moment. He lowered his arms and leaned forward to rest his elbows on his knees. It eased the phantom ache in his chest. "Not enough to be any good to us now."

It wasn't an answer. He knew that. Cade still accepted it as one, with a twitch of his mouth to suggest he was disappointed.

"Fair enough," he said. "What—"

"Piper always had a good reason for what he did," Marlow said. "He never came out and asked if you wanted to make a shit load of money doing crimes. He just eased you into it, one blind eye turned at a time. It always made sense. So he let some gangbangers walk instead of arresting them? We were Night Shift, not Vice. Besides, it was useful to have people who owed us on the street. Yeah, Adam Rodriguez should have been charged when he killed his girlfriend—it was borderline, the courts should have had their say—but his father Carlos fed Piper info about people trafficking. We saved more lives than were lost by giving the kid the benefit of the doubt. Okay, Piper took a backhander from some guy in the Reserve to escort his null girlfriend in and out, but he gave a chunk of it to Harris to rebuild his goddamn shoulder after a wolf near tore it off. Seems fair enough, right?"

Marlow heard his voice crack and stopped. Old guilt, finally unstoppered after all these years, felt sticky as it filled the back of his throat.

"This might not be the time to mention it," Cade said. He straddled the arm of the couch, close enough that Marlow could feel the heat of the wolf under his skin. "But like I told Bennett, Cold Winds offers excellent medical benefits to our null employees."

"Asshole," Marlow said.

Cade chuckled, short and husky, and cupped his hand around the nape of Marlow's neck. Maybe to a wolf it would have meant something specific, tapped some instinct pulled up close to the skin by the moon. Marlow just caught his breath from how hot the possessive grip of practical, callused fingers was.

"What made you draw the line?" he asked.

"I don't know if I did, if I would have," Marlow admitted. "I wasn't part of it. I heard about it later. Franklin told us all about it like it was a joke. People on the Reserve used to pay for *extras*. More patrols, discretion if any of their kids acted out, that sort of thing. Money for nothing, Piper called it, since he never did any of it. Which is why one guy, a local politician, decided not to pay after his son got Crated and charged the next day. Deliberate Endangerment. Franklin grabbed this guy off the street before the moon rose, drove him up into the mountains, and kicked him out just when he started to shift. The wolf probably had a good time, but the poor bastard had no idea where he was when he woke up the next morning."

"Did he die?"

"I think I would have turned them in for that. For murder," Marlow said.

Even as he said it, though, he could hear Piper's easy, believable voice in the back of his head. He'd call it an accident and say they'd learned their lesson, that Marlow would be within his rights to turn them in, but… There was always a "but," always a greater good that Piper was somehow on the right side of. He might have talked Marlow round, even with a dead man on a slab. That wasn't something that Marlow wanted Cade to know, though.

"No, the park rangers found the guy the next morning. He was dehydrated, and he had sunstroke, but he was alive. Paid what he owed from his hospital bed, Franklin said, now that he'd been shown who was boss. I told myself I'd go to IA and tell them everything… but first I'd talk to Piper, let him tell me his side of things. Only, I never got the chance."

Cade absently grazed his thumb over the sensitive hollow under Marlow's ear. The caress cut through the smog of old guilt with a much more immediate distraction. His mind should have been on how to clear his name and make Franklin pay for everything he'd done. Instead, Marlow leaned into Cade's hand, and Cade scruffed him to pull him to his feet.

"Come on," he said. "I want to show you something."

"Any chance it's a bed?" Marlow asked. It might have passed as seductive if he'd not immediately yawned hard enough to make his jaw pop.

"Next time," Cade promised. He picked up a tablet from the dining table pushed against the wall and tapped at the screen for a second. Once he'd pulled up what he wanted, he handed it to Marlow. "What do you see?"

On the screen, Night Shift officers—anonymous in full gear to the point even Marlow could only pick out a few of them—loped in and out of the shot. Bennett, helmet off and blood on her face, walked next to the stretcher they'd loaded Franklin onto. He held her hand, head tipped back against the board and mouth set in a grimace.

"Franklin making a meal out of me *not* shooting him?"

Cade reached over and tapped the screen to pause it. "Look at the bruises."

Blue and purple spread over Franklin's chest and up over his shoulder. The marks looked livid under the glare of the incident spotlights set up around the ambulance. Marlow frowned and pinched the screen to zoom in.

"They're not fresh bruises," he said.

"No," Cade said. "That's because I shot him over a week ago. At SKINNED. This guy was there too."

He flicked the video to the side and pulled up a picture of a fresh-faced man with acne scars on his cheekbones.

"The rookie?" Marlow said.

"George Cook," Cade said. "He tried to start a fight with me in the club that night, but he wasn't quite up to it. Once I broke his wrist for him, he lost interest."

"He always hesitated before he committed to a course of action," Marlow said. Habit made his voice dry and critical, as if he was in O'Hara's office to give his feedback on the rookie's progress. "He's lucky you only broke his arm. If he doesn't have the confidence to risk a mistake, he'll get someone killed one day."

"A friend?" Cade asked.

Marlow shook his head. "New guy," he said. "Bennett was his training officer. Franklin took him under his wing. In more ways than one, I guess. But I don't see how it helps. We could have the full roster of dirty cops in the department, but without evidence, we can't do anything with it."

"Trust me," Cade said. "You don't need evidence when you have leverage. Cook here has 'weak link' written all over him."

That was true. He did. If the rookie didn't have the confidence to commit for fear of mistakes, he wouldn't have bought in to Franklin's con. Not yet. But…

"It could work, but leverage takes time, and I don't have that," Marlow said as he handed the tablet back. "Franklin isn't going to let me talk to Cook or anyone else if he can help it. Even if I turn myself in to O'Hara today—so Franklin can't make sure I get shot 'resisting arrest'—I won't last the night. No one is going to ask too many questions about a 'disgraced Night Shift officer who couldn't live with the shame' headline. It's what they want to hear."

"Leverage doesn't have to be legal," Cade pointed out. "And how are we going to clear your name without taking Franklin down? He says you killed Lyons, you say he did—but you're the one who ran."

"Franklin didn't kill Lyons," Marlow said.

"That leaves you," Cade pointed out. "I can get you a good lawyer if you want to confess, but it's the opposite of clearing your name."

Marlow snorted.

"I had no reason to kill Lyons," he said. "And I didn't. He was dead when we got there. So if I find out who did kill him, that's a hole blown right through Franklin's story. Then we can expose him… even if it means making a deal with Piper."

Cade shook his head at the concession. "We'd be in a lot less trouble if you'd come to that conclusion *yesterday*," he pointed out.

"Do you want me to say you were right?" Marlow asked.

"Yes."

"You were right," Marlow admitted. "I should have listened to you."

Cade nodded in response. "Thank you," he said. "Not as satisfying as if you'd resented every word, but still, it's the principle of the thing."

"I was wrong," Marlow said with a shrug. "I've experienced it before. The stakes were even the same. Piper deserves to be in jail, and not just for what he did to me. I stand by that. But Franklin needs to be there more. He's hurting people now, not in the past, and you saw that when I couldn't look past my own grudge."

Cade reached out and cupped Marlow's face in his hand. He grazed his thumb over Marlow's lower lip, and Marlow caught a ragged breath as heat shivered through him.

"All I saw is that you'd be safer if we used Piper," Cade said, his voice low and rough. "So don't give me too much credit."

"Got it."

They looked at each other for a second. Marlow could feel the tension between them. He knew he should say something. There were things he did want to say. He could feel them wedged in his throat—heartfelt, honest, emotional—but he couldn't get any of them out.

"So," Cade said. "You're the cop. What do we know about this Lyons guy?"

Marlow hesitated for a second. *Got it* was a hell of a note to leave it on with the only person in the whole city you trusted—but murder was easier to deal with. He made a note of that for later.

O'Hara was going to send him back to the department shrink once this was all over, and that would give them something to talk about.

"I know there's only one person in town whose house he ended up dead in," Marlow said. "If anyone killed Lyons, it had to be something to do with Clemons."

Cade nodded. "What do we know about him?"

"Nothing," Marlow said.

"Then that's where we start," Cade said. He fished his phone out of his pocket. "I'll give Lem a call and see what he can dig up."

He turned away as he lifted the phone to his ear. Marlow finally thought of something to say.

"Thanks," he said.

"I told you," Cade said. "I don't like being used, and I don't like people endangering my business. Franklin did both."

"I meant for the coffee," Marlow said.

It was for the thought behind the cold Americano and the fact that Cade had remembered what Marlow drank and that he'd probably appreciate it after the last few hours. The whole package. Of course, if Cade wasn't on the same wavelength, it would sound like Marlow *actually* thought a tepid beverage was worth more than aiding and harboring a fugitive.

Cade half turned to look at him. The corner of his mouth tilted up in a brief smile. Either he understood what Marlow wanted to say, or he thought Marlow was an idiot. He might not be wrong.

"You're welcome," Cade said, then sighed. "Not you, Lem. I need you to find some information for me. No, you didn't. I found Marlow on my own. I'll give you one more chance. Get me any background information you can on Victor Clemons. Start with his hotel booking last night and work backward from there."

"While he's doing that," Marlow said as he sniffed himself, "I'll have a shower."

Cade nodded and moved the phone away from his mouth, his hand cupped over the mouthpiece.

"I'll have to go," he said. "Make sure I'm seen not to be in your company. I'll come back later if I can make it before moonrise."

That was fine.

It wasn't like Marlow had hoped Cade would join him in the shower or anything like that.

"Nothing?" Marlow repeated the assertion. "How can there be nothing. He rents a house. He had mail. Dated a man."

Cade sprawled on the couch, a bottle of beer dangled from his fingers. He'd unbuttoned his collar and cuffs, his sleeves folded back along his forearms. His eyes were bright, gold rims around the irises as the wolf moved restlessly under his skin. The moon wasn't up yet—it would take more than one bad night to throw Marlow's internal clock off enough to lose track of that—but the difference between him when he'd left and when he came back was notable.

Blue moon, an imaginary Bennett insisted in the back of Marlow's head; *things get weird.*

"According to Lem, Victor Clemons started his life as a Grindr account two years ago. Before that, he didn't exist. Afterward, he got a job, drew a paycheck, and swiped left until he got to Barney."

He took a drink. Despite the situation, Marlow stopped thinking for a second to watch the line of Cade's throat move as he swallowed. Heat stung the back of Marlow's neck, and he had to give himself a mental kick to get his brain back on track.

"That sounds like someone who's running from something," he said.

"It sounds like me," Cade pointed out. "If you looked, you could find my birth certificate and a few early years' medical records, but before I left Alaska, my employers mostly paid me under the table. Even when they didn't need plausible deniability, they didn't want to pay the taxman."

"Why did you leave Alaska?" Marlow asked.

Cade laughed, a low, rich sound, and took a drink of beer. He wiped his mouth on the back of his hand.

Mind on the job, Marlow reminded himself.

"It could be described as running from something," Cade admitted. "Mostly my dad. A little bit the chance of a moose encounter. Fair enough."

"That could be the problem," Marlow said. "If he moved here from somewhere else. Franklin moved here from San Francisco, and he nearly got fired a couple of years ago for insurance fraud when they couldn't access his record of employment automatically. Shame it didn't go through now, obviously, but public records aren't set up to talk to each other because people don't move much."

Cade straightened up on the couch and looked thoughtful. "Wolves don't," he agreed. "Maybe from city to city, like Franklin, but not states. It didn't bother me, I think the wolf hated Alaska as much as I did, but most people find it hard to leave their territory. Nulls?"

Marlow shrugged. "We can move," he said. "Most don't. Either they have wolf family and friends, or it just doesn't occur to them since no one else does. The few who do… it's usually because of a fixation that was too persistent for the usual techniques to cope with."

"The same thing that got Barney Lyons killed?" Cade said. "That's… not evidence, but it's a theory."

Marlow nodded. He chewed his lower lip absently as he thought the idea through. "It makes sense. If Victor Clemons had to leave his whole life behind once because a wolf wouldn't leave him alone, and then it happened again… When we talked, he was angry, and he didn't want to make any compromises or try anything to wean Lyons off his attachment. Maybe because he'd tried it before and it didn't work? In that situation, he might decide to take things into his own hands."

"Self-defense?" Cade said. "Why let you take the blame, then?"

"If he had silver bullets to hand," Marlow said, "that's premeditation. Even if he can prove he used them to save his own life, he'd still get a few years for that. And just owning silver is a federal crime. If I hadn't set an extra patrol on the neighborhood, he would have probably come back in daylight and got rid of the body if wolves hadn't taken care of the remains for him."

Cade pulled a face. It probably wasn't something he wanted to imagine, Marlow supposed. He needed to start to think before he spoke.

"I mean—" he stumbled over an attempt to retract what he'd said, and Cade waved it away.

"Valid theory," he said, setting the bottle down by his feet before he stood up. "Still no evidence, though."

Cade stretched, one arm folded behind his head as he tried to loosen a knot. His shirt was tight over his shoulders and snug across his chest, and it rode up at the sides as Cade twisted to reveal taut, tanned skin. Marlow's mouth went dry.

"We need to talk to his first boss," he said. "Find out anything he said about where he came from."

Cade flashed a lazy grin. His teeth looked very sharp.

"Tomorrow," he said. "Unless you want to have to set me on fire again?"

"I'd rather not," Marlow said in a dry voice. He stood up, awkward as he wondered what the etiquette was. When he'd been a kid, Gran had just kissed him goodnight, given him his dinner, and locked him in the safe room.

It didn't seem entirely appropriate to this situation.

Cade stripped his shirt off over his head and dropped it onto the couch. He unbuttoned his jeans and had them halfway down his hips, thumbs hooked around the waistband, when it occurred to him to glance at Marlow.

"You know it's rude to stare," he said.

"Yeah," Marlow said, "I know."

That didn't mean he was going to look away. Cade laughed, a throaty, satisfied sound, and stripped the rest of his clothes off. He looked just as good as Marlow remembered from the… start of the month. It seemed longer than that.

"You going to be okay?" Cade asked. "Not your usual full moon."

Marlow glanced around and shrugged. "It's weird to sit it out," he admitted as he puffed out his cheeks on a sigh. "I might just get drunk and feel sorry for myself."

"I can think of something else you could do," Cade said as he idly scratched his jaw.

"What?"

Cade closed the distance between them in one stride and hooked his fingers into the waistband of Marlow's jeans. He dragged him in close so Marlow could feel the heat of all that naked skin. Marlow caught his breath, harsh and hot in the back of his throat, as he grazed his hands up Cade's bare, lean hips.

"Think about me," Cade growled, the scrape of the wolf thick under his words. "All night."

He clenched his hand around the back of Marlow's neck and kissed him, a quick, hard scrape of his mouth. Marlow sucked in a startled breath, the hot taste of Cade's mouth on his tongue, and before he could decide how to react, Cade pulled away from him.

There was a pause, and Cade glanced over his shoulder.

"I half expected Bennett to kick the door in," he admitted. "Based on her track record."

Marlow gave a snort of laughter and leaned in to kiss along Cade's collarbone. The skin under his mouth tasted like salt and was almost hot to the touch. Wolves ran hotter before the shift. He'd never been this close to one this close to the full moon.

The thought of it made something between arousal and uneasiness tug at his gut. Arousal had the edge.

"Once this is all over," he said, "maybe I'll visit that ranch house of yours."

Cade snorted. "I've already bought the coffee," he said, "so you better. If you still want to get drunk, whiskey is in the dresser."

Cade let the door slam behind him as he left. Marlow stared at the dresser for a second but decided against it, so he was sober when Cade's phone rang from the pocket of his abandoned jeans.

Who'd call a wolf on the full moon?

Marlow hesitated for a second as he debated the best thing to do, then reached down to grab it.

"Yeah?" he said. It wasn't a deliberate attempt to disguise his voice, but his throat was still thick with the taste of Cade.

"Piper says he'll call," Maria said, the words quick and stressed. "He said he'll talk to you, Marlow. Just you. Now you're off that high horse."

She hung up.

That explained why they'd called while the moon was up.

CHAPTER FIVE

CADE WOKE UP smug.

He lay on his back, concrete cool against his ass and shoulders, and peered up at the blue strip of sky overhead. Most of the time, the wolf gave him back his skin and a general sense of a night well spent—mornings he thought he'd eaten someone he knew aside. He'd never woken up and felt quite so ridiculously self-satisfied.

Last night he'd probably done something stupid.

Cade sat up, stretched until something popped, and looked around. An alley somewhere, smudges of graffiti on scar-scored brick walls, and a sheep's head left balanced on the fire escape. The mild gaze of milky eyes made Cade feel—briefly—guilty, but if he hadn't eaten it, someone else would have.

There was dried blood on him, crusted on his stomach and smeared down his legs. It was hard to tell if it was his, the sheep's, or someone else's, but it didn't look fresh either way. Cade scratched his stomach and turned to go. He nearly tripped over the tangle of cloth he'd apparently curled up on while still furry.

Black, shredded, and tangled around his feet. He kicked it loose and bent down to pick it up. That explained where the blood came from, he supposed, as he unknotted it and smeared more blood over his hands. He shook it out, and…

Shit.

The TAC team logo was splashed over the back, with NIGHT SHIFT in white block letters underneath. It looked like his grudge against the SDPD had carried over into the night. He hoped he hadn't killed anyone.

Not really. Not yet. He was sure he'd feel that way at some point, though.

Cade draped the ruined coat over the sheep's head. The alley was muddy and wet underfoot as he headed toward the street. He stopped on the pavement, one hand up to shade his eyes, and took a second to orient himself.

A man stood on one foot by a bank of lockers as he tried to pull his trousers on and juggle a phone call at the same time.

"What do you mean your mom was called into work?" he said. "Did she take you to your grandfather's? Well, who's with you, then? I have… Your mom knows I have to go to work this morning; are you sure she won't be back until— No. No, it's fine. I'll be home in twenty minutes, be ready."

He hung up and threw the phone back into the locker in frustration. It bounced off the metal, and he stood there for a second, half-dressed and exasperated, with his head in his hands. Cade left him to it as he turned right on instinct and headed down the street.

The plan had been to get a cab and maybe a cup of something hot to wash the sheep down. Instead, Cade stopped at the end of the street and stared at the low gray-and-yellow building opposite.

It looked like he hadn't gotten far last night. That didn't mean anything, but… the apartment was a business expense and the neighborhood was new to him. The only thing here that Cade cared about enough to bleed over into the wolf was Marlow.

That would be a problem at some point. It was the textbook example—literally, *Romeo and Juliet* was on nearly every school syllabus in the country—of why null/wolf relationships could be difficult to navigate. And Juliet hadn't even been Night Shift.

Cade scrubbed his hand through his hair and decided to worry about that later. He had a crush. It might feel like more—maybe it would become real—but he'd known Marlow a month. Cade would hold off on comparisons to famous tragic romances until they'd at least fucked.

That was a bad train of thought. All the excess energy leftover from the wolf headed for his cock as half-finished fantasies of Marlow under him flashed through Cade's mind. Scars and sweat-salted skin, lean muscle and tight flesh under Cade's mouth, and long legs wrapped around his waist—

Cade cleared his throat, shoved those thoughts back into the box for later, and started across the road to the apartment building.

"How did Piper know Marlow was here?"

The phone lay on the kitchen counter. The last call had been from a burner phone the night before. It had lasted under a minute. Piper wasn't in a rush to follow up with his promised call.

Lem shrugged and poured himself a glass of lemonade. "Lucky guess? It isn't like your friend has a lot of friends in town right now. If he wasn't with you, then he was in the wind." He boosted himself up onto the kitchen table and swung his sneakered feet over the tiled floor. "So, when you go to jail, do I get to run the company?"

"No."

"Who does?"

"Becky."

Lem snorted. He took a long drink of lemonade and admitted, "She'd do a good job." He put the glass down and wiped wet hands on his jeans before he pulled a folded-up envelope out of his jacket. "Addresses. Victor Clemons's old boss thinks you're doing a background check for some government agency. He is expecting you. It looks like Clemons is still at the Hilton, or his credit card is anyhow. He *has* booked a ticket to Portland for next week, though… which supports Officer Marlow's theory."

"I thought you didn't believe him," Cade said as he took the envelope. He slid his nail under the flap to open it. "That you were Team SDPD."

"I'm Team Mind Our Own Business," Lem corrected. "The police are paid to investigate crimes, to find out whodunnit… whether the 'dunnit' is murder or 'just' aiding and abetting a fugitive, by the way, so let them do it. That said… I pulled his disciplinary record."

Indignation was probably the appropriate response if this *was* something more than a crush. Cade wasn't that far gone, though.

"And?"

"He is in the bottom twenty-five percent for use of deadly force," Lem said. "His psych report from when he applied to Night Shift actually cited his positive relationship with his wolf family as a possible problem for him doing the job. Then there's the fact he's licked your tonsils, which isn't in the file but does suggest that he's got no problem with wolves."

Cade flinched at the mention of the psych report. It looked like that was where he drew the line. He didn't think he'd heard anything so far that would make him need to confess the transgression to Marlow, and he wanted to keep it that way.

He dragged the conversation back on topic.

"And?"

"And Officer Franklin's file reads real different," Lem said, the "real" drawn out between his teeth like taffy. "I still don't see how it's our business, though."

"That's because it's my business," Cade told him. "Also, you might need glasses because thinking Franklin wouldn't be gunning for us next is short-sighted."

Before Lem could argue, Marlow came out of the other room. His hair was styled back from his face with colored wax, streaks of gray worked into the dark waves, and the navy suit Lem had grabbed for him fit like his tailor wanted to fuck him. The combination somehow managed to look more severe than the all-black Night Shift uniform, more controlled, and Cade forgot how to swallow for a moment.

"Yeah," Lem muttered to him. "Okay, I can see that."

"The hoodie would draw less attention," Marlow said as he fidgeted with the cuffs. "I don't look like a cop; I look like I'm late for someone's wedding."

Late for our *wedding?* The dopamine-sodden part of Cade's brain tried to drop that idea into the mess it had already made in there. Cade squelched it. For one thing, he'd be livid if Marlow was late to their wedding, and they'd not be wearing navy either.

"The hoodie might pass on the street," Cade said. "Not in an office. You look like a detective."

"Most people say court," Lem said. "Or a funeral."

"I wear my uniform to both of those," Marlow said. He pulled his glasses out of his pocket and slid them on. That didn't help Cade drag his mind out of the gutter. "But that doesn't pass unremarked on."

Cade picked up the phone and tossed it to him. Marlow caught it out of the air one-handed and raised his eyebrows.

"Piper said he wants to speak to you," Cade said. "Let's not give him a chance to play keep-away games with us."

Marlow held the phone like it was a loaded gun for a second before reluctantly sliding it into his pocket.

"I'll see what else I can dig up on Clemons," Lem said. "If you find out anything from his boss, let me know. If I know where to look, I should be able to track him down."

Cade slapped his shoulder. "And keep the SDPD off my back?"

"Always."

Gavin Hackett was a sweaty man. It made his collar slump and beaded on his forehead, just under where his hairline had started a slow retreat to. When he unbuttoned his jacket, he flashed wet, dark patches of it under his arms.

Whatever he'd done wrong, he was not confident he'd done it well.

If Cade had been a genuine government official, he'd have immediately opened an investigation into Eye in the Sky Photography. He might not be able to say why straight out of the gate, but he was sure there was something.

"Don't worry," he said. "As far as we know, you're not involved in Mr. Clemons's situation."

Hackett shifted on the seat opposite and then shifted back again. Cade imagined the swampy squelch of sweaty ass and regretted it almost immediately.

"I'm not," he said. "Look, Clemons quit four months ago. No notice. Nothing. And after I went out on a limb to give him the job. Whatever happened at his house, between him and that wolf or that psycho Night Shift officer, it's nothing to do with me."

Cade paused as he glanced briefly at Marlow to try and assess his reaction to that. It didn't seem to have struck a nerve, maybe because he knew he was innocent or because he'd heard it before. Most people either hero-worshipped or at least appreciated Night Shift, but there were a minority who hated them. Cade's father had. He'd never liked any limits put on his behavior.

"That's not why we're here," Marlow said. He sipped his sweet-and-sour broth and sat back in the chair. "It's taxes."

Hackett exhaled, and his mouth twitched into a quick, relieved smile. He was a lousy liar. A good liar would know better than to be relieved that the taxman was there. No one was ever relieved to know it was something about taxes. Not unless they had something a lot worse on their conscience.

"Oh, well, I'm all paid up," Hackett said. "My accountant deals with all of that. I can give you her—"

"You hired Mr. Clemons when he first came to San Diego," Cade said, ignoring the attempt to palm them off. "Why?"

"What?"

"Why?" Cade repeated. "Did you know him previously?"

"No," Hackett said. He took a quick drink of his broth and nearly dripped some on himself. "I mean, he contacted me."

"From?"

Hackett glanced between them. "From where he lived."

"And where do you *think* that was?" Cade asked with just a hint of emphasis. Under Hackett's eye, a twitch started as Hackett realized there was a wrong answer to give.

Most of the time, back in Alaska, Cade had a petty thief or some idiot who'd thought he could sell company secrets on the other side of the table. It had also been in a small gray box of a room—everywhere he worked, no matter the company, had a room like that—not a coffee shop franchise with students and hipsters queued up in the background.

So far, the differences didn't matter. The old pressure tactics still worked. Even good liars got nervous at the idea someone else had lied to them.

"… Portland?" Hackett said.

"Is that a question or an answer?" Cade asked.

"I mean, he was in Vegas when he contacted me," Hackett said. "But he, um, came from Portland, I think. His most recent references were from there."

"Did he say why he wanted to move?" Cade asked. "Was it for someone or…"

Hackett licked his lips. "Man trouble," he said. "He, um, said he'd broken up with someone, and he needed a fresh start. I mean, hey, some guys just can't pick 'em, right? That's why I like girls."

"Not women?" Marlow asked.

That little nerve by Hackett's eye was going to tire itself out. "That's what I meant."

"Course," Marlow said in that mild voice that was somehow worrying. "Did you ever meet anyone from Victor's past? Did he go home for the holidays?"

Hackett started to shake his head before Marlow finished the question. "No. Nope. He never did. Up until he quit, he was the best photographer on staff. He worked weekends, and he worked late. He'd do the holidays and never had any conflicts. Hell, the most surprising thing about this business with Lyons is that he actually *had* a life outside of work."

"Why did he quit?"

There was a napkin folded up under Hackett's plate. He unfolded it and blotted his face with the grease-stained tissue.

"He said he'd got a new boyfriend," Hackett said. "They were going to move in together, but the new guy lived in… Santa Barbara? I don't remember. We were yelling at that point. Who moves for sex, right? Like you couldn't get your dick wet in town?"

He looked from Cade to Marlow for agreement. Neither of them obliged. Cade took a business card out of his jacket—plain white on the front with, when he turned it, a number printed neatly across the back—and handed it over.

"If anyone asks what we talked about, tell them to call me," he said. "It could be risky if anyone thinks you know more than you do."

They stood up. Marlow paused as he lifted his jacket from the back of the chair. "Do you still have Clemons's CV?" he asked.

Hackett shook his head. "Sorry, you should have asked last month. We got a virus. IT guy said it just lay low until it had infected everything—computers, backups, even the stuff in the cloud—and then scrambled it all when it triggered. Most of the footage and stills I still have, on cards, but everything else is gone."

"That's… inconvenient," Cade said.

They left Hackett to salt his broth with his own sweat and headed outside. A parking enforcement officer stood in front of the car—pulled from the Cold Winds pool of vehicles—and Marlow paused. His weight shifted slightly onto his back foot as he slowly exhaled.

"Left or right? Cade asked.

Marlow laughed, a short huff of sound. "I haven't decided yet."

"I'd go right."

"Huh."

In the end, Marlow didn't have to decide. The PEO moved on down the line of cars. Cade thumbed the fob to unlock the doors and headed over without incident.

"Eye in the Sky Photography," Marlow read off his—well, Cade's—phone as he pulled the seat belt over his chest and clipped it in. "They do drone photography. Corporate PR videos. Weddings. From the damp patch that Mr. Hackett was sitting in, I'm going to assume they also peep at sorority girls."

"That, or someone had the idea to use drones to case rich people's houses," Cade said as he shifted gears. "It's not a bad idea."

Out of the corner of his eye, he saw Marlow glance at him. "Career change?"

"No, it's the same one," Cade said. "Sometimes clients need to *see* the breakdown of the security flaws in their current system. The more dramatic, the better. Lem's number is in the phone if you want to send Clemons's last address through to him."

Marlow made an absent noise in the back of his throat as he tapped his thumbs over the phone. It wasn't the text screen that the phone was open on.

"Two moves, three states. At least," Marlow said.

"It happens."

"But it doesn't fit my theory," Marlow said. "Clemons didn't leave his whole life behind once, he did it twice. This would be the third time. That's not unlucky."

No, it wasn't. He was right.

Cade took a right onto Gramercy to avoid the traffic cameras.

"It's a pattern," he said. "Good. That's something we can track."

CHAPTER SIX

THE SAFE HOUSE had started to feel like more of a prison. Marlow could feel the pressure of the walls on his shoulders, as if he'd been shoved into a closet instead of a luxury basement apartment. The rent was probably three grand a month, and Marlow wanted to dig his way out with a spoon.

He wasn't used to this. Patience wasn't something you had to practice much in Night Shift. From the minute he clocked in until he finally handed his kit over to the armory, he was either in motion or asleep. Marlow had spent a few nights, as he dragged banged-up bones from one incident to another, wishing for boredom. Now he had it, and it sucked.

It hadn't been that long. Hours, not days. The closer they got to the moon rising, though, the slower time seemed to pass.

The click of a key in the front door interrupted his self-pity. He turned, one hand halfway to the gun that wasn't there, and had a second to think he should have been careful what he wished for and plot the quickest path to the knives in the kitchen.

"Yeah, hold on," Cade said as he let himself in, a bag of fast food in one hand and keys in the other. He had the burner phone he'd picked up tucked between his shoulder and his ear. "Let me put you on video."

He dropped the paper bag on the coffee table and lowered the phone.

Marlow let the breath he'd held out on a ragged sigh. He went over to move the food before it marked the finish on the table—the memory of his gran's fingers sharp on his ear—and Cade set the phone down in the middle of the table.

"… limb to go out for some guy you've known a month," Lem said.

"Lem," Cade snapped.

"He's not wrong," Marlow said. "But it's too late to change your mind now. So what did you find?"

Cade gave him a wry look for that as he sat down, but it was true. The smart move would have been to turn Marlow in and hope Franklin would take that as a truce. Instead, here they were. Marlow appreciated not being locked up—or dead—but he couldn't fault Lem for looking out for his brother.

"I run the company and my life," Cade said. "I didn't ask for anyone else's opinion. Lem, you said you found other cases that fit Clemons's pattern in Portland and Vegas?"

"Nope," Lem said.

"Do I sound like I'm in the mood for you being a smartass?" Cade asked.

Marlow shook his head and walked around to perch on the arm of the couch next to Cade. He was too tense to actually sit down, but this seemed like a good compromise. "You found something, though?" he said.

"See?" Lem said. "That's how you do it, Cade. A little bit of theater, let me showcase how smart I am."

"Yeah," Marlow said. "I worked with Franklin for years. He needed to let his ego out for a run before he told you anything too."

"Kind of spoiled it now," Lem said, "but that's fine. I didn't find cases that matched Clemons's MO—what we think is Clemons's MO—in Vegas and Portland… But I found *cases* that matched in Vegas, Portland, Salt Lake City, Sacramento, and San Jose. Five dead wolves over ten years. Six, if we count San Diego on the list. Every one follows the pattern you laid out: break-up, complaints about a wolf with a fixation, dead wolf found the morning after the full moon in the ex-boyfriend's kitchen. Always the kitchen. Maybe he lured them in with his signature pasta."

Lem laughed at his own joke and then stopped. "Sorry," he said. "This is just… Do we think this guy is a serial killer? That we unmasked a serial killer?"

He sounded like he couldn't decide whether to be stunned by or skeptical of his own research. Marlow could sympathize. He'd just wanted to prove *he* didn't kill Barney Lyons. Now he could do that… *if* he could pin a murder on a man who'd gotten away with five of them.

"And Clemons was never a suspect?"

"He was always a suspect," Lem said. "Well, Clemons, Williams, Butler, and so on were suspects. Never the same name, never a name that tracked outside of the city it started in. Every time, though, he was quickly ruled out because he had an air-tight alibi. He swiped into work before sunset, there was security camera footage of him getting on a train that afternoon, and one time he'd gotten himself arrested and spent the night in jail. I can send through the news reports I pulled."

"Yeah," Cade said. "Do it."

"Send it to Bennett too," Marlow said. "If you can spoof your ID enough she can't track it back to you."

Lem gave him a dirty look. "She'll think the tooth fairy sent it. If I send it?"

The question was for Cade, who scowled as he looked at Marlow. The fact he thought it was a lousy idea was obvious. He could be right. Marlow still gave an insistent nod, and Cade gave in with a growl.

"Her too," he said. "You need her email?"

Lem snorted his opinion of that and hung up. Cade leaned back and raised his eyebrows at Marlow.

"You sure that's a good idea?" he asked. "Even if Bennett's not involved, she could go straight to Franklin."

"She's not stupid," Marlow said. "The minute she realizes there's a chance I didn't kill Lyons, that means Franklin could be a liar."

Of course, that didn't answer the first part of the question. Was it a good idea? Fuck if Marlow knew, but Franklin hadn't expected her that night in Clemons's house. So at the very least, he didn't think he could trust her either. Not if he went too far.

That had been Piper's mistake, after all.

"If you think this is such a bad idea," Cade asked. "Why involve me at all? Just because I had resources—"

Marlow leaned over, took Cade's face in both hands, and kissed him to shut him up. He caught a muttered something that slipped between their mouths, and then Cade leaned into it. His shoulders relaxed, and he sank back into the couch cushions. He curled one hand around Marlow's thigh and idly stroked his thumb up the seam of his trousers in a lazy, distracting caress.

"Of course it's a bad idea," Marlow said as he tilted his head back. He was still close enough to feel Cade's breath on his kiss-damp lips. “Until a month ago, the only time you’d spoken to me was to call me a heavy-handed, tongue-tied idiot—”

Cade winced. “That was you?”

“It was. I’m glad you’re here, but you’d be better off if you had just walked away.”

Something dark caught on Cade’s expression. It was his turn to pull away. “So what? Now you’ve worked out who killed Lyons, now you don’t need my help anymore?”

Marlow heaved an exasperated sigh. “Is the only way to stop you making up reasons to feel insulted to just keep your mouth busy?” he asked.

Cade tilted his head to pin Marlow with an intent stare. Something went tight and wet in Marlow’s stomach at being caught under that gaze. People always made a fuss that his eyes were gray-blue, but they never struck him as anything special. It was Cade’s—whiskey shot through with bronze—and the slow, sly warmth that flickered through them that made the breath catch in Marlow’s throat.

“I don’t know,” Cade said. “You could try?”

The bed was huge. Marlow hadn’t bothered to make it the night before; the sheets were still tangled up in a messy nest, and the pillows tossed onto the floor. He kicked them out of the way as he dragged Cade across the room, kisses snatched between the removal of items of clothing.

Marlow cursed under his breath, the huff of annoyance bitten off his lips by Cade as he fumbled with the buttons on his shirt. It wasn’t exactly a difficult job. The neat little mother-of-pearl buttons just seemed smaller and slippery, his fingers clumsy and impatient.

Finally he just pulled himself away from Cade and dragged the shirt up over his head. He got stuck for a second, the too-tight fabric caught over his shoulders, and then Cade grabbed the tails of it to help pull it off the rest of the way. It lost a few buttons somewhere in there, they hit the ground and skittered off under the furniture, but Marlow didn’t care.

He tossed the shirt aside and stepped back to give Cade—still mostly dressed—a slow up and down look.

“Your turn,” he said.

“You’ve already seen me naked,” Cade pointed out, even as he worked the buttons on his shirt free one after the other. “Don’t tell me it’s slipped your mind?”

“I’ve seen *Die Hard*,” Marlow said. “I’m still going to watch it again at Christmas.”

Cade looked amused. “I’m not sure if that’s a compliment or not,” he said. “It’s not—”

Marlow grabbed the loose collar of the partially shed shirt and pulled Cade down into a kiss. He had warned the man. The grumble died between their tongues, and Cade ran an appreciative hand up Marlow’s side, over taut muscle and slatted ribs. His thumb grazed over a thread of old scar tissue and found the hot, tender splash of purple bruised down his side. Fresh, livid marks blended in with the old faded stain from the last time he nearly died. The kiss stalled for a second as Cade gently traced the boundaries of the bruise with careful fingers.

“I always forget that your bruises last,” he said. “Do you ever heal up, one month to the next?”

Marlow reached up to cup Cade’s cheek, fine golden stubble prickly against his palm, and pulled him back down into the kiss.

“It’s been an eventful month,” he said before Cade claimed his mouth. “It’s not always this bad.”

That wasn’t a lie. It was a very carefully phrased truth, though. Marlow couldn’t remember the last time he’d not either had his knee strapped up or had to nurse scrapes and bruises. If his lip wasn’t split, then he’d wrenched his back. It was just the job. Most full moons Marlow didn’t have to worry about his own team trying to kill him, but he couldn’t remember the last time he’d finished a shift where he didn’t limp home.

That was just the job. Night Shift collected scars and popped painkillers—contraband, but the higher-ups turned a politely blind eye to usage—so they could pull their weight on the streets. Until they couldn’t anymore.

Marlow knew that. He accepted it. In his experience, though, it wasn’t much of a pickup line. People wanted to sleep with a badass, not feel sorry for someone with the knees of a sixty-year-old.

Well, one knee.

Marlow veered away from Cade's mouth and kissed his way down his throat to the bony jut of his collarbone. He bit bruises into golden skin that tasted of salt and the flat metal tang of lust, although the marks would be gone by tomorrow. A fresh start every twenty-eight days.

Impatient hands pulled at waistbands and fumbled at buttons. Cade's tongue clashed with Marlow's, wet and slick and hungry, as they tumbled back onto the bed. The sheets smelled of the soap Marlow had borrowed and the faint, sharp smell of whiskey sweat.

Cade twisted his hand in Marlow's hair and pulled his head back, the line of his throat tight and vulnerable as he swallowed. He took one last kiss from Marlow's mouth, teeth sharp as he chewed along Marlow's lower lip. Then he sat back, knees straddled across Marlow's hips, and unfastened the last few buttons on his shirt. He stripped it off his shoulders, tanned skin pulled taut over long, heavy straps of muscle.

"Now, where had we gotten to when we left off last time?" he asked as he bent back down. Warm lips skimmed over Marlow's throat as he murmured, "Remind me? Wasn't it—"

He slid his hand down Marlow's stomach and under the waistband of his pants, then swore, sharp and surprised, as he yanked it back out.

Fuck. Marlow's brain shrugged off the fog of lust a minute too late.

"I forgot," Marlow said. He propped himself up on his elbows. "Fuck, I'm sorry. Are you okay?"

Cade shook his hand like he could shed the sting. His fingertips were blistered, distinct watery stripes raised under the skin, and his hand trembled visibly for a second until he clenched it into a fist.

"What the hell does the Night Shift keep in their pants?" Cade asked.

Old, flustered embarrassment made Marlow flush, a hot wash that started at his collarbones and rose from there. He scrubbed his hand through his tangled hair.

"We get them when we're rookies," he said. "If we survive our first full moon on the streets, then we get drunk enough that that seemed like a good idea. Is your hand okay?"

Marlow tried to grab Cade's hand to check it, but Cade pulled away from him. He clenched and relaxed his fist a couple of times, and then he reached out to brush his fingertips over Marlow's mouth.

"Kiss it better," he suggested. "Then we'll see."

Heat caught in the back of Marlow's throat at the suggestion. He opened his mouth, and Cade dipped silver-scalded fingers between his lips. Marlow laved the injury with his tongue as he sucked gently, his eyes intent on Cade as he worked.

His stomach tightened, his balls heavy and tight between his legs, as Cade pressed his fingertips down against his tongue. After a second, Cade pulled his hand back, fingers damp as he cupped Marlow's chin and tilted his head back.

"Let me see it," he said.

Marlow licked his lips. "It's not exactly legal," he pointed out, his voice scratchy with how much he *didn't* want to argue with Cade right now.

"I know, that's why it's hot," Cade said. He pushed himself off Marlow and sprawled back over the messy bed, shoulders propped against the padded headboard. He slid one hand down his stomach to cup the thick jut of his cock through his trousers. "And I'm already harboring a fugitive, so apparently I want to live dangerously. Show me."

He tucked his free hand behind his head and waited.

Marlow hesitated for a second and then scrambled up onto his knees. His pants were already unbuttoned, barely caught on his lean hips. He hooked his fingers in the waistband and pushed them down to his thighs.

His cock was already hard enough it ached dully as it jutted up toward his stomach. Silver glittered just under the head, a thick barbell pierced through the frenulum and secured with a black bead on either side. The sight of it made Cade catch his breath and shift his weight uncomfortably on the bed, even as his hand tightened around the bulge of his erection.

"Doesn't it hurt you at all?" Cade asked.

Marlow wrapped his fingers around his cock and lazily stroked it. His fingers slid over the metal, and he felt it shift under the skin. Most of the time he barely thought about it. But under Cade's fascinated scrutiny, Marlow was suddenly as awkwardly aware of the weight and thickness of it as he'd been for the first few days after he was pierced.

"It did at first," he said. "Now, not unless I catch it on something. Usually, I swap it out for a silicone placeholder, but…"

He trailed off with a shrug and flicked the bar with his thumb—a hot tug of pain. He tightened his grip around the base of it until he could feel his blood pulse against his fingers.

"So I can't touch your cock—"

"Not unless you have a pair of pliers," Marlow said. A sly smile tucked the corner of his mouth. "Or a heavy-duty condom."

Cade snorted and licked his stung fingers. Something about the gesture reached right down Marlow's suddenly parched throat and gave his cock a tug. He felt the twitch of reaction against his fingers.

"Yeah, Russian Roulette never appealed to me," he said. "I like to be in control."

"So do I," Marlow said. A slight hint of mockery cut through his voice as he cocked his head to the side. "Think that's going to be a problem?"

Cade cupped his hand around Marlow's chin and pulled him forward until Marlow's body was stretched out in one long, lean line and his hands braced on Cade's thighs. He grazed his thumb—rough-callused and damp—over Marlow's lower lip, and Marlow closed his eyes as he leaned into Cade's touch.

"I don't see why," Cade said. The low, roughly sensual scrape of his voice harked back to that first day in the lift. Pleasure tickled down Marlow's spine, from the nape of his neck to the small of his back. "I think, just this once, you're going to enjoy someone else being in charge."

"And next time?" Marlow asked.

There was a pause for a heartbeat, and then Cade leaned in for a slow, sweet kiss that filled Marlow with a warm, safe feeling.

"We can toss a coin," Cade said as he shifted from under Marlow. He swung his legs off the bed and kicked his shoes off. The bare span of his back, all sun-warm skin, freckles, and the taut bulk of muscle made Marlow's fingers itch. He gave in to temptation and measured the span of Cade's shoulders with his hands.

Muscles tightened under the skim of his palms and then relaxed as Marlow dug his fingers into the knots. Cade shimmied his trousers down over his thighs and off. Before he kicked them both away, he pulled a flat square out of the pocket of his trousers. He tore a corner of it off with his teeth, and the smell of strawberries was so strong it made Marlow's teeth hurt.

"You came prepared," he said.

"Fail to prepare, prepare to fail," Cade quoted, with the absent cant of someone who'd learned the saying by rote. Then he rolled back and tumbled them both back into the sheets. Marlow ended up sprawled on his stomach, his tender cock pressed into the comforter and the heavy sprawl of Cade's weight on his back. A kiss tickled the nape of Marlow's neck. "Applies to fucking too."

For a second, Marlow hesitated. This was a bad idea… for a lot of reasons. It wasn't too late to listen to sense and back out. Too late for it not to be awkward, but a couple of minutes of embarrassment as he grabbed his clothes and he'd be done.

Go back to work. Clear his name. That was probably what he should worry about.

"What?" Cade asked, his breath warm and tickly against the back of Marlow's ear.

Marlow took a breath and let the idea he might do the smart thing rest on the tip of his tongue for a second. It melted like cotton candy and left the aftertaste of strawberry in his mouth.

Fuck it. He wanted this. If he ended up in jail—or dead—he'd have plenty of regrets. This wouldn't be one of them.

"It felt like the last chance to change my mind." Marlow felt Cade start to shift his weight off him and reached to pull the wolf down. "I didn't, but I like to think my bad ideas through."

It took a second, but Cade's weight relaxed, his cock hard and warm as it pressed against Marlow's ass.

"I'm a bad idea?" he asked.

"Would you want to be anything else?"

Cade bit the back of Marlow's neck, sharp teeth and enough pressure to make Marlow gasp, and then chuckled. "Good point."

He ran a hand up the inside of Marlow's thigh. His fingertips bumped Marlow's balls and made him twitch.

"Careful," Marlow reminded him. "I don't want to have to Crate you."

Cade laughed. "Wouldn't be the first time."

Marlow felt a twinge of curiosity at that. Before he could pursue it, Cade moved his hand and pressed a blunt thumb against his ass.

Even coated with lube, the dull pressure made Marlow's breath catch in his throat. He twisted his hands in the comforter, the cotton pleated between his fingers, and groaned as he pushed his hips back.

The sensation of being spread—wide and then wider as the thumb twisted and was then replaced with fingers—was sweetly familiar.

Okay, it had been a while. When you lived on a different schedule from the rest of the world, it wasn't always easy to date. Not unless you wanted to dip into the company ink, and that was a bad idea. Nobody wanted the person they'd just cheated on—or fought with over who left an empty milk carton in the fridge—as their only backup against a moon-mad wolf. Still, his nerves tingled and twitched under his skin with expectation as Cade applied lube with slow, thorough self-indulgence.

"Maybe not spectacular," Cade remarked as he finally slid his fingers loose. He hooked his hand around Marlow's hip and pulled him up onto his knees. "But not a bad ass, all things considered."

Marlow hesitated for a second as he tried to focus through the fog of heat and pleasure to decide whether or not he'd insulted. It was possible. Cade took a prickly approach to flirtation.

That nudged his memory, just as Cade cleared his throat as if he'd just realized how that sounded.

"You—"

Cheap liquor and cold tiles and the warmth of Cade's skin under Marlow's mouth.

"I remember," Marlow said with a flicker of dry humor. "You should see Franklin's. Like two muscular pigs wrestling in a sack."

Cade nearly choked on a startled laugh. He gave Marlow a light slap on one ass cheek. It sounded harder than it felt, but it made Marlow squirm anyhow.

"Why?" Cade asked.

Marlow braced his elbows on the bed and grinned to himself. "Just because he's a crooked bastard doesn't mean he doesn't have a great ass."

"Better than mine?"

Marlow snorted. "Don't fish for compliments."

A warm, broad hand slid along Marlow's spine, from the small of his back to the nape of his neck. If Marlow were the cat that

Bennett always called him, that would have rubbed his fur the wrong way. Instead, he stretched up into Cade's touch as Cade scruffed him, thumb under Marlow's ear and fingers tight against the tendons of his throat.

"Any to catch?" Cade asked, but he didn't bother to wait for an answer. He rocked his hips forward and let his cock slide along the crack of Marlow's ass. The heavy breadth of it, soft skin and the dull throb of a pulse, slid along the crevice and back again. Each thrust smeared the lube, runny and messy as it warmed against Marlow's skin.

"Last chance for second thoughts," Cade said, his voice precise with control. "I'm not going to be a better idea tomorrow."

To be honest, Marlow didn't want to think about tomorrow. Just today, just this exact moment. He wanted to concentrate on the dry humor that sparked gold in Cade's eyes when he flirted—or whatever he wanted to call that—and the fact he still wanted to know what Cade tasted like.

"I mean, I thought we'd already established I was the bad idea right now," Marlow said.

Cade tightened his grip on Marlow's neck for a second, a flex of strong fingers. "Best idea I've had…" he said, then paused long enough that Marlow could almost hear the smirk that curled that stern mouth. "…today. Don't say I didn't give you an out."

His cock was thicker than the fingers he'd already had in Marlow. It spread him wide—his ass hot and tender as it stretched around the thick shaft—as Cade rocked his hips in slow, patient strokes. Marlow took a quick, ragged breath and dropped his head down between his arms. He licked salty sweat off his lips as the muscles in his stomach and thighs tightened in reaction to the pressure.

Scattershot bolts of pleasure fired off along Marlow's nerve endings, erratic pops of electric sensation that leapfrogged up his spine and tightened the still spit-damp buds of his nipples. He chewed his lower lip absently—impatiently—as he ached for *more.*

"I want you," he said, his voice scratchy and rough as he pushed back against Cade. "I'm not going to break just because I won't get a reset tonight."

Cade laughed. It jostled his cock inside Marlow and dragged a groan out of him.

"Trust me," Cade said. His hand shifted to spread over Marlow's shoulder, across the scar where the bullet had punched in. He traced the slick edges of it with his thumb. "That's not something I'm worried about."

Marlow looked over his shoulder. Under the circumstances, it seemed a little dumb to be taken aback by Cade's lean muscled beauty, but he was. Between the taut breadth of his chest and the clench of muscle in that sharply cut jaw, Cade made Marlow's mouth go dry.

"So, what are you waiting for?" he asked.

It was, more or less, a genuine question. Cade growled at him, a low rumble of sound that reached into Marlow's hindbrain and yanked a shudder raw and squirming up out of it. The hit of adrenaline that came with it would have been useful in the middle of a patrol, but right now just thickened his blood and stirred it up.

Cade tightened his grip on Marlow's hip and then buried himself deeper in Marlow with one rough, eager thrust. For a second, nothing fit, and it still felt good, a dark, sweet wash of pleasure that he could almost taste. Marlow's lungs squeezed tight around a gasp of air, and he slid forward on the bed, sheets rucked up around his knees. He reached out and braced his hand against the headboard, fingers dug into the padded fabric

"Fuck," Cade muttered. That fractured to something softer in his carefully modulated voice when he stretched forward and pushed Marlow's hair back from his face to stroke his cheek. "Are you—"

Marlow turned into the touch and pressed a damp, breathy kiss against the heel of Cade's hand.

"Not complaining," he said raggedly. "Don't stop."

Marlow groaned "Fuck" on an indrawn breath as Cade didn't. Each thrust pushed Marlow forward, the muscles in his braced arm tight, and pulled him tighter. The web of pleasure had spread slow and sticky under his skin—tingled in his lips and nipples under Cade's tongue—but now it contracted. His balls throbbed with hot pleasure as they pulled up tight to his body, and his cock was so hard it ached, that weird squirm of pleasure-pain you got from digging your thumb into a day-old bruise to see how deep it went.

After this was all over, Marlow swore to himself he was going to replace that damn silver bar with a stainless steel one. No one in the TAC team would be up close and personal enough with his genitals to tell the difference.

Cade pulled Marlow up so his back was pressed against Cade's hard, sweat-slicked body. The sudden shift in position pressed Cade's cock firmly against Marlow's prostate, and the jolt of pleasure was so intense it made the muscles in his thighs turn to water. A low, raw mewl of a sound escaped Marlow's throat as he dropped his head back against Cade's shoulder. He chewed on his lower lip as he tried to catch his breath, the air ragged and tight in his throat.

"You know, maybe you're not such a good idea either," Cade said, his voice warm and velvety against Marlow's ear, teeth sharp as he nipped at the lobe. He rolled his hips forward in a slow, controlled thrust that made Marlow arch his back and clutch blindly at Cade's shoulder for support. "You ever think about that?"

The angular line of Cade's jaw, sharp as if it had just been carved with a knife and banded with heavy, tight muscles, tempted Marlow too much to ignore. He scraped his teeth along the line of it, a hint of stubble rough against his lips.

"I'm Night Shift, and I'm TAC team," Marlow pointed out. "I'm the last bad idea anyone has before they marry an accountant."

Cade ducked his head down to slant a hard, eager kiss over Marlow's mouth. "My accountant's a lovely woman, but she's not my type."

"Once it was their car mechanic."

Cade's smile curved against Marlow's mouth. "Oh, well, that's different," he said. "He's actually hotter than you, and he makes good money."

Marlow hiccuped out half a laugh, the rest tangled up in a groan as Cade thrust into him again. The muscles in his thighs flexed, and he felt the pressure build—heavy and liquid at the same time—and spread from his balls and up into his stomach.

"Glad he wasn't free this afternoon, then," Marlow managed to get out, words strung together by luck rather than attention. Every breath he took tasted of Cade: sweat and musk and a hint of woody cologne. Marlow slid his hand up and around to tangle his fingers in Cade's expensively cropped curls. "Or I might have had to entertain myself."

Cade growled into the hollow of Marlow's neck. He closed his hands roughly around Marlow's hips and dragged him closer, his thrusts rough and impatient now. Marlow could feel the play of every muscle against his back and his thighs with each stroke. He licked his lips with his dry tongue and grabbed his own cock, that fucking unfuckable silver bar cold against his fingers as he pumped his fist along it in an erratic, broken rhythm.

Heat flushed up his spine, from his ass to the nape of his neck. Almost.

Cade spilled them both back down onto the bed, sprawled on their sides with his arm hooked over Marlow's chest. He pressed wet kisses against Marlow's throat and shoulder as he fucked him, teeth and tongue and enough pressure that some of them would leave bruises.

His fingers certainly would when they dug down into Marlow's hipbones as Cade buried his cock inside him and came. The wet, liquid spill of it sent sympathetic tremors through Marlow, clenched in the back of his throat and just behind his balls.

"Now," Cade drawled as he rolled over onto the pillows and pulled Marlow with him, sprawled along his chest and thighs. "Do what I tell you."

Marlow lolled his head back, sweaty hair stuck to a sweaty chest, and swallowed the lump in his throat.

"What?"

"I can't touch you," Cade said. He draped his arm over Marlow's shoulder and lazily grazed his nipples with a calloused thumb, proof that wasn't exactly true. He recognized that himself with a pause and an amendment. "Not there. But I still get to make you come. Give that piercing a tug."

Marlow stalled for a second as he thought about it. People thought he was easy to push around because he didn't push back unless it was necessary. They were wrong. But today he wasn't going to cut his nose off to spite his face.

Or his cock.

Marlow did as he was told and pinched the ends of the bar between his fingers as he pulled on it. The pulse of sensation that ran down his cock to his balls made him suck in a ragged Cade-scented breath and hold it.

Rough-voiced orders in his ear directed him as he worked his hand along his cock. After his initial pause, Marlow just obeyed as his brain hazed over with lust and pent-up pleasure. Cade's restless hands on his shoulders and along his thigh helped keep him unfocused as Marlow squeezed tight around the base and twisted his fist around the shaft on the downstroke.

It didn't take long. Marlow arched his hips up into his fist as he came, a messy spill of sticky fluid that dripped over his knuckles and onto his thighs. It left him boneless and lazy against Cade's chest.

Cade smoothed Marlow's hair away from his forehead and pulled his head back with it until Marlow looked up at him upside down. "Penny for your thoughts."

"I don't—"

On the bedside table, where it had been discarded, Marlow's phone started to ring. Not his phone, he remembered halfway through reaching for it, Cade's phone. The one Piper had the number to.

The screen showed a blocked number, and Marlow couldn't remember how to breathe.

"Die out there or die in here. Your choice."

The memory of pain spiked out from just under Marlow's collarbone and spread up into his shoulder. It didn't matter how many years passed; the moment Piper shot him was always raw and fresh under his skin, in his bones.

"I can try to talk to him," Cade offered. "Right now, he needs us as much as we need him."

Marlow made himself pick up the phone. The satisfying pop as the joints adjusted cut through the bitter slurry of old fear and anger. It had been a while since he'd felt panic. Been panicked, sure, but after years on Night Shift, his brain just tuned it out 99 percent of the time. It was like a drunk who couldn't get a buzz on beer anymore, but needed a shot of whiskey and a Baileys chaser.

The last time he'd felt panic the way God intended had been that night, and the memory bypassed his usual functional shortcuts.

"No," he said. "He doesn't get to think he can still manipulate me."

He swiped to answer and put the phone on speaker.

"What did I always tell you, Marlow," Piper said. The bite of reprimand in his voice—five years and an *attempted murder* later—still made Marlow's shoulders go back and his spine try to straighten. "Night Shift aren't lone wolves. We work in a pack for a reason."

CHAPTER SEVEN

CADE SAT UP and leaned back against the headboard.

The deal with Piper made sense. Whatever he'd done back in the day, he was the devil they knew and the one that was locked up. It was easier to remember that when Cade couldn't *see* the scars Piper had left Marlow with. Or the flinch that tightened Marlow's shoulders at the jibe, the muscles clenched under his skin.

"How long has Franklin been dirty?" Marlow asked. "Day one?"

There was a pause on the other end of the line; then Piper chuckled. "Almost," he said. "You're not giving him due credit, Marlow. Franklin was dirty long before I recruited him. You didn't actually believe him that he'd left San Francisco of his own volition, did you?"

Marlow made a visible effort to bring his shoulders down from around his ears. "No," he said. "I thought it was just because he was a jerk."

"It didn't help," Piper admitted. "No. It was nothing official, nothing that went on his record, but it was made clear to him he'd never be back on active duty. So he came to San Diego and applied here. One of the Night Shift brass in SF actually came down to give me a heads-up about him. They thought it was a warning. I took it as a reference. Turns out, my mistake."

Cade rubbed Marlow's back. His thumb grazed the neat shallow scallop of scar tissue he'd kissed before. It made his throat tighten with an odd retroactive clutch of panic—how close had he come to *never* even meeting Marlow. An inch? Less?—but it made Marlow relax back into his touch.

"This isn't a High School reunion," Cade said. "Don't waste our time with reminiscences, Piper. Your bargaining chip was Franklin's name, and the value of that just crashed. So what else do you have to trade?"

"I'm on speaker?" Piper said. "You should have said, Marlow."

"You shot me," Marlow said, his voice dry as dust. "Why don't we call it even."

There was a pause. In the background of the call someone coughed, wet and thick and prolonged. Piper waited until the cougher wheezed into silence. He exhaled, a tight, controlled noise.

"Fair enough," Piper said, his voice clipped as he got down to business. "I have all the time in the world to shoot the breeze, but I get that you've got more demands on your time. What I've got will give you Franklin wrapped up in a pretty red bow. Enough evidence to prove that Franklin was eyes-deep in what I was doing, and more. Enough no one is going to trust his word."

Cade frowned and rubbed the sweat off the back of his neck. The post-sex buzz that pulled lazy and liquid at his bones wanted to take that at face value. They were free and clear, and they could just spend the rest of the day in bed.

"If that's what you have," Cade said, "why did you only offer a name last time we talked?"

Piper snorted. "How did you end up with your own company when that's your idea of how to run a negotiation? I wasn't going to put all my cards on the table. If all I had to give you was Franklin's name, then I could get Franklin back on a short leash. Now, like you said, the situation has evolved, and so has my approach."

"Why should we believe you have anything?" Marlow asked. "You're a convict. You've nothing to lose by lying your ass off."

Marlow left the phone in the middle of the bed as he slid out of the sheets. The clothes he'd stripped off stayed on the floor, and Marlow grabbed the jeans he'd left folded on top of the dresser instead. He was still bruised from his fight with Franklin, the stain of color spread under his scars, but Cade could still pick out the marks he'd left. A hickey on his throat, still wet and fresh, would still be there tomorrow.

It was a *very* satisfying thought, and it felt… rooted. The idea made Cade squirm internally. He wasn't here—assisting in a felony and making deals with felons—*just* because he had a crush on Marlow. If he needed to at any point, Cade could justify the majority of his involvement over the last month for mostly pragmatic reasons.

The next person on Franklin's hit list—once he had Marlow out of the way—would be Cade and Cold Winds for the resources the company gave whoever was in charge. They would be loose ends, and Franklin had already shown a willingness to do whatever it took to tie those up.

Still, he could hear himself.

Majority and mostly.

So he had feelings for Marlow? That was hardly a surprise. They were completely appropriate feelings for someone you were into but had known only a month, that was all. Nothing that would tie his wolf to a half-mile radius around Marlow, as if Marlow had just become the heart of the wolf's territory. That would be stupid… and possibly one-sided.

So it was fine.

Cade scrubbed his hand roughly through his hair, damp at the roots and tangled, as he pulled his attention back to Piper's voice on the phone. The accent had sharpened since the last time they'd spoken as Piper picked up the old habits of speech from them.

"…know me better than that," Piper said. "You think I'd leave Franklin in charge without a leash on him? Even if I trusted him—which I wasn't dumb enough to do—he's not a predictable man. He's not one to stick to a plan."

Marlow snorted. He left the stolen shirt crumpled on the dresser and just grabbed the hoodie to shrug on over bare shoulders instead.

"You'd be surprised," he said, his voice grim.

Cade raised an eyebrow at Marlow, but just got a shrug in response. Whatever was eating at Marlow, he wasn't ready to share with the class just yet. That was fine. Cade had his own questions.

"How good can this information be?" he asked. "Franklin doesn't seem to be too worried about what you have on him. He doesn't seem to answer to you at all anymore."

There was a pause.

"Yeah," Piper said. "I can't explain that. It's up to you to decide whether you want to barter for it or not."

"And in return…"

"Same as before; I want out," Piper said.

"Can't do that," Cade said. He didn't give Piper a chance to argue. "What I can do is get one of the best lawyers I know on your case. I can't promise what the outcome will be, but it'll be the best you can get."

Piper snorted. "And what's to stop you telling them to let me rot once I deliver Franklin?"

"Because he doesn't like me that much," Cade said. "Trust me, if I told him I wanted to keep you behind bars? He'd turn up with a crowbar. Never mind the billable hours he can charge."

Piper inhaled audibly. "See," he said. "I'm not sure a 'best efforts' promise is worth what I'm risking. I want assurances that I'm not going to end up on the short end of this deal and that there's a life out there for me when I get out. Maybe—"

"Maybe you don't have anything," Marlow said. "You think you've been pulling Franklin's strings all this time? Yet you're the one behind bars, just where he wanted you."

Piper snorted. "What's that supposed to mean?"

"Franklin's the one who told you I was an informant, right?" Marlow said. "Convinced you that you had to shut me up."

"What do you want? An apology?" Piper snorted. "Maybe I should have asked more questions, but you fit the bill. I never did manage to buff all the shine off your conscience, and Bennett was the last person I thought would blow the whistle. Never expect an ex to keep your secrets, I guess."

Marlow rubbed his hand over his face. "There was no informant," he said. "No case being built behind your back. The only reason that Bennett went to the brass and dropped you in it was because you'd gone too far. All those rationalizations about what we deserved and how, really, what you did made our job easier? They all fell through the minute you shot me and chucked me to the wolves. She couldn't make that for the greater good. And ask yourself… how did she find out? Bennett wasn't there that night. I was in a coma, and I don't think you told her. So tell me something, did Franklin know you had something on him before IA knocked at your door?"

A slow, controlled exhalation was the only answer he got.

"Call your lawyer," Piper said, his voice flat. "Once he's *my* lawyer, I'll get you what you need to take Franklin down. Maria knows how to contact me."

He hung up.

Cade picked up the phone to set it on the bedside table. “Is it true?”

Marlow zipped his hoodie up slowly over his bare chest. He shrugged one shoulder. “I don’t know,” he admitted. “I think so. More importantly, it seems like Piper does too.”

“It worked,” Cade acknowledged. He kicked the tangled sheets out of the way and swung his legs over the side of the bed. The rug was rough against the soles of his feet. He studied Marlow as he tried to read how the conversation with Piper had affected him. It wasn’t easy. Marlow was reserved at the best of times. He didn’t look happy about it, but he *did* look resigned. “If we do this, Piper will get something out of it. Can you live with that?”

Marlow pushed the frayed cuffs of the hoodie up and crossed his arms. “I haven’t spoken to him since it happened,” he said. “He told me I was a good cop; then he had me thrown out into the street. If I lived with that…”

Cade wrinkled his nose. “That’s when you knew he was locked up, that he was paying for what he did to you.”

“Yeah, well, to be honest? The fact he let Franklin get one over him, that probably hurt Piper more than any one of those five years he spent inside,” Marlow said. “Five years, and he’ll never be Night Shift again? I can live with that. He’d have been up for parole in a couple of years anyhow.”

He didn’t sound entirely convinced. That was actually reassuring. It was honest, and Cade could work with that. People who lied well enough to fool themselves—for a while—were the ones who came apart at the worst times and in the worst places.

“I need to go and talk to Piper’s new lawyer,” Cade said as he collected his clothes off the floor. “We’ve got a few hours before the moon rises. He’ll want to speak to you.”

Marlow pushed himself up out of his slouch, even as he looked confused. “Why?”

Cade pulled his shirt on over sweat-damp shoulders. “Because he’s a bastard,” he said. “And it’s the sort of thing a bastard would do. There are T-shirts in the wardrobe if you want to borrow one.”

“One question?”

“Just one?” Cade asked as he leaned back in the slick metal-and-leather hammock chair. It felt precarious under his weight.

"What gave you the idea that I'd do *anything* to help you?" Justin asked as he sat down behind his desk. He picked up a pen and twiddled it between his fingers as he enjoyed the moment. "I'd not piss on you if you were on fire, Deacon."

They'd been friends once.

It had been for a month—drunk on adrenaline and disbelief they'd gotten bonus checks instead of coffins after they'd faced down with Russians. Just long enough to plan and commit money to the idea of their own security company. They'd quickly realized that being friends and business partners did not work. Not for the two of them, anyhow.

"Ned Piper," Cade said. He laid the folder he'd put together about Piper's business on the desk between them and flicked it open. Justin's fingers twitched, just once, as he looked at the plain cardboard. It was enough. Cade had played enough poker with Justin—in winter, half-pissed, just to keep their blood moving—to know his tells. He was at least eyeing the hook. "He was a Night Shift—"

"I know who he was," Justin said. "What does he have to do with you? He's pretty enough, but I'd hope you've not been reduced to Men Behind Bars dating sites."

"You know I can't after we both signed that non-compete clause," Cade said. "Although you *did* try and poach my employee, which is also against the conditions."

"Lem has a big mouth," Justin said with a thin, humorless smile.

"That's a surprise to you?" Cade asked, eyebrows raised. "You didn't pay enough attention to our day-to-day business."

Marlow cleared his throat. They both turned to scowl at him. He absorbed the glares placidly as he tapped his wrist.

"Can the dick-measuring wait?" he asked. "We don't have much time."

Justin snorted and then narrowed his eyes. He tilted his head to the side. "Do I know you?" he asked. "You look familiar."

"I'm wanted for murder," Marlow said, his voice mild and even. "You probably saw me on the news."

Justin's mouth hung open for a second, and then he closed it sharply. "I was just going to imply you looked like one of Cade's exes," he said. "But you're the killer Night Shift officer. So I'm going to call a tip line to turn you in—"

"I didn't do it," Marlow said.

"Everyone says that."

Cade snorted, "Probably not him," he said. "He's got a bad habit of telling the truth, like it or not."

"You believe him?" Justin said, an incredulous edge to his voice. "You? Believe someone is trustworthy? Fine. Convince me?"

He leaned back in his chair and crossed his arms as he waited. Cade leaned forward and tapped a finger against the photo of Piper's face.

"That's what he's for," he said. "I get you to agree to handle Piper's appeal, and he'll give us the evidence we need to prove a corrupt colleague framed Marlow. The same corrupt cop who tried to kill us both last full moon."

"Not sure whose side I should be on there," Justin said. He turned the pages absently as he talked, his eyes moving from side to side as he glanced over the State's evidence. "Why not get Beth on this? She's your go-to bought and paid for legal representative, isn't she? Do you not think she's up to the job?"

"She's more than capable," Cade said. "There's just one element I don't think she could deal with."

Justin looked up and waited expectantly, one eyebrow raised. "And that is?"

"Piper's guilty as sin. She'd have a problem with that."

"And I wouldn't?"

"I know you better than that."

Justin laughed, cheerful as always when his failings were pointed out. There was no reason for him not to be. Just because people knew what you'd done didn't mean they could make you pay for it. Justin was smart enough and knew precisely how to toe the line between unethical and illegal, so he'd rarely had to face the consequences of his actions.

"Why *would* I help, though?"

"I'll give you back the ten shares in the company you forfeited when you dissolved our partnership."

"So the board could outvote you," Justin said. "Even fire you as CEO, put in their own man."

They could. In the year Cade had spent locked in negotiations with Justin over every line and clause of the partnership contract, that had been where he'd always dug his heels in. The company was his. If he wasn't the asshole CEO of Cold Winds, then who was he? Just anyone, instead of "someone."

"I know," he said.

Marlow made a choked sound of protest and grabbed his arm. His fingers dug in. "Don't," he said, then turned to Justin. "That's not on the table."

"Too late," Justin and Cade said at the same time.

They traded a brief annoyed look.

"I don't want you to do this for me," Marlow said. His voice was tight with nervous concern. "Don't prove Lem right."

On the other side of the table, Justin snorted as he examined his nails. "Lem as the voice of reason," he said. "Things *have* changed."

Cade took Marlow's hand off his arm. "I like you, Marlow, but we're not married. You don't get a say in this," he told him. "And I don't need anyone in my life who thinks they can tell me how to live it. Do you want the stocks or not, Justin?"

He sounded annoyed. Probably because he was a little, that knee-jerk rejection of anyone who thought he wasn't capable of making good decisions because of where he'd come from or how he spoke. Make that "used to speak."

That would pass. What mattered was that he *felt* Justin take the hook. His old partner had already been interested in the challenge of getting a guilty man off and the payoff with the stocks—but the opportunity to cause issues in Cade's relationship with Marlow was just the sweetener he needed to bite.

"The stocks and my usual fee," Justin counteroffered. It was just for show. He didn't expect Cade to back out now. "No promises, obviously. I'll do my best."

"Done," Cade said. "A handshake good enough?"

Justin laughed. "For an asshole, you always had a good sense of humor," he said. "I'll get my assistant to draw up a contract. I assume that your friend outside is here to make sure we're not going to pull a fast one?"

"That's right."

Justin picked up the phone on his desk. "Brent? Bring through Mr. Deacon's guest."

A second later, the door opened and Maria walked in. She didn't look like she didn't belong—her makeup was flawless and her clothes good quality—but she held herself as though she knew better. Both hands were clenched around her purse, and she kept her elbows close to her side as the equally flawless but far more relaxed Brent directed her to a chair. She sat with her knees and heels pressed together and her back so straight it looked like it hurt.

"Don't worry," Justin said. "I don't bite."

"You're not what I'm worried about," Maria said, tension sharp as cheese wire in her voice. "My neighbors said Night Shift was at my house last night. The principal at my school thinks I'm dead because he can't find me and I'm not answering my phone. Night Shift is the only law there is during the full moon, and now fuck knows how many of them are looking for me. None of this is my fault—"

Cade snorted. "Didn't you facilitate criminal activities for a felon?"

"Yeah, for years," she said. "And it went fine until you came knocking on my door."

Justin chuckled. "I like her," he told no one in particular. Then he rested his folded arms on the table and raised his eyebrows. "So, what hoops do we have to jump through here?"

He didn't get an answer right away. Maria flexed her hands against her bag, the pleather pleated under her nails, and glanced around at them.

"What if I don't do shit?" she asked, her voice flat and stripped of the nice Spanish-teacher overlay. "I owe Piper, sure, but he can't do fuck-all to help me now. Maybe I should just walk out of here, give Franklin whatever he wants. I'd miss the extra money, but I'm a good teacher. I could get by, and I'd be alive to do it."

She had to know the answer to that. Everyone else in the room did.

"Then we tell Piper why his once-in-a-lifetime, limited time offer on some sort of future evaporated," Cade told her, just in case she needed to hear it out loud. "Maybe he doesn't have the pull he did before, but he's a careful man. Are you sure that Franklin is the only one he kept a stash of evidence on, just in case?"

Maria clenched her jaw. "Not on me," she said. "He trusts me. I'm not like Franklin."

"And Franklin's not like Piper," Marlow said.

"Piper shot you," Maria said. Her gaze cut toward Justin, and she stumbled over her tongue as she edited herself. "Allegedly, anyhow. Do you expect me to believe you think he's Robin Hood?"

"I think he was an asshole," Marlow agreed. "He was corrupt, and he hurt people—but it was a business for Piper. He was in it for the money. Franklin… he'll take the money, but it's not the point. He won't let you walk away. He'll take you down with him."

Maria opened her purse and reached inside. She came out with a switchblade, the pearl handle held competently in her fingers. She thumbed the trigger, and Cade grabbed her wrist and squeezed as the blade snapped out. Justin and Marlow both bolted to their feet.

Tendons flexed under Cade's grip, and Maria rolled her eyes.

"What do you think I'm going to do?" she asked. "Stab all three of you and run off into the night? I promise, if you let go of my wrist, I won't hurt you."

"Or yourself?" Cade asked.

She looked at him for a second and then flashed a grin that was all hard lines and sharp edges.

"Don't get me wrong, that's sweet," she said. "But ask Marlow, I'm a survivor. If I was going to kill myself, I would have let the gangs do it a long time ago. I just need something out of my bag."

She waited.

Cade stared at her for a second and then glanced at Marlow. He thought about it for a moment, mouth twisted, and then gave a short, sharp nod. At this point, Cade had trusted Marlow with his reputation, his business, and his cock. There didn't seem much point in drawing the line now.

He let go of Maria's wrist. She flipped the knife in her hand and dug the point into the thick strap of her purse.

"Piper said that he'll call you first thing tomorrow, Mr. Tanner," she said as she worked the blade along the stitching. "To discuss your approach to his case. He said you might as well have these now, since there's nothing you can do with them until tomorrow anyhow."

The length of the strap gaped open. Maria peeled it apart between her fingers and used her fingernails to pry three memory cards out of the glue, one after the other. She stacked them on top of each other and then set them on the table to push over to Justin.

"What's on them?" Justin asked as he picked them up.

"Enough to bury Franklin," Maria said as she stood up. "Piper said there was something good from San Francisco, but I told him I didn't want to know anymore. I've been a snitch enough times to know when it's best to stay in the dark. Like I said, I'm a survivor."

She let herself out, her butchered purse dangled from one hand. Cade let her go. His men could take her back to the hotel she was holed up in and make sure she didn't make any bad decisions.

CHAPTER EIGHT

"GIVE ME THE files," Marlow said.

Justin pinched the narrow wafers of plastic between his fingers. "I'm sorry," he said, in a way that made it clear he was not. "This could contain evidence that implicates my client. I would be *remiss* if I allowed anyone connected to law enforcement to view these before—"

"Remember those audits you used to run on our competitors?" Cade interrupted him. "That was a good idea. We still do it. Based on our last estimate, it would take five minutes for security guards to get to your office in the event of an incident."

Justin smirked. "My office in particular?" he asked, but didn't wait for Cade to answer. "But in case it slipped your mind, you had to surrender any weapons to security before you entered the building. I didn't."

He pulled his jacket back to show the gun holstered in an expensive tailored leather harness against his ribs. It looked black and dangerous against the crisp white of his shirt.

"Your move," Justin said.

Cade laughed at him and leaned back in the chair, arms crossed. "Hell, no," he said. "I'm not bad in a fight, but you don't date someone in Night Shift and punch fuckers yourself. Marlow? How much damage could you do in five minutes?"

He glanced over expectantly. Marlow tried to think of a pithy, dangerous reply, but his brain had derailed on the "dating" mention, and it was hard to get it back on track. It wasn't the time, but knowing that didn't actually help.

Marlow gave up on clever and settled for blunt. "Enough," he said as he stood up.

Annoyance lifted Justin's chin in a pugnacious jut. Cade's ex-partner—business, nothing else, Cade had assured Marlow on the way over—wasn't someone who liked to be underestimated.

Justin's jaw set. "I wear a nice suit, Officer Marlow, and I get paid a lot of money to be clever," he said. "Please don't assume that makes me soft or helpless. It would be a mistake."

People always thought that.

"It wouldn't," Marlow said bluntly. "Everyone is soft and helpless compared to a wolf, and I face them down three nights a month."

"With guns and silver bullets," Justin pointed out. "You've got neither right now."

That made Cade chuckle. He just smirked when Justin glared at him, sprawled and arrogant in the chair as if this was his office. "Inside joke," he said with a shrug.

For a moment, the back of Marlow's neck stung with heat. He was as awkwardly aware of the weight of the barbell through his cock as he'd been the first few weeks after he'd first gotten it. Marlow had done his job too.

"Okay," he said. "Try me."

Justin paused for a second. He had probably had a script for how this confrontation was going to go, and it most likely involved a good two minutes of posturing before they reached this point. It had left him flat-footed when Marlow skipped ahead.

People didn't like it when they didn't get what they expected, but it did tend to make them more reasonable. It also saved time, and they didn't have much of that right now.

"You're that confident?" Justin asked. "I'm a good shot."

Marlow shrugged and held his hand out. "It's been a bad couple of days," he said. "Why not just give me the cards and stop pretending you're going to shoot up your own office?"

"I've done stupider things," Justin said. He blew on the memory cards like they were dice and dropped them into Marlow's hand. "If you try and use *anything* on this against my client—"

Cade sighed. "We're the ones who hired you to represent him," he said. "What makes you think we would try and backstab him now?"

"I told you," Justin said. The chair creaked as he leaned back in it. "I know who Ned Piper is and what he did. He tried to kill Officer Marlow here. He might hold a grudge… And you always want to impress people you're interested in."

"Fuck off," Cade snapped.

Marlow folded his fingers around the cards. It felt like they should be heavier, that the information should have a weight of its own, but they were just thin plastic and even thinner metal.

"At this point," he said. "Who hasn't tried to kill me?"

Justin had given them an office and a computer in order for them to look over the files. He'd insisted that nothing—physical or digital—leave the building. It wouldn't have been easy to enforce since Marlow already had possession of the cards, but his demand actually worked in their favor. The moon would be up enough to trigger the first shifts in—under now—two hours, and the city's police force were still looking for Marlow.

So they didn't have time to go back to Cold Winds and access their equipment, and they couldn't exactly just drop into a nearby internet cafe either.

There were .doc files and spreadsheets, haphazardly named video clips—Marlow recognized a few police codes, but others just seemed to be strings of alphanumeric text and digits—and a dozen "copy of…" folders that been made without renaming.

Marlow didn't know why he was surprised.

"He always sucked at admin," he said. "It was an unofficial assignment for one of the team to write up the incident reports for him. He'd just sign them."

Cade snorted as he turned the screen toward him and used the mouse to drag the cursor up to the corner of the display. "It probably says bad things about me that I'm more offended by his sloppy approach to his insurance policy than I am his corruption."

"I mean, he did shoot me," Marlow pointed out as he leaned on the back of Cade's chair to watch what he was doing. "If we're dating, I might expect you to just be more offended by that on principle."

"I said almost."

"You did not."

Cade chuckled as he dragged all the files over into one folder and clicked up in the corner to organize them by date. An .avi jumped to the top. The structure of the file name looked familiar, and the date embedded was ten years ago—before Franklin came to San Francisco.

"That looks like dashcam footage," Marlow said.

"One way to find out," Cade said and double-tapped the file.

Someone had already clipped the extraneous footage out. The video started as the first punch was thrown. It wasn't what Marlow had expected. A dozen cops in a grim circle, illuminated by the headlights of the cop car, as they kicked the shit out of someone on the ground. The footage was grainy—ten-year-old technology and filmed at night—but it was good enough to pick up the splatter of red on the ground as someone kicked the victim in the head.

Human instinct was to either look away or watch the point of impact. It was one reason why eyewitness statements weren't as useful as TV cop shows made them look. People didn't focus on the face. They looked at the fists or the feet.

Marlow looked at the faces of the cops who had taken part in the beatdown. He didn't recognize any of them. Piper had promised them something to take Franklin down, but he wasn't there.

"Did you see that?" Cade asked abruptly. He stopped the playback and leaned forward to squint at the screen.

"No," Marlow admitted. "What?"

Cade clicked back three seconds, then five. He hit Play again and moved the cursor up to the victim's hunched-over shoulders. "Watch."

Two boots to the gut nearly lifted the man off the ground. He managed to get his elbow under him and tried to push himself up. Before he could, one of his attackers kicked it out from under him, and he went back down.

Marlow had already seen what Cade had, though.

"Shit," he said. "I thought you were bad with faces."

"Not when they matter," Cade said. He backed up frame-by-frame until he found the second that Franklin's face was visible on screen. It was him, although the scar in his eyebrow was still a split-open gash here. "I thought this was meant to implicate Franklin in something."

"He'd not appreciate anyone knowing he'd been assaulted," Marlow said. "Especially by wolves."

Cade glanced up at him, then back at the screen. "It's not the full moon," he pointed out. "Could be nulls."

"Not in San Francisco," Marlow said. "Nulls in active duty have to wear a medical alert bracelet for triage. The only one there with any jewelry is Franklin. Those are wolves, and there's no moon. Give me ten minutes?"

Cade looked at the time on the screen. "Make it five," he said. "You need to get back to the apartment and lie low. Otherwise, if the wolves don't get you, Night Shift will."

It was the sort of truth that should have stung, but it didn't. The idea that he couldn't trust his fellow Night Shift officers was… nothing new. Marlow hadn't trusted any of them for a long time. He'd just not admitted it.

"It won't take long. Phone?"

Cade handed it over, and Marlow stepped away from the desk as he dialed in to San Francisco PD.

"This is Captain O'Hara," he lied. "Can I speak to Lieutenant Randall?"

Randall was the longest-serving Night Shift lieutenant in California, and he'd held on to the job even after he'd lost a leg in the line of duty. He could have retired—most did; it was hard to be kept off the front lines—but he didn't. If anyone had driven down to San Diego to deliver the news, it would be him.

He paced back and forth as he waited for someone to pick up. Every click of the mouse as Cade worked his way through the other files made him fidget.

"O'Hara," a voice ruined by nearly twenty years yelling orders over wolf fights said. "Shouldn't you be naked somewhere?"

The lazy tease made Marlow blink. He hadn't realized they were friends, which meant his half-assed plan to lie wouldn't work.

"I lied," Marlow said. "This is Officer Kit Marlow, and I didn't kill anyone."

Silence for a second, and then Randall coughed out a dry laugh. "Yeah, well, you shouldn't call me at work for that," he said. "Hold on."

The line went muffled, and Marlow heard Randall excuse himself to someone in the background. He had a feeling Randall and O'Hara might be more than friends, which was significantly more information than Marlow wanted to know.

Doors closed and clicked, and then Randall came back. "Why the hell should I believe you?"

"The only evidence is Franklin's word," Marlow said. "And my best guess is that you know better than to believe anything you hear from him."

"Not a bad argument," Randall said. "It's not the only evidence, though. Apparently, you short-changed the armory more than once. The inventory on your bullets doesn't match up."

"That's a lie," Marlow said. "I've got the signed receipts from the armory clerk to prove it."

"You keep them?" Randall said, surprise tart in his voice. "Do you report every 'for your service' gift too? Don't answer that, I can guess. Typical of Franklin, he thinks that secretly everyone would do the same things he does if they could just get away with it. He doesn't believe some people are just Boy Scouts."

Marlow didn't know about that. He just preferred to be safe instead of sorry, and all it took was a single folder in his filing cabinet to do that. So why not.

"I'm not better than anyone else," Marlow said. "But I didn't kill that man. I swear."

"No offense," Randall drawled. "But I'm pretty sure that makes you better than Franklin."

"You think he killed someone up there?" Marlow asked. The background sound of Cade on the computer stopped, and the chair creaked as Cade got up and came over to join him. He gestured to his ear and then the phone. Marlow gestured for him to wait a second.

"I know he did," Randall said. "He just did it legally, as far as we could prove."

"Did it have something to do with the cops that attacked him?" Marlow asked. "I've seen footage of that."

He put the phone onto speaker and set it on the corner of the desk.

"How?"

"Better you don't know," Marlow said. "It's dashcam footage from an officer's car."

"His," Randall said. "It went missing before I could pull it, and Franklin said nothing happened; he just slipped and fell. So I could never prove he had a motive for what happened."

"What did happen?" Marlow asked.

"He did his job," Randall said. "He killed wolves… and the first one was clean. I was there, and he had no other choice. Some adolescent idiot and his girlfriend had snuck out to turn together under the first full moon of the year… except she didn't turn. Franklin saved her life—even if it wasn't something she appreciated at the time—when he took that headshot. I should have… it didn't bother him, you know? His first kill—even if it was righteous—and it didn't give him pause. Not until it turned out that the dead kid bled blue. Three generations of cops in that family. Good cops. Even one Night Shift officer, although he'd retired years ago."

"They didn't think it was righteous?"

"Would you?" Randall asked. "His father lodged a complaint. He came down to the armory to protest, tried to throw a punch at Franklin. His partner had to drag him out of there. Is she in the footage? Tall blond woman, looks like she belongs in a painting of the English countryside."

"Yes," Cade said. He shrugged when Marlow raised his eyebrows at him. "She got her licks in."

"That makes sense," Randall said. "He killed her three months later, second night of the full moon. Head shot. Justified—she attacked him right out on the street. Nothing but bad luck there. Grudges carry over sometimes. Then a month later, Sergeant Caulder goes to join his son, misadventure that time… he turned up dead in Golden Gate Park with a missing foot. Then the kid's uncle. His grandfather's last rookie too. Six cops in the end, and all of them tied to that dead kid somehow. So I confronted him, and he told me to prove it. Didn't even bother to deny it."

"But you couldn't."

"I could not. I couldn't even *explain* it. How did he know one wolf from the other? How could he set any of that up? And he thought that meant there was nothing I could do. He was right, officially. Unofficially, I told everyone who owed me anything—and that's a list—that he wasn't fit for active duty. He didn't get fired, but he was dumped into the armory to do work as an inventory clerk, and I made it clear that he'd stay there for as long as he was in San Francisco. A month later, he transferred to San Diego. I tried to put the word out about him, but it didn't take. I worked out why when Piper went down. That's everything I've got on Franklin, Officer Marlow, and it won't be enough. Like me, you'd have to prove it before you could take it to court. The dashcam footage provides motive, but you still have to explain the method."

"It's somewhere to start," Marlow said. "Thank you, sir."

"Anything I can do to help," Randall said. "Maybe you should talk to that reporter."

"Who?"

"Well, that's what she called herself," Randall said. "I looked her up after she called, and the only byline she had was on a podcast."

"She was looking into Franklin?"

"No. No. The kid's death," Randall said. "Or the tragedy around it, rather. Death as infectious disease or something ridiculous like that. I couldn't help her much, but maybe she turned up something that could help you."

"Maybe she already did," Marlow said. "Was her name Clara? Clara Walker?"

"Something like that," Randall said. The expectation he was about to hear something awful settled in his voice as he asked, "What happened to her."

"She killed herself," Marlow said. "Jumped off a bridge."

"Fuck," Randall said. "You know, I always wondered if I'd let him down, if this was something I could have stopped. He looked like a good cop once. That's why I took him on to the Night Shift. Now I think there's just something *wrong* in that man."

He hung up.

"Stay safe," Cade said. He kissed Marlow, hard and sharp and with the tang of blood mixed on their tongues as wolf-sharp teeth scraped Marlow's lips. "Stay out of trouble. At least until morning when I can do something about it again. The city can fend for itself."

"I'll be fine," Marlow said. He meant it. Probably. Seventy-five percent at least. After that, it was down to luck. "And so will the city. I'm not the only Night Shift officer, you know."

Cade snorted. "You're the only one I'd piss on if you were on fire."

"That's almost romantic."

"Yeah, well," Cade said as he stepped back. "We are dating."

"Oh?"

"We've been on three dates now," Cade pointed out. "You're practically my boyfriend."

Marlow tried to pretend that statement didn't make his breath catch just a little in his throat. "Am I, now? What's the tipping point on that?"

"Oh, you'll know," Cade said.

He was always an arrogant bastard, but this close to the full moon, he was cocky too. It was stupid how ridiculously cute Marlow found that. Even though it did mean Cade was about to shift into a killing machine that probably still wanted to tear Marlow's head off.

"Is there—"

The short, impatient whine of the taxi's horn interrupted Marlow's question. They had places to be and a deadline to get there.

"Don't eat anyone I know," Marlow said as he ducked into the car. The heavy door—bulletproof and reinforced—made a final-sounding clunk when he pulled it closed after him.

"No promises," Cade mouthed through the glass before he waved them off.

The inside of the cab smelled of fear, sweat, and curry—the take-out bag was on the front seat, strapped in with its own seat belt. Technically, night-hacks were only allowed to run until the first wolf hit the streets. A fare in progress could be finished, but then they were supposed to head back to their depots or home—whichever was closest.

Instead, they just stayed on the road as long as someone was willing to pay over the odds on a jacked-up fare. And there was usually someone who thought it was worth it to get that contract delivered *technically* before the deadline or sneak in a last-minute bid to undercut a wolf competitor.

Mostly it was an edge-of-the-seat ride through the city. If something did happen, then the hacks depended on their cabs being sturdy enough to keep the wolves out long enough for the Night Shift to get to them. They'd have to pay a fine, but they'd be alive and probably still come out ahead.

The fares were moonlight robbery, in Marlow's opinion. Even for this trip, which should have Marlow dropped off just before the cutoff point, the price had been enough to make Marlow wince… and it wasn't his account.

It wouldn't, he thought grimly to himself, be Cade's for much longer either once the stocks were transferred.

Guilt settled onto Marlow like a heavy blanket.

"No one ever tell you it's a bad idea to date a wolf?" the hack asked. She angled the mirror so she could see him in the back seat. "You'll lose your heart the old-fashioned way."

"We're not dating."

"Not what he said," she pointed out with a chuckle. "Eh, I've got a few exes running around out there with their asses all furry tonight. Some of them are wolves too."

She cackled at her own joke and turned her attention back to the road.

Marlow sat back and watched the city roll past. He rarely saw it like this, in the calm before the storm. The marks of the last few nights were still on show—scored walls, broken windows, blood not quite scrubbed off the pavement—but it was quiet and oddly peaceful. More so because you knew that was about to break.

The radio crackled. Habit made Marlow focus on it as adrenaline kicked his heart rate up a notch and pulled at his shoulders. He expected to hear the familiar clipped delivery of Dispatch come out of the speakers. Instead, it was a flat midwest drawl that opened with, "Hey, hon."

Marlow pushed his shoulders back and tried to relax. He rolled his head from one side to the other, the bones in his neck noisier than was healthy.

"We had a call from Pippa," the woman on the radio said. The driver straightened up at the name. "One of her clients is in labor. They aren't advanced enough to justify an ambulance, but Pippa says the baby won't wait all night. Baby five, apparently. Can you take the call, Bets? No one else is in the pickup area."

Bets glanced over her shoulder at Marlow. "Pippa's a midwife," she explained. "One of our clients. Look, I can still get you home before the first shift. The hospital is right on the way. I won't even charge you—"

Marlow raised his hand briefly. “It’s fine,” he said. “Go ahead. The full moon is no time for a home birth.”

Blood, screams, and the smell of a newborn—they might as well set up a ‘Fresh Food Here’ sign with a neon arrow pointed to their house.

“Thank you,” Bets said with relief. “Hopefully, she won’t give birth back there with you, eh?”

“It wouldn’t be the first baby I’ve delivered,” Marlow said with a dry smile. “And I’ve nothing else to do tonight.”

CHAPTER NINE

JUSTIN WAS OUT on the long balcony that wrapped around the outside of his office when Cade went back in. He didn't look around at the sound of the door closing, but he raised his hand and gestured for Cade to join him.

Back when they'd worked together, that had always put Cade's back up. It had always felt like he was being given an audience with his boss, not a meeting with his partner. Now they were competitors…

It still made Cade want to push him over the railing.

"I'm not saying a corner office was why I took Bear Arms up on their offer," he said. "It didn't hurt, though."

"It's our building," Cade pointed out. "You could have any office you wanted."

"I prefer people to seagulls," Justin said. He lifted a cigarette to his mouth and inhaled, the tip cherry bright against the dim light. "Plus, I get to run their entire West Coast operation, including protection detail for the diamond companies reps. I already have my eye on a promotion to the East Coast."

"More money?"

"Old money," Justin said. "That comes seasoned with influence, and that opens the sorts of doors I've always been interested in. What do you think? Congressman has a ring to it. For a dirt-poor lad made good."

He offered the cigarette to Cade, who took it after a moment's hesitation. The paper was dry under his fingers as he took a drag and filled his lungs with hot, mellow smoke. It didn't taste as good as the lingering taste of Marlow's kiss, but the wolf didn't need any reminders of him.

"Your dad's a doctor."

"He worked in the fishery."

"Yeah, when he was a teenager."

Justin snorted. "It's a lot easier to impress my new partners. They don't know me."

There it was, the reason they'd never worked long term as friends. That hollow thing in their gut they tried to hide under success and nice suits. It was hard to like someone when you suspected they could see right through you.

"Can you get him off?" Cade asked. "Piper. I know you cloned the files off the computer already."

"My client. My files," Justin said. "Do you want me to get him off?"

"Does it matter?"

"No," Justin said. "Not more than my reputation. As a congressman, I want to be able to boast that I never let a wealthy client face the consequences of his actions."

"Piper isn't rich."

"Maybe. Maybe not. Who knows, I'm sure he can pay me back somehow."

"Tell him if he comes back to San Diego, I'll make him miss prison," Cade said. "He wants his life back, he'd be advised to start it somewhere else."

Justin finally pushed himself off the rail and turned to look at Cade. "Are you *actually* doing all this for him?" He waved his hand vaguely, a thin trail of smoke tangled through his fingers. "Didn't you get your crush on the school jock out of your system when you were a teenager?"

He had not. The various humiliating scenarios that he'd played out in his head had been too vivid to even think about taking that risk. Even in the unlikely event the feelings had been mutual, he would have had to introduce someone with a normal family to his dad. Back then, Cade would have picked public humiliation and mockery over pity.

Still would.

"I'm doing this for me," Cade said. "And maybe I think what's best for me includes keeping Marlow around. But it's not the only reason. Franklin's a problem that I'll need to deal with eventually, and it's a lot easier with a Night Shift officer at my back than… Lem."

Justin pursed his lips and snorted. "Fair."

"Threatening Piper, though, that's all for Marlow," Cade said.

"At that point, it's not my problem," Justin said. "My interest in him ends the day I have an impressive legal victory in court. Oh, and it starts tomorrow. I've already set up a press conference."

"You spoke to Piper."

"Not yet, but he shouldn't have to say much," Justin said. "I want to establish myself as a passionate crusader for the truth before I have to try and rewrite Piper's history to sell him to the masses. He's not a palatable man."

"He's a charismatic one," Cade said. "That's the other reason I picked you and not Beth. She'd have liked him."

"And I won't."

"You will," Cade said. "It just won't matter to you."

Justin put his hand to his chest. "I'm hurt," he said. "And, not to be a bad host, but if we're down to insults, I assume we don't have any actual business left to discuss? So you should probably go. We still aren't friends, and wolves aren't pragmatic about that sort of thing."

It was a good point. Most wolf fights ended up with chunks of fur on the road and bloodshed, but the wolves involved all still alive. Hate complicated things. Along with love, it was one of the things that carried over during the shift.

"Stop trying to poach my brother," Cade said as he headed back inside.

"No," Justin said.

Bastard.

At the side of the play park, a group led by an elderly Asian lady did Tai Chi naked. Cade watched them with idle interest as he waited for the moonlight to reach critical mass. He assumed the Tai Chi practitioners were early shifters too. Otherwise, they were shortly going to get a rude interruption to their practice.

People claimed that the slow, measured movements worked to keep the wolf in a more relaxed state after the shift. Cade doubted it was true; he'd tried yoga last time it was in and got nothing out of it. But he supposed it didn't matter if they believed it.

It wasn't like they'd ever know.

Cade stretched and felt his spine loosen as the tension seeped out of him. He made an effort not to think about Marlow—alone in the city on a blue moon, his only possible allies out to get him—and focused on the acrid film of smoke left on his tongue.

It was an illusion of control, the same as the one the naked practitioners chased on the grass, but it was all he had. He couldn't *not* shift, and he had no idea what he'd do once he was a wolf. Any more than the wolf could influence what he did the rest of the month—otherwise a lot more contract negotiations would end with his teeth in someone's throat.

"Mr. Deacon?"

The sound of his name was unexpected. It wasn't a secret that Cade came here on full moons when he wasn't out in the country, but it wasn't somewhere people came to talk to him either. He turned and stared at the red-haired woman who picked her way over the uneven grass toward him. She was a cop, he could tell that from the uniform, but not Night Shift.

"You're Cade Deacon, right?" she said. Her eyes were wide and wet with anxiety, her pulse visible in her throat. The moon was high enough that the thought of blood—salty and hot as it spilled from the vein like soda water from a tap—made Cade's mouth water. "Officer Marlow's… friend."

"That's one word for it," Cade said. "Who are you?"

She swallowed and took another step toward him. Cade resisted the inexplicable urge to take a matching step back as a growl scraped at his throat—impatient to get out.

"I'm a Night Shift clerk," she said. "In the Armory. I… someone's altered my records to make it look like Marlow stole silver. I don't know who, but it had to have been someone on Night Shift, and if I can't trust them—"

Someone screamed. It was from pain, not fear. There was a difference in the timbre of it. Cade glanced around and saw the Tai Chi group stagger away from each other as the wolf pushed out of them. He felt the poison-ivy itch of it on his skin as thick, coarse patches of wolf fur sprouted from his skin.

His bones felt *hot*, as if the wolf was in the marrow, and his vision was suddenly filmed with blood as his brain was pulled apart to be knit back together.

"You—" He doubled over and spat out a tooth on the ground. He'd swallow some of them; he always did. Mostly they got broken down between now and the morning, but not always.

It was hard to think. His nerve endings were on fire as his body pumped out adrenaline like candy, and the recognition of the red-haired clerk as a person frayed. She was just meat and rich, healthy organ meat to shred between his teeth and fill his gut.

"R… run," he snarled through teeth that didn't feel like his anymore. The sharp edges shredded his tongue, and even the taste of his own blood made him hungrier. "Stup… stupid…"

"No," the clerk said. "I'm the one who stays *smart*."

She pulled a stun baton from behind her back, heavy-duty Night Shift kit some wispy bit of *Cade* recognized, although he didn't have any control over his muscles and feet anymore. She screamed in a mixture of panic and adrenaline as she rammed it into his neck.

The wolf convulsed as the electricity ripped through it and disrupted muscles and nerve endings that weren't quite functional yet. It hit the ground hard as its limbs spasmed and twitched against its will.

Still screaming, the red-haired woman hit the wolf with the shock baton again. And again.

"I've done it," she yelled, her voice high and shrill in her throat as she looked around. "Come and help."

It was angry.

It was hungry.

It hurt.

Mostly it was hungry.

The wolf tried to lunge at the woman, jaws agape. Its legs, weak and jerky still, wouldn't cooperate, and it flopped back down onto the ground. Then the rest of the woman's pack ran up, sticks in hand, and pinned it in place until they could sting it with the sticks again.

"You know where to take him," the leader of the pack said.

He smelled like something the wolf wanted to eat. Everything did, but him especially. The wolf snarled at him as the world went soggy around it and lashed out blindly. He wasn't quite close enough to reach.

"Yeah," the leader made the noise with his mouth. He pulled his gun and shot another wolf—old wolf from the smell. The wolf could have killed it if it had needed to. "Not my first rodeo. Muzzle him and get him into the truck. Now. Move."

Rough gloved hands rolled the wolf onto its back and tangled it in something that bit at its wrists and ankles. It panted, hot and wet, as it fought against the sluggish pain in its head.

"I'll do it," the woman said. The fear had almost left her voice. Out of the corner of the wolf's eye, it saw her bring a thing toward its face. Even before it touched skin, the wolf could feel the *itchstingpain* of it on its tongue and behind its eyelids.

It snarled and snapped at the thing. This time it caught meat between its teeth. The woman shrieked in shock and snatched her bloody hand away. The wolf swallowed the three fingers in its mouth. Then the pack hit it with their sticks again and shoved the thing on its face.

It took all of them to lift the wolf's limp weight.

The leader had to shoot two more wolves to get them back to the truck. The woman, her bloody hand clutched to her chest, cried the whole way.

CHAPTER TEN

MARLOW DIDN'T HAVE much family. There was an aunt out in Julian, a couple of cousins. They traded Christmas cards once a year and sent birthday wishes online if they were in time.

He knew more about Jenny Oldman's life.

She was single, a realtor, loved musicals and shoes. The worst thing about pregnancy was how much she had to pee. Her wife had been the one who talked her into IVF—"I had four kids and custody of the gerbils. I didn't need any more appetites in my house."—and then broke up with her for a dental hygienist, "living the cliche!"

Jenny could also juice pineapples with her bare hands. Her fingers dug into Marlow's arm hard enough he was sure he'd have a bruise later as she breathed through her contractions.

"Fuck fuck fuck," she panted as sweat dripped off her face. "Fuuuuuuccccck."

Pippa, the midwife, timed the contraction on her phone.

"Nearly there," the hack said over her shoulder. "Fucking construction! What did the wolves *do* last night, dig up the fucking roads?"

She braked hard in front of the blocked-off section of road, reversed, and took the detour that pointed down the road to the right. The back of her neck was sweaty, and there were already wolves on the street. Two of them had nearly run the cab off the road a few minutes before when they'd side-swiped it in the middle of their fight over a torn-up deer carcass.

"Talk to me!" Jenny demanded in a thin, anxious voice. Her fingers pinched Marlow's arm as she squeezed. "Tell me what's going on!"

"That Night Shift killer is still on the streets," the hack offered up. "I heard he'd *eaten* parts of the body."

Jenny made a thin, discontented noise in her throat. "What?"

"I didn't see that on any of the news channels," Pippa said, with a disapproving glance at the hack. "It's just fear-mongering. The truth is bad enough."

She gave Jenny's knee a reassuring pat. Jenny swore at her, and the hack finally turned onto the road into the hospital. It was already in lockdown; shutters slammed down over the doors and windows and armed guards on the roof.

They weren't Night Shift, Marlow reminded himself as the back of his neck crawled with panic. They wouldn't recognize him from up there. Not even through the scope of a rifle.

The hack spun the wheel and screeched into the bay in front of the entrance. Just as she straightened out of the turn, a wolf—fur gray-streaked black in the flash of the headlights—charged them. Marlow felt the jolt of impact as the car hit the wall of muscle and fur. It snarled and smacked its hands down on the hood. Long talons dug into the metal.

"Son of a bitch!" the hack cursed and slammed her foot down on the gas. The engine screamed, the smell of burnt oil sickly sharp in the back of the cab, as she tore through the forecourt with the wolf hunched on the car like a hood ornament. She turned hard to circle back around. The wheel spun under the flat of her palms, and the wolf was thrown from side to side. It hunched down, dug in, and wrinkled black lips back from ragged teeth in a snarl that showed the flesh caught in its teeth.

"Jenny," Marlow said. "Could you hold on to Pippa for a second?"

She panted—whether from fear or labor, Marlow wasn't sure—and transferred her death grip from Marlow's arm to Pippa's leg.

"Oh, my—" Pippa choked off whatever she was going to say with a wince and put her hand over Jenny's.

Marlow unbuckled the seat belt and leaned into the front of the car. Slaver coated the windscreen, thick and viscous, as the wolf snapped and scraped at the glass.

"What are you doing?" the hack asked as she reached up to shove at him.

"Helping."

Marlow braced his hand against the steering wheel and leaned on the horn. It blared out, an angry goose honk of machine-generated noise, and the wolf flattened its ears to its head. Yellow eyes narrowed—it wasn't Cade under the fur, his amber-gold eyes were distinct—and it howled at him. Marlow kept his hand on the horn. The wolf shook its head, and its ears flapped wildly.

"Ha!" the hack said gleefully. "I should have thought of that."

"Brake," Marlow ordered as he braced himself against the passenger seat. Pippa and Jenny were already strapped in.

The hack took a deep breath and slammed both feet onto the brake. The car screeched to a halt, rear tires fishtailing and the sour smell of burnt rubber in the air. Jenny made a startled noise—half eep and half urp—and the wolf was thrown off the hood of the car. It hit the road and rolled twice, skin and fur scraped off on the tarmac. The wet, raw flesh had already started to heal as it scrambled onto all fours.

This time the hack didn't need to be told what to do. She hit the gas, and the car roared forward. Marlow hung on to the passenger side headrest as he was thrown backward. This time the sound out of Jenny was definitely a retch. The bull bars caught the wolf just under the shoulders and flipped it up in the air. It landed on the hood hard enough to dent the metal and bounced up onto and over the roof. It hit the road with the sort of smack that broke bones, and this time, it took longer to get up.

The hack kept her foot down and jerked the wheel around hard as she U-turned back into the forecourt. This time, when she hit the brakes, Marlow let himself fall back into the seat.

Jenny had been sick on Pippa. It was mostly bile, but it smelled foul. The hospital doors opened, the hack popped the back door, and they maneuvered the awkward off-balance bulk of Jenny's belly through the door ahead of her. On the other side of the doors, nurses waited, hands poised over the emergency lock button as Marlow and Piper hustled Jenny in. The hack brought up the rear with a running commentary of what the wolf was doing.

They got Jenny inside just in time. The doors closed behind them, and the nurses sprang into action, with wet wipes for her chin and chest and a wheelchair for her to lower herself into. She gripped Marlow's hand so tight he couldn't *feel* his fingers, never mind pull himself free.

"Thank you," she said. "Thank you so much. You were… fuck it, fuck me… so calm. If you have a sister, I will totally date her once my divorce comes through!"

She finally let go, and Marlow fell back as the nurse wheeled her away. Pippa followed along after a quick stumbled-over, "What she said." Marlow rubbed his hand gingerly and flexed his fingers to be sure they still worked.

So much for a quiet night. The sound of his name made him look around, a second before he realized it wasn't someone in the room. It came from the flat TV mounted on the wall. Annabeth stood on the pavement outside her mother's house, hands knotted together in front of her and a slight deer-in-the-headlights look on her face as she stared at the camera.

"...Marlow saved my baby," she said. "He could have shot me, and he didn't. I don't believe he'd shoot someone for no reason. He was kind to me."

The TV flicked back to the studio, and the anchorman provided a potted history of... earlier that month. It felt like longer. Marlow felt his chest warm with quiet appreciation for Annabeth standing up for him. Then it went cold, brittle as old wood, as the image on the screen shifted to drone footage of the Old Town Market.

"In an update to the ongoing situation at the Old Town Market," the anchor said solemnly over the footage, "the unexpected foci of wolf activity in this area has been tracked to deliberate vandalism, with a keg of goat blood thrown through a local shop window. In the confusion, Officer Jay Bennett has still not been contacted. Fears are growing that something—"

Marlow didn't wait to hear the rest. He loped over to where the hack stood with one of the porters and put his hand on her shoulder.

"How much would it take to change my destination?" he asked. "Because I'll pay it."

Marlow couldn't remember the last time he'd been to the Old Town Market. It was a tourist trap, not somewhere the residents regularly went. There must have been a call down here at some point over the years, but his team hadn't taken it.

He paused on the edge of the Night Shift cordon. In the dark, lit by the strobe of the patrol cars and back in his uniform, no one gave Marlow a second look. He'd always said that his eyes weren't *that* noticeable, but nobody had listened. He eavesdropped discreetly on the argument between Captain Gil and a lieutenant. The lieutenant wanted to go in after Bennett, but Gil was reluctant.

"Public feeling is high enough," she said, her voice grim with reality. "We can't afford to kill twenty wolves just to save one Night Shift officer. That 'thank you for your service' shit, it used to be 'thank you for your sacrifice.' That's what people expect of us."

Marlow pulled the black neoprene gaiter up over his mouth and nose, tight and already claustrophobic as he tasted his own breath bounced back at him, and buckled his helmet. The back of his neck stung with imagined eyes on him as he ducked under the strung yellow tape and into the incident.

Torn banners flapped from shop fronts; ripped-down pennants, triangles of bright frayed material strung on thin rope, tangled in knotted tripwires in the narrow alleys. Blood splashed over the clay tiles, and disturbed birds shrieked furiously from windowsills and under the roofs.

A boar, heavy-shouldered and bristled, shrieked like an angry woman as it charged out of a side alley. Pastry crumbs covered its face, and there was blood on its tusks. It was followed by two others and a farrow of piglets on their heels.

Marlow backed up to give them space.

Someone had turned the city's sties out onto the streets. Usually the stockmen turned out a couple of pigs *a year*. They did too much damage otherwise, and they sometimes survived the night. No one wanted to be the one who had to hunt down pissed-off pigs in the sewers and back alleys.

The last piglet charged across the broken tiles. Marlow waited a second—just in case—and then pushed himself into a lope.

Growls and snarls, the occasional squealing shriek of an enraged boar, bounced off the walls and glass windows. Despite that, it still *felt* quiet to Marlow. He was used to the crackle of the mic in his ear, the call and response of the rest of his squad as they moved through the space.

He was on his own, and it occurred to him that—grand gesture aside—he wasn't sure he was actually going to be able to help Bennett. What could he do that a dozen other Night Shift TAC officers couldn't?

All he had was that he knew Bennett. He'd dragged her out of the weeds before, and she'd done the same for him. He knew how she acted in the field and how she reacted when things went wrong. Most of all? He knew Franklin was involved.

Something snarled behind him—a wet, rough cough of a sound—and he spun around. A wolf crouched on the counter of the taco stall. Stippled gray-and-red fur stuck out in matted, sticky chunks around it, and the searchlights of the drones overhead caught reflections of green sparks in its eyes. Thick strings of bloody slobber dripped from its mouth and matted in the sparse fur on its chest.

It chewed the air, lips peeled back from its teeth as it worried at nothing, and hunched down, ready to spring.

There was something wrong with it.

Marlow touched the gun on his hip, but went for the baton instead. People already believed he was a cold-blooded murderer—no reason to give them more reason to think that. The weight of the baton settled comfortably into his hand, and he snapped it to the side to extend it to its full length.

"You could go for easier prey," he said. "I saw piglets."

The wolf ignored the offer and lunged at him. Marlow threw himself out of the way. He felt the claws catch in his hair but ignored the quick flick of hot pain as he hit the ground shoulder first. The wolf tripped over him and made a frustrated guttural noise as it caught itself. It spun around on the balls of its feet and stooped over him. Spit dripped on his face, thick and…

Why did it make his skin itch?

Marlow swung the baton in a short, vicious arc. It cracked into the wolf's jaw and snapped it with an audible pop. Its eyes bulged, and a small choked whimper escaped it at the unexpected pain. It reared back. Marlow shifted his grip on the baton and drove the end up into the soft skin under the wolf's broken jaw.

It gagged and recoiled as it clawed at its broken throat, raw stripes of flesh where it dug its claws in. Marlow scrambled to his feet and ran. He wasn't there to clear the market, just to find Beckett. His feet pounded on the tiles as he wove in and out through the maze of stalls and small shops.

The wolf gave chase for a while, but it quickly lost interest. Marlow stopped for a second and leaned back against a wall to catch his breath. He gave his T-shirt an absentminded tug to straighten it. He paused as it stuck to his hands.

Honey?

Marlow pulled the T-shirt up to taste one of the stiff patches. It stung the tip of his tongue; the sweetness cut through with heat.

Okay. He wiped his sleeve over his mouth and pushed himself off the wall. Spicy honey. That gave him something to work with.

He found a map of the shops in the market in a pile of pamphlets crumpled and torn under an overturned stall. There was only one shop that sold “artisanal honey, gifts, and crafts.” Marlow folded the flyer, tucked it in his back pocket, and headed that way.

Bennett perched clumsily on top of the shop’s counter, broken leg awkwardly splinted with metal struts from a scavenged set of shelves and strips cut from her uniform. A makeshift baton—caked with blood and dented—was clutched in one bruised hand, and she hefted a broken jar of ghost-pepper honey in the other. Blood dripped between her fingers where the glass had sliced her fingers open.

“Who the fuck are you?” Bennett rasped out as she saw him. Bruised lips twitched back in a snarl as she hefted the honey, ready to throw. “Did Franklin send you to do his dirty work? Should have known he wouldn’t have the balls to do it himself.”

Marlow held one hand up and used the other to pull the gaiter down to his throat. The bridge of his nose itched where the seam had dug into it.

“It’s me,” he said. Then he realized that might not be entirely reassuring, seeing as he was a wanted killer. “I didn’t kill Lyons.”

Bennett’s expression whiplashed from near tears—her eyes wet and her lower lip trembling—to exasperated annoyance.

“You *didn’t*?” she said, mock surprise layered as thick as… honey… over her voice. “Wow. But who else could have? Maybe Franklin would know, but he hasn’t been back since he *broke my leg and left me here to die*.”

“No need to yell,” Marlow said.

“You’re a fucking muppet,” Bennett told him. Sweat broke on her forehead as he scooted to the edge of the counter. He jogged over and helped her down, her weight braced over his shoulder. Both of them pretended not to notice the choked sound of pain

Bennett made as she tried to stand. She managed to steady herself against the counter long enough to slap him around the back of the head. "Why didn't you tell me Piper still had his fingers in the department?"

Marlow shrugged. "I figured if I brought them down, it would make me a shoo-in for that promotion," he said.

Bennett stopped mid-rant and stared at him; her mouth hung half-open. "Fuck off," she said after a second. "You thought it was me."

Marlow put his arm around her waist, and they stumbled over to the door to look out. The blood that had started the whole thing caked the square in thick, clotted puddles. Wolf footprints tracked through it, and it seeped under the doors of the few shops not busted open.

"Would you have suspected Franklin of being the mastermind?" he asked.

She glared at him. Marlow could tell she wanted to argue the point, but she'd be lying. None of them would have thought of Franklin.

"When did you realize it wasn't me?" she asked. "I assume you did, and that's why you sent me those files on Clemons."

Marlow nodded. "You saved my life when you turned up at Clemons's house the other night," he said. "Franklin was going to kill me, but your arrival distracted him enough I could get away."

"I could have still been involved."

"You would never have worked for Franklin," Marlow said.

Bennett made a rude sound under her breath. "That bastard," she breathed out raggedly. "He set this up. We were called in to investigate a wolf pack formation and found that mess. He waited until my back was turned and then—"

She stopped and sniffed hard, her face twisted in an odd expression to hold back the tears.

"He was your friend," Marlow said.

"No," Bennett said. "If he was, then he would have had the common decency to kill me clean, not leave me for the wolves."

Marlow hesitated. He didn't care to defend Franklin's reputation, but he remembered the sting of betrayal from when Piper tried to kill him. The weird let-down feeling that he hadn't merited a bullet, that someone he'd admired would let him die badly rather than do it themselves. There was nothing he could do about that with Piper, but…

"He's in love with you," he said. "Franklin. For years. Maybe he just couldn't—"

Bennett pinched his ear.

"Don't be such a fucking boy," she said, the words still thick with tears under the contempt. "He stamped on my leg until it snapped. Oh, he sniveled like a bastard the whole time, but it didn't stop him. Would you do that to someone you loved? To your wolf?"

"I set him on fire," Marlow pointed out.

It startled a laugh out of Bennett. Then she swore and dug her fingers into his shoulder as it jarred her leg.

"Fuck," she muttered under her breath, her voice thready and cracked. Then she sniffed, cleared her throat, and tried again. "Fuck him, okay. It pisses me off that I trusted him. Even after I checked into those murders? When I knew it was Clemons who murdered that man? I didn't think that Franklin was… I thought that there'd been a mistake. Except I knew better, didn't I? I'm smarter than that, but I wanted it to be a mistake. And when I showed him, he said all the right things and promised to fix everything. He just asked me to wait until… Until he could set this up, I guess. I never knew him."

Her eyebrows pleated together, and she looked away, shoulders hunched.

"Now I've got us both killed," she said.

"Not going to tell me to leave you and save myself?" Marlow asked.

Bennett snorted. "I've gotten good at chucking these jars," she said. "I could lay you out before you got across the square."

Based on the fragments of bloody, sticky glass outside, she probably could. The news had said she'd been in here for an hour, and she'd kept the wolves at bay that long.

"You're right," Marlow said. "Franklin never knew you at all if he thought it would be this easy to kill you."

"I just figured if I got out of this, I was a shoo-in for that promotion," Bennett repeated his claim with a sharp, bloody-toothed grin that had no humor in it. "As long as no one snitches on me for drowning Franklin in a fucking toilet. Thing is, Marlow, I don't see how we can get out."

"We don't need to," Marlow said. "We go up. They've got the drones out, and you might be an acceptable casualty, but right now, I'm the most wanted man in San Diego. They'll come to get me."

Bennett stared at him for a second, and then she smiled, wide enough that the scab on her upper lip split. She dabbed the blood away with the tip of her tongue.

"Cocky bastard," she said. "But it might work."

"Better hope it does. It's all I've got," Marlow said. He turned her around, and they headed for the back of the shop. "I get my name cleared, and you get that leg set—"

"Don't be stupid," Bennett said flatly. "After this, we're going to be toxic. There's no smoke without fire, Marlow, and this is the second time we staggered out of the smoke. So… let go of that idea of a house and family. It's rented apartments and partners who'll eventually realize you're never going to live up to your potential."

The idea stuck in Marlow's throat. It was true. They both knew it was, but that was something to face up to tomorrow.

"I have to drag your ass up two flights of stairs and onto the roof," Marlow said. "Maybe not the best idea to try and convince me to lie down and die."

The staircase was narrow and the steps piled with stock not out on the shelves yet. Of course it was. Marlow tightened his grip on Bennett's belt and got his shoulder under her armpit. They could do this.

"Reverse psychology," Bennett said raggedly. "Make you want to do it from spite."

"That works on you, not me."

Bennett hiccupped out a laugh. "You're dragging my broken ass up the stairs," she said. "Don't try and tell your granny how to suck eggs."

At the top of the stairs, the doors were locked. Marlow kicked one open and dragged Bennett, who'd gone silent except for the rattle of her breathing, through the small storeroom to the window. The smash of broken glass made the wolves outside look up, the glitter of a dozen eyes suddenly fixed on them, but it had to be done.

"Maybe you should leave me," Bennett said, breaking her silence at last.

"You don't mean that."

"No, I fucking don't," Bennett said. "But I'm not sure I can get up there. My leg—"

"It's broken. I don't think it's going to be right again," Marlow said bluntly. Over an hour with a smashed leg she'd had to splint and drag herself about on? That wasn't… ideal. Marlow could remember the conversations the doctor had about his knee. "So I'm going to boost you out the window, and you're going to get on the roof. It's going to hurt, but—"

"Tomorrow, you put your boot up Franklin's ass for me," Bennett said.

"For you, anything," Marlow said.

They scrambled up onto the sloped roof, tiles sharp against their fingers, and the drones picked them out immediately. Marlow tilted his head back so the cameras could see his face and handed his gun to Bennett.

"The wolves are going to get here before help," he said. "You take this side. I'll get the other."

Bennett made a rude noise in the back of her throat. "This is what it is to be Night Shift," she said. "We don't even get to die in peace."

"Maybe they'll put that on next year's recruitment poster." Marlow pulled his backup gun and scrambled over the bird-shit decorated roof to the far side of the building. He stood on the edge and looked down. A wolf—mostly white under the grime and blood matted into its fur—hauled itself up the side of the building. Thick black claws dug into the walls, the stucco render torn away from the frame in chunks.

He shot it in the shoulder. Blood sprayed out from the wound, bone splintered and flesh tore, and its arms went weak. The wolf screamed like a hurt child and dangled for a moment. It tried to drag itself the rest of the way up on three limbs but couldn't quite make it. After a second, it lost its footing and fell back into the street.

It wouldn't kill it, the fall or the bullet, but the silver in its shoulder would hobble it for the night. Hopefully.

Marlow should have taken the headshot. That was how Piper had taught them.

"A crippled wolf can still rip you apart," he'd said. Marlow could remember the drill-sergeant bite of it on his nerves during the qualifying target practice for the Academy.

Franklin wouldn't have hesitated. They were right: hesitation got you killed. It would get other people killed along with you.

Marlow was just sick of it.

The wolves didn't care. More came out of alleys and around corners, heads up and noses flared to show red flesh as they sniffed the air. The injured white wolf tried to defend its claim to the hunting ground, but with one ruined arm it was soon driven off. It fled with its tail between its legs. And that just left Bennett and Marlow.

It felt like hours. It was probably minutes.

The Black Hawk choppers swooped out of the cloudy sky, the chuff-chuff of the rotors loud enough to deafen. Weighted ropes dropped, straight as plumb lines, and Night Shift officers in full TAC gear swarmed down them onto the roofs and into the streets. Their guns stayed slung over their backs as they waded into the pack of wolves with batons and tranq guns.

The last thing Night Shift needed right now was a slaughter.

A few wolves got through the cordon, though. Gil dropped them from her perch on the landing gear of the chopper, boots braced and harness pulled tight as she swung out for a better angle.

Marlow recognized the tactics. It was straight out of the playbook. Clear the space you wanted to control and then—

The first gas canister arced in and smashed through the window of the shop opposite. Gas leaked out in a thin white cloud and sank toward the ground. It settled over wolves who retched and tore at themselves as their skin burned. Another canister bounced off the street and got stuck in the muck of spilled honey and blood. The gas sprayed out at ankle level and spread.

They'd have to cordon off the block for a week to decontaminate it. The local shop owners would have to be compensated for their time. It worked, though.

The wolves, blind and blistered, took the path of least resistance away from the gas and the masked Night Shift officers. A few—

hungrier or angrier—veered back and smashed themselves against the wall of Kevlar and silver-laced batons.

Marlow lowered his gun. His hands weren't shaking, they never did until later, but they'd gone numb with the build-up of stale adrenaline.

He turned to check on Bennett just as her leg went out from under her. She landed badly, broken leg awkward and stiff as it overextended to the side, and sank her teeth into her lower lip to try and stifle a scream.

"A minute," Marlow said as he headed over to her. He grabbed her under her arms, the edges of the Kevlar vest rough against his fingers, and hauled her back to her feet, more or less. "Just hold on another minute, Bennett. We'll be out of here."

She jabbed an elbow back into his ribs. "What the fuck do you think I'm going to do?" she asked. "Just decide to die instead?"

"I wouldn't put it past you."

She laughed, a ragged hiccup, and didn't deny it. On the chopper, Gil glanced their way. Marlow couldn't see much—between the distance and her helmet—but he could imagine her expression. She acknowledged them with a tilt of her head and twisted to yell something at the pilot. After a second, the Black Hawk pitched forward and headed their way.

Something pale and quick moved, just in the periphery of Marlow's field of vision. He turned and saw the white wolf—shoulder still raw meat but the rest of its injuries healed—as it launched itself off a nearby roof.

Marlow lifted his gun and squeezed the trigger in one smooth, practiced motion. The gun clicked on an empty magazine, and the wolf crashed into the roof. Dislodged slates rained down on the street below as the wolf scrambled to its feet.

The angle of the Black Hawk meant that Gil couldn't see them. Not yet.

Black lips wrinkled back from jagged yellow teeth, gums bright red, and the wolf swung at them with one long, thick-muscled arm. The hooked claws caught in Marlow's sleeve as he dragged Bennett out of the way and scraped a thin paper-cut painful sting of a cut from his elbow to his shoulder.

"Fuck this," Bennett snarled. She took a hobbled step forward and threw a roundhouse punch—her fist weighted with her empty gun—at the wolf. The crack of impact did more damage to her hand than to the wolf, but it stumbled backward and lost its balance. It took a second to drop to street level, and Bennett nearly followed it.

Marlow grabbed her collar, a jolt of pain shooting up into his shoulder as he took her weight and yanked her back.

They both fell backward and sprawled, sweaty and panting, on the remaining slates.

"Thanks," Marlow said.

The Black Hawk swung in over them, and Gil kicked two ropes down. The thick, weighted skein of black webbing swung back and forth over the roof.

"We've got to rescue ourselves?" Bennett asked. "What the hell. Give me a hand."

Marlow pushed himself up, grabbed her wrist, and dragged her up. The dregs of gas that reached them stung his throat and made his eyes itch. It didn't have the same potency on a null as it did on a wolf, but it was still an irritant. Usually it set Marlow's hay fever off as well.

They limped over to the ropes. Marlow steadied the first as Bennett clumsily wedged her uninjured foot in the loop. She twisted the rope around her hand and looked at Marlow.

"You know, either of us would have been a fucking amazing lieutenant," she said.

"Still could be," Marlow said as he grabbed the other rope.

It was a lie, but it was a nice thought. Both of them hung on grimly as the pilot took the Black Hawk up and out of the hot zone. When it landed, the paramedics grabbed Bennett and Gil stalked over to Marlow.

"You're under arrest," she said. "What the hell did you think—"

"It wasn't him," Bennett said. She wrenched her arm away from the medic before they could slip a needle into the crook of her elbow. "Franklin did it and framed Marlow. He tried to kill me too."

Not quite the whole story, but it was close enough. It would do until they got back to the station and Marlow could lay it all out for them.

He nodded when Gil looked at him. "I didn't kill anyone," he said. "Franklin can't say the same."

It was morning, but there was no rest for the wicked. Or for anyone else.

Gil leaned against the back wall of the office and drank cold, thick coffee as if she couldn't taste it. Her eyes were red-rimmed, and her hands had a slight, noticeable tremor.

"So you see," she said as O'Hara stared at his desk. "Clemons is a serial killer. Franklin is a murderer, a wannabe cop killer twice over, and a corrupt cop, and Piper's lawyer is a fucking shark. So, busy night."

Technically, Marlow was still under arrest. His hands were cuffed, and they'd taken his weapons when they brought him in. He slouched down in the black leather chair and spread his hands as far as the cuffs would let him.

"Don't forget that Bennett's in hospital," Marlow added. "And the Old Town Market is in ruins."

O'Hara sat back and rubbed his hands over his face.

"Why didn't you just turn yourself in, Marlow?" he asked. "You know I knew there was still corruption in the Night Shift."

Gil pushed herself off the wall. "You knew what the fuck?" she said.

That made O'Hara wince. He pinched the bridge of his nose between his fingers.

"I didn't know who else was dirty," Marlow said. "Every single Night Shift officer in this precinct came up with either Piper or Franklin. Any of them could have been dirty."

"Even me?" Gil asked.

"You turned a blind eye to Piper," Marlow said. "You knew he bent the rules. Why should I assume you didn't know he'd broken them?"

"I…"

"He's right," O'Hara said. "We didn't clean house last time, Gil. Not enough. We just brushed stuff under the rug and tried not to look down. I wouldn't have trusted us either, I guess."

He flicked through the file in front of him: Clemons's other victims. There was a map that Bennett had made of Clemons's route that turned up three more potential targets and then the information on Franklin that Justin had sent over. A lot of problems for first thing in the morning.

"You're still suspended for now," O'Hara said. "Until I can do this officially, but go home, Marlow. Get some rest."

Easier said than done. Marlow held his hands out to be uncuffed and pushed himself up from the seat.

"Piper's going to be a problem," he said. "He didn't hand over that stuff for free."

"It's our job to worry about that," O'Hara said.

Gil nodded. "I won't make the same mistake twice."

"And I'll send the Day Shift to pull in Mr. Clemons," O'Hara added. "Until we can find out exactly what he has and hasn't done, and where."

Marlow was a bit surprised to realize that he didn't care. Maybe it would come later. He limped down to the armory to collect his belongings. Erin was on duty again, and she didn't meet his eyes as she passed over the bag with a bandaged hand. It looked bad.

"They're doing an audit," Marlow said as he emptied his phone, wallet, and keys onto the counter. "You think you covered your tracks, but are you positive?"

Erin stared at him. "I did it for Jay," she said. "Out there, every night. She deserved more than they gave her. More than you getting the promotion that should have been hers."

So he'd been right. Marlow tucked his wallet in his pocket and still didn't care. The department would deal with her. He didn't have to.

"What Franklin got her was a broken leg and compartment syndrome," Marlow said. "He tried to kill her."

"No."

"You don't have to believe me. You could ask her yourself," he said. "Once you do, though, it will go easier on you if you cooperate. Bennett might even forgive you."

Erin stared at him. "No," she said slowly. "She won't. But I can tell you one thing that Franklin did."

There was venom in her voice, clotted anger, and fear. Marlow finally felt something other than exhaustion as he looked at her. The corner of her mouth twisted into a grimace of a smile.

"We took your boyfriend," she said. "And you won't see him again to ask him anything."

Marlow took a step toward her but changed his mind. She didn't matter. It wasn't a "we," it was a "he," and Franklin wouldn't have trusted Bennett's girlfriend with anything.

"You know why he recruited you?" Marlow asked. "To hurt Bennett. That's all."

He turned on his heel and stalked out. There were eight missed calls from Bennett on his phone, and halfway to the lift, he got the ninth.

"What do you want?" he asked.

"They kept you talking until *now*?" Franklin said. "After the night you had? I'd get the union on it."

For a moment, the unexpected voice stalled Marlow. He started to wonder how the fuck Franklin had Bennett's phone, but he supposed the red-haired answer to that was weighing up her choices behind him. It took him a second to swallow the knot in his throat enough to speak.

"What. Do. You. Want?" Marlow repeated, each word enunciated clearly.

"I didn't want to hurt Bennett," Franklin said. "Despite everything, I'm glad she's okay."

This time Marlow didn't bother to ask. He just waited as he got on the lift.

"Your boyfriend won't be so lucky," Franklin said. "I checked your computer while you were… gone… so I know that you know how I deal with people I need to… go away."

"Yeah."

"You are a frustrating asshole," Franklin said. "The fine art of conversation is lost on you, huh. All right, I want money. Deacon has money. You get someone to give me Deacon's money."

"How much?"

"All of it. Liquidate it. I want everything," Franklin said. "Oh, and could you drop by my apartment and feed Curly?"

"What?"

"The guinea pig," Franklin said. "I figure Bennett will take him in, he can hang with the rats, but she's not exactly in a fit state to go up and down stairs right now."

"There's something wrong with you," Marlow said.

"Maybe," Franklin agreed. "But I'm not into hurting animals, so I'm not psychopathic. And Curly likes the food in the blue tin. Not the red."

Marlow leaned forward and rested his forehead against the cool metal of the doors.

"When and where?" he asked.

"I'll text you the address."

CHAPTER ELEVEN

HOT OR COLD? Which was better?

In Alaska right now, Cade would probably be hypothermic and halfway to frostbite in *all* his extremities. That wasn't pleasant.

On the other hand, neither was the parched, sticky ache in his throat and the hot pinprick itch of the sunburn that glowed under his existing tan… on *all* his extremities.

What took longer? Death from exposure or sunstroke?

Cade would have to look that up if he got a chance. He kept his eye on the horizon and stalked across the hot, gritty sand in a straight line toward it. It had been hours so far, with a few brief stops by rocky outcroppings as he sheltered from the sun. He had to admire Franklin's thoroughness. The corrupt bastard had taken the time to make sure that Cade woke up in the middle of fucking nowhere. He wasn't the only one Franklin had given this one-way treatment to either. The chain and manacles were well-made, but they'd obviously been there for a while. The workmanship on the hook sunk into the bedrock had reminded Cade of the one they'd found on the Reserve.

Heavy enough to hold an angry wolf—and Cade had been angry, he had torn the ground around him up like a plow—but easy enough for a human to slip their foot out of.

Franklin wanted the bodies found. Missing people started searches. Corpses found changed out in the desert—that made it look accidental.

The problem with that, though, was that Cade had grown up in the *ass-end* of nowhere. This wasn't the first time he'd woken up with no idea of where the wolf had left him, and he was pretty sure that, at least here, he didn't have to worry about bears.

So Cade wasn't going to panic or get lost or fall off a cliff. He picked the most straightforward direction to stay true to—east, toward the sun—and started to walk. Eventually, he'd find some sign of civilization, or he'd die.

They were the only two choices.

He kept walking.

Overhead a vulture companionably followed along; black wings spread to catch the hot air as it rose. Cade glanced up at it occasionally when he needed motivation to keep walking.

"Eaten by animals" was what happened to a miserable teenager with a shit dad and a stepmother whose best wasn't going to be enough. Not that he begrudged the bird a meal, but this was not how he planned to die. He had money and influence. People who owned a Lexus didn't die in the desert, and he wasn't going to be the exception that proved the rule.

He kept going, one foot in front of the other, until the hot, sandy rocks of the desert gave way to the flat, even hotter surface of a cracked backroad. Cade stopped and looked down at the potholed concrete, its road markings scraped and faded until they could barely be seen.

Then he looked up.

The vulture dipped a wing and turned away. It felt like a sign, even though there was probably just a dead coyote that would take less work somewhere nearby.

Cade stood on the road for a second and then started walking again.

One foot in front of the other.

"You fucking lost or what?" the kid at the register said. He leaned his elbows on the counter and pushed himself up and forward to give Cade a once-over from head to red, blistered feet. "And on the last day of the full moon! You're going to have to live with that."

Cade pulled the cap off a bottle of water and took a drink. It was a bad idea to drink too much when you were dehydrated. He knew that. The minute the water hit the back of his throat, though, his body decided it was a lie. He gulped down half the bottle before he could pull it away from his mouth. The rest he tipped over his head. It soaked his hair and dripped down onto his shoulders.

The shock of cold made his stomach cramp, and the water he'd just swallowed retched back up into his throat.

"You going to be sick?" the kid asked as he recoiled back to his side of the counter. "Don't puke on the floor. There's a toilet out back."

"I'm not going to be sick," Cade said grimly.

"You sure about that?"

No.

Cade braced his hands on the counter and let his head hang forward as he waited for the wave to pass. His skin felt too hot and tight to sweat.

"I can't pay right now, but—" he said.

"Don't worry about it," the kid said. "We have a fund for anyone that loses their tags and can't pay. Water and sweats, use the store phone."

Huh.

Cade wiped his mouth on his arm and straightened up.

"Happen often?" he asked

"Once," the kid said. "Guess that was enough. Some guy came in, ranting and raving that he'd been kidnapped? He wanted us to call the police, but fuck sake. Wolf chases a coyote into the desert; you don't call the cops for that… unless you're the coyote. We don't have a payphone anyhow, so… The guy got real mad or scared and took off. He went the wrong way and, well, died. Awful. But his friend or brother, or something? He heard my boss talking about it on the radio and turned up a couple of weeks later. I guess he didn't want that to happen to anyone else, so he gave us money to keep things stocked and even bought and paid for a phone so that people could call for help if they needed it. Bad reception up here, though. I used it a couple of times in an… um… medical emergency, and it just kept cutting out."

"Huh," Cade said. "And what happens if I just take the water and the clothes?"

"Nothing? You don't have to pay it back or anything," the kid said. He pulled a phone from behind the counter and pushed it toward Cade. "I just call the guy's brother, and he gets it all restocked."

"How much would it cost for you not to call him?"

"I… I don't know. Fifty bucks?"

"Lend me your phone," Cade said. "I'll give you a hundred."

Cade transferred the money, waited for the kid to get confirmation, and then headed over to peer out the dusty, fly-specked door as he made the call.

"Who the *fuck* is this?" Lem snapped. "I don't have time to play games, so—"

"Lem, shut up."

He did as he was told. That wasn't a good sign. Cade heard Lem take two deep, unsteady breaths before he cleared his throat.

"Holy crap, man," Lem said, his voice relaxed into a laid-back drawl. "I've had the shit scared out of me. We've been putting together a ransom."

"We?"

"Yeah. Me and that cop of yours," Lem said. "FYI? I may have embezzled some money. I'm good, so I don't think anyone will notice if I move it back. But if they do mention it—"

"Shut up," Cade told him again. He pinched the tender skin of his nose and tried to think through the pulse of his headache.

Ransom hadn't been the plan. If it had, they would have put him somewhere he had to stay put, wolf or man. Franklin had dropped him off in the middle of the desert to die. So, whatever was going on with Marlow was… improvised. And a ransom drop for an already dead victim—or that's what Franklin assumed—would end with two.

"Tell Marlow not to go," he said.

"Too late," Lem said. "He's on his way there now."

"Are you sure?"

"I'm not a complete asshole," Lem said. "I've not let him go alone. He could be in on it for a start. I followed him. The meet is in some roadside cafe out in the sticks, *Sunny's Side Hustle.* They're in there now. I'm parked in the gas station next door. Want me to go in and tell Franklin he's a shit kidnapper?"

"No," Cade said. "He's a pretty good murderer. Stay there."

He hung up and went back to the counter. The kid tried to look like he hadn't been listening.

"Do you want to earn some more money?"

The kid shrugged. "Sure," he said. Belated suspicion flickered over his acne-scarred face. "How?"

The truck was bright blue except for the primer-red doors. Cade parked it in an empty row at the back of the lot outside *Sunny's.* The kid at the counter had told him to order the Chorizo Hash, but not to listen to a word the waitress said about the pancakes.

Cade didn't plan to stay long enough to finish anything.

He got out of the truck and shambled toward the front door of the diner, a big man with a sunburnt neck and a stained Food Lion T-shirt tucked into a pair of too-long jeans. The god-awful straw cowboy hat had been part of the thousand-buck package deal he'd struck with the kid in the Food Lion. It made his head itch, which he hoped was just the sunburn.

The chime over the door jingled as he let himself in. Five or six people scattered between the various booths and tables turned to look at him. Cade ignored them and kept his hat pulled down over his eyes as he headed toward the counter.

"Hey there, darlin'," the heavyset man behind the counter drawled as he cleared away the cups in front of Cade. "Breakfast?"

"Give me a stack of pancakes and bacon," Cade said. He'd not *asked* the kid's opinion, and he made his own decisions—even if it did involve getting pancake food poisoning. The name tag on the man's shirt said "Susie." There was probably a quirky story there. "And a lemonade. Busy in here."

Susie shrugged as he grabbed a fresh glass and filled it up. "Morning after the blue moon," he said. "Everyone's in to lick their wounds and wonder how the hell they got Ms. Gardner's gnome wedged where they wedged it."

He laughed at his own joke. "Locals?" Cade asked.

"You ain't."

"I'm not asking about me," Cade said. "This is police business."

It was. Cade just wasn't the police. That was a technicality, though. Susie hesitated and looked around as he pushed a small bowl of sweeteners over the counter.

"The big blond man's been in before. Always gets his food spicy as hell and then can't eat it," Susie said. "Tips like shit. I don't know the guy with him. The two at the door and the kid in the corner with the cast just drove up an hour ago, been nursing their coffee ever since."

Null at least, then. Probably whatever members of Franklin's crew he trusted to be okay with outright murdering one of their own.

"Could I borrow your pen?" Cade asked.

Susie hesitated for a moment and then shrugged and handed it over, along with his order pad. The first stroke of the pen didn't work. Cade scribbled in the corner of the page until the ink came through and then wrote a quick message to Lem. He tore it off, folded it in half, and handed it over.

"Take that and two—" He glanced at the menu out of habit. It didn't matter. The food was an excuse, but some stuck-in-the-past part of his brain wanted to make sure he fed his baby brother something nutritious. "Chorizo and egg tacos over to the car parked in the gas station. Nice car, blond guy in the front seat. He'll give whoever takes it over fifty bucks."

"For that tip, I'll take it," Susie said dryly. "I don't want any trouble here. The bank might own this place, but sometime in the future, they've promised to sign it over to me."

Cade shrugged. "There's going to be trouble," he said. "One way or another. This way you make sure the right guys win, and I'll make sure the SDPD compensates you for any damages."

"Shit," Susie muttered. "If you turn out to be a serial killer, I will be so pissed."

He turned away and beckoned the waitress over to give her the order and the note. Hopefully, the distraction of a pretty girl and a bag of food wouldn't slow Lem down too much.

Cade slid off the stool and slouched through the tables. He walked like his feet hurt after a long night—they did after his walk through the desert, and in these broken-down boots—and after a quick look, the three he'd pegged as Franklin's men dismissed him as nobody.

It was stupid—and Cade hated to admit it—but that bugged him.

Maybe Franklin wouldn't have been so quick, but he was busy holding forth to Marlow.

Who could, like Lem said, be involved. Cade didn't believe that but disproving it gave him a reason to take a nearby table and crane his ears to listen in on what they said about him. That wasn't the only reason—he needed to give Lem time to get into position—but he could have done that from the counter.

"…I am sure you have a whole speech about how I'm better than this, that underneath it all, I'm a good cop," Franklin said as he dug into his hash with enthusiasm. "But—"

"I don't," Marlow said. "You're a bad person and a corrupt cop. We're on the same page."

"Huh." Franklin speared a crisped chunk of chorizo. "Questions about where I went wrong? Started down this path?"

"No, worked that out," Marlow said. "You aren't that special, Franklin."

Franklin forked the food into his mouth and chewed it irritably. "You've always been like this," he said. "Never let me have anything. But I think you're lying. You've no idea…"

"I spoke to Randall," Marlow said. "I found those people you killed—"

"Let die."

"Your lawyer can argue that in court," Marlow said. "Only thing I don't know is, did you kill Clara Walker because she found out what you'd done, because you were scared she'd expose you? Or did you kill her because you thought she'd find out why you did it?"

Franklin grinned.

"Little bit of both," he said. His shoulders hitched in a shrug. "I didn't plan that one out, not properly. I thought I'd get caught, to be honest—instead, nothing. So next time one of Piper's old clients spoke to me the way they thought they could speak to me? I… handled… him too. Piper noticed that, and that's when I found out he'd kept an insurance policy on me. I couldn't live with that hanging over my head, could I? I'd been loyal. Sure, I made a mistake—"

"Killed people."

"So have you. That's the job," Franklin said. "Maybe some of them I didn't miss. Piper threatened to turn me in—to ruin me. Bennett would have found out; my career would be over. I could have ended up in prison."

He sounded genuinely offended, as if the unfairness of it still ate at him.

"I still don't care," Marlow said. "The only reason I'm here is because you kidnapped my boyfriend."

Cade tried not to grin. It wasn't the time. That felt good, though.

"Boyfriend?" Franklin said. "You move fast."

"I thought about waiting for six years and then trying to kill him," Marlow said, "but I didn't want to step on your toes."

Out of the corner of his eye, Cade saw Franklin's face curdle with a quick black rage.

"That's good," Franklin said. "Because he's dead, so I don't think it would have worked out."

Marlow grabbed the fork from next to his untouched plate of food and jammed it into Franklin's hand in one smooth movement. The tines tore through the skin and jabbed down into the meat. Blood dripped from his palm into the eggs. For a second, Franklin just stared at the fork that jutted up from between his knuckles, his face slack with surprise.

Then he swore and ripped the fork out.

"I would have let you live," he said as he tossed the bloody cutlery down. Blood oozed out of the wound as he wrapped a napkin around it. "But this works too. It's how those old plays always end, isn't it, the moon-crossed lovers apart even in death."

Marlow scrambled out of the booth and away from him. The waitress stepped back to avoid the cutlery and hesitated, her brain stuck between the everyday event of a dropped fork and the not-at-all-common splatter of blood. She flinched and splashed coffee on the floor when the chef stuck his head out to yell at her about curdling eggs. One of the tables, an old couple with weather-beaten faces and worn collars on their clothes, tucked folded bills under their half-eaten breakfast plates and made for the door.

"Stop them," Franklin snapped angrily. His voice cracked, and the desperation oozed out from the words. Whatever he'd expected today, it had probably gone smoother than this. After weeks of everything going to plan for him, the world had suddenly started to close in around Franklin. "Don't let them just walk out."

Franklin's people did what they were told and then traded uncertain looks. It wasn't hard to see where this was headed. The woman—tall and lean, with a scar that ran along her jaw like a seam—looked around the diner. Her gaze touched on the old couple, the woman's arm protectively around the man's back, and then bounced away.

"Now what?" she asked. "Marlow's one of us. Half these people are nulls. This isn't why we—"

"Do I have to do everything myself?" Franklin asked as he stalked over. He grabbed the gun she'd kept under the table and lifted it. Someone screamed, and a chair was knocked over as the rest of the diner realized what was going on. Marlow dodged to the side, between the tables, as Franklin took potshots at him that pocked the floorboards. He finally ducked down behind an overturned table, knees hunched up to his chest. He stared straight at Cade for a moment and then finally believed what he saw.

What he mouthed at Cade was less touching than "boyfriend."

"You can't just—" someone protested.

The retort of the gun silenced the protest, and someone else screamed, this time with feeling. Probably the scarred cop.

"I'm done," Franklin said. "There's no coming back from this. So, I am taking the money, and I am walking out of here. You want to be the ones that survived me shooting my way out or not?"

The guy in the cast broke and dashed out the back. Franklin sent two bullets after him. His aim was half-hearted. He missed the man's back and killed the wall instead.

"The money's already gone," Cade said as he stood up. He took the hat off. It felt a bit dramatic, but his head itched. "I had my brother steal it back from that offshore account you had him send it to."

Franklin stared at him, jaw set in a furious, exasperated expression. He started to say something and stopped, his lips pinched together in a thin, twisted line.

Cade pulled the gun from his waistband and held it loosely by his thigh.

"If I was you," he said, "I'd forget the money. Run, Franklin. It's your last chance."

Franklin shifted his weight from one foot to the other and then grabbed a woman from where she cowered in a booth. He dragged her over and pressed the gun to her temple. "I still have hostages," he said. "You can't—"

The chime rattled behind him. He swung around and yanked the gun away from the woman's head to aim it at Lem, who yelped, "Son of a bitch," and threw himself back out again.

Cade lifted the gun, steadied it, and squeezed the trigger. The bullet blew through Franklin's wrist and left a mess of splintered bone and flesh behind. He dropped the gun. The waitress darted forward and kicked it away with a nervous flick of her toe. It skittered away under a table.

"I've called the cops," Lem yelled from outside. "They're on the way."

Franklin laughed, an exhausted huff of sound, and went down on his knees. He held one arm up in the air.

"Of course you did," he said. "What else. Could someone get me a tourniquet?"

The scarred woman and her companion glanced at each other and then at Franklin. After a heartbeat they made their decision and headed for the door. Outside Lem yelped in surprise as the two of them shoved their way by him.

Marlow ignored them all as he scrambled to his feet and staggered over to grab two handfuls of Cade's bought-used and sweaty T-shirt.

"You fucking asshole," he said. Then he dragged Cade down into a desperate, hungry kiss that felt like he *needed* Cade's breath in his lungs. "I thought you were dead."

"Now you know what it feels like," Cade said. He realized that was a mistake immediately and pulled Marlow back. "Sorry. I'm sorry. That was a stupid thing… for your boyfriend to say. I told you that you'd know."

Marlow relaxed into Cade and wrapped his arms around him.

"You're still an asshole," he said. "But I'm glad to see you."

"Me too," Cade said. "Should we bandage Franklin up?"

"No," Marlow said. His breath was warm against Cade's throat. "Someone else can deal with him."

The way he said it sounded oddly final. Cade would have questioned it, but he decided to just enjoy the fact it was all over.

EPILOGUE

VICTOR CLEMONS HAD played the innocent victim in all this so many times that he had it down to an art. Not too vulnerable, a little bit angry. Indignant, even. They'd picked him up at the train station, with a one-way ticket to Phoenix in his pocket.

"I wasn't even at the house during the full moon," he said and jabbed a finger at Marlow. "I took Night Shift's advice and checked into a resort."

The feds had been called in for this one. It crossed state lines, and the ensuing fight over jurisdiction was easier to just dodge. The agent from the LA sub-office, who'd asked Marlow to sit in on the interview since he had a prior relationship with Clemons, shuffled through the file in front of him as if he hadn't already memorized it.

"The Hilton by the Bay," he said. "You checked in before sunset and ordered take-out after the hotel locked down for the night."

Victor looked satisfied and sat back. He rested his hands on the table in front of him.

"Exactly," he said. "So there's no way that I could have been the one to kill Barney. I mean, don't get me wrong, I didn't shed any tears when I heard the news. Whoever killed him did me a favor, but I'm not a violent man. I don't even own a gun."

The agent flicked a page over.

"Victor Clemons isn't registered as having bought or owned a firearm," he said. It sounded like agreement. It wasn't.

"In that case, if you had nothing to do with Barney Lyons's death," Marlow said, "why did you book a ticket to leave town?"

"I. Took. Your. Advice," Clemons repeated himself, each word enunciated with a jab of his finger against the table. "The only way to break a fixation is to move. So I decided to move cities, get a new start."

"Handy enough that you'd already quit your job," Marlow said. "You'd done the same just before your ex, Sammy Goodwin, was shot in Portland, wasn't it, during the full moon."

That was not part of the script. Clemons's face shut down as his confidence took a hit. He crossed his arms and licked his lips.

The agent pulled a photo out of the file and pushed it across the table. No one would have said that Goodwin and Lyons looked alike, but they were still somehow the same type. Same social class. Same background. In the photo, Goodwin had his arm around Clemons's shoulder.

"Or, for that matter, Jensen North," the agent said as he pushed another photo across the table. They hadn't been able to find one of North with Clemons, who avoided cameras for obvious reasons, but his corpse made the point. Another photo joined the pile, this time of a man slightly older than the others. "Claude Jollet. Not quite your usual type?"

"I don't…" Clemons paused as he tried to work out how much they knew and what he could still deny. "People die."

"Sure," Marlow said. "But around you, they drop like flies… with restraining orders."

Clemons took a breath and shrugged one shoulder. "So I have bad taste in unlucky men," he said. "Like you said, they all died during the full moon—"

The agent clucked his tongue. "You mean," he said, "they were found dead after the full moon."

It was Marlow's turn to pull something from the folder, a grid of clothes laid out on a table with tags next to them. Chinos, socks, corporate-themed blue T-shirt, and well-worn sneakers.

"Why did you have Barney Lyons's clothes in your suitcase?" he said.

"They're my clothes."

"Wrong size."

Clemons's smile had started to show the strain around the edges. "They're my clothes *now*," he corrected himself. "I borrowed them from Barney at some point, and, well, we weren't exactly on good terms. I didn't even think."

"You took them off Barney's dead body," the agent said. "Admit it."

It had been Franklin who made Marlow realize the truth. He didn't intend to ever thank the other man.

No one asked too many questions when someone died during the full moon. They assumed the obvious, but sometimes they shouldn't have.

"The pathologist checked time of death," Marlow said. "They do that, once suspicions have been raised. Barney died before you checked into the hotel. You shot him, stripped him, and left him for us to find, didn't you?"

Clemons leaned forward and finally unfolded his arms. "I want a lawyer," he said, clearly for the tape.

That ended the interview, but it didn't matter. He was already tied up with a bow.

Marlow was a city boy at heart. He'd trained in all terrains—all the Night Shift did—but cities made sense. They had landmarks. Street names. Buildings to hide in. He knew some guys in Search and Rescue who'd say the same about the wilderness, but if push came to shove, he'd bet they'd all take shelter behind a reinforced door over a hollow tree stump.

Still.

He lay naked on his back, sweaty and lazy with that boneless, satiated feeling of well-being, and watched the clouds drift in front of the stars.

The view out here was as good as advertised.

Marlow took a break from stargazing to steal a glance at Cade, sprawled out on the blanket next to him. Moonlight stole the gold from his skin and darkened the shadows, the spread of his broad shoulders and chest picked out in exaggerated contours.

Actually, the view might be even better than he'd been promised… now he came to think about it.

"And Clemons?" Cade asked. There was a bruise on his throat, worried into the tendons that stood out in taut lines against his skin. It would last this time, at least until it faded on its own. "Did you find out who he really was?"

It wasn't as pleasant a subject as how much Marlow enjoyed looking at Cade, but he supposed it was relevant.

"Harry Gowdy, originally," he said. "From Mount Hood in Oregon. When he was a teenager, his mother was murdered by her abusive boyfriend. She'd broken up with him, but the wolf couldn't read the writing on the wall, and Night Shift had palmed off her complaints with platitudes. None of which turned out to be helpful when a wolf ripped you apart."

He heard the anger in his voice. Cade did too, from the way he turned his head to look at Marlow. He left it for now as he stayed on Clemons.

"So she was the one who ended up dead, not the wolf?"

Marlow shrugged and sat up. He hitched one leg up and hooked his arm around his bare knee. His fingers grazed the old, neat surgical scars, and he idly poked at the joint. Even with being on the run from his fellow officers and climbing onto a roof, it didn't hurt nearly as much as it usually did.

"The forensic psychologist the feds sent in said that he was 'relitigating the event' so it happened how he thinks it should have. He moved to a new city, found a lover with the same profile as his mom's boyfriend, and proved that what happened to her wouldn't happen to him."

"So, crazy?"

Marlow shrugged. "He knew it was wrong," he said. "He tried not to get caught or blamed other people. That will go against him."

"Maybe he'll end up in prison with Franklin," Cade said.

He might.

Marlow unfolded himself and sprawled over Cade's body. He brushed a kiss over the sun-warmed, stubbled jaw, and Cade made a lazy, satisfied sound as he ran his hands up to cup Marlow's ass.

"I've been meaning to ask," he said. "Do you still have job openings for nulls with training?"

Cade chuckled. "You aren't the first person to ask me that," he said. "Justin wants me to hire Piper. I turned him down, so there's at least one empty slot. Why? Bennett looking to change careers?"

"No," Marlow said.

Cade hesitated for a moment and then sighed raggedly. He cupped his hand around the back of Marlow's skull, fingers tangled in the curls, and held him for a quick, hard kiss. It ended with Cade tilting his head back against the ground so he could search Marlow's face.

"Maybe that's a bit… soon?" he said.

It was.

Marlow didn't care. He'd handed his notice in to O'Hara and left. It had been terrifying, and he'd nearly walked back in and snatched the incriminating resignation off the secretary's desk

He'd also felt free, almost weightless. He couldn't remember the last time he'd felt like that.

"If I want to be with you, I can't be Night Shift," he said. "That would end with one of us dead."

A hint of panic flicked over Cade's face. "I mean, that's a lot to put on the line," he said. "I don't want… I don't want you to sacrifice that for me."

"It's not," Marlow said. He ran his thumb over Cade's cheekbone. After what happened with Piper, he'd just gotten better and gone back to work. He'd never thought about the fact that there'd been five cops at his apartment that night, that it had been Piper who shot him but not who dragged him naked to that car. Every day he'd gotten up and not thought about that. "I'm not. That's the point. When this happened, you were the only person I had to call because I didn't trust anyone I'd spent the last six years working with. I need a break from Night Shift, and that's been five years in the making. You're not the reason, just the one who made me realize."

Cade exhaled.

"I just don't want this to be something you regret," he said.

Marlow leaned down and pressed a kiss to Cade's ear, and then he whispered, "I could go see if Justin has work for me—"

He choked on laughter as Cade growled under his breath and rolled them over. The grass, coarser than it looked, scratched against his back as Cade glowered down at him.

"Not funny. You want to do something stupid and ill-advised; you do it with me," he grumbled.

"It has worked so far," Marlow pointed out. "I need something new, and maybe it could be working with you."

Cade stared at him for a moment, his jaw set. "For," he corrected stiffly. "You'd be working *for* me."

Marlow rolled his eyes and laughed. "You should see your face," he said.

Cade's face tried out a few expressions before he settled on resigned amusement. "Well, being a spectacular asshole has worked for me so far," he said with a wry smile. "I didn't want to change it up when things are going so well."

"Maybe pull back a bit?" Marlow suggested. "I'm trying to—"

Marlow's phone rang, muffled in the pocket of his discarded jeans. The habit of decades made him grab for it.

"It's a text," he said. "I'll just… huh."

There was a pause, and then Cade asked, "And?"

Marlow glanced up from the phone and snorted. "You remember I saved that pregnant woman?"

"Instead of staying out of trouble," Cade said. "It's on the list."

That invited questions. Marlow didn't indulge Cade by asking them. "Apparently she was grateful and called the station to get my name."

"Another Kit in the world?"

"No," Marlow said. "Apparently, some wires got crossed at some point, so there's another little Bennett in the world. Bennett Crane."

That was the second time Bennett had grabbed the glory after Marlow had done the work. It didn't matter anymore; if it ever had. Still, one baby named after him! Was it too much to ask?

Cade looked amused. "Parting shot, huh?"

"I guess. She's—"

This time when the phone went off, Bennett's name flashed over the screen. Marlow went to answer it, but Cade plucked the phone out of his hands. He answered it.

"He's busy," Cade said.

Then he chucked the phone away into the long grass and turned his attention back to Marlow.

"Now, where was I?"

"Telling me you loved me," Marlow said. "Which is good because I love you too."

Cade stared at him for a moment. "Good," he said. A grin spread over his face, and he leaned down to kiss Marlow, their bodies tangled together as he ran a hand down Marlow's thigh. "Good to know we're on the same page."

Somewhere in the long grass, Marlow's phone started to ring again. This time he ignored it.

ABOUT TA MOORE

TA MOORE is a Northern Irish writer of romantic suspense, urban fantasy, and contemporary romance novels. A childhood in a rural, seaside town fostered in her a suspicious nature, a love of mystery, and a streak of black humor a mile wide.

Coffee, Doc Marten boots, and good friends are the essential things in life. Spiders, mayo, and heels are to be avoided.

TA Moore can be found at the following locations:
Blog: www.tamoorewrites.com

If you've enjoyed this book, please consider leaving a review for TA Moore on Amazon and other book retailer sites. Actually, it would be great to leave them for any book you've enjoyed. Authors truly appreciate it.

To catch up on all Rogue Firebird Press authors, please visit www.roguefirebird.com
For other TA Moore's Dreamspinner releases, visit www.dreamspinnerpress.com

Readers Love TA Moore

Bone to Pick (Digging Up Bones #1)
"If you like mystery, crime, super steamy sex scenes between two antagonistic men, and lots of intrigue, Bone to Pick definitely must be your next read."

—Love Bytes

Dog Days (Wolf Winter #1)
"… Flawlessly written… Each page was a new surprise, and this story was unlike anything I have read—I had no idea what would come next. Quite simply, I want more."

—The Novel Approach

Stone The Crows (Wolf Winter #2)
"… the second novel in the Wolf Winter series by T.A. Moore, and it's a stunner at every level and element. Horror, urban fantasy, and romance. There is nothing this author and book doesn't excel at."

—Scattered Thoughts and Rogue Words

Wolf at the Door (Wolf Winter #3)
"Cold and dark. Ferocious and unforgiving. Brutal and beautiful. This last instalment in the Wolf Winter trilogy takes all the pieces from the previous books and twists them some more into a finale that will take your breath away."

—Paranormal Romance Guild

Cash in Hand
"Cash in Hand is a fast-paced, twisty turn of a story that really kept me in its clutches to the very end."

—Love Bytes

Hex Work (Babylon Boy #1)
"If you enjoy a good mystery with lots of twists and turns and some surprising chemistry with some magic thrown in, I think you'll like this kickoff to Babylon Boy."

—Love Bytes

Wanted – Bad Boyfriend (Island Classifieds #1)
"This is the perfect comfort food… I love Moore's books and her way of writing. This author always manages to infuse warmth and humanity to both the characters and the story, as well as humor."

—Joyfully Jay

AUTHOR CATALOG

Published by Rogue Firebird Press and Other Publications

NIGHT SHIFT

Shift Work
Split Shift
Shiftless

ORANGE NORTHERN WOMAN SHORT STORY PRIZE WINNER

Island Life
(Ulster Tatler)

ORANGE NORTHERN WOMAN SHORT STORY PRIZE FINALIST

Words of Wisdom
(Barefoot Nuns of Barcelona & other short stories)

ADDITIONAL PUBLICATIONS

Labyrinth of Stone

Red Milk
(Requiem for the Departed)

The White Heifer of Fearchair
(The Phantom Queen Awakes)

A Different Kind of Monster
(Blood Fruit)

Published by Dreamspinner Press and DSP Publications

DIGGING UP BONES

Bone To Pick
Skin And Bone

WOLF WINTER

Dog Days

Stone The Crows

Wolf At The Door

LOST AND FOUND

Prodigal

BLOOD AND BONE

Dead Man Stalking

THE PRODIGIUM

Cash In Hand

STAND-ALONE NOVELS

Liar, Liar

Every Other Weekend

Swipe

Take The Edge Off

ANTHOLOGIES & SHORT STORIES

Collared
(Devil Take Me)

Elf Shot
(Bad, Dad, & Dangerous)

Made in the USA
Monee, IL
17 September 2023

42843924R00207